LOVERS OF THE DAMNED

DEVIL'S Mate

COLETTE RIVERA

Love's price is redemption

Edited by Hummingbird Editing

Proofreading by CJ Editing

Cover design by We Got You Covered Book Design

People depicted in the cover image are models and should not be associated with the book.

Interior Illustrations by Angelika Süto, Angki.s_

ISBN

Print: 978-1-991284-12-9

Kindle: 978-1-991284-13-6

AUTHOR'S NOTE

Dear reader,

This book deals with adult themes and is intended for mature audiences. You may wish to note that there are some Dom/Sub elements in this couple's relationship—mainly in the bedroom—but they don't adhere to a strict Dom/Sub dynamic.

If you wish to view a list of possible triggers, they can be found in the final paragraph of this note. Please take care and use your discretion.

Devil's Mate is part of a series with an overarching plot. If you haven't started the *Lovers of the Damned* series, it's recommended to begin with *Demon's Mate* even though each book features a different couple.

The romance in *Devil's Mate* stands alone and ends in a happily ever after. This is the fourth and final book in the series and will *not* end in a cliffhanger.

Content & Trigger Warnings: (may contain spoilers) Main character whose parents died in a boating accident in the past. Grief associated with deceased loved ones. Main character who unjustly imprisoned others in the past. Mention of witches who worship Satan. Magical and physical violence. A main character violently attacked a side character in the past. Blood-drinking demons—similar to vampires. One instance of a main character over-indulging in alcohol due to a low mood. Sexual content: intended for mature audiences. Some of the following acts may be presented unrealistically due to characters' use of magic and should not be taken as representative of real-world situations: Primal play. Biting kink. Public sex acts. Orgasm control. Bondage. Consensual non-consent: one main character asks the other to disregard him if he says no during certain play sessions. This is discussed beforehand with safe words in place.

DEVIL'S MATE

COLETTE RIVERA

1

____

LUCIFER

It was past time to leave this miserable city. Lucifer would never be welcome in Shearwater Landing, the home his brothers had claimed, and good riddance. Luc didn't need to be welcomed. He'd find somewhere better.

As soon as this last detour was out of the way.

Luc stood outside an eclectic little coffee shop in the Banks, invisible and lurking in peace. It was far from his first time here.

He'd initially discovered the coffee shop while following Ash's little obsession, Harper. When that jig had been up, there'd been no reason to return, and yet the café had nagged at Luc's consciousness.

Seaside Coffee.

It wasn't by the sea, though the smell of coffee was unmistakable. Not that human beverages held much appeal. Even the food on offer was nothing special, and the charm of the mismatched tables and chairs wasn't to Luc's taste.

No individual element of Seaside Coffee stood out, so why was the place impossible to overlook?

For some damn reason, Luc had been here yesterday as well.

His fingers tightened around the ceramic mug he'd inexplicably purchased and then carried around with him for the last twenty-four hours.

Sunlight caught on the earth-red glaze.

The coffee shop sold an array of similar items. This mug's asymmetrical glazing pattern and unglazed base had caught his attention. That, and it had been the sole red item on the shelf.

Luc brushed a thumb over the stamp on the bottom. *Colt Ceramics.*

There was no handle. Instead, two shallow, stylistic grooves circled the middle. Luc smiled, soft tingles winding their way up his arm. He'd never been so pleased by an object, especially one devoid of magic.

He should discard his invisibility illusion and buy the rest of the items in the shop, but he had nowhere to put them unless he brought his haul back to the Realm of the Damned. The idea left a sour taste in Luc's mouth. He needed a place to live in this realm.

But why bother? No one wanted him here. Was he seriously considering setting up in this city—his brothers' boring city—for the sole purpose of collecting pleasing mugs? What the hell was wrong with him?

Luc's brothers wanted nothing to do with him. They'd made that clear. Onyx might have been tempted to give him a chance, but the others had probably changed his mind. Luc hadn't heard from him since leaving his phone number.

If Onyx didn't want to call, then Luc wouldn't force himself on him. It was the correct—insufferable and selfless—thing to do, and Luc reserved the right to be bitter about it.

Unlike with Onyx, Luc had been warned to stay out of Ash and Dante's lives, which meant avoiding Seaside Coffee, a place their little mates frequented.

It wasn't fair. He wanted to be here even if he didn't know why.

Luc's demon fire sparked, and he clenched his teeth, the urge to crush the pretty mug overwhelming him.

He'd ruined everything, so why not ruin this? He didn't deserve anything nice.

Luc drew back his arm and flung the mug away. It sailed across the street and crashed into the sidewalk in front of the café door, shattering into countless pieces.

A human seated at one of the outside tables startled, glancing around in confusion.

Luc's heart clenched, the sinking regret instantaneous.

Bits of ceramic glittered on the sidewalk, red like blood—broken like everything else in his life—and Luc's throat thickened.

He glared at the smashed mug. There was no point sweeping up the pieces and mending them with a spell. It wouldn't be the same.

"I'll see you tomorrow," a man called over his shoulder as he exited Seaside Coffee, his voice cutting through Luc's seething thoughts.

His attention shifted.

The man pulled off his apron and balled it up, tucking it under his arm as he scanned the street. His pale gray eyes seemed to linger on Luc, even though there was no way the human could see through his invisibility.

Luc froze, momentarily caught in the man's magnetic stare. His eyes were electric, bright, and haunting. The hairs on the back of Luc's neck stood, and a shiver wound through him.

Long, dark lashes fluttered as the man blinked and looked down. He stopped short at the sight of the smashed mug, a frown cutting his delicate face. He kneeled and grabbed one of the larger pieces, a crease deepening in his brow. Muttering something Luc couldn't make out, he stood and retreated inside.

The man's departure was like a bereavement, leaving Luc hollow as the urge to follow pulled on his chest.

Before Luc could dwell on the feeling, the man returned with a dustpan and brush, his apron nowhere in sight. Luc's tense muscles eased. With a few deft strokes, the mug was swept away and the man disappeared again, scowling like the shattered mug was a personal offense.

Luc's insides twisted. He was no stranger to regret. It clawed at him so frequently, he was permanently ripped apart. Breaking the mug was nothing compared to everything he'd destroyed in his long life. It shouldn't cut so deep. But it did.

The man strode back out of the café and turned down the street without stopping. Luc crossed the road and followed as if this were the reason he'd been waiting all along.

He pushed his regret over the broken mug away. It shouldn't matter. It didn't. Not like this did.

As Luc followed, he relaxed, his bitterness fading. Tailing the man soothed him.

Luc's pulse sped up, his momentary comfort vanishing. Was this man the reason he kept returning to Seaside Coffee?

No. He couldn't be.

Luc hadn't noticed him working at the café before. How could he be waiting for someone he hadn't known existed?

But following the man was even more pleasing than holding the mug. He was captivating even though he wasn't doing anything interesting. The mug's appeal paled in comparison. Of course it did, but the two felt connected, which shouldn't be possible when neither possessed magic.

It made no sense.

Yet Luc's magic responded as if merely gazing at the man had activated something deep within him. Power hummed, its frequency increasing the longer Luc followed. Luc hated not seeing the man's face. He needed those sharp eyes on him.

Not that there wasn't plenty to appreciate about his current view. Luc's quarry walked with confidence, his jeans flatteringly cupping his ass, but the man's beauty wasn't the reason Luc's fire sparked. He'd seen countless beautiful men over the millennia. This man was something more. Something...

Bitterness eclipsed the sweet tug on Luc's heart. Something more like what? Luc's mate? Ha.

Luc's brothers may have found their fated mates, but him? The Devil didn't deserve happiness. He was the villain. It didn't matter that he chose to take on that role. That it had been a necessary front. The only way forward. He'd worn the title proudly, and after so long, he couldn't pretend he wasn't genuinely bad.

The man paused and looked over his shoulder, light brown cheeks flushed with the late-afternoon heat. Luc halted, his breath catching as the man scanned the area, then continued on.

Luc followed in his wake like he was under a spell. He'd never been captivated by a random stranger. Ever. It had been more than a thousand years since his emotions had stirred for anyone at all, other than in anger.

Chest tightening, Luc's stride quickened.

He might not deserve to find his fated mate after leading the way to destroying the balance of magic and mortality in the universe, but Luc wasn't leaving Shearwater Landing until he figured out if, against all odds, he'd found his mate anyway.

2

DEX

Dex reached his building and paused at the entrance, unable to go inside. He hadn't been looking forward to leaving work, then he'd found one of his mugs shattered on the sidewalk, and his low mood had gone subterranean.

The red mug hadn't been on the shelf that morning, meaning someone must have bought it on Dex's day off yesterday. How had it ended up smashed in the doorway? Had the person brought it back? Seeing something he'd made broken and discarded was the last thing Dex needed.

He turned away from his building, bypassing the bakery on the ground floor, and continued down the street. His condo was not the place to be when he was down.

Pulling out his phone, Dex considered his options as he walked. His best friend, Ollie, was still at work. Fuck, all of his friends were. Starting and finishing early suited Dex, but not many jobs began at six a.m.

Dex turned down the street that ran along the river. His friend, Violet, worked at a tiny hole-in-the-wall bar close by and should be starting her regular shift about now.

When he arrived, a few people sat at the tables outside Dorthy's, drinking and vaping. Dex pushed the door open and searched the space as he entered. An older man was reading at a table by the window, and a couple who seemed like tourists sat at the bar.

Violet was nowhere to be seen.

Heart sinking, Dex headed toward the bartender. He was new, and Dex couldn't recall the guy's name. "Hey, is Violet working today?"

"Nah." He gave an apologetic smile. "We swapped shifts. Can I get you anything?"

Dex ordered a beer because it seemed rude not to. He dropped a tip in the jar and took the pint to a stool at the opposite end of the bar.

Well, this was a bust. Now he was day drinking alone.

Dex pulled out his phone and opened his chat with Violet.

DEX:

You're not working this afternoon?

VIOLET:

No. I'm out of town for Luna's cousin's wedding. We'll be back tomorrow night.

DEX:

That's right. Have fun!

He'd forgotten the wedding was coming up. Luna was Violet's girlfriend. They'd been together since all three of them graduated from college. Violet had studied art with Dex, and he'd met her in a pottery class in their first year.

One of Violet's steel sculptures was mounted on the wall behind him, her work as bold as she was. Dex loved it, even if he personally hated using metal as a medium. Welding was not his thing. But Violet kicked ass at it.

Dex sipped his beer and opened his email app, reading

through his messages. His realtor had sent one a few hours ago outlining the open home she'd organized for this weekend. Dex hit reply and stared blankly at the new message field.

Knowing his first open home was around the corner released some of the tension from his shoulders and immediately filled him with guilt. What would his parents think of him selling the home they'd loved so much?

He remembered painting the living room with his parents in high school. His dad had stepped in a paint tray and ruined his shoes, and his mom hadn't stopped laughing.

Dex's chest tightened, and he rubbed his sternum. That weekend had been so fun, but these days, seeing the soft blue accent wall left him cold and empty.

He had a long sip of beer and replied to the realtor. Getting out of the damn condo was well overdue. It was a time capsule that he couldn't bring himself to change, and it was stifling him. He had to escape. It was hard to believe he'd found living there soothing a few years ago.

With the email sent, Dex placed his phone face down on the bar. That was his life admin done. Maybe he should head over to his pottery studio after he finished his drink.

The stool next to Dex scraped along the floor, and he turned, finding a tall man beside him.

"Mind if I join you?"

Dex blinked.

Had this guy walked off a fall photoshoot or something? He wore a black coat that no one in their right mind would wear during summer, and it looked expensive as hell. His hair was perfectly sculpted, effortless waves framing his chiseled face, and he stood as if he were posing, but in a way that seemed natural, like he was so used to displaying himself in the best light that he didn't need to think about it.

Dex's body flashed hot, and he cleared his throat. "I don't mind."

The man set his beer on the bar and unbuttoned his coat, revealing dark slacks and a dress shirt undone at the collar. Even as he sat, their height difference was apparent.

Dex's face heated, and he sipped his drink. Hooking up hadn't been on his radar for the afternoon, but damn, it was now.

"I'm Luc." He extended a pale, long-fingered hand with blunt wine-red painted nails.

Dex swallowed, his throat parched despite the recent sip of beer. "Dex." He shook Luc's hand, his palm warm and grip firm, but not in an obnoxious way.

Luc's thin red lips turned upward. He had to be wearing a lip stain to get that kind of color. "Dex. Is that short for anything?"

"Dexter. It was my grandfather's name."

Luc nodded. "Dex suits you better."

He snorted. "I know."

Luc held eye contact until Dex had to look away. Luc drummed his fingers on the side of his glass. "I've never been here before. It's very appealing."

Out of the corner of his eye, Dex could tell Luc was scanning the room. The space was unmistakably queer, especially when you got a closer look at the pictures on the walls, or read any of the messages scrawled on the bar top.

"Appealing is one way to put it."

Luc turned to face him. "How would you put it?" He cocked his head slightly as if he were waiting eagerly for an answer.

Dex squirmed. Luc's brown eyes were intense. His focus wasn't unwelcome. Just a lot. "I don't know. I've come here so much that it's more familiar than anything."

"But you agree on the appeal?"

"Yeah, totally."

Luc nodded. "I had a good feeling about coming in here."

This conversation was bizarre. That last statement could almost be a line, but Luc didn't add a cheesy, *and seeing you, I know why,* or whatever to bring it home.

"So you wandered in on a whim?" Dex asked.

Luc shrugged. "What brought you here?"

Dex's insides twisted. There was no way he was admitting his home was so depressing, he couldn't stand going inside. "I came to visit a friend, but she isn't working today."

"Did that make you sad?"

Dex's eyes widened. Blunt much?

"Sorry." Luc's smooth brow creased. "That was rude, wasn't it?" He sounded like he was genuinely unsure.

"Maybe not rude, just very forward."

Luc nodded, his brief confusion evaporating. "I meant to be direct, so I'm not misunderstood. If I want people to believe me, I have to speak plainly and tell the truth."

"Uh-huh." Dex sipped his beer. He'd totally stereotyped this guy, thinking he'd be smooth and socially adept because he was hot. He had also assumed Luc came over to hit on him, but it didn't feel like that at all.

"Do you not usually tell the truth?" he couldn't help asking.

Luc's mouth tightened around the edges. "Depends on who you ask."

"I'm asking you."

Luc smiled, his intense eyes gleaming as his cheeks flushed slightly. "I'm trying to tell the truth more than I used to."

Weird to basically admit to a stranger that you were a liar, but okay. At least Luc was trying to do better.

"Good for you. Personal growth counts for something."

"Hmm." Luc didn't sound convinced. "In that case, I should

admit that when you asked if I came here on a whim, I evaded your question."

Dex shifted on his stool until he was squarely facing Luc. "Why?"

"Because I didn't want you asking the reason. It wasn't a whim."

Dex leaned forward. "Well, now I have to ask."

Luc swallowed, his gaze unfaltering. "I saw you and wanted to talk to you, so I followed you inside."

A shiver wound down Dex's spine. That should have been borderline creepy. Instead, it was thrilling. "You wanted to talk to *me*?"

"I did." Luc looked down, trailing a red nail along the bar. "But I'm out of practice with small talk." He frowned like this was perplexing, and it was kind of sad.

Dex had the urge to rescue him. "I engage in small talk all day. I'm a barista. It comes with the hospitality territory, so feel free to practice."

"Really?" Luc's attention lifted from the bar.

Dex's insides twisted at the look of hope in Luc's eyes. "Yeah, no problem. So, what do you do?"

Luc's face fell. "I don't have a job."

"I'm sorry. Didn't mean to hit a sore subject." Dex couldn't blame himself. Looking at Luc, he seemed well-off rather than struggling. It wasn't as if Dex could afford clothes like that.

"No need to apologize. I don't need a job, but work is what people talk about, isn't it?"

Why did Luc seem to be referring to people as a foreign concept? He must not get out much.

"Someone's profession is a key small talk component. But we could move on to the weather, or our star signs if you want to get interesting."

"I don't have anything to say about the weather or star signs."

Dex laughed, prompting a smile from Luc. "I'm starting to see the issue. How about you tell me what you're doing in town? Do you live in the city?"

Luc hesitated. "No. I followed my brothers here, but they'd rather I didn't stay."

Damn, that was an honest answer. Luc appeared to be taking his not-lying resolution a little too seriously. But that wasn't bad. Social awkwardness didn't put Dex off. Not forcing yourself to act like everyone else was an attractive quality.

"That sounds like a story." Dex smiled encouragingly. "Want to talk about it?"

3

LUCIFER

How could Luc talk about his brothers without lying? This wasn't going how he'd imagined. Luc had entered the bar confident, only for Dex to shatter an illusion he hadn't known he'd been upholding.

For far too long, whenever Luc interacted with someone, he decided who to be in order to bend the situation to his will. If he needed to be cruel, so be it. If he needed to placate, that was easy. It was only recently that being genuine aligned with his desired outcomes.

With his brothers, being genuine was straightforward. He was sorry even if no one believed him. He'd told the truth when they'd found him at the tower in the Realm of the Damned, and ever since. It was all he could do until he was given the chance to offer more.

But when faced with someone who didn't know him, someone who had no grudge or preconceived notions of who he was, how could he be genuine? Who was he without his mistakes?

Luc didn't know.

He hadn't been anyone other than the Devil in far too long.

Dex was a blank slate. This man, who drew Luc in like he always imagined the fated mate connection would. It inspired him to show Dex nothing except his purest self, but he came up empty.

Maybe he was nothing more than the being who'd damned thousands and destroyed the universe's magical balance. When Luc looked, he couldn't find anything beneath that truth.

He cleared his throat.

Should he tell Dex what he could about why he was in Shearwater Landing? No matter how much he wanted to avoid lying, even by omission, the full story was impossible to share. Dex would assume Luc had lost his grip on reality if he started talking about the fall to Earth and magic.

But he had to start somewhere if he wanted Dex to know him eventually.

"I betrayed my brothers' trust some time ago, and it doesn't seem like they're interested in an apology."

Dex bit his lip and took a moment to consider, his sharp gray eyes narrowing slightly. The assessing nature of his attention was refreshing. No one had seen Luc in forever. Or at least, no one had seen anything he hadn't curated.

He'd tried with Onyx. Luc had let his distress surface, but it had angered his younger brother. Onyx hadn't believed him, and that was no one's fault but Luc's.

"Did your apology fit the, uh, betrayal, as you called it?"

"I don't know if that's possible."

There were no words to encompass Luc's regret for stealing his brothers' magic, and that was only the beginning of his trans-gressions.

Dex's lips parted, but he snapped them shut like he'd recon-sidered. "Maybe you need to keep apologizing."

"Even if they asked me not to?"

Dex's nose scrunched. His face was soft-featured and

boyish, a hit of stubble preventing him from being completely baby-faced. "If they asked you not to, you should respect their boundaries."

"That's what I suspected." Boundaries were annoying. Luc would rather not deal with them, and that was part of the problem. "One of them said he'd hear me out."

"That's good. If he's willing to talk, then there's hope. It'll take time."

Dex's encouragement was sweet, but Luc couldn't take solace in it. He might not mean it if he had the whole story.

Unless being Luc's mate meant Dex would understand.

Were they mates? The question was a thorn in Luc's heel. He wanted to believe the signs, but hope did terrible things to him.

He tamped it down.

"I suppose I'll have to find a place to stay in the city while I wait and see. But enough about my problems. I didn't follow you in here to burden you."

Dex snorted. "I can't believe you're admitting to following me."

"Does it make you uncomfortable?" Luc's heart skipped. He hated the idea when he normally wouldn't give a shit.

Dex shrugged one shoulder. "Not unless you're planning on following me anywhere else."

"I won't," Luc promised. Damn it, now he'd have to stick to that.

Usually, he wouldn't care about the ethics of stalking or false promises. With Dex, it seemed vital to care. If there was one thing in his life Luc could get right, it had to be this.

Each honest piece of himself Luc offered up, each promise not to lie, seemed to ignite something inside him. A flame wrapped around his heart, urging him on like he was headed in the right direction.

He'd never felt anything like it. Not even when he'd fallen to Earth and been sure beyond all doubt that he was on the path to his mate. Luc had no idea anything could feel as right as sitting next to Dex and trying to figure out what lay beneath his vast array of masks.

They had to be mates.

Dex hopped off his barstool. "Glad I won't have to worry. I'm going to get another drink. Are you good?"

Luc glanced at his nearly full glass. "I'm fine, thank you."

He should have bought Dex his next drink. That was a thing humans did when dating. Right? Luc didn't know much about modern romance. He should have done more research.

Luc's stomach dropped at the idea of asking Dex on a date and being turned down. He wasn't ready for his mate, not without a plan to win his heart. Luc always had enough plans to fill a book, accounting for every scenario.

Guaranteed outcomes were all Luc tolerated. Hoping things would work out was for fools.

Maybe he should say to hell with modern dating. It brought no guarantee. Instead, he could show Dex magic, prove it was real and not a delusion, and seduce him with power and possibility. Promise Dex the world. Anything he desired.

He could whisk Dex away and pleasure him senseless, then mate him, and keep him forever.

If Dex truly was his mate, Luc couldn't let him slip from his grasp. Four thousand years was too long to miss his chance now. He could go a step further, bind them together, and explain later. That way, Dex would be his, and it could never be undone.

The smoldering around Luc's heart flared painfully.

It was wrong—immoral and selfish—but keeping his mate captive until he accepted the truth was a guarantee. Luc wouldn't have to hope for Dex's acceptance. Being fated meant they would work out in the end, no matter what. Dex would want to be Luc's. And Luc could always use magic and illusion to ease the way.

Shame doused the fire around his heart and sent a shiver through him. Was he really considering kidnapping Dex and forcing him to fall in love? Luc couldn't cheat his way through this. Even contemplating it proved how unworthy he was. Manipulating Dex wasn't love.

And Luc wanted real, pure love more than anything.

Not that he deserved it. But if he was so unworthy, why would he find his mate now? Why was he being given this chance after everything?

Was he worthy?

Not likely. But the more he considered, the more Luc acknowledged that capturing Dex and forcing him to bend to his will wasn't anything more than a fantasy, one in which Dex's cooperation was key to the allure. Dex, his willing captive. Anything else was revolting.

No, Luc wasn't seriously considering forcing anything on Dex. He was just scared.

Dex returned to his seat with another beer. "I didn't see this on tap when I first came in. I love a sour." He sipped his new drink. "So good on a hot day."

Luc smiled, his bitterness and shame cracking and falling away. He could do this the correct way. When Dex's gaze held his, he didn't doubt himself.

A tether seemed to form between them, reeling Luc in. Fuck, they really were mates. This could be nothing else.

Dex is my mate. Mine.

Fire turned to light within the depths of Luc's soul. It burst forth, setting his hidden wings and tail tingling. It was happening. Luc was with his mate at last—four thousand years of heartache were at an end—and for the first time since Luc could remember, hope felt good.

It wasn't poison. It was life.

"I've never had a sour beer," Luc admitted, trying for something to say that wasn't completely unhinged.

"Here." Dex slid his glass along the bar.

Luc had a sip and pursed his lips. "I'm not sure about that." He grimaced, handing the drink back.

"It's not for everyone." Dex took the glass, his fingers a hair away from touching Luc's.

Luc needed more. To be closer. He turned in his seat, facing Dex in a mirror of his position, their knees brushing momentarily. "You said you work as a barista. Do you enjoy it?"

"I do." Dex lifted his chin like his statement was a challenge.

"I'm glad."

"You're not asking what I *really* want to do?"

Luc didn't understand. "Why would you want something else if you enjoy your work?"

Dex huffed. "I don't know. People always assume it's a temporary job, like everyone has to aspire to work in an office."

"I'd never work in an office." Luc would die of boredom before he figured out what humans did in offices all day.

In some respects, he was knowledgeable about the modern human world, even though he'd been in the Realm of the Damned for a thousand years, but in other respects, current human society was baffling.

Dex rolled his eyes. "Of course you wouldn't if you don't need a job to begin with."

That was true enough. "Tell me more about your work. I assume you like coffee?"

Dex laughed. "Yeah, I love coffee as much as the next person. I've been at the same coffee shop for years and wouldn't want to work anywhere else. The team is great, and it's the perfect job to give me time to do my pottery."

Luc leaned closer, repositioning his legs so his knees bracketed Dex's but didn't touch. "Pottery?"

Dex shifted slightly, resting a knee against Luc's inner thigh. The touch sparked and smoldered. Dex didn't pull away. "I make pottery and sell some of my pieces at work. Mugs and bowls and things. I'm opening an online shop."

So, Dex and the red mug were connected. Luc hated himself for breaking it, but even that couldn't bring him down while Dex's knee pressed against him. "I love that. Handmade items are precious. Do you have pictures of your work?"

Dex's eyes widened a fraction. "I can show you my website. I haven't promoted it yet, so no one's really seen it."

"I'd be the first?" Luc could have purred.

"Pretty much." Dex grabbed his phone and unlocked it. As he clicked around on the device, he rested his other hand on Luc's knee, leaning in to show him the screen. As if he'd suddenly remembered himself, Dex stiffened. "Sorry." He snatched his hand back.

Luc's lips twitched. "You have my permission to touch me."

Dex cleared his throat, a slight flush bringing a rosy undertone to his soft brown cheeks. He refocused on the phone and his hand returned to Luc's knee, his touch delicate. "This is my site. I've only got a few items listed so far. Mugs are always popular at Seaside Coffee, so I'm hoping they will be online too."

Luc could hardly concentrate on Dex's words. Another man's touch had never been this captivating, never called for more the way Dex's did. "I like the mugs. The earthy colors you've chosen are striking."

Dex chuckled softly. "Thanks."

"Show me the other items?"

Dex clicked the back button and brought up a bowl, scrolling through the different glazes, his other hand unmoving on Luc's knee.

Did he feel the tug between them as acutely as Luc? Dex's touch filled Luc up, proving he wasn't an empty shell after all. Perhaps he could show Dex who he was without words. They could connect in the most pure sense.

Luc leaned closer. "Can I touch you?"

Dex's gaze snapped from the phone to him. "Yeah."

Luc snaked an arm around Dex's shoulders, and Dex's breath stuttered. He squeezed Luc's knee before sliding his hand higher.

Luc swallowed a growl. His little mate was forward. Luc loved that. Not shy in the face of their connection. Dex must feel it too, even if he had no clue what it was.

Dex set the phone on the bar, his lashes fluttering as his fingers stroked Luc's inner thigh. He angled his face ever so slightly upward as if he couldn't help being a little needy.

Luc's voice dropped low. "You have gorgeous lips."

Dex's breath caught. "Kiss me?"

Pulling Dex in, Luc slid him off his stool and nestled him between his thighs. After the briefest pause, he covered Dex's lips with his.

Stubble scratched Luc's cheeks. Dex didn't hesitate, meeting Luc motion for motion. He fell into it, licking Dex's sweet lips, the hint of sour from his beer sharpening his senses.

Dex smelled earthy and rich. Luc breathed deep, then plunged his tongue into Dex's mouth. Dex's fingers stroked his thigh, not quite high enough to brush Luc's growing arousal, and his other hand settled on Luc's hip.

Luc tangled his fingers in Dex's short, thick hair, deepening the kiss. He should hoist Dex onto the bar and make a meal of him, show him what the Devil's wicked lips could really do, then claim him in front of any humans who dared look at them.

My mate. Mine.

Dex pulled back, his lips wet and swollen, gray eyes dark with lust. "Who needs small talk when you can kiss like that?"

Luc let out the ghost of a laugh. "I can be a charmer when I want to be, but it's refreshing to be real."

Dex dragged his teeth over his bottom lip. "I don't think I've ever met anyone quite like you."

"Oh?" Pride expanded in Luc's chest. "I'd say you're right about that, and I know for a fact that I've never met anyone like you, Dex."

"There's the charmer."

"I mean it," Luc said seriously. "I won't charm you for the sake of it."

Fuck, was he killing the mood? It was immaterial. He wanted Dex to know that he wasn't putting on an act. Screwing up and falling into his old habits was unacceptable.

Forget claiming Dex on the bar. This was his mate. Luc had to do better.

He couldn't accept Dex's affection under false pretenses. Nothing but truth for his mate. Nothing that wasn't real. Dex had to choose Luc, knowing who he was, with nothing clouding his judgment.

Dex ran a hand along Luc's shirt buttons. Perhaps the mood wasn't dead after all. "Will you charm me if I ask you to? Say, back at my place? I live less than ten minutes away."

Luc's fire raged, his cock fully hard and fangs aching to drop. He burned to go home with Dex and fuck him until neither of them could think. "You want to take me home?"

"I sure do. A little fun is exactly what I need today."

Luc could grant his wish. He wanted nothing more than to give his mate everything he desired, large and small. But if he had sex with Dex now, and later revealed he was the Devil, that would be its own kind of lie.

Dex had to choose *him*. He had to climb into bed with him with his eyes open, and Luc couldn't reveal it all in one afternoon.

Luc ran a finger across Dex's knuckles. "I'd like to go on a date first."

"A date? You don't need to wine and dine me. I'm down."

Luc reveled in the flush deepening on Dex's cheeks. "Your willingness is intoxicating, but I'd prefer to get to know you before we're intimate. I like you. I like talking to you as well as kissing you, and I'd like more than an afternoon with you, if you're willing to have me."

"Oh." Dex paused like he wasn't sure what to do with this turn of events. "You're not into casual hookups?"

Luc ran a hand down Dex's spine, unable to stop touching him. "Not with you."

Dex's flush spread to his ears, and he withdrew his hand from Luc's thigh, rubbing the back of his neck. "Um. I don't usually date, but I like the sound of more than an afternoon." He made a cute face, lip quirking on one side. "I'd like to get to know you, too."

Luc prayed Dex wouldn't regret it once he did.

4

DEX

On Sunday morning, Dex woke and smiled at the ceiling. Fuck, that was a novelty. Sundays were always good because it meant brunch with Ollie, but his mood didn't usually lift until he'd left the condo.

Apparently, having a date to look forward to that night was all it took.

While Dex had initially been disappointed when Luc hadn't come home with him, the anticipation coiling inside him over the last few days had been a welcome change. He hadn't been on a date in years.

He wasn't usually as forward as he'd been with Luc. Dex almost didn't know what had come over him, other than a burning need to offer his body to Luc. With any luck, he'd get the opportunity tonight.

He got up, crossed the hall to the bathroom, and turned on the shower, careful not to mess up anything before the open home later.

The condo was a two-bedroom, two-bathroom set-up, which he'd managed to keep in good condition in the years since his parents had passed away. Dex still used the hall bathroom and slept in his childhood room rather than move into his parents' old room, the one with the ensuite, which he'd left completely unchanged.

He'd have to address that soon.

Dex pushed packing his parents' belongings to the back of his mind. No need to stress over that today.

After showering and wiping down the bathroom, Dex got dressed and headed downstairs to the bakery. The sweet smells had his mouth watering. He hadn't bought a coffee cake in ages, and Ollie had said Dante liked sweets, so it seemed like a good bet.

When the cake was secured in his canvas bag, Dex headed out and turned toward Ollie's apartment.

Dex had met Ollie's boyfriend, Dante, briefly at an art show a while back, but hadn't seen much of him since, and was looking forward to getting to know him better at brunch.

Should he tell Ollie he had a date? Butterflies swarmed in Dex's chest. Best not to. There'd be too many questions. He should see how dinner with Luc went before saying anything, in case it turned into nothing but a hookup after all.

Honestly, Dex wouldn't be disappointed if that's all it was. Part of him preferred it. Dinner and getting off sounded pretty damn good. Dex didn't do attachments, and any time he seriously considered having a boyfriend, with real feelings involved, his chest constricted.

What if he fell in love with Luc and something happened to him? Dex barely scraped through his parents' deaths without dropping out of school and losing his job.

But he needed a change, and not a small one. The things that had kept him safe were starting to hurt, like living in his parents' condo as if they might come home at any moment and thank him for looking after it.

Dex wasn't comforted by familiarity anymore. It haunted him, and being alone was starting to feed his fears rather than soothe them. He had to sort himself out. Holding back and distancing himself from people wasn't protecting him from anything.

Selling the condo was a healthy decision, even if the process was hard. Dex wanted to embrace his life and make it into something, not merely get through it.

A date with a hot, disarmingly upfront guy like Luc was unequivocally a step in the right direction, and after this first step, who knew? Dex might finally confront the other things he'd been holding back from.

There'd always been something missing with the guys he'd dated and had sex with, and the missing piece wasn't exactly a mystery. Orgasms were great, sure, but Dex could never ask for what he truly wanted.

He longed for his sex partners to get rough with him, tie him up, whisper twisted things in his ear, and that was only the start. But he was never able to broach the topic with anyone—fear of judgment always silenced him—and he was too intimidated to seek out kinky spaces. Everyone would be experienced, and all he had were fantasies, which led to a whole other realm of anxiety.

It was easier to ignore his desires, but Dex was tired of nothing in life feeling as good as it should.

He reached Ollie's building and buzzed to be let in, then slogged up the endless flights of stairs to the top floor.

Ollie answered the door so fast, he must have been hovering on the other side, waiting. "Hey." He beamed, smile blinding and hair disheveled.

Dex stepped inside. "What's up with you?"

"Huh?" A guilty look flashed across Ollie's face. "Nothing. I'm good. What did you bring?"

"Coffee cake." Dex followed Ollie down the hall and into the kitchen, where he unearthed the cake from his bag. "You haven't made coffee yet?"

"Shit, sorry." Ollie quickly grabbed a bag of coffee grinds and was about to dump them into the machine without a filter. He caught himself in time, laughed, and quickly found the filters.

Dex switched the oven to preheat. Something was up. Ollie wasn't usually scattered. "Where's Dante?"

"In my room. He should be out in a second."

As if on cue, Dante appeared. "Hi, Dex. It's nice to see you again." He stuck out his hand.

Dex shook it. "You too. Hope you like coffee cake."

Dante's face lit up. "Cake? I love cake."

"Ollie mentioned you prefer sweet breakfasts."

Dante gave Ollie a tender look. "I love sweets for every meal, but it's easier to get away with having cake for breakfast than dinner."

Ollie laughed and poked Dante in the side, his demeanor more relaxed. Maybe Ollie was worried about all three of them hanging out. This relationship was a big deal for him.

Harper, Ollie's roommate, sauntered into the kitchen as they poured their coffee—none for Dante, who made himself a hot chocolate complete with marshmallows and whipped cream. Once the coffee cake was plated, they trooped into the living room.

"What are we playing today?" Dex asked as he sank into the couch. Ollie and Dante were on the opposite end, with Harper in the armchair. "I hear you're a gamer, Dante."

"Sure am. I'll play anything and everything." Dante took a sip of hot chocolate and licked the cream from his lips.

Ollie fidgeted beside him. "Why don't we chat and eat first, then game later?"

"Okay." Dex frowned at Ollie's renewed nervousness.

"How's selling the condo going?" he asked.

Dex's gut twisted. "The first open home is today, thank god, but I can't stop feeling shitty about it."

"There's nothing to feel shitty about," Ollie said.

"I know. I'm not having second thoughts. I need to do this to move on, and I'm ready. But being ready doesn't mean it's easy. You know?"

Ollie squeezed his shoulder. "I know." His gaze wandered to Harper and lingered.

That was odd. Maybe Ollie had told Harper about his parents' deaths? Dex didn't mind. He got sick of explaining it to people. Maybe Dante knew, too.

Ollie's attention returned to Dex. "I've got something to tell you."

The air in the room seemed to shift, settling heavily over them. Dante placed a hand on Ollie's thigh as if in support.

What the fuck. Did Ollie have bad news?

Dex's heart raced, and his palms broke out in a sweat. Was Ollie sick? What if he had cancer? What if it was terminal? For a second, Dex couldn't breathe.

"What is it?" he choked out.

Ollie took the mug from Dex's hand and squeezed his fingers. "I'm okay. I didn't mean to scare you. Fuck, it's not bad."

Dex sucked in a lungful of air, not bothering to pretend his mind hadn't gone exactly where Ollie suspected. He nodded and got himself under control.

"It's something Dante, Harper, and I all want to share with you, actually," Ollie went on.

Huh?

Dex looked around at each of them. The tone was serious, but it wasn't like Ollie was about to make some big announcement about the three of them. Maybe about him and Dante, but

Harper had his own boyfriend, so including him seemed random.

Ollie turned to Dante. "I don't know how to start without sounding like I'm pulling a prank."

"Want me to try?" Dante asked.

Dex couldn't take the suspense. "Please, someone tell me. I don't care how it sounds."

Dante turned to him with a soft expression, wrinkles forming around his eyes and reminding Dex that he was older than the rest of them. "Ollie learned a secret several weeks ago, and he'd like to share it with you."

"A secret?"

"Yes, one that Harper and I are already aware of. That's why we're all here."

Dex looked to Ollie for guidance.

Ollie smiled, but his dimples didn't appear. "Keep an open mind."

"Sure. Of course. I won't judge you guys." Maybe they were all into some obscure secret sex thing? Dex definitely wouldn't judge them for that.

"Magic is real," Ollie blurted out. "Harper and Dante can both do magic."

Dex wasn't sure his mind could open *that* far. He laughed. "I see why you were worried. Come on. Don't mess with me."

"We're not," Ollie said earnestly. "I want you to know the truth, so I don't have to hide anything from you. This way, you can get to know Dante and Harper for real. Magic is part of who they are."

Dex shook his head. "Magic isn't real. It can't be."

If it were, why did his parents die in a stupid boating accident? Why couldn't magic have saved them? Unless... Maybe it wasn't too late to change the past if magic were real.

Ollie squeezed his hand again. "It is real, and we can show you so you don't have to take our word for it. But magic isn't perfect. It can't do everything." Ollie hesitated, tone serious. "Some things are still impossible and can't be stopped or undone."

Was he saying...? No. Dex didn't believe this. He couldn't. Except Ollie's expression was so tender that Dex's heart cracked. Ollie would never joke about his parents' deaths, and that had to be what he was referring to.

Tears welled in Dex's eyes, and his throat clogged. "What can magic do if it can't bring people back?"

Fuck, had he said that out loud? Was he entertaining the possibility that Ollie wasn't full of shit?

"It can protect you and help heal you." Of course, Ollie started with the things that would soothe Dex's worries. "Magic potions can help you sleep. Illusions can make you invisible."

Yeah, right.

"And what? You're going to show me?" Dex's stomach roiled. He didn't need this today. Worrying about Ollie having bad news and then being blindsided by the stupid shred of hope that magic could undo the worst thing to ever happen to him was too much.

"I can make myself invisible," Dante said as if it were perfectly normal. "Should we start with that?"

"Sure. Why the fuck not?" Dex blinked his unshed tears away.

There was no way it would work. He didn't know why he'd gotten so emotional over this dumb...whatever it was.

Of course this wasn't real.

Dex had been prepared to like Ollie's boyfriend, but now he wasn't sure. If Dante had dragged Ollie into some delusional nonsense, Dex would have words with him.

Dante had another sip of hot chocolate, then cleared his throat. He was there, sitting on the couch on Ollie's other side, and a second later, he was gone.

Dex's stomach dropped.

Dante reappeared. "Ta-da." He released his mug, but instead of it falling and spilling hot chocolate everywhere, it floated in front of him.

It had to be special effects. If this were a video, Dex would have rolled his eyes. But how did you pull off this sort of thing in person?

"So you're a carnival magician?" Dex crossed his arms, heat flooding his cheeks. "You think I'm gullible? What's wrong with you guys? I'm not in the mood."

Ollie grabbed his hand. "We're not tricking you."

Harper stood from the armchair and grabbed a candle from the coffee table. "I have a talent for alchemy and potion brewing. Want to see me turn this wax into wood?" He held out the candle.

Dex touched it, the wax tacky beneath his fingers. Harper had always been quiet and nothing but sweet-natured. As far as Dex was aware, he wasn't the type to mess around.

"Fine. Let's see."

Harper cupped the candle in both hands and murmured words under his breath. There was a flash of light. Dex blinked, and the candle had transformed from wax to what looked like a thin branch, the wick sticking out of the top.

Dex reached for it, and Harper passed it over. Tugging on the wick, Dex couldn't get it to budge. "How do I know you didn't swap out the candle for this?"

"Where did the candle go?" Harper held out his arms. He wore a tight tank top and shorts. He couldn't exactly hide anything up his sleeve.

Dex inspected the ground around them and found nothing,

but that didn't mean it wasn't a trick. He faced Ollie. "How did they get you to believe? Show me what you saw."

It couldn't have been these parlor tricks, not with how confident Ollie sounded. Dex didn't know the details, but everything he'd seen could be faked. The candle had to be somewhere.

Ollie's expression darkened.

Dante put a hand on his shoulder. "I can show you one of the things Ollie saw, but we'll have to go outside."

Ollie whipped around. "What do you mean?"

"You saw my wings when you first learned about magic. I'll show Dex what I really look like."

Ollie nodded, seeming relieved.

"Let's go to the roof and I'll fly around." Dante stood, and Harper followed him down the hall.

Dex wished he were back in bed. Why couldn't they play video games and eat too much coffee cake like he'd expected?

Ollie pulled Dex to his feet. "I'm sorry. This seemed like a good idea, but you look like I ruined your morning."

"No. Don't apologize. I want to know what's happening." Dex was grateful Ollie had shared whatever this was. That way, he could protect Ollie if Dante and Harper were taking advantage of him somehow.

He let Ollie lead him to the roof, where Dante was standing with his shirt off. Harper sipped his coffee as if this were any other Sunday.

"I've cast an illusion over myself so no one but you three can see me," Dante explained.

Dex would have rolled his eyes, but what they'd said about flying hit him in a new light. His blood ran cold. "Wait! You aren't jumping off the roof, are you?"

"No." Dante smiled reassuringly, but Dex didn't feel any less terrified.

Ice pooled in his gut. Fuck, he had to make sure no one got hurt. Why had he agreed to come out here?

Dante turned away, showing Dex a full back tattoo of folded wings. Surely, he didn't believe he could fly because of a tattoo? Dex opened his mouth to double-check that Dante wasn't going near the edge of the roof when the tattoos changed, rippling through Dante's brown skin and disappearing.

Wings burst from Dante's back and spread wide, gray feathers sparkling in the sun, his wingspan stretching at least ten feet across.

Dante turned to face them and horns sprouted from his hair. Dex gripped Ollie tight. Dante's wings flapped, and he lifted off the ground, hovering a few feet above the roof.

It couldn't be a trick. There was no way to make tattoos disappear like that, or for wings that big to sprout out of nowhere.

Suddenly, it was like Dex was on a tilt-a-whirl ride at the fair. "Are—are you an angel?" His voice shook. He tore his eyes from Dante, focusing on Ollie.

He knew what this meant, right? Holy shit. *An angel.* That meant...

Ollie smiled softly, a hint of sadness unmistakable.

Dante landed and folded his wings against his back. "I'm not an angel."

"But you're not human." Dex pointed at his wings.

"No, I'm not."

Dex rounded on Harper. "Do you have wings?"

"No." Harper laughed. "I'm a witch. A person who can do magic. I can't do everything Dante can."

Dex would think about that later. "What are you, Dante?"

"A fallen Eternal being. What you'd consider an angel doesn't exist."

What did that mean?

Something seemed to be slipping from Dex's grasp, and he scrambled to capture it. "What does exist? Does Heaven?"

"Not in the way you think. There is an afterlife. An Eternal Realm. This"—Dante spread his arms wide—"is the Human Realm."

Dex's hands shook. His chest tightened, and something bubbled inside him. He needed to lie down. "So—so people go to an afterlife when they die?" That was the important thing. Who cared about semantics and if Heaven didn't exist *in the way he thought?*

"Yes." Dante stepped closer and clasped Dex's shoulder, the word echoing around them. "All humans enter the Eternal Realm when they die, and eventually reincarnate."

Dex couldn't breathe.

"That's why I wanted to tell you," Ollie whispered. "Yeah, I want you to know Dante and Harper, and I don't like keeping secrets from you, but with you selling the condo, it seemed like a good time to share all this with you. Maybe it'll help."

Dex's vision blurred, his throat too thick to speak.

"I hope I'm not making everything harder for you."

Dex cleared his throat. "You aren't. I've been thinking about them a lot. And—and now you're saying my parents are in an Eternal Realm. I'll see them again?"

Dante squeezed his shoulder. "Human souls aren't the same in the Eternal Realm as they are on Earth, but I'd say your parents will likely wait for you before entering the sacred process of moving on."

Dex burst into tears, huge choking sobs coming out of nowhere, his entire body shaking. Ollie hugged him tight, holding him as his knees went weak. Dex clung to him, his fingers digging into Ollie's back. Dante's grip on his shoulder didn't falter. They held him firm. Held him through it.

This had to be the greatest gift anyone had given him. Hope

ripped Dex into pieces, the pain so overwhelming it was impossible to do anything but feel.

He hadn't been religious like his mom. He'd gone to church when he was young, but when his parents had died, he hadn't been able to make himself believe they still existed somewhere.

"Thank you," he sobbed into Ollie's ear. "Thank you."

5

———

LUCIFER

Pickings were slim in the housing market in the Banks, where Dex lived, especially when Luc ruled out all the cramped apartments that wouldn't accommodate his wings.

He decided to make do with a recently renovated warehouse in the adjacent neighborhood. Having his own building was ideal, and pretty much essential once he and Dex consummated their mateship. Luc intended to make the sweet young man scream.

His pleasure would echo through the loft nicely.

Luc refused to admit he'd copied Onyx. His brother wasn't the only demon allowed to live in a loft. Besides, Luc's new home was located in the Docks. Onyx was in the South Banks. They were completely different neighborhoods.

Sitting on his new bed, Luc tipped his face toward the sun streaming through the high-set windows. Dex's lips haunted him. Sweet and soft, and oh-so adept. Where else on Luc's body might he like to put his mouth? Luc intended to map every inch of Dex with his.

But he wouldn't be fucking Dex tonight. Luc wouldn't go further than kissing. Not until Dex knew.

Luc deserved a medal for his restraint.

If his brothers were aware of how well he was treating his mate, maybe they'd give him a chance. Though probably not. He was sure his intentions were selfish deep down. Luc wanted to do right by Dex, but only so long as it led to him accepting the mating bond.

Luc had to reveal his being the Devil in the most appealing way. Before their relationship went too far, but not before Dex was attached and willing to continue what they'd started.

It was a delicate balance. Nothing had felt so fragile in Luc's life. This was his chance to share his side of the story, reveal his mistakes as he saw them before judgment was cast.

Luc's phone vibrated in his pocket, and his heart skipped. Was Dex messaging about their date? Hopefully not to cancel. Luc hurried to unlock the phone.

No. The text wasn't from Dex.

UNKNOWN:

This is Onyx.

Luc saved the number, his fingers trembling, which was absurd.

So, Ash and Dante hadn't poisoned Onyx against him. What fucking luck. This was all he needed. A chance. He could work with this. Maybe in time, he'd have his mate and brothers.

Luc called Onyx. The phone rang and went to voicemail. Luc hung up, scowling.

Onyx had texted less than a minute ago. Why hadn't he picked up? Luc called again. And again.

"What?" Onyx snapped, answering at last.

"You texted me."

"I know."

There was a long silence.

"Can we meet?" Luc asked.

Onyx growled, and Luc braced himself. "Fine. I don't know why I assumed you'd play it cool. Meet me at my loft. Stay on the roof and I'll see you there." Onyx hung up without waiting for a reply.

Luc rubbed his temple, fire raging inside him. Play it cool? Apparently, it was too much to expect Onyx to be glad to see him, even after he'd reached out. How was he supposed to fix anything if he was fighting Onyx's temper the entire way?

The flight to Onyx's loft was short, the city blurring beneath Luc, his wings beating steadily while his heart thundered. He landed on the empty roof of Onyx's building and shot off a text announcing his arrival.

Luc rubbed his chest, a strange hollowness spreading through him. Relinquishing control of the situation wasn't something he usually tolerated. Onyx better appreciate the gesture. This was big and should help prove that he wanted to fix things.

Eventually, Onyx landed beside him, folding his shimmering blue wings at his back. "So, you're hanging around town. Why aren't you off on a tropical island or something?"

Luc raised a brow. "I told you I'd be here." Never mind that he'd planned to leave. He'd have come back when Onyx called.

"Don't say that like not lying this one time means anything. Wow, you're here. I'm so impressed." Onyx rolled his eyes.

Luc clenched his teeth. His brother didn't make anything easy. It was best to get right to it. "I'm sorry, Onyx. I had no idea you felt left behind."

"But you should have. We've been over this. I didn't *feel* left behind. I was going to *be* left behind. I told you that I didn't want to go, and you ignored me."

Luc still couldn't believe he'd missed it. When he'd been preparing to leave the Eternal Realm, he'd been sure Onyx was as committed to following as Ash or Dante. He'd hardly spared it much thought.

"I don't understand how you couldn't have wanted your mate."

Onyx's cheeks flushed crimson, and he clenched his fists. "That's your problem, Luc. You can't understand anyone who doesn't agree with you. Your way is the only way. You're the most arrogant motherfucker I've ever met."

The extent to which Luc's self-absorption had blinded him was hard to wrap his head around. Onyx had seen everything in a completely different light. It threw Luc off balance. He wanted to say it wasn't possible, that Onyx was wrong, which seemed to be the root of his problem.

Onyx wasn't wrong, and Luc's inability to see his truth wasn't his brother's fault.

"I'm sorry I didn't listen. You're right. I'm arrogant. My confidence blinded me to everything else."

Onyx's brows shot upward, and he shoved a hand through his hair, his horns hidden away as usual. "Your confidence? What is this, some sort of my-strengths-are-my-weakness bullshit?"

Luc snorted, and Onyx's eyes flashed with blue fire. "No. That's not what I meant. I used to think my unwavering conviction was a strength. I believed I was right because I held logic above all else. I was right about finding our mates—they had to be on Earth if they weren't in the Eternal Realm. Even when I realized I was wrong, I still believed I knew the best way forward. I saw no other path because I was so full of myself that nothing else existed. No one else's opinion mattered. That's not a strength."

It was obvious now, even if it hadn't been back then.

"You can say that again." Onyx scowled. "But how was letting magic seep into humanity the best way forward?"

"It wasn't. I already told you that I didn't father the first witch. Fixing that mistake was the only way forward."

Onyx scoffed. "I don't believe you didn't create witches. You wouldn't fix something for someone else."

"Maybe not entirely. Would you believe it was, in part, my arrogance that led me to take credit for creating witches, even though I didn't do it? I believed myself so important that the council would punish me and spare the rest of you."

Onyx's eyes narrowed. "I still don't see it. You wouldn't stick your neck out for anyone."

Luc tamped down his growing frustration. "Don't think of me as you know me now. Not as the one who imprisoned you. Think of me as I was before. Wouldn't that Luc have sacrificed himself to protect others?"

Onyx's brow furrowed, his eyes widening ever so slightly.

Luc pressed on. "If I'd been the one punished as I'd hoped, then I'd never have betrayed you."

Onyx's tentative surprise vanished. "How the hell do you figure that?"

"If the council never created the Realm of the Damned, I'd never have needed to trap anyone."

Onyx shook his head. "Creating Hell didn't mean you needed to trap us there. What the fuck, Lucifer? The council didn't make you do shit. Their decision was questionable at best, and yours was even worse."

Could Luc ever make Onyx see?

Back then, his brothers might have believed he'd taken the fall for a fellow demon. He should have told them what he'd done before it all went bad.

But his arrogance had gotten in the way. Why consult them when he'd already decided?

When Nox came to him and confessed that he'd fathered a half-human child, Luc feared the Eternal Realm's wrath. Nox didn't deserve to be punished for loving a human who wasn't his mate, so Luc took responsibility. How much more could the council hate him? He'd led the fall. He was already their number one enemy.

But he wasn't the one punished. Witches were. They were banished to Hell after death for the crime of being born. And the other demons hated him. They saw having that child as a betrayal of their quest for mates.

Luc should have told the truth then.

But the first step away from being a trusted friend had already been taken. Once everyone's anger had become clear, Luc suspected they'd no longer believe the truth, and Nox wasn't backing him up, too afraid to be the one cast out.

Nox had more offspring, and others saw no point in resisting. There were no consequences to their actions, and there was no fear when the Eternal Realm punished the resulting witches. Luc's pleas to do the right thing fell on deaf ears. They all considered him a hypocrite.

Only one way to mitigate the damage had remained.

Demons didn't need to hear how their mates were out there. They didn't need to feel seen and sympathized with in their heartbreak. Luc had tried for centuries, and it had done nothing but lead to the current mess. Demons needed to be forced to do the right thing.

There needed to be consequences.

"Creating Hell didn't mean I had to trap you. You're right, Onyx. But the Eternal Realm punishing witches for what we'd done meant someone else needed to punish us. I couldn't let magic completely overrun humanity. If we'd stayed on Earth and demons had offspring left and right, how long would it have been until magic infected all of humanity and completely stopped the cycle of reincarnation?"

Onyx took a step backward, his feathers ruffling. "I don't know. We wouldn't have all had children."

"That's not the point, and you know it. Things were going wrong, the consequences reaching far beyond us. Falling should have hurt no one but *us*. We were ruining things we never should have touched, damning innocents to Hell. I asked demons to stop and think, and no one bothered to listen."

Onyx stalked forward, jabbing Luc's bare chest with a finger, the touch disproportionally painful. "Why would they listen to you? If it wasn't you who started it, you should have said."

"That was a mistake, but I can't take it back!" Luc heaved a breath. He was yelling and had to rein it in. "If everyone had to hate me—fear me—to ensure humanity wasn't destroyed, then that was the price I had to pay as the one who led you all here."

Onyx's mouth fell open. "Why didn't you say that? Why didn't you come to me? Why not confide in Ash or Dante? All you did was spout bullshit about a prison."

Luc's tail thrashed. "It wasn't bullshit. We had to be imprisoned to stop the spread of magic. To stop more souls from being banned from the Eternal Realm. I said that. The logic was sound. This time, it was you who didn't listen, like I didn't listen to you about not wanting to fall. You, Ash, and Dante cried about was how unfair it was to imprison those who hadn't procreated."

"It was unfair."

Luc's fire sparked, his eyes itching as they burned. "So I should have weeded out the guilty demons? How? After that first demon came to me, no one else would confess. I tried to figure it out and asked for cooperation. It didn't work, so I did what needed to be done."

Onyx clenched his jaw. "What needed to be done. That's

one hell of a way to say you violated me and stole a piece of my very essence."

"I know. And you might never forgive me for what I did to you. That's your right. But I need you to know that I'm sorry. I regret it. Hurting you, Ash, and Dante was a line I never should have crossed."

Once he'd crossed it, nothing remained sacred, and there seemed to be no point in doing the right thing. Luc was bad, and he leaned into it. He had to embrace being the enemy to control the enraged demon population. There was no room left for kindness, and no one would have believed it was real if he'd tried.

"I don't know what to do with you, Luc." Onyx seemed to deflate, his wings drooping. "Even if what you say about not fathering the first witch is true, it doesn't make the rest okay."

Fuck, there was no fixing this, was there? No apology would undo the harm he'd caused the three men he loved most in all the realms.

"Give me more time." Luc couldn't help begging. "Let me talk to you like this again."

"I don't know." Onyx swiped a hand over his face. "Even if I can get my head around the reasons you didn't ask for help, stole my magic, and imprisoned me, that doesn't excuse what you've done since returning to the Human Realm."

"Onyx, please—"

"I have to go." His wings snapped out, and he leaped into the air. "Don't try to justify hurting Harper and Ollie. It'll make the hole you're trying to crawl out of deeper."

Onyx took off toward the river, disappearing into the distance.

The memory of Dante's snarling rage filled Luc's mind, and the smell of Ollie's blood permeated the air. Luc took a gasping breath. He was sinking to the bottom of the sea, and he deserved to drown. To be buried in a hole he could never crawl out of.

He stood like a statue until the light began to change.

At last, he shook himself. He had to get ready for his date. It was better to focus on his mate anyway. If he could get Dex on his side, maybe he could help Luc mend things with Onyx.

And if not, at least he wouldn't be alone.

6

——

DEX

Perhaps Dex should have canceled this date. Everything was different after the morning he'd had, like his world had been flipped upside down.

His insides were in knots as he reached the park by the river. He'd managed to de-puff his eyes and didn't think it was obvious he'd spent the day crying, so at least there was that.

Dex sighed and reminded himself of the reason he hadn't canceled: he didn't want to miss his chance with Luc. Getting his life back seemed more important than ever. He wanted to hope, not wallow. But he wasn't sure he could talk to someone normally after finding out magic and the afterlife were real.

Dex's steps felt disorientingly light, given the mess inside him, almost like he'd drift away. Was that good or bad? God, everything was just so strange right now. Like a dream.

A cool breeze came off the water and caressed his over-heated body. The park was quiet. Most of the benches were empty, as were the play structures, noticeably absent of children. Most of the people here were clustered around an ice cream truck parked at the far end, the smell of fresh waffle cones filling the air.

Luc stood with his back to Dex, leaning against the stone wall lining the riverbank. He was dressed more formally than Dex, similar to how he'd looked at Dorthy's. His dark gray slacks hugged his ass, and his dress shirt fit him like a glove.

As if he sensed Dex staring, Luc spun around. He ran a hand through his night-black hair, pushing the waves out of his face, and smiled.

A pleasurable thrill wound down Dex's spine, and the knots constricting his insides unraveled.

"Good evening." Luc approached, his strides graceful. The sleeves of his dark red shirt were cuffed at his elbows, the neck unbuttoned, revealing a few wisps of dark chest hair.

"Hey." Dex suddenly had no idea what to do with his hands.

Luc towered over him. He had to be well over six feet tall, maybe even a full foot above Dex's five-foot-seven, if that was possible.

Dex's pulse picked up. What a man like this could do to him. If he asked nicely, would Luc chase him down, pin him to the ground, and—

"How was your day?"

Dex cleared his throat and banished the erotic images flooding his mind. Hopefully, his flaming cheeks passed as a reaction to the warm night. "My day was kind of draining. How was yours?"

Luc's lips twitched downward. "It was all right. Would you like to go for a walk before dinner?"

"Sure." Dex didn't know where they were eating, but he could easily be talked into skipping the meal altogether.

"Let's head along the water." Luc placed his hand on the small of Dex's back and steered him toward the path that ran along the river, heading upstream. "How about an ice cream?"

Dex glanced at the bright pink truck. "Yeah, sounds good."

They detoured to stand in the small line.

Dex swore he caught a whiff of campfire smoke as Luc bent to speak in his ear. "What's your favorite flavor?"

"Mm, anything with caramel or fudge."

Luc turned to the menu posted on the side of the truck. "Should we get salted caramel?"

"That's what I'm getting. You'll need your own."

Luc chuckled. "All right. I'd like tonight to be my treat, but I know these things can be tricky on dates. Would you be comfortable with me paying?"

It was considerate to ask rather than assume paying would be fine, and Dex found he was comfortable when he wouldn't have been otherwise. "I don't mind you treating me." Especially if it pleased Luc as much as his smile suggested.

"Excellent," Luc said in a low rumble.

Something seemed to sizzle between them, and renewed heat flooded Dex.

Did Luc feel it, too? The gleam in his eyes had Dex thinking he did.

Luc ordered a scoop of strawberry in a waffle cone, and Dex got his salted caramel. "I figured we could share," Luc said once they both had their cones.

"Did you?" Dex grinned. How cute.

"If you want." Luc's attention traveled from the ice cream to Dex. "Or I can taste it off your lips. I'm fine either way."

Dex's heart skipped. "I like your thinking."

Mischief lit Luc's expression. He licked his ice cream, tilting his head as his tongue wrapped around the scoop. He hummed, closing his lips over the tip. "Tasty."

Fuck, Dex's mind was back in X-rated territory. "Careful. If you treat that ice cream any better, you're going to need some privacy."

Luc's eyes seemed to flash in the low light, reflecting the red of his shirt for a split second. "This is nothing, my dear Dex. But I like where your head is at."

Dex's stomach swooped, and he almost lost his footing. "Can't wait for you to deliver on that promise."

Luc chuckled. "Waiting certainly won't be easy. Oh, careful. Yours is about to drip."

Dex quickly licked his ice cream. Thank fuck he hadn't canceled this date. Being around Luc was exactly what he needed after the day he'd had.

They ambled slowly along the path, eating their ice creams, and every time he looked over, Dex caught Luc eyeing him.

Dex stopped at a small lookout nook with a bench and leaned against the wall. "Here, let's swap."

He held out his cone to Luc, urging him to hand his over. Dex held Luc's stare as he licked the ice cream, the strawberry a fresh burst of sweetness on his tongue.

"You're beautiful," Luc murmured, the caramel ice cream forgotten.

Dex sucked his bottom lip between his teeth. "Right back at you."

Luc was wearing his subtle red lip stain again. It suited him perfectly, even without any other makeup. He shifted closer to Dex and swiped ice cream from the corner of Dex's mouth. Bringing his finger to his lips, Luc sucked it slowly.

Oh, dear god. Dex was ready to get on his knees.

"Why was your day draining?" Luc finally tasted the caramel ice cream and hummed, considering the flavor.

His question brought Dex's heated thoughts to a halt. It wasn't what he'd expected Luc to say after licking his finger like that.

Was he not trying to seduce Dex? Was the whole *you're beautiful* and sharing ice cream not a move? Could this be how Luc acted normally? Fuck, that made it hotter, and made his question seem sincere. Like he wasn't asking why Dex's day was draining out of social obligation, but because he'd considered it and wanted to know.

"I've had a draining week, to be honest." Dex had another taste of Luc's ice cream. "Actually, a draining month. I'm selling my condo."

"Is that stressful?"

"Yeah. I've never dealt with anything this major. The money will go right into buying a new place, but still. I didn't buy the condo myself, so I don't know what I'm doing." The financial transaction was out of his depth, that was for damn sure.

Luc swapped their ice creams back. "Do you have anyone to help you?"

It was sweet of him to ask. "I found a good realtor and got advice on the financial stuff. I have it under control."

Luc nodded in approval, his tone serious. "It still sounds like a great deal to handle. Are you moving away from the city?"

"No." He'd never do that. Dex had a bite of ice cream before continuing, "I love living here. It's my condo that I can't stand being in any longer."

He'd never said the words out loud, not even to Ollie. He'd always danced around how bad it had gotten.

Luc's brow furrowed. "Why can't you stand it? Is it unsafe?"

"Not at all. The building is great. Way better than anywhere I'd normally be living at my age."

"That's good." Luc seemed relieved, though his concern remained. "What upsets you about it?"

"It's my parents' place. They died four years ago, and I've been living there by myself. And I mean, it's a privilege to even own a condo. I know that. But I hate it." Dex's throat tightened.

He'd never let himself acknowledge how true that was. It was time to move out and move on, yes, but it went deeper. It was painful sitting amid so many reminders. Hate summed it up perfectly.

Luc shifted subtly closer. "Why have you stayed if you hate it?"

"I didn't always. It helped me feel connected to my parents for a long time. Sometimes, I wish I could get that back, and other times, I wish I'd left years ago, but that feels like a betrayal."

Luc placed a hand on Dex's shoulder. "You can grieve however you want. It's not a betrayal to move on and look after yourself, or change your mind."

"I realize that now. Selling is the right thing, even if it's exhausting for reasons beyond having to deal with open homes and legal shit."

"They say nothing worthwhile is easy. Though I think that's stupid. Suffering doesn't make something superior, and easy can be a sign that you're on the right track. But not in this case."

A shaky laugh bubbled out of Dex. "Was that supposed to be comforting?"

Luc shrugged, surprisingly bashful. "Not really. I was thinking out loud. Sorry."

"Don't be. I wasn't planning on saying any of this. Guess you can say it's been on my mind."

Luc ran his hand down Dex's arm. "We can talk about it. Would you like to tell me about your parents?"

Butterflies surged through Dex, and he took another bite of his ice cream to give himself a moment to think.

This had gotten personal fast. Maybe that's what Dex liked about it, even if the butterflies seemed to set off a twisting discomfort deep within.

He laughed unsteadily. "My family doesn't feel like the right topic for a date."

Luc seemed disappointed, his face falling. Fuck, it was like he actually cared. "Is it not a good topic because you don't want to talk about them or because it isn't what the arbitrary rules of dating tell you to do?"

"Damn, way to call me out. The second one."

"I wasn't calling you out." Luc's expression softened. "We don't have to follow a script or censor ourselves. I'd like to hear about your parents if you'd like to talk about them."

A soothing feeling replaced the butterflies and knots inside Dex. "All right. Let's keep walking."

Luc fell into step beside him, finishing off his ice cream, and Dex did the same. "I'm guessing you were close to your parents?"

"Yeah. I don't have any siblings, so growing up, my parents and I had lots of fun. They were genuinely supportive people, and not just when I did what they wanted. They listened when I told them how I felt."

Luc made a surprised sound. "I can't say the same. My parents, like many, I'm sure, supported what aligned with their vision for my life, and nothing more. I'm glad you weren't raised that way."

"Yeah, I was lucky. When I was younger, I didn't understand why my friends complained about their parents controlling their lives. I assumed they were upset they had to follow rules and curfews, and I wondered if I was a goodie-goodie. But then they were forced into careers they didn't want, doing degrees they hated, and I got it."

Different parents wouldn't have supported Dex's pursuit of art, and that was depressing. Yeah, making and selling pottery was a less stable career than others, but Dex loved it. He loved working at Seaside Coffee and never tolerated anyone looking down on his choices because he hadn't been brought up by people who cast those kinds of judgments.

And yes, Dex was probably romanticizing his family,

remembering the best parts and turning his parents into more perfect people than they'd been, but that seemed natural when he loved and missed them as much as he did. The fact remained —they had been good to him.

As they reached the end of the path, a smaller park marking its conclusion, Dex told Luc how his parents had encouraged his artistic side, and how they'd turned creativity into a family endeavor. He admitted, "I was devastated when they died. I'm only starting to move on now, to be honest."

Knowing his parents weren't gone forever lit the path to his future when it had been dark and murky for so long, but finding out he'd see them in the afterlife one day didn't erase his grief. It didn't make not having them around any easier.

Luc was quiet for a long moment. He seemed to be mulling over everything Dex had said, but it wasn't awkward. No one had ever put so much effort into listening to him.

"Your love for your parents is refreshing. Even if it hurts, it's a beautiful thing. I'm sorry you lost them."

Dex couldn't believe he'd shared so much. Even with Ollie, he'd avoided talking about most of this for years. "Thanks. Refreshing is a good word. For this, I mean." He gestured between the two of them.

The heavy emotions he'd been carrying around all day—all year—seemed to filter through a positive lens, highlighting what he'd loved rather than lost. It was a shift in perspective he wouldn't have had on his own, and he was grateful.

This was how today of all days should end.

Luc took Dex's hand. "I'm glad you think so."

The touch was warm, the heat welcome even on a summer evening. As if he couldn't stop now that he'd started, Dex added, "I regret holding back so much after they died."

Luc squeezed Dex's fingers. "What do you mean?"

"I've gotten paranoid." Dex swallowed. Fuck, this was not

the kind of thing you shared on a first date, but Luc didn't seem to judge, and that was so fucking rare. "I worry about things happening to my friends all the time, and that gets in the way of doing things. Today, I saw my best friend and he had some news. I immediately panicked, positive he was dying."

"Was it bad news?"

"No. Not even close." Dex rolled his eyes and glanced away. No way he could tell Luc what the news actually was, but that was all right.

Luc brought his fingers to Dex's chin, delicately nudging him until they were face to face. "How does worrying get in the way of doing things?"

Dex fidgeted under his gaze. "I don't date much."

Luc's furrowed brow softened. "I'm glad you put your fears aside to give me a chance."

Dex's cheeks flamed. "Same. I'd have regretted it otherwise."

"Me too." Luc's fingers tightened on Dex's chin, his voice painfully earnest. "I have more regrets than I can count, but you won't be one of them. I promise."

Fluttery warmth bloomed in Dex's chest. "Yeah. No regrets."

Luc hadn't promised that nothing bad would happen—he couldn't, no one could—and that still scared Dex. Having to grieve someone, especially a boyfriend, would be crushing. Knowing an afterlife waited wasn't the same as having someone in your life. It would still be a loss. But living a life ruled by fear was a loss too. And Dex wasn't letting that happen.

Not anymore.

7

LUCIFER

"Want to skip dinner?" Dex asked in a low voice, sending shivers from Luc's head to his toes.

Luc bit back a groan. *I'll make a meal of you.*

Dex's expression went from heated to eager, almost as if he'd read Luc's mind. "We can go back to my place and order in later."

Yes. Luc pulled Dex close, their bodies pressing together. "I love the sound of that, but I'd like to take this slow. There are things you need to know about me before we go to bed."

Dex cocked his head. "Like what?"

"Like who I am. It's a long, complicated story."

Dex opened his mouth, and Luc hurried on. He couldn't allow Dex to talk him out of this. "I want to get to know you, to know as much as I can about you. Sex has too often been an empty pleasure for me. I don't want that with you. I'm greedy—it's one of the things you should be aware of—and I want more from you than bodily release."

Dex's pupils blew wide, and he gripped Luc's shirt. "Saying stuff like only makes me want to fuck you more. You being open and understanding is why I want to skip dinner. Though your looks don't hurt."

Luc chuckled, a smoldering heat building inside him. "I promise the anticipation will make it better when we finally give in."

"*Ugh*, fine. If that's what you want, I won't push. I respect wanting to wait. But to be clear, I'm good to go the second you are."

Luc hummed in appreciation. "Noted. I love that you say what you want and aren't shy about it."

Dex opened his mouth once more, hesitated, and abruptly closed it, his smile faltering. "I like that you aren't afraid to want more than sex and stick to your convictions."

Luc had the impression that wasn't what he'd originally intended to say. Perhaps there was something Dex was shy about.

Before he could ask, Dex's voice dropped back into that sultry tone. "Most guys would take a sure thing and put the get-to-know-you stuff second."

"Oh, you tempt me to," Luc rumbled, letting Dex's moment of hesitation go. There was plenty of time to discover his secrets. That was the whole point of taking it slow. "But I've learned that temptation isn't everything. I mean it when I say you won't be another of my regrets. And I don't want to be one of yours."

Dex laughed. "Not possible."

Was that true? Luc hoped so; his desire for Dex burned from the inside out.

Would a sweet man like Dex go to bed with the Devil? Would a man who'd known pure love find anything to love in him? Luc was a terrible person. Not flawed, but rotten. He'd known it for a thousand years, but maybe he didn't have to be rotten forever. Maybe he could change.

Luc tilted Dex's chin and kissed his sugar-sweet lips. He'd

guard Dex like the precious soul he was. Luc's demon senses flared, hidden wings scorching his back. Dex was his mate, and Luc never wanted to let him go.

But he had to.

Luc let that truth wash over him as they kissed.

He could never mate Dex. If he bound them together, he'd regret it more than anything else in his life. Mating would prevent Dex from ever entering the Eternal Realm, where his parents waited. Luc knew he would never be allowed to return, no matter what he did, and refused to drag Dex down with him.

Dex deserved to see his beloved parents again. He needed to complete the sacred journey of passing from one mortal life to the next, healed of all the hurt this lifetime had caused him. Luc would not rob him of that.

Letting Dex go would be the first truly selfless thing Luc had ever done. It seemed there was something redeemable in him after all.

He should be raging at the unfairness of not getting to keep his mate—of being denied the eternal connection that he'd fallen to Earth to find—but how could he? What Dex needed was more important.

Luc wanted to give Dex everything. He wanted to love Dex, take care of him, explain the nature of who he was and what magic meant for Dex, and do anything he asked of him. If Dex wanted him, Luc would be his partner until the day he died.

But he *would* die.

Perhaps Luc would find Dex again after he reincarnated. Not if the council held his soul back, but even if they did, after his death, Dex would heal from this life and experience all the magic of the universe, and that was what mattered most.

The time Luc had on Earth with Dex deserved to be treasured, starting now.

Luc withdrew from their kiss. Dex's gray eyes were hazy, his lips plump and shiny. Luc ran a hand through Dex's hair. "Would you like to go to dinner?"

Dex cleared his throat. "Yeah. I'm ready."

An invisible string wrapped around Luc's heart and pulled tight, as if his yearning had manifested into a physical force. Knowing Dex would be wonderful, even if it wasn't forever.

Luc brushed a thumb across Dex's cheek. "Perfect."

And he was. Luc's sweet, delicate human was perfect, flaws and fears and all.

Dex slipped his arm around Luc and turned toward the street. "So, what's the long story? I'm dying to know more about you, and—"

"*Dex!*" someone shouted.

Dex whipped around, and Luc followed suit.

Across the street stood Dante and his mate.

Luc's heart stopped at the murderous look on Dante's fine-featured face. This was Ollie and Harper's neighborhood, but Luc had never run into any of them by accident before.

"Dex!" Ollie screamed as he frantically checked for cars, his face splotchy red and eyes wild. When the traffic was clear, he launched across the street, Dante at his side.

The scent of salt air and blood filled Luc's nose, washing away Dex's earthy musk. Luc froze, ice in his veins.

No. Wait. How did Ollie know Dex?

"Hey, Ollie..." Dex pulled ever so slightly away from Luc. "What's wrong?"

Ollie and Dante reached them in a rush, and Luc's chilled blood pounded in his ears.

Ollie glared at Luc, naked fear lining his face. "Get away from him!" He grabbed Dex and yanked him from Luc's embrace.

Dex stumbled into Ollie's arms. "What?" His gaze volleyed from Ollie to Luc and back.

Luc hadn't looked into Ollie's face that day on the beach, not until he'd been bleeding out in Dante's arms.

Coward. Couldn't even face the man before trying to kill him.

Now, Luc saw red blood splatters where there were none. For a flash, Ollie was cold and broken, and Luc hated himself.

"What the fuck are you doing?" Dante growled, his eyes flaming. He got in Luc's face, chest to chest, fisting Luc's shirt. "I told you to stay out of our lives."

"What's going on?" Dex sounded frantic now. He hadn't disentangled from Ollie, and Luc missed his touch like he'd lost a piece of himself.

Luc couldn't move. His insides quivered, brittle and breaking like a paper-thin ice sculpture.

They all knew each other? How?

Dante shoved Luc in the chest, and he stumbled against the river wall. "I'll ask you one more time, what the fuck are you playing at?"

Luc had eyes for no one but Dex. Their stares locked, Dex's piercing gray gaze confused and edged with panic.

"We're on a date." Dex pulled away from Ollie, but Ollie wouldn't let go. "What's happening? Ollie, how do you know Luc?"

"*Luc?*" Ollie heaved a ragged breath, voice breaking. "He's not *Luc*, he's the Devil. He tried to kill me."

"What?" Horror broke over Dex's face, cracking Luc's heart. "Kill you?"

Ollie grabbed Dex with both hands. "At the beach. When I said I was attacked, I couldn't tell you everything. He—he—I would have died if Dante hadn't saved me with magic."

"*Died?*" Dex rounded on Luc, not letting go of Ollie. The two friends clutched each other fiercely, as though the thought of letting go was impossible. "You hurt Ollie?"

Dex didn't react to the mention of magic. Ollie must have told him. If Luc had known, he could have...fuck. He needed to say something, but his thoughts were sluggish, like the ice in his veins really had frozen him.

"What are you doing with Dex?" Dante was in his face again, smoke tinging the air. "Hurting Ollie and Harper wasn't enough? You had to go after their friend, too?"

"N-no." Luc choked on the word.

"You hurt Harper?" Dex's features twisted into hard lines. "Is that why you followed me into Dorthy's?" He shook Ollie, panic bleeding into his tone. "What do you mean, the Devil? You said angels weren't real."

"They're not. But he is. Luc is a nickname."

"Wait." Glass seemed to tear Luc's throat apart as he spoke, the word no better than poison.

"No." Dante shoved him aside. "You have ten seconds to get out of here, Lucifer, or I'll knock you out and throw you in that prison after all. Fuck your truce. I should have known it was a lie."

"*Lucifer?*" Dex whispered, recoiling and moving further into Ollie's trembling grasp.

"Dex, please." Luc took a shaking step forward, but Dante dragged him back.

"D-don't listen." Ollie pulled Dex farther away, his voice shaking. "He can trick you with illusions, mind control."

"No. I wouldn't," Luc pleaded.

Dex trembled. "Mind control? This date wasn't real? You tricked me with magic?" His devastation shook the earth beneath Luc's feet.

Dante grabbed Luc by the collar, shocking him with invisible lightning. Luc's body went rigid, his heart stopping. He would have fallen if not for Dante's hold.

"Ollie, call Ash. Now."

Ollie scrambled for his phone.

No. Luc had to explain. But how could he? Facing Ollie now, it had never been more apparent that he was utterly irredeemable. He'd betrayed Dex before he'd even met him, hurting a friend he clearly loved. Dex, who was so afraid of loss that he held himself back. Luc couldn't have done worse if he'd tried. There was no fixing this.

Dex looked at him like he was a monster, and he wasn't wrong.

The second Luc's heart restarted, he fled, disappearing to the Realm of the Damned, where he belonged.

8

———

DEX

Dex gaped at the spot Luc had been, his nails digging into Ollie's arm.

Luc could do magic. One second, he'd been standing there, the next, he was gone. No, not Luc. *Lucifer.*

Dex might be sick. "Is he invisible? Like you were, Dante?"

Dante cursed under his breath. "No. He's run off to the Realm of the Damned."

Ollie spoke urgently into his phone before hanging up. He trembled against Dex, more afraid than Dex had ever seen him.

Why was he scared? Had Luc—Lucifer—been planning to hurt him like he'd hurt Ollie?

A man approached Dante, asking what the hell was happening, and Dante pulled him aside.

"Did that guy see Luc disappear?" For some reason, Dex couldn't get Lucifer past his lips. It hurt enough the first time.

Ollie took a long, slow breath like he was trying to calm himself. "He might have seen. Don't worry, Dante will wipe his memory."

Dex's stomach twisted. *What the fuck?* "You didn't tell me magic could do that."

"I was going to. I swear, but there's so much to explain." Ollie's already broken expression crumpled further, and guilt overwhelmed Dex.

Dante wrapped his arm around Ollie as the random man walked away, all his concern seemingly vanished. "Come on. We're going."

Ollie kept hold of Dex, their grips so tight they'd both have bruises tomorrow. Not that it mattered. Screw tomorrow. Dex was having enough trouble wrapping his mind around everything in front of him.

Mind control. Illusions. *The Devil*. Ollie, saying he'd almost *died*.

"It'll be all right," Dante said with calm authority. "Let's get home. Then we can figure this out."

He guided them down the street. Strange hiccupping sounds came from Ollie. Shit, he was in bad shape, but Dex didn't know what to do. Luc had hurt Ollie. And Harper. Fuck, he had to stop thinking of him as Luc.

Dex was numb, his feet heavy as he was dragged along. "How can the Devil be real?"

"I told you about Eternal beings, but that's only the beginning. Telling you everything today was too much." Dante cut an apologetic glance at Dex. "We aren't angels; however, Lucifer did lead a group of us to fall to Earth."

Sweat gathered at the back of Dex's neck as something else Dante had said finally registered. "Wait. Is the Realm of the Damned the same as Hell? You didn't tell me that either. How do you know my parents aren't in Hell? They stopped going to church long before they died."

Dex's dad had never been big on attending. He'd accompanied his mom when she'd asked, and she'd stopped going after Dex had come out.

She'd never made a secret of her disagreement with their

church's exclusion of LGBTQ+ people, but finding out that Dex had still worried over what she'd think of him had affected her deeply. Later, she'd talked about finding an inclusive congregation and rekindling her faith, but had never gotten the chance.

"It's not about going to church," Ollie said, steadier than before. "Hell is for witches. It's about magic, not sins or moral failings. Witches can't reincarnate, so they go to a different afterlife. There's no fiery pit of punishment."

Thank fuck. Dex would have lain down on the sidewalk in relief if the others hadn't kept dragging him along.

He glanced around, surprised that they'd arrived at Ollie's apartment already.

After trudging up the stairs, Ash greeted them inside, looming tall, his eyes glowing orange.

Shit, he was terrifying. Dex shrank back. He didn't know Harper's boyfriend well, and he could obviously do magic.

Ash wordlessly stepped out of the way, and Ollie guided Dex to the couch, not letting go when they sat down.

Harper hovered near the kitchen. Dante and Ash headed straight for him, talking in low tones.

How was this happening? Everyone was so tense. This was bad, obviously, but Dex couldn't seem to put it all together.

He held Ollie's hands tight. "What did he do to you?"

Ollie closed his eyes, tears spilling over. "Lucifer almost murdered me when I was at the beach with Dante. He r-ripped my throat out."

Dex gasped. His whole body went cold, and his stomach rebelled, almost expelling the ice cream he'd eaten. He choked the nausea down. *Ollie's throat?* Ripped it out with what? It was something a bear would do, not a man.

Ollie went on, "I'm Dante's mate. We have a magical connection, and Lucifer attacked me because he believed Dante was lying about it. If Lucifer had been right, I would have died."

"No." Dex grabbed Ollie's shirt like he could hold him here and save him from what had almost happened. He didn't know what mates were, but that didn't matter. He'd almost lost Ollie.

"It was horrible." Ollie shuddered. "It hurt so much. I was drowning in my blood."

Dex made a strangled sound.

"I still have flashbacks sometimes. It's better than it used to be, but some nights, I can't sleep. I feel his hands on me. Seeing him with you, I was terrified of what he'd do. He targeted you. He must know we're friends."

Luc had been planning to hurt him? Dex couldn't see it, not with the sweet way Luc had held him. But he didn't doubt Ollie. His pain was tangible between them, and it scared the hell out of Dex.

"How could he know we were friends?"

Harper settled beside them on the couch. "Lucifer has been stalking our group. He started following Ash, and then me. He threw me off the roof."

Dex covered his mouth, his hand trembling.

He'd kissed Lucifer. Had practically begged to have sex with him. Dex's skin crawled. He wanted to wash the memory of his desire away. How had he not realized he was in the presence of a monster?

"H-he's evil," Dex managed.

Harper and Ollie shared a grim look, neither denying it.

Ash came up beside the couch, resting a hand on Harper's shoulder. "Luc wasn't doing anything good hanging around you. That's for damn sure."

His growly tone set Dex's senses on edge even though Ash was clearly on his side. Being afraid now was a joke after missing any sign that Luc was dangerous, but Dex couldn't help it.

"I still don't understand. How is he the Devil if Heaven and

Hell aren't what I think they are?" *And how could I have fallen for Lucifer?*

Dante joined them, and he and Ash explained who the real Lucifer was. How they had been as close as brothers and had fallen to Earth together. It wasn't like any story Dex had ever heard. They'd been looking for their mates—Ollie and Harper—and Luc had betrayed them. He'd betrayed nature and magic and mortality, and damned all the Fallen to become demons.

That part Dex didn't understand. Magic and mortality? It sounded big, but his brain was fried.

And that wasn't all. Lucifer had gone on to violate Ash and Dante, cutting out some of their magic. He'd seized power over his fellow Fallen—demons—and trapped them all in a prison. Hell.

It wasn't fire and brimstone, but it wasn't sunshine and flowers either.

Still, the story didn't seem to fit. Luc had been this sweet, disarming guy that Dex had met by chance. Except he hadn't been that at all. The part that didn't fit was their time together at Dorthy's and walking along the river. The rest of it all lined up.

Luc was the Devil. He'd stalked and hurt Dex's friends over the last few months. He'd ruined Ash and Dante's lives for years and tried to recapture them after they escaped. They'd been fighting this whole summer.

Had Lucifer planned to hurt Dex as part of his war with Dante, Ash, and their mates? Dex still didn't understand what they meant by mates, but he didn't need to. All that mattered was that Lucifer had almost killed Ollie because of it.

Why had Luc been so understanding and willing to listen to Dex's problems? Why hadn't he fucked him and laughed in his face when Dex realized he'd betrayed his best friend?

Their connection had felt so real. Realer than anything Dex had experienced with another man.

"Did he put a spell on me?" Dex asked the room at large. "Is that why I felt so good around him?"

Ash's gaze narrowed. "Felt good how?"

Dex balled his hands into fists. "I don't know. It was easy. We clicked, and I was willing to give him a chance when I hadn't been on a date in four years."

Ash's scowl deepened. "Do you still feel that way?"

Dex's face flamed, and his stomach dropped out. "I hate him. How could I like him knowing what he's done?"

Dante raised a calming hand. "Of course you hate him. What we mean is, when thinking back to meeting Luc or being near him, how does it feel?"

"I don't know." It was like a tangle of contradictions had grown inside him.

"We can cast a spell on you that will break any lingering illusions," Ash suggested.

"Okay. Yes, do it." *Wash it away.* Dex was sick, thinking Lucifer had coerced him with magic when he'd seemed nothing but respectful.

The demons cast their spell, and magic swirled around Dex in a hot wave.

Ollie watched him closely. "How do you feel now?"

"The same." Dex had no more clarity, his feelings as scrambled as ever.

"When you think back to meeting Luc, it's the exact feeling as before?" Ash pressed.

"Yeah. Is that bad?"

"No." Dante looked concerned, nonetheless. "It means you weren't under any kind of illusion or magical thrall."

Dex sank further into the couch and covered his face. "So, I fell for the Devil out of my own stupidity?"

Ollie tugged at Dex's wrist until he uncovered his face. "Don't beat yourself up. You're not stupid, Dex."

"Luc is a charmer," Ash agreed. "He could seduce anyone, even without magic. Hell, he had us fooled until it was too late."

But it hadn't been like that. What caught Dex's attention were the awkward moments, not Luc's charm. Though there was nothing to say it hadn't all been an act.

"Why would he do this?" Ollie turned desperately toward Dante. "You said he wanted a truce."

"That's what Luc claimed. We shouldn't have believed him, even after he gave our magic back." Dante pulled out his phone and read something on the screen. "Onyx wants to come over."

Harper nodded. "Good idea. Is he bringing Nico?"

"Wait." Dex sat straighter. "Onyx as in the owner of Gallery Four?"

Ollie patted Dex's knee. "He's a demon, too. He, Dante, and Ash are like brothers."

No. Dex didn't want Onyx here. He was a mess. His pottery might never be shown in Onyx's gallery, but that didn't mean he wanted someone so connected to the art world seeing him like this.

Before he could figure out how to voice this new concern without sounding silly, his phone vibrated in his pocket.

LUC:

I'm sorry.

Please let me see you. I have to explain.

Explain? There couldn't be an explanation unless Ollie was wrong about what happened to him. Which he wasn't.

Dex showed Ollie the messages.

His eyes widened. "Luc is back in this realm already? Dante, look at this."

Dante shifted to the arm of the couch, and Dex showed him the phone. "He didn't stay away long."

"I can't believe he wants to meet," Ollie all but growled.

Dante laid a hand on Ollie's shoulder. "It would be good to figure out what he's planning. See if he'll meet with all of us, Dex, and maybe we can figure it out, but he's not getting you alone. It's not safe."

Luc had been scheming, using Dex like a pawn, and it was pathetic how much that truth cut Dex up. He didn't want to accept it.

"We'll protect you," Dante added as if he assumed fear kept Dex silent, rather than a crushed heart.

Dex's anguish fueled the fire of his shame. He was disappointed about his ruined date, even knowing Luc had almost killed his best friend. What was wrong with him? He should be enraged and nothing else.

Why did Dex's first chance at seizing life after years of holding back have to happen with Lucifer?

"He might not agree to meet with all of us," Ash said.

"You think he's messaging, hoping I'll meet him alone so he can..." *Hurt me.* Dex couldn't finish the thought out loud. And he was disappointed about their date? He was definitely broken inside.

Harper looked at Dex with heart-wrenching sympathy. "We don't know what he planned to do. See what he says."

Dex's stomach roiled as he typed.

DEX:

> You can talk to me with the rest of the demons or not at all.

He pushed down the hope that Luc could explain this all away. Nothing could excuse trying to kill Ollie. Every time Dex remembered that's what Luc had done, he feared he'd pass out.

"He agreed." Dex looked up to find surprise lining Ash's face. "He says he didn't know we were friends."

Dante snorted. "Yeah, right. This wasn't a coincidence."

Ash's surprise settled into a scowl, but he didn't comment.

Dante and Harper began coordinating Onyx's arrival and discussing where to meet Luc, with Ash weighing in, but Dex tuned them all out.

He pulled Ollie into a hug, whispering, "I'm sorry."

Ollie squeezed him tight. "You didn't do anything wrong. I'm glad I saved you."

Dex's heart jolted. Saved him. Like he'd been about to suffer the same gruesome fate as Ollie. Somehow, Dex couldn't believe it.

Or more like he didn't want to.

9

LUCIFER

Luc flew to Ollie and Harper's apartment building. His brothers were graciously allowing him entry to the roof. They'd less graciously mentioned that their protective spells would stop his heart if he attempted to enter the building, as if reaching out to Dex was nothing but step one in his latest deception.

He'd prove otherwise.

Luc didn't want to belong in the Realm of the Damned, and never should have fled after their failed date. He couldn't fix things with Dex from there, if he could fix them at all.

From the sky, Luc spotted seven figures on the rooftop. Dex stood in the middle of the group, protected on all sides. Even Ollie had shown up.

Shame burned Luc's throat like acid. What a brave human.

Dex and Ollie held hands, their shoulders pressed together. Luc's chest constricted as if his heart had shriveled. He'd had that once, the fierce love of family, and he'd pissed it away, favoring his own importance and conviction that he was right.

He felt more alone than he had in centuries.

Luc landed, folding his wings at his back. He stood before his mate in his true form, red horns curling along his head like a ram's, tail poised, and eyes glowing crimson. He did not hide, but laying himself bare didn't feel like enough.

Dex's gaze swept over him, colder than Luc thought possible, and his lips parted in disbelief. A visible tremor traveled through him, and the knuckles of the hand clutching Ollie turned pale.

"You tricked me." Dex's tone was accusatory, betrayal written all over his face.

"Dex, please." Luc dropped to his knees, the sudden movement causing Ash, Dante, and Onyx to surge forward. "I didn't know you and Ollie were friends."

"You t-tricked me," Dex repeated, voice shaking.

Luc's skin burned hot, his voice coming out in a whisper. "I didn't. I never used magic on you. No illusions. I showed you my human form because it was the only option. I said there were things about me that you needed to—"

"Stop." Dex shook his head. "It doesn't matter. Even if you didn't cast a spell on me, you still deceived me. I thought... But there's no explanation, no excuse. All I want to know is if you hurt Ollie?"

The words stuck in Luc's throat. Dex was right. There was no hope here. No coming back from what he'd done.

"Well?" Dex snarled, clutching Ollie tighter. "Did you try to kill him or not?"

"I did." Luc's gaze fell to the floor.

How could he look at Dex, let alone Ollie? That day at the beach had become a blurry memory. He'd been nothing but cruel, discarding Ollie's life without a care for anything except his anger at Dante and Ash. And proving he was right.

"Then I don't need to hear anything else. Ollie, let's go. I don't want to be here."

"C-come on." Ollie's voice came out strangled and small, and Luc shriveled with shame.

He couldn't watch as the two young men walked away, their footsteps echoing like the gavels of judgment. How had he deluded himself into believing he could fix this? No truth would make Dex love him when he wasn't even worthy of forgiveness.

"I'd like an explanation." Dante's hard tone cut through the air.

Luc's gaze rose, finding Dante's arms crossed over his bare chest and his eyes blazing with black fire.

"Why did you try to kill Ollie and Harper?"

Luc shook his head. "Dex is right. There is no excuse."

A growl ripped from Dante's throat, and Ash and Onyx closed in around him, Nico at Onyx's elbow. It seemed Harper had left with Dex and Ollie.

"So it was mindless violence?" Dante snarled.

Luc's fire sparked. "Why are you so desperate for me to justify myself? You think I have a reason that will satisfy you? No answer is acceptable, and I won't pretend otherwise."

"Stop twisting your words so that we can't argue with you." Ash's eyes flamed orange. "What about our truce? We agreed to move forward if you stayed away. You expect us to believe you didn't know Dex was connected to Ollie? Please. The two of them are like family."

Dante rumbled in agreement. "The truce is off."

"I swear I didn't know." Luc rose to his feet, wings twitching in growing agitation. "This wasn't a move against you or Ollie. I was leaving town, but I couldn't seem to get this coffee shop out of my head. I saw Dex there, and I knew."

Onyx stepped closer. "Knew what?"

"Dex is my mate."

Stunned silence fell over the group. No one seemed to move a muscle.

Saying it out loud seemed to solidify it. A pain far greater than when he'd realized he would have to let Dex go lanced through Luc. He'd still let his mate go, but he hadn't wanted it to be like this. He wanted the chance to love Dex, and he'd never get it.

"Bullshit." Dante's voice shattered the calm.

Luc's internal fire raged, hollowing him out as pain consumed him. "It's not bullshit. Dex is my fated mate. I felt it before I even saw him. I was drawn to the ceramic mugs he makes and sells at Seaside Coffee, as if the art holds a piece of his essence. I was mooning over a handcrafted cup the day I saw Dex for the first time."

"So you say." Dante sounded impossibly more enraged. Fuck, this was a lost cause.

Why would they believe Luc when he had initially doubted their claims of finding their mates? Violently so.

Ash grabbed Dante's arm. "Wait. It makes sense."

"Excuse me?" Onyx gasped as Dante shouted, "What the fuck?"

Ash didn't back down. "I wondered if Dex was another mate, remember?"

Onyx snorted. "Yeah, mine, and you were totally wrong."

"Clearly." Ash's glaze flicked to Nico, his flames snuffing out. "But I was right about the mates being connected. Harper brought Nico into the group, same as he brought Ollie. There had to be magic helping him find good people when he was in need. There must be a fated connection between us all."

"But Luc isn't one of us." Dante's words cut Luc's heart open, even though he was already painfully aware they were no longer family.

Ash's gaze sharpened in Luc's direction. "He was our brother for a long time. Longer than he's been our enemy."

"So?" Dante sneered.

"So, there's a connection among us, and the connection

between Harper, Ollie, Nico, and Dex feels as meant to be as each of us mating them."

Luc's heart skipped. Ash believed him?

Nico shook his head. "It *feels* meant to be, but that doesn't mean it is. Concocting an explanation isn't proof. Dante is right. Luc isn't part of your group anymore. And you've been wrong about Dex before. Don't be so quick to believe because it sounds good. Lucifer has been hunting you all summer and broke the truce he supposedly wanted so fast that it seems to have been a ploy all along."

"It wasn't a ploy." Luc tamped his anger down. He couldn't let rage rule him. It was part of what got him into this mess. He took a breath. "I was never hunting anyone down."

"Bullshit." Dante threw up his hands. "Everything you say is crap. Do you think we're stupid?"

"No." Luc clenched his fist. "I can prove it's not bullshit. If I were hunting you, you'd have been back in the Realm of the Damned months ago. I've known where your house is all along, Dante. On the clifftop within the protected nature reserve. I saw through the illusions hiding your heavily guarded sanctuary as easily as I saw through your invisibility all these years."

Dante's mouth dropped open.

Luc didn't stop. "My plan to release the demons from Hell was set. Had been for a century. I rebuilt Hell to mimic Earth in preparation, so we could all adjust, and came here to find you three, to reveal my plans and offer you a chance to structure a new society with me. As I said before, I intended to hold onto your magic—hold onto the threat of reimprisonment. I was still scheming when I first showed up. *But I wasn't hunting you.*"

Ash raised a brow. "Then you were stalking me for what, fun?"

Luc's gut twisted. It was all coming out. "No. It was far from fun. Seeing you three after two hundred years affected me more than I expected. I was angry. Lonely. And pissed off when I saw you spending all your time with some witch."

"Harper is not some witch."

"I know, Ash. He's your mate. But you know what? Harper claiming he was your mate was the first time anyone had uttered the word *mate* to my face in over a thousand years. No one dared mention our failed quest once I locked everyone in Hell. And when Harper did, I snapped."

Ash seemed stunned, Dante and Onyx too.

Luc's fire wrapped around his miserable heart, and his voice rose. "I took out a millennia's worth of rage on your poor mate because he had the audacity to tell me something I didn't want to hear. There was no way it was true. I hated Harper and you, Ash, for bringing the reminder to the forefront."

Luc heaved a breath, his chest tightening. His tail flicked back and forth, wings begging for the open air, but he stood and faced this.

"I stewed over your claim of finding your mate for weeks, alone in that cursed place where I'd imprisoned everyone. Being there after returning to Earth set my senses into overdrive. The wrongness clawed at my insides. I couldn't take it, and the second I fled back to Earth for relief, I found Dante playing mates. But this time, it wasn't rage that sent me spinning. Hope broke through, and it fucking broke me. Hope, when I knew better, wasn't something I could endure. The only way to be sure was to kill Ollie and force Dante to see the truth. To see the truth for myself. And I'm sorry. Not because Dex loves Ollie and everything is ruined, but because intending to kill him to get answers was my most selfish act. Despicable. There's no excuse and there will be no forgiveness, but Dex is my mate regardless."

Dante's nostrils flared. "You're right, there will be no forgiveness."

Onyx closed his eyes, his expression tight. Was he disappointed? Surely he wasn't surprised by Dante's stance.

Dante went on. "I don't care if Dex is your mate. I won't convince him to hear you out, and neither will Ollie."

"I don't expect you to." Couldn't Dante see that wasn't why Luc had explained? At least Dante wasn't arguing against them being mates anymore. "Please, don't tell Dex. I hate that everyone knows he's my mate except him. I need to be the one to explain, if he ever wants to hear it. This needs to be worked out between us."

Dante shifted his weight, uneasy perhaps? "Fine. That is your right. We can't hinder your connection without breaking an ultimate rule."

Ash and Onyx both nodded.

At least they believed Dex was his mate. Not that it mattered when Luc would never bond with Dex. Maybe it was best if Dex never found out. The knowledge would only cause further harm.

Luc spread his wings. "Now that's been cleared up, and you know I wasn't stalking Dex to get to you—that I was never hunting you—I take it our truce stands?"

The three exchanged a heavily loaded glance. At last, Ash said, "It stands."

Luc launched into the sky.

10

———

DEX

The universe hated Dex, so of course, he had work Monday morning. He'd usually have the day off, but one of the team was out sick. Ollie suggested Dex call in sick, too, but Dex couldn't do it. Wallowing wouldn't help.

The morning rush would do him good. No need to feel sick over kissing the Devil when there was coffee to brew.

"Office Daddy is back," Justine whispered as Dex frothed milk.

He rolled his eyes. "Shush. What if he hears you call him that?"

"He won't. He's at the back of the line." Justine handed a customer their muffin with a *have a nice day* before turning back to Dex. "I swear, he's going to ask you out. Today's the day."

Luckily, Justine had to serve the next person, who seemed to be ordering coffee for their entire office, allowing Dex to finish making this latte in peace.

He shook out his wrist before moving on to the next order. Everything ached as if his bad night's sleep had beaten him up.

He looked from the machine to the growing line of customers. 'Office Daddy'—who was actually named Holt—wouldn't ask Dex out. He was hot, older, worked in insurance, and always wore a stylish suit and glasses, hence the nickname Justine had given him.

Holt had been a regular at Seaside Coffee for months. He was admittedly flirty, but Dex didn't get the impression it was more than that. Besides, he couldn't have been feeling it any less today if he tried.

The line progressed steadily, and Dex turned his full attention to the stream of orders, losing himself in the familiarity of it all.

"Dex." Holt smiled as he moved away from the register to wait for his coffee. "Don't often see you on a Monday."

Dex smiled reflexively. "Right? It's throwing me off."

Holt's gaze dragged over Dex in a way that usually felt good. "I'll take it as a good sign. My week must be looking up."

The familiar ego boost didn't hit. Dex laughed awkwardly and turned toward the coffee grinder.

Not feeling it was right. Holt's comments had never put him off-balance before.

Maybe Holt sensed Dex's discomfort because he didn't say anything else until thanking him for his coffee before leaving.

As Dex kept pace with the incoming orders, he imagined Holt making a move, asking for his number, or saying he wanted to take Dex to dinner.

Not a hint of excitement stirred.

Why was that? Holt was Dex's type, and a hookup would be hot, no doubt about it, but Dex had no desire to go on a date with the man. Suddenly, he wasn't any more open to the idea of a relationship than he'd been before.

Hadn't Dex decided he was ready to get back out there? Why did the temptation of *more* seem to be exclusive to one objectively terrible man?

It must be too soon to try again. Once Dex recovered from

the shock of who Luc was—never mind the shock of magic existing—he'd be all for dates with hot older guys with arms that looked like they could bench-press him...or other things. If Dex figured out how to ask.

On his break, Dex collapsed onto a worn couch in the staff area with a coffee. He checked his phone, surprised to find he'd been added to a new group chat by Onyx of all people. Or should he say of all demons?

Dex hardly remembered talking to Onyx yesterday, other than exchanging numbers at Ollie's insistence. Everything after seeing Luc with horns and wings was a blur.

He opened the chat.

Your Favorite Group Chat:

Dex Colt has been added.

ONYX:

Welcome, Dex. You're now part of the cool crowd.

HARPER:

Dex is here? Isn't this a mates chat?

ONYX:

It's your favorite group chat. See the name change? Besides, you don't see Nico here, do you?

HARPER:

No, but he's your mate.

Anyway. Welcome, Dex!

OLLIE:

Yay! This is so much better. Now Dex can join our food tour.

ONYX:

Good idea. Who wants to go out tonight?

HARPER:

Me!

OLLIE:

I'm down.

Here they were, talking about mates again. The three of them seemed like good friends. When had that happened? Dex had no idea Ollie had become close with Onyx.

He replied.

DEX:

Hey. Thanks for adding me. I'm free tonight.

ONYX:

That's what I like to hear. Do you have any food allergies I should know about?

DEX:

No. All good.

HARPER:

Are we going somewhere fancy?

ONYX:

That could be arranged.

HARPER:

Yes, please. I have a new outfit.

ONYX:

Perfect! Harper and I are dressing up. Take note and act accordingly.

OLLIE:

I'm not dressing up. You'll be lucky if I do laundry and have a fresh shirt.

Dex chewed his nails as the messages streamed in, feeling like he was intruding. Going out for fancy dinners wasn't his usual thing. Ollie's either, as far as he knew. Maybe it wouldn't be *that* fancy. It's not like Ollie or Harper were in the same income bracket as Onyx.

DEX:

Are Ash and Dante coming to dinner?

ONYX:

Eww. No.

HARPER:

Hey…

ONYX:

Sorry! Habit.

While I love not hating Ash so much, this is an *us* thing.

What did that mean? Harper had said something about the chat being a mate thing, but now that Dex was here, it couldn't be. Whatever. It didn't matter.

HARPER:

You mean a short people thing? Oh, no. Wait. I'm here. *devil emoji*

ONYX:

I'm starting to see why you're Ash's mate.

HARPER:

Sorry. Was that mean?

I can't help it. You get so prickly, and literally no one cares how tall you are.

ONYX:

Mean? You think I can't take a little teasing? Brace yourself for my retort.

Dex never would have guessed that being in a group chat with someone who ran a renowned gallery would be so…normal.

He could almost forget what a big deal going to dinner with Onyx was. Everyone in the Shearwater Landing art world had heard of him and Gallery Four, and anyone Dex went to school with would kill for this opportunity.

HARPER:

…

I'm waiting.

Guess you've got nothing.

ONYX:

You're a bit of a brat.

I like it.

OLLIE:

He is not. Harper is pure sweetness.

HARPER:

devil emoji

ONYX:

I think we scared Dex away.

@Harper you know there are other emojis right?

DEX:

I'm still here.

HARPER:

devil emoji

DEX:

Gotta get back to work. See you tonight.

DEX ARRIVED at the restaurant right on time in a button-up shirt he couldn't remember the last time he'd worn. He was lucky it fit.

He'd walked to the Arts District, hoping to clear his head, and had only gotten sweaty for his trouble. The restaurant was intimidating, to say the least. Everything screamed expensive, from the brushed silver door handle to the upholstered chairs and elegant light fixtures.

Dex smoothed his shirt and gave the hostess Onyx's name. She smiled and led him through the mood-lit room and up a set of stairs to a rooftop patio, where an honest-to-god harpist sat in the corner, plucking at her instrument.

Dex hurried to close his gaping mouth. Good thing he was selling his condo if he was buying dinner here.

The hostess showed him toward a round table overlooking a garden where Onyx was seated alone, focused on the music. Dex shouldn't have bothered dressing up. He looked like he'd come for a job interview, and Onyx looked like he'd walked out of a magazine.

The demon's blue hair was perfect, his posture reminiscent of Luc's easy grace. He wore a sheer white blouse and a silver choker, looking every bit the influential gallery owner.

Dex's stomach flipped. He should have met Ollie and Harper at their place and ridden with them so he wouldn't have been caught alone with Onyx.

"Here we are," the hostess announced.

Onyx's attention snapped toward them. "Thank you, Claire."

She nodded and left.

"Um. Hi." Dex pulled out a chair. "Thanks so much for inviting me."

Onyx waved off his thanks with a careless hand. "My pleasure. Ollie tells me you're a bit of a foodie."

"Yeah?" Dex sat, trying to ignore the twist settling in his gut. He didn't know *that* much about food.

"Me too." Onyx leaned in conspiratorially. "This place has one of the best tasting menus in the city."

"Great." Dex glanced at the menu. There were no prices. *Fuck.*

Should he ask Onyx about the cost? He took the glass of water closest to him and sipped, wetting his rapidly drying throat.

Onyx had apparently already ordered a bottle of red wine, which sat on the table next to three glasses. The demon lifted the bottle. "Do you like pinot noir? Claire went ahead and opened it so it could breathe."

Dex shifted in his seat, folding his hands on the table, then on his lap. "Sure, thanks."

Onyx deftly poured what seemed like a tiny amount of wine into Dex's admittedly massive wineglass. "We need to go wine tasting to nail down the others' preferences. Harper had never even heard of pinot noir or pinot grigio, bless him."

Dex laughed shakily as Onyx set the wine aside. "Don't you want any?"

Onyx wrinkled his nose. "I don't drink human beverages. Wait..." He leaned in once more, his voice dropping to a whisper. "Has anyone told you about the blood drinking?"

Dex swallowed. "No." *Blood drinking?* He would not panic. Not in front of Onyx. He would remain still and calm.

"Don't fret. No one is asking you for a sip. We demons require blood to maintain our immortality in this realm, but we source it all ethically these days."

Dex had a large gulp of wine, choking slightly. "Immortality?"

What. The. Actual. Fuck.

Onyx's brows rose. "Ollie didn't tell you?"

"No. He told me about magic and the afterlife," Dex whispered, glancing around to make sure no one was listening.

Yeah, he'd had trouble processing everything yesterday, but no way he'd missed something this major. Ash and Dante hadn't mentioned how much time had passed when explaining Luc's story, and Dex hadn't wondered, even though falling to Earth made him think of the Bible and things that would have happened a long time ago.

Fuck, maybe he had missed some important cues.

Was Onyx saying he, Dante, and Ash were immortal? Was Luc? Dammit, his name was Lucifer. Dex had to stop thinking of him as Luc.

And stop thinking about him, period.

Onyx ran a hand through his hair, his congenial expression cracking. "Sorry. I'm freaking you out. Revealing all this to a human is actually quite involved." A furrow appeared on his brow. "I should have cut Dante more slack."

Dex didn't bother asking. "What do you mean *immortal?*"

"Exactly what you think: demons live forever unless we're permanently destroyed."

"How do you destroy a demon?"

Onyx raised a brow. "Planning on becoming a hunter?"

Heat flooded Dex's body. "No. Definitely not. Shit. Sorry. And sorry for swearing."

"It's all right. Relax. You can't out-swear me. And I was teasing about hunting. There's no way you could do anything to a demon that we wouldn't bounce back from."

Dex had another sip of wine.

Onyx's expression sobered. "I'm sorry about yesterday. Dante and Ash said you were on a date with Luc when Ollie ran into you."

Dex's stomach sank so rapidly, it nearly fled his body. He

scrubbed a hand over his face as it grew hot with shame. "I can't believe I let him fool me like that."

Onyx gently tugged Dex's lingering hand away and met his eyes. "Don't beat yourself up. No one thinks you did anything wrong."

"I betrayed Ollie." Shit, he'd admitted it out loud. Forget this being any kind of art-related networking opportunity. Dex was coming apart at the seams.

Onyx's grip tightened on Dex's hand. "You didn't betray Ollie. He doesn't think that, and neither does anyone else."

But Dex *had* betrayed Ollie. Going on a date with Luc and kissing him wasn't the half of it. His attraction to Luc lingered. Dex hated Luc, but his hate was incomplete. Part of him regretted walking away from Luc without hearing him out.

"Whatever you're thinking, don't guilt yourself," Onyx continued. "Everything to do with my brother is complicated. Give yourself a chance to process. Talk to Ollie. Talk to me if you want. It'll all work out in time."

Heat faded from Dex's face. Onyx sounded so sure, but then, maybe everything worked out when you lived forever and time didn't end.

"I can't get rid of the feelings I had when I first met him," Dex whispered before he could stop himself. There was no point trying to be professional, and he feared he'd explode if he didn't admit it to someone.

Onyx squeezed his hand again before releasing it with a soft little smile. "That's okay."

But it wasn't okay. How was Onyx not shocked by Dex's feelings for his best friend's would-be murderer? That was so far from okay, it wasn't even funny. Dex's stomach cramped, and he hated himself.

He desperately wanted to believe the Luc he'd met at Dorthy's was the real Luc. Not the man who'd hurt Ollie and

Harper. But he was wrong. It was a foolish, selfish thing to hold onto. He was a terrible person.

"Hey, sorry we're late." Harper pulled out the chair next to Onyx.

Onyx looked him up and down. "The wait was worth it. Look at you."

Harper beamed. He looked stunning in tight pants and a flowy, vintage pastel blouse with pearl buttons. He even had glasses to match. "I kept ruining my eyeliner and had to use magic in the end."

Onyx laughed.

Ollie sat next to Dex, giving him a one-armed hug. "How was work?"

"Good, but I'm going to crash after dinner."

Ollie's smile was replaced with a sympathetic frown. "What—"

"Oh, Satan, your nipples are pierced!"

Dex couldn't have been more thankful for Harper's shriek, which stole Ollie's attention. Ollie gaped at Onyx. Dex hadn't even noticed the piercings.

The demon rolled his eyes. "Yes, little mates. There are many things you don't know about me."

"It's hot." Harper cleared his throat. "Sorry, I'm staring." He quickly grabbed a menu and averted his eyes.

Onyx grinned. "Don't apologize for complimenting me. You think I didn't see this reaction coming when I put on a sheer top?"

"True." Harper shared Onyx's smile, turning to Ollie and Dex. "Maybe I should get a piercing or two. Not my nipples, but maybe my ears. I could have bought earrings to go with this outfit. What a missed opportunity."

"Give yourself time," Ollie said to Harper as Onyx poured their wine. "There's no rush to try everything at once."

"You're right. I'm lucky time's on my side. Pole dancing is next level difficult. It's going to take me ages to get any good." Harper pouted.

Dex hadn't realized Harper was into pole dancing. Good for him.

Onyx handed Harper a glass of wine. "Isn't that the best part? Think how much fun you'll have practicing."

"I already know how much fun I'm going to have. Ash said... Never mind. What are we eating tonight?"

Onyx opened his menu. "The five-course tasting is a must. Unless you want to go for eight."

"Eight courses?" Dex's eyes nearly popped out of his head. "How much will that cost?"

"Don't worry about that. I'm paying for you little m—I mean, young men."

Harper snorted. "You can't call us little mates now that Dex is here."

"Maybe not, but I reserve the right to call you young, given I'm more than a hundred times older than you."

Ollie choked on his wine. "When you put it that way, you sound ancient."

Onyx put his nose in the air. "I am ancient."

Should Dex bother asking about mates? Maybe it would come up enough that he'd finally get what the big deal was. "You don't have to pay for me," he told Onyx.

"Nonsense." Onyx glared, his smile fittingly demonic. "I want to pay. This was my idea. I like sharing meals with these two, and I'm glad we can include you now."

"But—" Dex began.

Onyx showed no sign of having heard him. "You wouldn't prevent an old man from spending money on his friends when it makes him happy, would you?"

"I guess not." But why did Onyx seem excited to include

him? He wasn't a demon's mate. He'd tagged along because of Ollie.

Dex wasn't really part of this group. His heart clenched, and he swallowed the unexpected lump forming in his throat.

Luckily, Harper asked Onyx something about the menu, distracting him.

Dex turned to Ollie. "Onyx told me demons live forever. You forgot to mention that."

Ollie blinked. "Oh. Yeah. I was getting there, I swear."

"Isn't it weird being with a guy who's ancient and will never age?" How was Ollie so relaxed? He'd been wary of relationships for years, and suddenly, he was all in with this wild shit. Dex had to be missing a boatload of details.

"It's not weird at all." Ollie shifted in his seat. "It's like dating anyone else. We game, get coffee, and—well, I can't say sex with Dante is like anything I've ever done before because it's not. Um." Ollie's cheeks bloomed with color, and he cleared his throat. "You should join Dante and me online. This is why I wanted to tell you. So we could all get to know each other for real. You'll see."

Dex wasn't sure he would. He agreed anyway. It was better than focusing on his own confused feelings.

Would he ever look at Ollie and not feel guilty for the lingering pull Luc seemed to have on him?

11

———

LUCIFER

Luc's phone had to be lying. He stared at the new message.

ONYX:

We need to talk.

This must be for someone else, sent to Luc by mistake. But a second later, another text came through.

ONYX:

Now, Luc. Where are you?

All right then. Not a mistake. He replied with his address and waited, tail twitching impatiently.

It was late in the evening. Not that Luc was busy doing anything except obsessing over Dex walking away on the rooftop. A visit from Onyx would be a welcome change of pace.

A short time later, someone banged on the door, and Luc went to open it.

"A loft? Really?" Onyx curled his lip as he sauntered in, wings out and horns and tail hidden away.

Luc slammed the door. "I'm not copying you."

"Whatever. This place doesn't hold a candle to mine." Onyx

made a cursory inspection of the mostly empty loft before facing Luc. "I had dinner with your mate tonight."

Luc's throat ran dry. Was Onyx taunting him? "How nice for you."

Onyx's eyes flashed. "Nice? Don't start walking on eggshells now. Say what you're thinking, dammit."

The tightness in Luc's chest released, and he staggered forward as if Onyx's permission had opened a floodgate. "How is Dex? Was everyone there? No one told him, right?"

Onyx's expression softened. "No one told Dex anything about mates. Ash and Dante haven't even told Harper and Ollie. They're staying out of it completely."

"And you?" Luc's heart beat faster, hope threatening to take hold, even if he wasn't sure why. There was nothing Onyx could do. Luc had ruined this beyond repair.

"Does it look like I'm staying out of it?"

Luc shook his head. No, it didn't.

Onyx sniffed, seemingly satisfied with the acknowledgment. "I won't lie, Dex is upset and confused, but he's your mate. You need to fix this. What's the plan?"

Luc's pounding heart clenched painfully. "Plan? There is no plan. What am I supposed to do?"

Onyx threw up his hands. "Figure it out. Anything other than give up."

"Gee, having you on my side is helping already."

"Fuck you, Luc. You miserable piece of shit. I have a dozen better places to be than this lame, definitely-copying-me loft of yours."

A grin tugged on Luc's lips despite his best efforts to scowl. Onyx's attitude could be exhausting, but his candor was amusing. "I'm not copying you."

Onyx didn't dignify that with a response, unless you counted pointedly ruffling his feathers.

Luc's amusement didn't last. "Dex hates me, and I don't blame him. There's nothing I can do. I won't stalk him if he doesn't want to see me."

"You won't?"

"Don't look surprised. How would that help?"

Onyx shrugged. "It probably wouldn't. So, how do we get him to talk to you?"

"We don't. I'm not forcing anything on him."

A growl ripped from Onyx's throat. "Did I say you should? Dammit, Luc, you wanted your mate so badly that you dragged us all to Earth. You aren't giving up on him. We need to figure this out."

Dragged them all to Earth? As if he'd been the only one willing to forsake their home. He'd dragged Onyx, not everyone.

"I'm not giving up. I'm respecting Dex's boundaries. I'm capable of doing the right thing on occasion."

"Yeah, when it allows you to feel hard done by," Onyx muttered.

Luc's wings twitched, his fire smoldering. He forced it down and let the comment go. "Is Dex doing any better than yesterday?"

Onyx paused, considering. "He seemed okay. We didn't really discuss you. Though he did mention he feels like he's betrayed Ollie."

Shame burned hotter than Luc's internal fire. "Does Ollie agree? What does he think of you keeping me around?" Perhaps Ollie didn't know Onyx was giving Luc a second chance. If he found out, then Luc would lose Onyx, too.

Onyx paced to a nearby window and gazed out. "Ollie isn't holding my decision to see you against me. He understands that your attack is one piece of a long history, and trusts me as a friend to do what's right in this fucked up situation."

Luc swallowed his surprise, the taste bitter. "So what? The boy is a saint?"

Onyx whirled around. "No, but he's certainly less petty than either of us. Did you know he asked Dante not to kill you? No one would have blamed him for wanting vengeance, but he had compassion instead."

Onyx's words hit Luc in the chest, knocking the wind out of him.

Onyx wasn't done. "If Ollie knew you and Dex were mates, he'd understand eventually. I bet he'd even believe that you weren't trying to hurt Dex yesterday. Maybe you need to work things out with Ollie before you try with Dex."

"Work things out with Ollie? Oh, is that all? Simply ask the man I nearly killed to forgive me?" Luc would have laughed if he didn't feel dead inside. "That'll never happen. Dante will stop my heart the second I approach his mate."

"Then don't sneak up on him, genius. Tell Dante you want to explain being Dex's mate to Ollie. If Dex doesn't feel like he's betraying his friend, I think he'll talk to you."

"So I need Ollie's forgiveness and a favor? To see if he'll put in a good word with Dex for me?" That was even worse.

Onyx clenched his jaw so hard, Luc heard his teeth grinding. "Is there a way to figure this out without involving Ollie? If so, I'm all ears."

No. There wasn't. If Luc ever wanted to see Dex again, he had to mend fences with the others and their mates. But that was impossible. They wouldn't forgive him, no matter what Onyx thought Ollie was capable of.

"None of it matters." Luc turned away, staring blankly at the nearly empty loft. "I'm never mating Dex. Even before I realized he knew Ollie and that I'd fucked this up, I was never bonding with him."

"*What the hell?*" Onyx grabbed Luc and pulled him

around, glaring, nose in the air, and eyes flaming. "You have no intention of mating with the man that you destroyed everything for?"

Luc's own fire raged back to life. "I didn't destroy everything."

"Yeah, yeah. You didn't father the first witch. Big whoop. I told Ash and Dante that, by the way, and they believe your story. They're softening. Seeing things in a new light matters even if it doesn't excuse everything you've done. We need to understand what the fuck is happening in your head, Luc. If you'd shared from the start, maybe things wouldn't have turned out this way."

Was that so? Luc doubted it, but he had nothing to lose now. "What's happening in my head is this: Dex lost his parents and struggles with grief. He needs to pass into the Eternal Realm to reunite with them at the end of his life. I refuse to take that away from him. So we aren't mating no matter who forgives who."

"Oh..." Onyx's aggravated expression smoothed out, leaving him almost blank.

Being right brought no satisfaction. "You see? There's no need to harass Dex into giving me a chance. No need to torture Ollie. Dex and I aren't going anywhere."

Onyx's lips twitched into a ghost of a smile, his eyes sad as his hand came to rest on Luc's forearm. "Maybe not, but I think you should talk to Ollie anyway. Tell him what you've just told me."

Why? So Ollie could point and say, *See, this is what you deserve?* Luc shook Onyx off. "No."

Onyx smacked Luc's upper arm, all tenderness gone as if it had never been. "If you're as sorry as you say and want to make amends, this is your chance. Show everyone what kind of person you are."

"Haven't I? I'm someone who kills innocent humans when he gets angry."

Onyx smacked him again. "If you don't want to be that person anymore, then be someone else. Stop feeling sorry for yourself and make up for it. Do something other than complain about how misunderstood you are. Apologize to Ollie if you regret hurting him."

Luc took a step back, spreading his wings, the urge to fly almost overwhelming. "Ollie won't want to hear it. There's no way to apologize for what I did to him."

Onyx stalked closer, pointing an accusatory finger. "Why don't you let Ollie decide if that's the case? You have to try, Luc. You asked how to prove your remorse is real. This is how. You have to actually do something. I've heard you out and I believe you, but that's not the end of it. If you want our relationship to grow and improve, you need to make an effort with me and everyone else. Dante, Ash, me, and our mates are a package deal."

Luc closed his eyes. He didn't want to hear it. And he didn't have to. He could easily convince himself that Onyx had it all wrong. That Onyx was unreasonable. The argument was on the tip of his tongue. Luc could twist this until he felt like the wronged one. But why? What was the point in being right and feeling sorry for himself?

What Onyx was asking for was impossible. But Onyx was right. Luc had to be different. He had to do what scared him, even if it wouldn't be enough.

He had to try.

Nearly a week later, Luc stood outside Onyx's loft. He was

a fool for agreeing to this, and his expectations were lower than low, but that wasn't stopping him.

He knocked, heart banging louder than his fist on the metal.

Onyx opened the door. "Come in and don't fuck this up."

"Thanks," Luc muttered, his stupid heart leaping at Onyx's version of encouragement. He was lucky to have him.

Luc followed his brother into a huge room cluttered with books and art. Even though Luc hadn't been inside the loft on his previous visits to the building, the space seemed familiar, as if Onyx's essence was embedded in everything around them.

A cozy seating area was arranged near a full wall of windows. Ash and Harper sat on a couch, Ollie and Dante on another, and Nico, Onyx's mate, sat in an armchair. Onyx flounced into Nico's lap, who wrapped an arm around his waist.

What a sweet picture of everyone with their mates. This was a sight Luc had lost hope in ever seeing, and yet here it was.

Too bad the simmering tension radiating off everyone tarnished it.

Luc remained standing at the edge of the sitting area, his hands in his pockets, appearing human in the hopes he'd seem more approachable. His brothers had their wings away, though Ash and Dante sported their horns.

Luc's attention landed on Ollie.

The young man sat with his back ramrod-straight, his gaze fixed on Luc's shoes and hands clutching Dante's. Luc didn't need to look too closely to know Dante was glaring. His stare was like fire on Luc's skin. Ash's too.

Onyx had told Luc that Ash and Dante had filled their mates in on everything, except for Dex being Luc's fated mate. Luc doubted revealing that truth would do anything except anger Ollie. Still, it was best to tell him. Dante would eventually, Luc was sure.

He cleared his dry throat. "Thank you for letting me come over. I have something I'd like to tell you, Ollie."

His hazel eyes snapped to Luc's face. "I don't care if hearing about mates after a thousand years made you lose your mind. You didn't have to take it out on me or Harper."

Fuck. Luc fought not to look away. "I know. I'm sorry. It's not enough, but I'm sorry. I regret hurting you more than anything I've ever done. If I could take it back, I would, and I swear, I'll never hurt you or anyone like that again."

Ollie sniffed, lifting his chin. "Is that all?"

Luc let Ollie's cold dismissal burn through him. He deserved it. "No, that's not all I came to say."

Ollie seemed to grip Dante tighter. "Then spit it out. This is a waste of my day off."

The more Luc learned about Ollie, the more he respected him, and regret sank deeper into his bones. "I swear, I wasn't with Dex to hurt you, and I never considered hurting him. I don't have ill will toward any of you. All I want is a truce and to make amends. Onyx believes me. Dante does too. I think..." Luc's gaze landed on Dante.

He grunted.

Luc's muscles seized, his fire cold. "I'd like to tell you why they believe I wasn't hurting Dex or any of you through him that day."

Ollie shivered, and he swallowed audibly before saying, "Fine," his voice tight.

Cool water seemed to slither down Luc's spine. "Dex is my mate. I was drawn to him at the coffee shop where he works. I swear, I had no idea you two were connected. I stayed in Shearwater Landing once I sensed our bond forming. Otherwise, I would have left."

Ollie remained still for a long moment, then shook his head like he was trying to dislodge the knowledge from his brain.

"No. That can't be true. Dante, you actually believe this?" He looked at his mate, betrayal in his eyes.

Dante ran a hand through Ollie's hair. "I believe him. Dex and Luc are mates."

A strange, high-pitched sound emanated from Ollie, and he whipped around to face Luc. "So what? You want my permission to mate with Dex? That's not up to me."

Luc's heart clenched, his pulse slowing until he was light-headed. "No, it's not. It would be Dex's decision. But I'm not here to smooth things over so I can mate with him. I'm not asking you to tell Dex to call me or agree to meet with me. I'm here to tell you that I'm not mating with Dex. I never planned to, even before you saw us that day. He told me about his parents."

Ollie seemed to deflate, his posture sagging, emotion ripping across his face too fast to read. Dante pulled him close, and Ollie seemed to melt into his comforting touch.

"You're going to let Dex die?" Harper asked, his tone harsh against Luc's oversensitive nerves.

"Don't say it like I'm dooming him." Luc gritted his teeth, forcing his temper to remain in check. "If this weren't a colossal mess, I'd have eventually told Dex the truth about magic and the afterlife, and let him decide. But I know what he'd choose. He wouldn't pick eternal life over the alternative, even if he didn't hate me."

"Th-then why are you here?" Ollie's voice wobbled. "Why tell me Dex is your mate if it doesn't matter. This isn't fair. I wanted Dex to have a mate, but I didn't want *you* to be the one for him."

Ash leaned forward, catching Ollie's attention. "It makes more sense for Dex to be Luc's mate than any other demon. Harper brought all four of you together to match the four of us.

But, you're right. It doesn't seem fair. I can't believe a mate wouldn't choose to form the bond."

"Maybe he will," Ollie said desperately. "Maybe he'll want to stay with us."

Luc dropped onto the ottoman beside Ollie. "Do you really think that?" he asked gently.

Ollie closed his eyes. "No. I told Dex about magic so he'd know his parents were out there. He's not giving up the chance to see them. He needs it." Ollie's eyes popped open. "There has to be another way."

Luc pulled back, not realizing how close he'd leaned. "Another way for what?"

"To keep Dex with us. He's supposed to be, isn't he? That's how all this fate stuff works."

Luc shook his head. "No, fate wouldn't force Dex into something that's not best for him, and I won't allow it to."

Ollie blinked in shock. Letting go of Dante's hands, he leaned forward. Closer to Luc. "You want everyone to forgive you, don't you?"

It was Luc's turn to be surprised. "Of course, but I don't expect you to."

"Yeah, well, you're supposed to be part of the group. Even after all the shit that's happened, that's what this means."

"I don't know if we want him," Dante grumbled.

"No, but that could change. We're all going to live forever. Who knows what the next century will bring?" Ollie's gaze sharpened. "If I forgave you and told Dex it was okay, he'd give you a chance."

"I appreciate that, but how could you ever forgive me? Dex won't believe you're suddenly okay with him dating someone who attacked you. And you can't tell him we're mates. That's for me and him to discuss."

Ollie frowned. "I want to argue, but fine, I won't tell him. You still need my support if you ever want to see him again."

His support? Ollie would give it?

Luc braced himself. None of this changed the fact that he couldn't bond with Dex, but maybe he could still be in Dex's life. "How would I get your support?"

"Fix it. Fix everything and make it so Dex can mate with you and still go into the Eternal Realm to see his parents. That way, he can stay with me, with our group like he's fated to, and he can heal from his trauma."

"Fix everything?" Luc laughed, sounding more like a bark. His insides seized painfully as bitterness burst forth, sarcasm lacing his tone. "Why didn't I think of fixing my mistakes? I should have realized the Fallen and their mates deserve to return to the Eternal Realm. It's so simple."

Rage burned through Luc. What Ollie proposed was preposterous. Of course, he'd spare everyone damnation if he could.

"It won't work." Ash shook his head, the motion as heavy as the stone forming in Luc's gut. "Ollie, that's not within Luc's power. None of us will ever return home, and any mate that binds themselves to a demon will be trapped on Earth forever."

"If we'd never fallen, Dex would have found Luc in the afterlife. He'd have healed and had it all," Dante whispered.

If Luc hadn't already believed he'd been wrong to fall, nothing could have made it clearer than that simple truth. He should have waited.

Ollie's back straightened once again, his glare more determined than ever. "I don't care. Make it happen. I want Dex to have a mate—someone better than the Devil—but if you two are fated, you must deserve Dex. It must be there deep down. Fix things so you can mate because Dex deserves everything regardless of your mistakes. He deserves a love he'll never lose, and he deserves to reconnect with his parents. You have to figure it out. You *will*. It's fate. That's what this means, right? You will figure it out."

Ollie's tone turned fevered, the sound resonating deep within Luc's broken soul.

Dex deserved all that and more. He deserved the universe on a silver platter. But what someone deserved wasn't often what they got. It didn't make returning to the Eternal Realm any more possible.

"I want this as much as you do, Ollie. But how? The council won't change its mind."

"You don't know that. You have to try. *Please*."

Luc's heart clenched. "I'll try. But I need you to understand how impossible this is. Don't hope too hard."

"Too late," Ollie snapped like he didn't care if hope ripped him apart.

Luc ran a hand through his hair. Hope had done nothing but destroy him, and he'd sworn to never let it in again. But if this hurt, so be it. He'd take it. "Fuck, it is too late. I don't think I've ever hoped for anything more."

Letting Dex go when there was no other option was heartbreaking, but easy. It allowed Luc to feel sorry for himself, to be hard done by, and rage at the world.

Luc was done with easy. Self-pity served no one.

Onyx challenged him to act, and Ollie presented his greatest challenge of all. Luc wouldn't shy away, not if there was a sliver of a chance that it could work out.

Hope cut through Luc more sharply than it ever had.

Was there a way to bring the Fallen home? What about the witch souls damned unfairly to Hell? They deserved to enter the Eternal Realm even if the rest of them didn't. Luc had to try for Dex. And for himself. Perhaps he could counteract some of the harm he'd caused in his long life. If he could fix any part of this, then maybe he deserved Dex after all.

Just because mating Dex would have worked out if he'd stayed in the Eternal Realm, it didn't mean Luc couldn't make it work in this changed world. Fate didn't dictate one predetermined future. He may have missed one chance to connect with Dex. That didn't mean it was the only chance.

Maybe Luc didn't have to be alone and hated. He could change. If he'd decided to be the villain, then he could decide to do good.

He'd changed the shape of the universe when he fell, regardless of who fathered the first witch. And he could change it again, for the better this time. With intention, not blind mistakes.

"I'll try my best," he promised Ollie. And meant it.

12

———

DEX

Buying a house was officially worse than selling one. That, or Dex was the problem. As he gazed out the window of a condo located right on the river, he suspected the issue was him.

The view was spectacular, with shimmering water below and the river walk along the opposite bank. The condo was directly opposite the park where Dex had met Luc for their date. Technically, it was in the South Banks rather than the Banks, but it was close enough, or so the realtor had argued.

"What do you think?" Ollie nudged him with his elbow. "You're on the top floor, but four stories isn't ridiculous, and we can get Dante and Ash to move your furniture with magic."

It had been two weeks since Dex's disastrous date, and on the surface, things were back to normal. He'd met Ollie for brunch that morning, same as last Sunday.

Today, Ollie seemed a thousand times more relaxed than the previous week, and much less distracted. He'd been evasive about his change in mood and hadn't let Dex brush off his offer to come house hunting, even though Dex had tried.

Dex turned away from the window and inspected the open-plan living and kitchen area. "This place is all right. Not the neighborhood I wanted, though."

"Technically, but you're literally a river's-width from the Banks, and the footbridge is right there. You'll be as close to work here as your old condo."

True, and he was closer to his pottery studio. Dex rented space in a co-op, giving him a private workroom, somewhere to store everything and dry his pieces, as well as access to a kiln. This was the best condo he'd seen. By far. If it didn't have a view of the damn park, it would have been perfect.

"I don't know. Maybe I shouldn't downsize. One bedroom feels small."

Ollie opened the sliding door to the balcony. "Seriously? Small? Even with indoor-outdoor flow like this? A balcony is the dream. Can you imagine sitting out here in the evenings? It'll be great. And what do you need two bedrooms for? You don't want a roommate, do you?"

"No." Dex cringed. He was used to his own space.

"Then what?" Ollie shut the door. "Why is downsizing and saving the extra cash not the plan anymore?"

Dex pretended to be interested in a throw blanket on the couch, running his fingers along the stitches. "It's still the plan. I guess this place is fine."

It wasn't as if he would look out the window and pine after Luc—wishing the kind man he'd met was real—for the rest of his life. Fuck. He shouldn't be pining at all. If only this mess of feelings would leave him alone.

Ollie moved closer until they were shoulder to shoulder. "Whatever it is, you can talk to me. This must be hard. But is moving what's bothering you? You haven't been yourself lately."

Dex's fist clenched around the blanket. "How can I be myself after kissing the man who hurt you?"

Ollie went completely still. "You don't have to feel bad about kissing Luc."

"Why not?"

Ollie glanced around the room, maybe checking that the realtor was still giving them space and hadn't snuck in from the hall. "Dante and I may have overreacted when we ran into you. I'm sorry."

"What?" Dex's heart rate skyrocketed. Was this a joke? There was no overreacting after what Lucifer had done to Ollie. Of course Dex should feel terrible for kissing *the Devil*.

Ollie crossed his arms defensively. "I really am sorry, Dex. I was so sure Luc was planning to hurt you, but it turns out I was wrong."

Sorry? Ollie was sorry? Dex braced himself on the back of the couch, a weight pressing on his chest. Ollie was *wrong*? Luc hadn't been planning to hurt him? "How could you possibly know Luc wasn't going to hurt me like he did to you?"

Ollie hesitated, and Dex's heart sank. Ollie didn't know. He was speculating. But why? What was happening right now?

Ollie had a turn avoiding eye contact and inspecting the blanket. "Luc hasn't contacted you, has he?"

Dex shook his head, fresh guilt for being both relieved and hurt by Luc's radio silence swallowing him whole.

Ollie ran a hand through his messy curls. "We were wrong about Luc going after you because of me. He proved to Dante that he didn't know we were friends. He really wanted a date with you. There wasn't an ulterior motive."

Dex had to be dreaming. Ollie wasn't making sense. "Fine, say he randomly wanted to date me. That doesn't change what he did to you on the beach."

Ollie winced. "No. It doesn't." He paused, lines forming around his eyes. "Do you want to talk to him again?"

Why did it sound like Ollie already knew the answer?

Blood rushed in Dex's ears. Ollie had guessed he was a terrible friend, conflicted when he shouldn't be.

Ollie gripped Dex's arm. "It's okay if you want to talk to Luc. We never gave him a chance on the roof. But Dante did, and he doesn't think it would be a bad idea for you to call Luc if you want to hear him out, and I agree."

Dante wanted him to call the Devil? After growling at Luc and shoving him away?

"You agree? You can't seriously want me to talk to someone who attacked you."

"It's not that simple. I hate Luc, but I can't grasp the extent of the conflict between him and the other demons. Not really. It's impossible to get my head around knowing someone for four thousand years. They hate each other now, but that could change. Who knows what the next decade or century or millennia will bring? I talked to Luc, and he's sorry for hurting me."

Dex should want to hear this, but his blood boiled. "So what if he's sorry? That's bullshit. You almost died. Being sorry doesn't make it okay."

"Do I have to hate him forever? What if Luc can make up for what he did? Show that he regrets it enough to do better."

"I don't know." Why hadn't Ollie felt this way two weeks ago? Sure, one action didn't define a person, but ripping someone's throat out wasn't a small misstep.

How could Luc deserve a second chance after that?

Ollie ran his hand through his hair once more, a nervous habit of his. "All I'm saying is, if you want to hear Luc out, do it. I did, and I'm glad I gave him a chance to talk."

Jitters erupted in Dex's chest. Not excitement. It was too frantic and off-putting, threatening to overwhelm him. "What did Luc say to you?"

Ollie broke eye contact. "It's hard to explain. He'd do a

better job of it than me. I don't want to speak for him, you know?"

Fair. Though Dex would rather get a clear answer. This was such a huge shift from the last time they'd talked about Luc. Ollie was saying it was safe for Dex to see Luc alone, when last time, he'd been trembling with fear, dragging Dex away. How did Ollie and the demons go from snarling about protecting him to this?

Ollie squeezed Dex's hand. "Follow your heart."

Could he? It was as if Ollie understood Dex's inner conflict and accepted it. Fuck, that didn't make sense. Dex had kept most of his feelings to himself.

His gaze was drawn to the park across the river. "I don't understand why I can't get Luc out of my head. I shouldn't be obsessing over him. That's why this condo sucks. All I see when I look at the park is him."

Ollie's eyes widened.

Shit, he shouldn't have admitted that Luc had been on his mind all this time. It was still a betrayal, no matter what Ollie said about following his heart.

"You're obsessing?" Ollie asked, his demeanor turning soft and maybe even understanding.

What?

"Is it magic?" Dex lowered his voice. Even though they were alone. "I know Dante and Ash proved that Luc didn't trick me with an illusion, but could magic be making me feel this way?"

"No. Magic doesn't create feelings. I got really hung up on that when I found out I was Dante's mate, but whatever you're feeling is all you. Luc isn't tricking you. Magic isn't making you think about him."

"That's not what you said before. You were certain he was lying to me."

"I know, and that's why I'm telling you to talk to Luc if you want. I don't think he actually lied to you. I was wrong."

So everything Dex liked about Luc was real, and not a trick?

Dex wanted to scream. Even if Ollie had been mistaken before, not everything had changed. "I get what you're saying about the other demons coming to an understanding with Luc one day, given how long they live, but why are you on board? Luc not lying to me doesn't erase his attack."

Couldn't Dante hate Luc until he and Ollie broke up—or if their relationship lasted, until Ollie went to the afterlife—then reconcile with the Devil if he'd really changed his ways?

Ollie gripped Dex by the shoulders. "I'm going to live as long as Dante. I'm his fated mate. We bonded, magically. All his problems and history will be mine too, in time. Even Lucifer. That's why I'm on board."

Dex couldn't speak.

But Ollie didn't stop there. "Bonding with Dante is what saved me on the beach, and it took me a while to understand it, but having a fated mate is a good thing. Believe me. Fate doesn't dictate anything. It gives you what you need to make the right choices and the confidence that things will work out in the end. I realized that it's *fated* for Luc and the other demons to work things out, and I want to be open to that, no matter what happened between me and him."

Dex didn't follow. Nothing Ollie said made any fucking sense.

The front door opened. "Are we ready to view the last property?" the realtor asked with a sunny smile.

"We'll be out in a minute," Ollie said, and she disappeared to wait in the hallway. "Follow your heart, Dex. Let me worry about Luc's attack. What he did isn't okay, but I want to forgive him no matter how much time it takes."

Time that Ollie apparently had no lack of, even if Dex did.

THE LAST CONDO WAS A BUST. Dex wouldn't buy it if it were the only place for sale in the city.

"Want to come over for dinner?" Ollie asked as the realtor sped off in her car, leaving them on the corner.

Dex rubbed the back of his neck. "No, I've got to pack. The offers on my place are coming in fast."

"That's great. Want help packing? We could order in."

"No, don't worry. At least one of us deserves a fun night."

Ollie looked like he wanted to argue, so Dex added, "Let's see when Onyx wants to go out next. Maybe we can all do something tomorrow night, or later in the week."

"Yeah, let's do that. I'm sure Onyx can make time. There's an art show at his gallery soon, too."

"Awesome." Dex tried to sound excited.

They said goodbye, and Dex turned toward home, his smile falling as soon as he was safely away from Ollie.

He dragged his feet.

A night alone in his condo was the last thing in the world he wanted. He hadn't even started packing, and shouldn't have pushed Ollie away. Avoiding his best friend shouldn't feel like the safest option, but every time they talked, Ollie dropped yet another confusing, half-explained truth on him, and Dex needed a break.

Instead of going home, Dex detoured to Dorthy's despite knowing Violet wouldn't be working. He ordered a beer and found a stool at a high table in the back corner. Drinking alone wasn't a great habit, and this wasn't the first time he'd been here that week.

Oh well.

There was no point denying that he was doing worse than

he'd been a few weeks ago. Dex could have sworn he'd been on the right track, dealing with his issues, selling the condo, and making choices that promoted better mental health. But the whole process of moving sucked, and finding out about the afterlife hadn't helped as much as he'd have imagined. Dex still had to get through life missing the people he'd loved most.

The beer disappeared, and Dex ordered another.

How had Ollie assumed it was okay to slip that he would live forever into their conversation? Dex focused on death way too much. He didn't want Ollie to die. It terrified him. But knowing Ollie would never die scared him too. He'd never see Ollie in the afterlife. Eventually, he'd lose him.

It wasn't fair.

The beer went down too easily, and the whole day looked stranger the longer Dex stewed.

How had Ollie guessed that he couldn't get Luc out of his head? Why suddenly support hearing the Devil out? It was impossible to imagine what Luc had told Ollie and the others to change their minds.

Dex unlocked his phone. He had to figure this out, and if Ollie wouldn't explain, that meant seeing Luc. He opened their chat and typed.

DEX:

I'm at Dorthy's.

Maybe not the best opener, which was entirely the beer's fault. He'd had three, or was it four? Five? Shit. The fact that he couldn't pin down his beer count meant he'd passed three a while ago.

His phone buzzed.

LUC:

Hi, Dex. Did you mean to send this to me?

DEX:

Yes.

I want to know what's going on.

LUC:

Would you like me to meet you? Is that why
you told me where you are?

DEX:

Obviously.

LUC:

I'll be there soon.

A tightness released from Dex's chest. He didn't see how Ollie could support this, but knowing Luc was on his way felt better than anything had in weeks.

Figuring out what was happening was one reason to see Luc. The easy reason. The other was harder to face.

Dex burned for the closeness he felt during their date. Something about their connection was calling out to him, even after all this time.

It was ridiculous. No matter what Ollie said, Dex shouldn't want Luc like this.

He wouldn't act on it. All he'd do was hear Luc out. Then leave. That way, he could move on from this and date literally anyone other than the Devil.

Mind made up, Dex ordered another drink and emailed his realtor, saying he wanted to make an offer on the condo across the river. He wasn't letting Luc ruin a good property for him.

"Dex, I'm so glad you messaged me."

Dex whirled around at the sound of Luc's melodic voice, and there he was in slacks and a dark-gray sweater that seemed unnecessarily cozy for a summer night. Maybe demons couldn't feel the heat.

A flash of Luc with his horns and wings crossed Dex's mind, and his heart skipped. He looked so normal now. Well, maybe not normal. Luc still looked like a model, and towered over Dex even more than he remembered.

"May I sit?" Luc gestured to the stool opposite him.

"No, stand there." Dex had no idea why he said it. What an asshole move.

"All right." Luc leaned an elbow against the high table, angling toward Dex. "Are you comfortable being around me without your friends?"

Dex swallowed, mouth dry, and had a long sip of his drink. He was comfortable. He couldn't seem to help it, even if he shouldn't be.

Eventually, he nodded, stifling a hiccup.

Luc's gaze zeroed in on the beer. "Have you had a few?"

"Maybe," Dex muttered, taking another sip out of spite. "Is the Devil going to judge me?"

"No, but your state of mind is important."

Dex snorted and had another sip. "God forbid you take advantage."

Luc pushed off the table and crowded Dex's personal space. "I'd never take advantage of you."

"No? You'd only kiss me, knowing you almost killed my best friend." Fuck. Dex's vision blurred. Maybe he was too drunk for this. He should have had dinner or at least some water.

"I didn't realize Ollie was your best friend. I'd have done everything differently if I'd known." Luc's voice was low and harsh, his gaze intense. Dex swore he caught a flicker of red within his brown irises.

"Why does Ollie suddenly believe you? He said you weren't going to hurt me, but the other day, he was terrified. I don't understand." Dex turned away and finished his drink as if that might help.

It didn't.

Luc was too close, and Dex didn't hate it.

Luc took the empty glass and set it aside. "There's a great deal of history to fill you in on before any of this will make sense. Dante, Ash, and Onyx's belief that I wouldn't hurt you is rooted in our shared past and a new understanding of how I acted over the years, something their mates understand."

"Can everyone shut the fuck up about mates?" Dex jabbed a finger at Luc's chest. "That's another thing that makes no sense. Explain it to me. Now."

Luc grabbed Dex's hand, surprisingly gentle. "We can't do this here."

Dex glanced around, suddenly aware of how loud he'd been. "Take me back to your place then. I hate being home. Anywhere would be better, even if you have some sort of creepy evil lair."

Luc's gaze remained stern, but his lips twitched. "I don't have an evil lair. Sorry to disappoint."

Damn him, Dex almost smiled. He hopped off his stool and swayed. *Shiiiit.* Luc caught him with an arm around his waist, and Dex grabbed onto Luc's sweater.

"Steady there."

Dex's head spun, and he tangled his fingers in the fabric. *So soft.* He buried his face against Luc's chest, rubbing his cheek over what had to be a cloud.

The spinning sensation ceased. Luc smelled like a campfire on a cold, clear night. Rich, smoky, and bright. Goosebumps broke out on Dex's skin as memories of childhood trips to the woods with his parents overwhelmed him. He could almost taste roasted marshmallows and feel the heat of the fire. His chest expanded as the sweet sting of happiness filled him.

Dex breathed Luc in, and the sting faded to something as soft as Luc's sweater. Comfort. Like Dex was living in his memory. Transported to a place he longed to be more than any other.

A hand came to rest on the back of his head. "Dex," Luc murmured.

He didn't want to go. He was home. "I need you," he said into Luc's chest.

Luc's breath caught, and the hand teasing Dex's hair stilled. "We should talk. I'll get you something to eat, and we can go to my place. All right?"

Dex disentangled from the sweater, realizing he had both arms wrapped around Luc's waist in a vice grip.

"Come on." Luc pulled one of Dex's arms out so he could slip his around him, guiding him away from the table.

The bar blurred around Dex. "I want to wear your sweater. It's soft."

Luc chuckled. "You can borrow it."

He led Dex outside, pausing to say something as they headed out the door. Dex didn't catch it, but he didn't think Luc was talking to him. A moment later, Luc said, "You aren't going to be walking far, are you?"

"No, carry me." Dex buried his face in Luc's chest once more.

That last drink had hit hard, but he couldn't bring himself to care. Everything was easy right now. Luc was here, and he didn't have to worry. Ollie told him it was okay.

Luc's hand returned to the top of Dex's head. "I can carry you, or we can get a car."

"Can't you decide? Can't you just..." Dex couldn't find the words.

The pause stretched, and Luc's arms seemed to tighten around him. "I'll take care of you. Don't worry. But answer one thing for me. Would you like me to fly you to my place, or will that scare you?"

Dex considered lifting his head, but rejected the idea. He breathed in more of Luc's smoky scent. "Fly me."

"Okay. Come on. A little farther."

Luc guided Dex away from Dorthy's, and he didn't bother paying attention to where they were going. He felt safe in Luc's arms, which had to be due to the alcohol.

This man had almost killed Ollie. He was *the Devil*. Not to be trusted. Dex might not understand everything happening with the demons and Ollie's cryptic encouragement, but he didn't need to. He was being reckless and didn't care.

Something cold pressed against Dex's back, and he yelped, opening his eyes. When had he closed them?

He and Luc were in an alleyway, and Luc had him pressed against a wall.

Luc pulled his sweater over his head, and Dex's thoughts ground to a halt. Luc loomed over him, bare-chested, his hair disheveled, and Dex's insides melted.

A shiver wound down Dex's spine. "Are you going to fuck me?"

"No." Luc's red lips twisted into a smile, and he handed Dex the sweater. "Put this on. You wanted to borrow it."

"Oh." Dex tried not to pout. Not very hard. He'd rather Luc fuck him than dress him.

"Don't be sad, Dex. You're too intoxicated to consent. But that doesn't mean I don't desire you. You're beautiful and deserve better than being penetrated against a wall in a dank alleyway."

Heat bloomed in Dex's cheeks, and he pulled the sweater on, getting caught momentarily, and glaring when his head finally emerged. "There's nothing wrong with wanting quick and dirty. There's nothing wrong with what I want."

Luc cupped Dex's cheek. "No, there's not. I didn't mean to shame you. If filth is what gets you going, I understand the appeal, believe me. But know that you deserve the best, whatever that looks like."

That was more like it. "The best dirty sex?" Dex grabbed Luc's waistband and pulled him closer. *The best kinky sex.* But he couldn't say it.

"Only the best, but not now. I'm flying you home. Remember?"

Dex shook his head, setting everything spinning. "I don't want to go home. I hate being there."

"I know." Luc's gaze turned tender. "We're going to my place. It's a loft. Not as exciting as an evil lair, but it will do. I'm going to release my wings and horns now."

"Okay." Dex didn't let go of Luc's waistband. It wasn't as if Luc told him to. Besides, he might slide to the floor if he did.

Luc didn't pull away. His body was so warm, his smoky scent nearly overwhelming. Suddenly, deep-red horns sprang from the sides of Luc's forehead, curling outward like a ram's. The skin seemed textured, and Dex reached out, running a finger along the base of one.

"Leathery." He petted the other horn, confirming that they matched.

Luc chuckled. "It's very presumptuous of you to touch my horns without asking."

"It's pre-presumptuous to push me against a wall," Dex countered as his hand found its way back to Luc's waist.

"I didn't want you to fall." Luc pulled back, and Dex went with him, refusing to let go of Luc's waistband.

He stumbled forward. Dammit.

"See?" Luc caught him and hauled him against his chest.

"Yeah, fine. Hold me," Dex muttered, pretending it wasn't exactly what he wanted.

Luc's eyes locked on his, expression unreadable, and red

wings rose from his back without further warning. Dex gasped, longing to touch Luc's feathers surging through him.

"Let's go." Luc hoisted Dex up, and he squeaked as Luc maneuvered him into a bridal carry. "Hold onto my neck."

Dex did as he was told, not even sneaking a brush of feathers along the way. Luc was so strong. Carrying Dex didn't seem to strain him at all.

"How much can you bench press?"

Luc made a sound like he was choking and dissolved into laughter. "I don't know. I'm inhumanly strong. It's a demon thing."

"You don't even go to the gym?" That wasn't fair. Nothing seemed fair these days. Dex didn't go to the gym either, but he wasn't trying to bulk up or lift full-grown humans. He should probably still go—

"Dex?"

"Hmm?" His eyes fluttered open. Shit, he'd closed them again.

"I'm going to take off now. We'll be in the air for a few minutes before we land."

Oh, right. Flying. Dex closed his eyes on purpose this time. "I like your arms around me."

Luc's hold tightened. "Me too."

A moment later, Dex's stomach lurched, and he gasped, air rushing around him. His eyes popped open, revealing a blur of buildings as they shot into the sky.

He clamped his eyes shut.

"It's all right. I've got you."

Dex took Luc's word for it. This was the kind of reckless thing he shouldn't be doing. No way flying back to Lucifer's not-evil lair was a good idea, but it was happening, and Dex couldn't hold on to his worry. Luc's wingbeats lulled him into a daze.

With a jolt, everything stopped.

"We're here," Luc said, but Dex didn't open his eyes to check.

Luc carried him without complaint. It sounded like they went through a few doors and maybe along some stairs. Eventually, Luc laid Dex on something soft, and he opened his eyes.

Luc's deep brown gaze and red horns filled his vision. "What would you like to eat?"

Dex's fingers found their way into Luc's hair, to his horns. Was he on a bed? Luc's bed? They were going to have sex after all.

He wanted Luc, but a twinge of disappointment cut through his desire. Luc had brought him to a bed rather than use him out behind the bar like a whore. Did Luc think he wanted soft lovemaking? Whatever. If Dex couldn't ask for what he wanted, he couldn't expect Luc to fulfil his fantasies. Sex would still be nice.

Would Ollie be mad? No, he said it was okay. He might have suggested talking to Luc, not fucking him, but could Ollie blame him? He'd started this. Dex never would have texted Luc if Ollie hadn't told him to.

Dex pulled Luc closer, needing to feel his big body pressing him into the mattress, but Luc didn't budge.

"Food, Dex. We aren't kissing now. I'll get you some water and order pizza." Luc pulled away, and Dex whined.

Luc stood over the bed, doing his looming thing again, and tapped on his phone.

"Is looming a hobby of yours? You're very tall."

Luc's gaze tore from the phone and landed on Dex. He covered his mouth and laughed, his whole body trembling.

Dex grinned like an idiot. Look at him, making funny jokes.

Luc pulled his hand away from his mouth, revealing the most beautiful smile. It was as if he had transformed. He seemed younger and more at ease, even compared to the careful poise Dex had observed when they'd first met.

Luc turned away, taking his smile with him. Dex wanted it back. He wanted to get up and follow, but the bed was so soft, and moving required energy.

Something brushed against Dex's forehead, and he realized his eyes were closed again. He opened them, finding Luc sitting beside him. Had he been asleep?

"Feel like sitting up and having a sip of water?"

Dex reached out a hand. "Help me."

Luc pulled, and Dex's vision blurred as he sat up. It was a good thing he didn't have work in the morning. He accepted the water and drank it down, then Luc took the empty cup and exchanged it for a pizza box.

Dex's stomach growled. "Oh my god, thank you." He opened the box and peeled a slice from the pie, cheese stretching.

"I didn't know what toppings you liked, so I got plain cheese. I hope it's okay."

Dex nodded, his mouth full, and offered the box to Luc.

He selected a slice. "Looks like we made it to dinner after all." He had a bite and smiled at Dex, but it seemed sad.

"It's a date." Dex finished his slice and grabbed another. "Does that mean I'm spending the night?"

Luc licked sauce from his finger. "You can sleep here."

Dex narrowed his eyes. "Why are you saying that like you won't be sleeping with me?"

"We've been over this. You've had too much to drink for anything sexual to happen. Staying here isn't changing my mind, so if you'd rather go home, I understand."

"You're stubborn." Dex took a large bite and chewed. "I don't want to go home. I have to pack, and I really don't feel like crying."

Luc's brow furrowed. "Are you regretting selling your parents' house?"

Dex's stomach cramped. Ugh, he'd had too much beer. "I'm not regretting leaving. I'm regretting having to go through all my parents' stuff to pack it up. It's still in their room. And in the hall closet, and... I get sick every time I think of dealing with it."

"Do you need someone to go through it with you?"

Dex considered his pizza crust before popping it in his mouth. "I don't know. I should have dealt with it years ago, and I've already committed to moving. That should have made being in the condo and dealing with it easier."

"But it hasn't?"

Dex shook his head, his eyes suddenly burning. He blinked rapidly to stave off his tears. Fuck. Why was he even talking about this?

Luc set the pizza box on an empty, upturned crate by the bed and handed Dex a napkin. "Have you talked to anyone about how you're feeling?"

Dex wiped his face. "Sort of. Ollie knows most of it."

"Not all of it?"

"I can't whine to him about my sad life all the time. It's been years. He doesn't need to know every detail." Dex was sick of himself at this point. Why would anyone else want to deal with his never-ending issues?

Luc scowled as if he didn't like what he was hearing. "You know Ollie wouldn't mind."

Dex reached for more pizza. Talking about Ollie reminded him that he had questions for Luc, but he couldn't talk and eat, and the pizza was his priority. Everything else was too complicated.

"Would you like me to help you pack your parents' things?"

Dex jolted, almost dropping his slice.

He stared at Luc, whose head was cocked to the side, black

hair tumbling over his brow, his red lips in a serious line. Luc wanted to help him pack up his trauma? Or maybe unpack, depending on how you looked at it.

Unpack while packing up...?

Dex cleared his throat. "It's not boxing up their stuff that's the issue. I...I don't want to keep it. I'm not taking my same old shit—metaphorical or physical—to my new place. But I don't want to throw it all out either. I need to sort through things and figure out what to keep."

It was a huge, emotionally loaded task. Dex was exhausted even thinking about it.

Luc seemed to mull this over for a minute. "What if you hired someone to pack the house for you and stored everything that isn't yours until you were ready to go through it?"

"I guess. Too bad putting it off is why I'm here in the first place. More of the same can't be good."

Luc shrugged. "If you're dreading it this much, maybe a little more time isn't a bad thing. Some distance could be all you need."

It wasn't a terrible idea. If he didn't feel like he had no choice but to go through everything, maybe he would, but it wasn't practical. "Seems like a waste of money to store stuff I'm going to end up donating or throwing away."

Luc's nose wrinkled. "Cost shouldn't stop you."

Dex laughed. "Do you know anything about the world? Money or lack of it impacts everything." Dex was well off compared to most people his age, but that didn't mean he wasted money.

Luc's look of annoyance turned to a full-on scowl. "I know how the world works. Luckily for you, I happen to have an excess of space and no need to exchange money to use it."

Dex glanced around the loft. The bed sat on a mezzanine level, and the entire area below was empty. It was enormous.

The bed was about the only thing in here. Luc might not have an evil lair, but this was closer to one than anything Dex had ever seen. It would be freezing in winter.

"You want me to store my parents' stuff here?"

"Why not? You can't argue that it'd be an imposition. And I promise I'll look after it. Magic can keep everything perfectly preserved, so there's no need to worry about moisture." Luc tilted his head toward the ceiling. "I'm not sure if the roof leaks or not."

Dex gaped at the demon sitting next to him, his head suddenly clear of beer-fog. "That's very kind of you to offer."

Luc shrugged, avoiding Dex's stare. "I'd like to help."

It really seemed like their date had picked up where it had left off. This was the same Luc that Dex had met in Dorthy's, the same man who'd bought him ice cream. Could he trust it was the real Luc? Everything in him screamed *yes*.

"Thanks. I'll take you up on the storage. I want to buy new furniture. Start completely fresh. If I can put everything here, that would be such a relief. And I promise I'll deal with it eventually."

Luc rested a hand on Dex's knee. "No rush."

Dex's stomach twisted. "No, I suppose there's isn't when you live forever."

13

DEX

Dex groaned as he woke, not bothering to open his eyes. A dull ache pounded behind his temple, and he pulled the blanket over him, blocking out the light.

Why had he drunk so much? He had to get his shit together. No more solo pity parties.

Letting out one more miserable sigh, Dex promised to take better care of himself.

An unfamiliar scent filled his nose. Something faintly smoky. Dex froze. He wasn't in *his* bed.

The rest of the night came rushing back. Texting Luc. Seeing him. Clinging to him. *Oh god.* Going home with him.

Slowly, Dex peeked out from beneath the covers. The other side of the bed was empty. No surprise there, since Luc had refused to play along with his advances.

While Dex was relieved Luc wasn't the type to take advantage, his own behavior was humiliating to remember. Had he rubbed himself against Luc's chest like a cat? Multiple times. Why?

Sitting up, he wiped the sleep from his eyes. Sun streamed in from a row of high windows, illuminating the bed and otherwise empty mezzanine floor. Beyond the metal railing lay nothing but shadow and empty space.

Luc was nowhere to be seen.

Dex couldn't remember going to sleep. Apparently, he'd decided to wear nothing but his boxer briefs and Luc's gray sweater. He'd even taken off his T-shirt and put the sweater back on.

Had he said something about being wrapped in Luc's scent? *Ugh.*

Where was Luc? Had he spent the night next to Dex and snuck off before he woke? Did Luc wear anything to sleep, maybe a pair of underwear and nothing else?

Dex groaned even more pitifully than before, hating himself for going there almost as much as he hated that he might have missed seeing Luc undressed.

Ollie's encouragement wasn't some sort of free pass. Drunk Dex had an excuse for forgetting Luc was a bad person; sober Dex didn't. He shouldn't be attracted to a violent man, no matter how much Luc offered to help with his moving-related trauma.

If Dex were smart, he'd see Luc's caring side as the other half of a red flag. The Devil had two completely different personalities, and there was nothing to say he wouldn't flip his switch and become the man who'd had Ollie trembling.

A door banged open and shut, echoing through the cavernous space. Dex stiffened, his heart jolting as his pulse picked up.

Footsteps sounded on the stairs, even and unhurried. Dex's heart leapt. For a second, he had the urge to run.

Maybe Luc's sweetness was an act to lure him here—a lie, like Ollie had first said—and a far more sinister man was stalking up the stairs, coming to do whatever he wanted to Dex. And he wouldn't be able to stop him.

Heat flooded Dex from head to toe. Would Luc chase him if he ran? What would he do when he caught him? What did Dex want him to do?

Dex had fantasies of being overpowered. The desire had blossomed along with his awareness of sex. When he was young, watching wrestling or physical fight scenes in movies excited him, and as he'd gotten older, he couldn't deny that the idea of being dominated aroused him more than simple thoughts of kissing or touching another man. Dex wanted to let go completely and be at someone else's mercy.

Part of Dex was desperate for Luc's sweetness to be obscuring something darker. Not as dark as what happened to Ollie, but something more in line with his needs.

Would Luc give Dex what he'd longed for? Could he even admit his desires outside of his private thoughts? Doubt weighed Dex down, as strong as ever.

He shouldn't want to be overpowered, held down, and taken roughly by Luc. Not given everything else the Devil had done. Wondering if Luc would play along because he'd proven himself violent was all kinds of fucked up. Dex knew that, but it didn't dampen his desire.

If Luc took control, Dex wouldn't have to worry if what he wanted was right or wrong, and that was the most tempting thing of all.

Dex just wanted to let go. Get out of his head.

"I've got coffee," Luc announced as he appeared at the top of the creaking metal stairs, looking completely harmless, carrying a coffee tray and a pastry box. "I need a dining table. Eating in bed is awkward."

He set the pastry box on an upturned crate and held out the coffees for Dex. "The one on the right is black, the other is a latte. I've got sugar in my pocket."

Dex reached for the latte reflexively, his pulse pattering as if saying *run, run, run*. He was dying to see if Luc would chase him. Catch him. Make him tremble. But he couldn't move. "Uh, thanks."

Luc sat on the edge of the mattress next to Dex and discarded the tray on the floor, keeping the other coffee for himself. He wore a soft-looking red sweater. It was so normal. Dex could almost convince himself he'd woken with a human boyfriend and not the Devil, but he didn't want to.

There was a complexity to Luc. He wasn't simply an attempted killer or simply a kind man. Could he really be both? Luc's concern for Dex's grief couldn't all be an act, and Dex didn't want it to be. Luc's care was part of the reason Dex was tempted to bring his fantasies to reality with him.

Dex had a strong urge to trust him.

Maybe the truth of Luc sat in between sweet and going too far, and that middle ground where care mixed with control and force was what Dex craved more than anything.

"How are you feeling?" Luc asked, his calm demeanor in stark contrast to the feelings warring inside Dex.

"I'm fine." But he wasn't, and he didn't want to play pretend. Luc could be sweet if it were real, but they had to address everything else. Not ignore it.

Dex discarded his coffee on the crate. He either had to confront Luc or leave. Fuck.

Luc eyed Dex's discarded coffee as if it had said something rude. "Would you like a muffin instead?"

"I'm not hungry," Dex lied, his stomach twisting with more than one kind of hollowness. "I didn't ask you to bring me anything to eat. Speaking of, you don't need food, right? Just blood. How often do you drink from people?"

Luc set his coffee on the floor with the air of discarding a pretense, unless that was Dex's imagination. "It depends. Once a week is more than enough."

Oh shit. He answered. Dex forced himself to act casual, as if his heart wasn't in his throat.

It wasn't enough. He could ask polite questions and get equally polite responses all day, but he'd always wonder how a sweet man could be the Devil. His mind stuck on how the two came together, who the *real* Luc was, and if he was who Dex needed him to be.

Dex cleared his throat. "Who have you been feeding on? Are they still alive?"

Luc went as still as a statue, his sharp attention giving Dex chills.

Was he going to say nothing? Explode with rage? He clearly didn't want to talk about this, and Dex was glad he'd asked.

At last, Luc spoke, calm and detached. "I've been feeding on random men, and yes, they're all alive. Before I met you, I'd give them a little pleasure for their sacrifice, if they were interested."

Something ugly congealed in Dex's stomach. Was he fucking jealous right now? Why? Luc had said *before* he'd met Dex. But why would meeting him affect whether Luc got off with others or not? It was too much to take in.

Dex was stiff with growing tension. "Pleasure? Drinking from them doesn't hurt?"

Luc remained unnaturally still, reminding Dex of a predator poised to pounce. "My bite can hurt if I want it to, or I can hypnotize my meals so they don't know what's happening."

His meals. What a way to phrase it. As if the men didn't matter any more than a muffin. Men that Luc got off with, even if they didn't know what was happening.

Confusion throbbed in time with Dex's headache. He couldn't take another contradiction. "Why were you so against taking advantage of me last night if you do it all the time?"

Luc's jaw seemed to tense, the muscles around his mouth twitching. "I don't do it all the time. Only when I have to. And it's not the same. They always agreed to sex of their own free will. It's the biting I did without consent. Without them even knowing."

So, Luc's refusal to take advantage of Dex wasn't a contradiction. There were lines he wouldn't cross. He fed because he had to, in the least traumatic way he knew how.

Possibility unfurled within Dex. He was all too aware of his own blood pulsing through his neck. "You didn't have to feed last night? I offered myself to you. You could have done whatever you wanted." Fuck, Dex's core tightened at the prospect.

Something like a growl erupted from Luc. "What I want from you isn't something I can take. I don't want to hurt you."

No, he didn't. Dex believed him.

His breaths turned shallow, and he gripped the blanket, suddenly lightheaded. "You said biting wouldn't hurt."

Luc's eyes flashed red. "Dex, what are you doing?"

He clutched the blanket tighter, his back rigid against the headboard. "W-what do you mean?"

Luc's nostrils flared, and he shifted closer, an unmistakable growl vibrating from his chest. "What did the others tell you about feeding on blood? You weren't talking about blood last night, and you *know* I won't take advantage of you. Why are you pushing me like this?"

It was Dex's turn to freeze, caught like prey in Luc's overwhelming presence. "No one told me anything other than demons drink blood."

Luc shifted even closer. "Then why are you acting like you're about to offer yours?"

Goddamn, that would be the ultimate surrender. Dex shivered, unable to suppress it, and Luc noticed, his gaze narrowing.

"I want to know who you really are," Dex said desperately. "I want to know what's real. You act so sweet, but I know you've done bad things. Which is it? How is it all connected? Are you pretending to be what you think I want?"

He needed to figure out if the real Luc matched the real Dex, but couldn't get a more direct question past his lips, or admit that what everyone seemed to think he wanted didn't fill his true desires.

Luc leaned in, inches from Dex, heat seeming to pour off his body in waves. "I'm not pretending or manipulating you."

Sweat prickled along Dex's forehead. "Okay. But you aren't telling me what you really want either. You're acting, at least to an extent. You can't be this perfect boyfriend and also be the man who almost killed my best friend. You can't be two separate things, like the other half doesn't exist."

Luc huffed, and the scent of smoke filled the air. "You don't get to tell me who I can and can't be."

Dex braced against the headboard. "Then show me who you really are."

"I am." Luc pressed forward, planting a hand on either side of Dex. "The real me wants to care for you, destroy your grief, and give you *everything*."

Dex swallowed a whimper. What a thing to say. "Is that all?"

"No." Luc caught Dex's chin between two fingers. "I want you to be *mine*. I want to keep you. You want to know who I really am? The pieces I've kept quiet? When I first saw you, I considered using magic to ensnare you and *make you mine*. I'm known for taking what I want—it's become a habit—but I can't with you. I'm determined to break the cycle I've trapped myself in. You have to choose me and *let* me give you everything. That's the only way I can possess all of you."

Fuck. Dex had to remember how to breathe.

"Your pulse is pounding." Luc's voice softened, his gaze falling to Dex's neck. "I can hear it. Am I scaring you?"

Dex wrapped a hand around Luc's wrist, but didn't pull him off. If anything, he held Luc in place. "Yes." The word came out breathy, and his whole body burned.

Luc smiled, sly and befitting the Devil. "And you like being afraid?"

Dex nodded as best he could, heat pooling deep inside him as his cock stiffened.

He wanted nothing more than to be *possessed*. By Luc. By fear. His desire to feel owned, to let someone else take charge, came alive under Luc's grip.

Dex's life had been out of his control for years, and for once, he wanted helplessness to be on his terms. He was desperate to give in to fear while someone else held the reins, and it wasn't death or loss terrifying him. Those were his real fears. They ruled him, and he hated it. He wanted to be scared and embrace it. Face the emotion and see what happened.

What if it set him free?

In one swift motion, Luc released Dex and climbed on top of him, straddling his legs and trapping them beneath the covers. "You like seeing this side of me?"

Dex squirmed. "Yes, I do. So much."

Luc caught his face once more, gripping tight around his chin, and Dex sighed into the contact.

"I can smell your arousal," Luc purred.

Dex shivered, his eyelids fluttering. Smell him? How humiliating. But at the same time, it wasn't enough. Dex didn't want this to stop. "Please."

"Please, what?"

"Do what you want. Not what you think you should." If this was the real Luc, then Dex could be his true self with him. He was so close to asking for what he wanted. So close.

Luc ran his thumb along Dex's jaw. "I'm trying to figure out who I want to be. I have a host of regrets to break free from, and

I refuse to regret anything to do with you. So I'm being careful. That doesn't mean it isn't real, or that I'm only doing what I think is expected of me."

"I believe you. But please, you won't regret it. Let loose. Show me. You can take care of me like you said, but I...I want this too."

Understanding dawned on Luc's face. "You want a demon who scares you, thrills you, and then holds you after?"

"Yes," Dex moaned. That was exactly what he wanted. Desire coursed through his blood like a raging river, begging to be mapped in vivid detail.

Dex wanted to give himself over to fear while Luc made sure it was okay. And he could. Luc's care was as real as his desire to possess Dex, and he wouldn't cross any lines Dex didn't want him to.

"I want all those things too." Luc peeled the covers back, exposing Dex's lap and tented boxer briefs. "I like the idea of letting loose with you. Of you embracing all of me."

"Yes, I want all of you. That's exactly it."

Luc loomed over Dex, pinning him by the jaw to the headboard, and Dex had never been so aware of his body, his vulnerability.

He arched into Luc's hold. "Feed from me. Show me what it's like when you hunt someone. When you won't let them get away."

Fire danced in Luc's eyes. "My actual hunting habits are far less exciting. Hypnosis and illusion take away all the fun, but I won't use any of that on you. You're dying to feel it all, aren't you?"

Dex nodded, his breath stuttering.

Luc licked his lips. "Good, because I'm dying to taste you."

Dex squirmed, ready to take himself in hand and fuck his fist. "Do it."

"We should probably have a discussion first. You said you had questions, but I don't feel like talking. I want you, and if you want a thrill, then that's what I'll give you."

"I want it."

"Good." Luc released Dex and slunk toward the end of the bed.

Dex's head spun. Where was he going? Before he could beg Luc not to leave, Luc whipped the covers back, grabbed Dex's ankles, and yanked him down the bed.

Dex yelped, the sweater riding up and exposing his stomach as he slid along the sheets. In a blink, Luc was on him, eyes glowing red and horns curling out of his hair where there'd been none before.

Luc bared his teeth, and his canines lengthened into sharp fangs. Dex's stomach flipped. They were so long. No way having those monstrous points burred in his neck wouldn't hurt. Luc growled, and the deep vibrations sent chills cascading through Dex.

He sucked in harsh breath after breath. When had he begun panting?

"Fuck, your pulse is thundering. Your arousal is so potent." Luc hummed as if satisfied. "Do you like feeling trapped?"

Dex closed his eyes, hoping to heighten the already intense sensation. "Yes, I—I do."

Luc's approving rumble had goosebumps erupting on Dex's skin. "I love holding down eager prey. Playing with a desperate boy who can't escape my hold. Will you be my prey, my desperate boy, Dex?"

Dex didn't even consider holding back. Admitting what he wanted was easy when he knew it turned Luc on, too.

"Yes," he moaned. "Hold me down. Restrain me. Please."

Luc's hands mapped his torso, and he gripped Dex's hips, pressing him into the mattress. Luc was in control, and Dex didn't have to worry. It was better than a fantasy. All Dex had to do was let Luc crush him. Hopefully, Luc wouldn't let go no matter how much he struggled.

The pressure of Luc's grip increased. "How will I know if it's too much? If you change your mind?"

Dex opened his eyes. The lack of menace in Luc's tone jolted him out of the moment. He wasn't stopping, was he? Dex might die if he did.

"It won't be too much."

Luc's smile stretched into a feral grin made even more chilling by his fangs and burning eyes. "Perfect, but if you say stop, I will. And don't hesitate to say it. I don't enjoy forcing myself on anyone. I'll get off on you enjoying this. On knowing you want it."

"What if I want to tell you no. To say stop and for you to keep going anyway?" This was a fantasy Dex had never planned to voice, but who better to share it with? Luc wouldn't judge him for wanting this, wouldn't tell him it was wrong.

Not when Luc desired to possess *all* of him.

Luc's eyes flashed. "If that's what you want, then we'll need a safe word."

Dex's breath heaved. "Red for stop. Okay? Otherwise, if I tell you no or to let go, keep going." He wiggled in Luc's hold.

Luc took the bait, his grip tightening. "Okay, eager little prey. Struggle all you want. You won't escape unless you safe-word."

Dex moaned, and Luc chuckled low and full of dark humor.

Dex rolled, grabbing for the edge of the mattress, but Luc pulled him back.

"Where are you going, Dex?"

Dex struggled, unable to form words. The fire in Luc's eyes flared. Dex pushed against his unmoving chest with both hands, but there was no breaking free from his grip.

Dex gave himself over to the urge to flee, letting it burn through him and take over every one of his reflexes, but Luc didn't relent, and that was exactly what Dex craved.

"I asked where you were going."

He sputtered. "N-nowhere."

"That's right." Luc held Dex's stare, his hand traveling slowly toward Dex's neck with clear intent to wrap it around his throat.

Dex arched, exposing himself and baring his throat as an uncontrollable shiver overtook him.

Luc accepted the invitation—gaze never straying, so intense there was no doubt he was absorbing every one of Dex's reactions—and covered his throat with firm fingers, lips curling in satisfaction at Dex's desperate surrender.

A sound passed Dex's lips, so obscene that his whole body burned. Luc didn't squeeze, didn't actually choke him, but the presence of his hand was impossible to ignore.

Dex wrapped his fingers around Luc's wrist and pulled with all his strength. "Let go."

Luc didn't budge. "No, you're mine."

"*Uhh.*" Electricity shot through Dex, hotter than anything he'd felt before.

He had no choice. No way out. All he could do was feel. Fall into knowing that Luc wanted him so badly, he wouldn't relent, no matter what. Dex's cock throbbed in time with his thundering pulse, sensation threatening to overwhelm him completely.

Dex's legs scrambled for purchase on the bed. He needed friction, but Luc's hips didn't connect with his. He hovered, watching Dex with fire in his eyes and satisfaction written all over his face.

"Luc." Dex bucked his hips against nothing. He'd never been more turned on. Fantasizing was nothing compared to being pinned down by the Devil. "No. Please. You can't. Let me go. *Let me go!*" Dex shoved Luc's chest, scratching at his neck, his arms.

Luc caught both of Dex's hands in one of his and trapped them against Dex's sternum, forcing the air from his lungs in a whoosh.

"Why would I let you go? You're so pretty when you struggle, and it's all for me. But don't worry. It's almost over." Luc nosed down Dex's neck and licked from his collarbone to his jaw.

A high-pitched whimper tore from Dex as he shivered with pleasure. He was helpless.

He could make this stop with a word, but that was the last thing he wanted. Luc wouldn't hurt him. It was safe to be afraid with Luc and give in like he'd imagined.

Luc's fangs pierced his flesh with a sharp stab, and Dex cried out. His vision blurred and he remained still, whimpering, trembling so hard he was practically vibrating. Luc growled and sealed his lips against Dex's neck. He sucked, groaning long and low, and pleasure exploded within Dex.

He screamed, struggling against Luc's hold without conscious thought, the desire to feel utterly possessed taking over.

It was as if his neck had a hidden bundle of nerves, like his prostate. Holy fucking shit. The more Dex struggled, the tighter Luc held him, the harder he sucked, the louder he groaned, and the closer Dex was to coming.

He hadn't expected it to be like this. "Luc, please."

Luc released Dex's trapped hands, his lips leaving Dex's neck. He pulled his head back, blood smearing his already red lips, and his tongue darted out to lick it.

"Don't stop," Dex whimpered. That wasn't what he meant.

"I'm not. We're just getting started." Luc pushed the

sweater to Dex's armpits and yanked his boxers down, freeing his hard cock. Luc inspected him, running a hand over Dex's flaming skin. "Mmm. That's better. No hiding from me."

"I want to see you too." Luc was still fully clothed.

"Too bad. I'm in charge, and I'm not done taking what you've offered." He bent back to Dex's neck, and Dex automatically turned his head to the side, exposing his throat.

Luc's fangs sank back in, the bite stinging as pleasure bloomed where they connected. Dex gripped Luc's shoulders, moaning and bucking his hips, humping the air. If only Luc would drop his weight on top of him, but he stayed hovering out of reach.

Holding back was impossible. Dex must've looked like a fool trying to fuck the space between them as he let Luc devour him. A slutty, desperate fool.

Remembering his hands were free, he gripped his cock and stroked without mercy, not caring how dry his palm was. It didn't matter when everything inside him from his neck to his ass lit up like a neon sign.

One stroke, two, and pleasure zipped down Dex's spine. His back arched, and he came, crying out as Luc sucked on his neck with no sign of stopping. The orgasm went on, cum covering Dex's hand and stomach. When it became too much, Dex released his dick, but the sensations didn't fade as they normally would.

Each pull Luc took sent a shock through Dex like another mini orgasm. Fuck, his body didn't seem capable of stopping. His insides clenched. Air burned in his lungs as he whimpered. This would break him.

He wanted it to.

At last, Luc withdrew, and the pleasure faded. Dex sobbed in relief, his eyes wet, and sweat coating his body.

Luc licked Dex's neck in slow, steady strokes, sending an

unexpected prickling sensation over his skin. "You taste better than anyone I've ever had. I could drink you dry."

Dex whined. He didn't hate the threat.

With one final lick, Luc pulled away and rocked back on his heels, peering down at Dex with glowing eyes. Dex's own lids grew heavy. He sluggishly raised a hand to his neck to see if the wound was still bleeding, and his fingers brushed perfectly smooth skin.

Luc's gaze fell to the mess on Dex's stomach. "Seems you wouldn't mind me drinking you dry, would you, dirty boy?"

Dex's face burned with hot pleasure and self-consciousness alike. His tongue seemed to have stopped working so he gave a small nod.

Luc's erection pressed clearly against the front of his slacks, and the evidence that he wasn't completely unaffected had Dex's growing embarrassment fading.

"Has this got your attention?" Luc undid his pants and pulled out his cock.

Dex groaned, and Luc wrapped a fist around his length with a smirk. He stroked himself with punishing intensity, and all Dex could do was lie there mesmerized as Luc grunted and came all over him, their release mixing on his clammy skin.

"Fuck." Luc let go of his cock and dropped forward, nuzzling Dex's neck with his nose.

Dex's world was irreversibly altered. He'd never regret it, but this didn't make anything easier.

What was he supposed to do now?

14

LUCIFER

Luc's face might as well be glued to Dex's skin. He never wanted to pull away from his earthy scent. It was nearly as intoxicating as his blood. Luc hadn't lied when he'd said he could drain Dex dry.

Even that wouldn't be enough.

Dex's hands found their way into Luc's hair, gently toying with the strands. His pounding pulse calmed, the hint of fear sharpening the scent of his arousal long gone. Dex was, by all accounts, satisfied.

Luc would never be satisfied. Not until he could make Dex his forever.

Despair threatened to smother Luc's afterglow. Dex would never be his. Mating wasn't any more possible just because Dex had embraced some of Luc's more selfish urges.

But there was nothing Luc could do about that at the moment.

"Let's clean you up." Luc reluctantly withdrew from the crook of Dex's neck and sat back, pulling the borrowed sweater over Dex's head and using it to clean the cum from his stomach.

"I wanted to keep wearing that," Dex grumbled, trying to prop himself on shaking arms.

Luc tossed the soiled sweater away and wrapped a supportive arm around Dex. "You can have another, but I like you without it. I want to keep you naked in bed forever."

Dex shivered. "Like a prisoner?"

It was hard to tell if he was teasing. Did he want to play that kind of game, or was he still trying to goad Luc into revealing all his darker desires?

Maybe a little from column A, and a little from column B. Luc could work with that.

"No, not like a real prisoner. That wouldn't be pleasurable for either of us." Luc pulled Dex's tangled underwear from around his thighs and tossed them toward the sweater. "We can pretend you're my prisoner, if you like."

Dex squirmed, a response that could go either way. "Have you thought about holding me captive?"

"You mean seriously?"

Dex nodded.

Luc frowned. He obviously wanted the truth. "I considered the merits of not letting you leave my bed until you agreed to be mine. But it wasn't a serious consideration. More a fantasy than anything." A desperate wish to soothe Luc's own fears.

Dex blinked dazedly, as if he were having trouble absorbing Luc's words. Unless was it the result of having his pleasure sucked out of his neck.

Luc went on, "It would be easier to look after you if I kept you close. Willingly."

Dex trapped his lower lip between his teeth. "That's what you want to do now? Look after me?"

"Yes." Fire burned in Luc's chest. "You need to eat something. That was more than a love bite."

Dex's cheeks darkened, and he covered the spot on his neck

where Luc's bite would have been if he hadn't healed it with magic.

Luc pulled Dex's hand to the side to stroke the unmarred flesh. Dex remained pliant, seemingly ready for Luc to do whatever he wanted.

After a moment, Luc tucked his soft cock away and zipped his pants, then stood to grab the pastry box, bringing it back to the bed where he sat against the headboard. He dragged Dex onto his lap, draping both his legs to one side, and situated Dex's bare bum on his crotch.

Dex didn't resist Luc's commanding touches. In fact, he seemed to settle in, enjoying the possessiveness. Luc almost purred.

He pulled the pastry box closer.

Dex squirmed. "You want me to sit here, eating naked?"

"I do. I have a hunch that you'll enjoy me ogling you as much as I will. You like when I'm not a gentleman."

Dex buried his face in Luc's shoulder and his earthy scent flared. "Oh my god."

Why was he bashful? Did his desires embarrass him?

Luc stroked Dex's hair. "Am I right, or would you rather cover up and leave me to my imagination?"

Dex huffed, pressing his face harder against Luc, like he was trying to burrow inside. "You're right, I'm enjoying this." His voice was strained, as if the admission cost him.

Perhaps he needed reassurance. To know he was safe and free of judgement.

"I'm pleased to hear it." Luc let the hint of a purr come through, hoping Dex could tell how much he meant it. "You can always tell me what you like. And what you don't. I want to know it all."

Dex's grip tightened. "All of me?" he whispered.

"All of you," Luc confirmed. "With no exceptions."

Dex relaxed into his hold, and Luc smiled.

He opened the pastry box and tangled a hand in Dex's short hair, pulling his head back. "Eat this." Luc handed him a muffin.

Dex took it and had a bite. Damnation, he was so obedient.

He finished his muffin quietly, and Luc handed him another. Remembering the coffee, he levitated the latte over and grabbed the cup from the air. With a silent spell, he reheated it and handed it to Dex.

He had a sip. "Wow, it's warm. Did you do that?"

Luc hummed, appreciating Dex's sense of wonder. "Magic is great for little things."

"Is it stupid that every time I see magic, I'm surprised all over again?"

His tone implied he thought it was stupid, so Luc set him straight. "Why would it be? All your life, you were told that magic was a fantasy. It's only logical for a part of you to resist believing."

"I hadn't considered that." He had another sip, shifting his position, his muscles going lax. "Can we stay like this for a while?"

Luc wrapped both arms around Dex. "Of course."

They lapsed into silence as Dex finished eating and drinking his coffee. Luc didn't mind. Holding him was enough for now.

When the food and coffee were done, trash levitated away, Dex wrapped an arm around Luc and tucked his face into the crook of his neck.

Luc had meant to fondle Dex, tease him until he was aroused, and suck another orgasm from him, though probably not through his blood. But as Dex cuddled closer, Luc's chest tightened.

So much sadness was trapped in his petite form. Luc wished he could extract it, banish it, or otherwise destroy it. Anything to get rid of it. But Dex wasn't being haunted by an enemy Luc could conquer with force. All he could do was be good for Dex, not hurt him, and help him on his journey.

And Dex seemed prepared to let him.

Luc's mate found comfort in him. Snuggled him so sweetly. He accepted Luc's soft side along with his domineering tendencies. Dex allowed Luc to be whole, not just a demon who fed on him and possessed him, but held his grieving heart.

Luc hadn't had intimacy like this in thousands of years, if ever.

Damn his worn-out soul. Not bonding with Dex would break him. Why couldn't there be a way to keep Dex without taking anything from him?

"What's the deal with mates?" Dex asked after a while, jolting Luc out of his reverie.

It was as if Dex had read his mind, and Luc panicked. He hadn't spoken out loud, had he? "What do you mean?"

"Ollie told me he's bound to Dante and won't die. He started going on about fate. Mates are some huge thing, aren't they? It's not just the demon word for partner."

Luc was grateful they weren't facing each other. Dex would read too much into his expression.

He held Dex firmly tucked against his neck, in case he had any ideas about peering at him. "Mates aren't the same as human partners. They're fated. All Eternal beings have a fated mate, or in the case of my polyamorous kin, more than one."

"What does fated mean?" Dex sounded frustrated, and Luc almost smiled.

"That the couple is meant to be together. Destined to share a powerful, magical bond. We can't see the future and don't know who our mates are before we meet them, but we know they're out there, that we're meant for each other, and will never part once we come together."

"So Ollie and Harper were destined by magic to be with Dante and Ash?"

Was that a hint of sadness in Dex's voice? Luc hated it. He had to obliterate it, but wasn't sure how. "Yes... Did Ollie or anyone tell you why I led the fall to Earth?"

Dex shook his head into Luc's neck.

Luc rested his chin in Dex's hair, securing both arms around him. "Finding your fated mate is political in the Eternal Realm, and many were denied theirs. I was denied mine more than once by my parents, who sat on the ruling council. It wasn't right. Restricting love and regulating connection is wrong, so I decided to find my mate on Earth."

"But you didn't?" Dex asked hesitantly.

"No. None of the hundreds who fell with me did either."

"And then magic infected humanity? That's what Ash said."

"Yes. A demon and a human had a child, and Hell was born to hold the resulting souls who couldn't reincarnate. I tried to stop magic from overtaking humanity completely by trapping every demon in Hell. I bowled over anyone who said there was another way. What did it matter if we were prisoners? We'd failed to find our mates. I'd doomed everyone who'd followed me. Some hated me already. What was a little more hatred cast my way if it stopped magic from wiping out humanity and destroying mortal life?"

"Right..." Dex's tone was flat, almost like he wanted to disagree. "But Ash and Dante have their mates now, so...?"

"So now, demons are free. They can find their mates and be happy. Ash and Dante mating was the biggest shock to everyone. I didn't believe them. Their claims enraged me. The hunt for mates died over a thousand years ago. Hope was buried and forgotten. I hadn't seen my brothers in centuries, and hadn't been close to them in much longer. It seemed like they were taunting me, and it broke me."

Dex went rigid in Luc's hold. "And Ollie?"

"I took out my rage on him, needing to prove Dante a liar, while secretly hoping he was right, and hating myself for believing. I forced Dante's hand in the cruelest way."

Dex swallowed audibly but didn't pull away. "Ollie said he wants to forgive you. He said it's fated for you and the other demons to work things out."

"Ollie can't see the future any better than the rest of us. Maybe it's fated, maybe it's not. But he's willing to give me a chance I don't deserve. So we'll see."

They were quiet for a long time. Dex seemed to be trying not to move. In fact, he hardly shifted a muscle. It wasn't natural for humans to be so still. Luc was desperate to know what was going through his mind, but was too much of a coward to ask.

He rubbed Dex's back until he relaxed. The playfulness had left the bed a while ago, so Luc drew the covers over his mate, hoping he felt safe rather than exposed.

Dex's finger traced a circular pattern along Luc's arm. "What's so bad about not reincarnating?"

Luc's brows rose. Dex's thoughts hadn't gone in the direction he'd anticipated. "It's a disruption to the natural cycle of human life."

"Sure, but so what? Why can't witches hang out in the same afterlife as my parents? Eternals live in the Eternal Realm forever, so not reincarnating can't be bad."

"True. There's nothing wrong with having one life. I don't know if there's a reason for banning witches beyond punishing them for being something that shouldn't exist."

"Existing isn't a crime," Dex said in disgust.

"You're right. Witches didn't ask for magic. They're being punished for demons' crimes, which is wrong any way you look at it. I suspect that we, as the Fallen, are supposed to feel guilty for witches' plight, and thus be punished further by our own regrets. There wasn't any other way for the council to punish us once they'd already banished us from the Eternal Realm. So they got creative."

"But witches are still innocent."

"I know. The council created the Realm of the Damned, not me, even if I trapped my kind there. If I could abolish the Realm of the Damned, I would. But granting witches access to the Eternal Realm isn't within my power."

"Ash and Dante said you'll never be allowed to return to the Eternal Realm. So you can't even go there to try and work something out?" Dex's voice was so quiet, Luc almost missed the hint of hope hiding within.

Hope. Was it for witches, or was Dex thinking about something else?

Luc couldn't keep the heaviness from his words. "No demon or demon's mate can enter the Eternal Realm. We've been banished, and anyone tied to us is tied to this realm with us. For what it's worth, I don't think a demon's mate could enter Hell either, or if they did, they might not return to Earth."

Dex's hand came to rest on Luc's arm and squeezed. "Ollie and Harper wouldn't want to go to Hell. I guess they wouldn't have any reason to go to the Eternal Realm either."

Not in the way Dex did.

Had he guessed that he was Luc's mate? If so, he didn't say, and Luc couldn't force the words out. It felt painfully obvious— why else would Luc want to keep Dex and give him everything —but admitting it outright would hurt Dex.

Luc didn't want the truth to pressure Dex or weigh him down with guilt. He should be free to complete his human life as the universe intended.

"Did you have witch children?" Dex sounded more curious than judgmental, and Luc was glad the subject had changed.

"No, I never had a child. But I brought demons to Earth. If I hadn't, this never would have happened."

"Leading demons here doesn't make witches or them being damned your fault. Besides, if it never happened, what would that mean for Harper? Would he never have been born?"

Luc had never considered. "He's Ash's mate, so he'd have to have been born."

Dex finally pulled from Luc's hold and met his gaze. "Would Harper be *Harper* if he'd had a different life? Would Ash still love him if he'd been a completely different person?"

Luc was about to say *of course*, but paused.

If Harper hadn't been a witch living the exact life that led him to Ash, Ollie, Nico, and Dex, would any of them have found their mates?

Yes, surely they would have. In an alternate timeline, everything would look different, but that didn't mean it wouldn't happen in its own way. It was hard to fathom, that was all.

"The bond between Eternal beings and their mates happens between souls—the part of you that doesn't change with reincarnation—so I'm sure a different, less magical Harper would still have found Ash."

"Hmm." Dex's furrowed brow said he wasn't sold.

At least the rise of witches hadn't destroyed magical souls' ability to mate. "If only there was a way to release the witch souls from Hell. There has to be something within my power that I can do to fix what I've ruined."

"I don't think you ruined anything."

"Thank you." Luc squeezed Dex, his loyalty warming Luc's soul.

"Do you have any ideas on how to help them?"

"No. I doubt I'd even be allowed to argue a case in their favor. The Eternal Realm will likely ignore my request to speak to the council."

Dex's eyes widened. "You can contact the Eternal Realm?"

Luc shifted his weight, jostling Dex but not letting go. He knew where this was headed.

"There's a gateway, like an in-between realm that facilitates human souls on their journeys. Whoever is guarding it these days might hear my request and pass my message on to the council, or they might attack me on sight."

Even if his message got through, Luc doubted it would be answered.

"You can only talk to the gatekeeper?" Dex looked at his hands, twisting them on his lap.

Luc covered them with his. "Only the gatekeeper. I can't contact your parents or any other inhabitants directly. If your parents were witches, a séance to the Realm of the Damned might reach them, but no communication like that exists with the true afterlife."

"Right. Makes sense." Dex made a strange sound halfway between clearing his throat and a hiccup. "I wouldn't know what to say anyway."

Shit, he sounded dejected. Hurt despite Luc's efforts to prevent it.

He hugged Dex closer. "It's not about saying anything in particular. You want to connect with them. I get that."

"Yeah." Dex buried his face against Luc's neck, and Luc's heart lurched. "I'll have to wait a while before that happens."

He would, even if a human lifetime seemed like the blink of an eye to Luc.

One way or another, Dex would see the realm that Luc was forbidden to enter. That would never change.

Dex set a latte and an iced tea on the counter where Holt was waiting. "Here you go."

"Thanks." He grabbed the drinks and lingered.

Did he have something to say? It wasn't busy enough for Dex to pretend not to notice.

Their eyes locked over the espresso machine.

"I know it's only Wednesday, but do you have anything exciting going on this weekend?" Holt asked.

A not-so-stifled squeal came from over by the pastry display. Damn Justine.

Dex shrugged. "I've got dinner with friends. How about you?" It was polite to return the questions, but fuck, maybe he sounded too interested.

He wasn't. Holt was hot, but not for Dex.

Holt's expression shifted, giving him an air of unexpected intensity that might have had Dex blushing under different circumstances. "I need to let loose. Heard there's a new club in the Docks that's having a leather night."

Well. Dex tried not to imagine it... Holt's glasses, those arms bare, and leather. Fuck. How was he supposed to respond?

Holt chuckled. "Hey, if it's not your thing, don't worry. I guess I won't be seeing you there."

Dex's face heated. "I know the place you're talking about. My cousin DJs there. But, I, uh... I'm kind of seeing someone."

"Oh." Holt's brows rose, and he ran a hand through his salt-and-pepper hair. "Sorry."

"It's okay. Wait, were you even asking?" Fuck this was awkward. Holt hadn't actually invited Dex to go with him.

Holt seemed to relax, his easy smile returning. "I was testing the waters. But it's all good. Maybe I'll see you and your *someone* around." He lifted his coffee in acknowledgement and turned to go.

Dex's shoulders relaxed. Somewhere along the way, they'd crept toward his ears.

Had Holt purposely come in later so he could catch Dex when he wasn't busy? He must have. It was the first time Dex had seen him outside the morning rush. Justine had been right about him after all.

She appeared at his side. "Um, what? Since when are you seeing someone?"

Dex's tension returned. "It's new."

"I'll say. You never date exclusively."

Dex gave her a pointed look. "I never date. Period."

"But that's what you're doing? You have a boyfriend?"

Dex had no idea. He and Luc hadn't talked about it. Could you call it dating when someone admitted they'd fantasized about ensnaring you with magic, only to hold back because you had to *want* to let them give you everything?

"Maybe. While I figure it out, I'm not interested in anyone else."

Justine squeezed his arm, her smile nothing but encouraging. "That's awesome. He better come in so I can meet him."

Dex needed to figure out what was going on before that happened, so he made a noncommittal sound.

The café was in a slow patch, so Dex restocked the milk fridge and cleared a few tables. More customers came in, and at the next lull, Justine went on her break, leaving Dex to stamp pastry boxes with the Seaside Coffee logo as he waited for his turn.

"Hello, Dex," a familiar voice called.

He spun around, finding Onyx and a man Dex vaguely remembered being introduced as his mate, Nico, approaching the counter. "Hey, what are you guys doing here?"

"We're finally allowed on the premises now that you know all our secrets." Onyx grinned mischievously, and Nico shook his head in loving exasperation. Onyx slunk closer, whispering, "Ollie wouldn't let me or my brothers visit. He didn't want to drag you into anything."

Dex laughed, his insides churning. He'd been dragged into their midst, all right. Even if Ollie hadn't told him about magic, he still would have met Luc. Almost like it was fate.

Fate. Dex couldn't get the notion out of his head. His palms prickled, breaking out in a sweat as they always seemed to when his mind wandered this week.

Had fate brought Luc into his life?

Luc openly admitted that he wanted to keep Dex. Care for him. He said he'd seen Dex for the first time and had an urge to possess him, and ever since, he'd behaved as if it was vital for Dex to see who he really was.

It was intense, but it wasn't an act. None of it had been. Luc had been truthful, just as he'd claimed the day they'd met. And once Dex finally understood the gravity of mates, nothing else seemed to fit.

Was he Lucifer's fated mate?

He swallowed the question, as he'd been doing for days, but

it was getting harder to ignore, especially with a demon and his mate right in front of him. "What can I get you now that you're here at last?"

"No drinks for me. I'm here to check out your mugs." Onyx craned his neck, looking around.

A flutter of anticipation surged through Dex. "My stuff is on display over there." He pointed toward the side of the room where his homewares were set out next to bags of coffee, boxes of tea, and other items for sale.

"Perfect." Onyx sauntered over, pausing along the way to inspect the paintings on the wall.

"Can I get you anything?" Dex asked Nico, who'd stayed behind.

"An espresso would hit the spot." Nico moved toward the register, a disproportionately fatherly air of concern coming over him. "How are you, Dex?"

He rang up the drink. "I'm good."

"No, really." Nico handed over his card, studying Dex a little too closely. "You've learned a great deal in a short time, and despite Ollie's efforts, your introduction to our world wasn't all that smooth."

Dex swallowed. "I've talked to Ollie. He said what happened when he found me with Luc was an overreaction."

Dex had a much better understanding of what drove Luc to hurt Ollie, but struggled to see how Ollie could forgive him. Even believing it was fated for Luc to be brought back into the fold didn't explain it. Why was Ollie willing to believe that? He hadn't seen the kind side of Luc that Dex had.

Nico folded his arms across his chest. "We were wrong about what Luc was doing with you, but many of the facts remain unrefuted. If you need advice or to talk, I'm always here."

Dex ran Nico's card, trying not to reveal his confusion. He didn't even know Nico. "Thanks, man."

"I mean it. If you need help dealing with anything, I'll be there."

Dex handed the card back, a sense of dread sneaking up on him. "Do you know something I don't?"

He couldn't take any more surprises. It was bad enough wondering if he was Luc's mate.

Nico's smile lost the serious edge. "No, it's nothing like that. I've made the same offer to Harper and Ollie."

"Why?" Was it because he was a mate too?

Dex's pulse jumped into his throat. All this damn worrying wasn't good for his blood pressure. He had to calm down.

"You're at a disadvantage when dealing with powerful beings. I don't want you feeling intimidated."

"Thanks, but you're one of those beings." Dex dropped his voice to a whisper. "You could trick me with magic as easily as any of them."

Nico seemed startled.

"Not that I'm accusing you," Dex hurried to add. He didn't actually think anyone, demon or witch, was tricking him with magic anymore.

"I know you're not accusing me, but I hadn't considered it that way."

"I still appreciate the offer." If they got to know each other better, Dex might feel comfortable sharing with Nico. Though, maybe not. He hadn't told Ollie what had happened with Luc.

Who was he kidding? He couldn't talk to Nico about what he was thinking any more than he could talk to Ollie. What would they think if he turned out to be Luc's mate? Would they be shocked? Unless... Did they already suspect? They must. All this shit made more sense to Nico and the rest of them than it did to Dex. He couldn't be the first to connect the dots.

Fuck. What was he supposed to do?

He couldn't bond with Luc like Ollie had with Dante. Forfeiting his time in the Eternal Realm wasn't an option.

Maybe he was wrong and there was some other explanation for Luc's behavior.

Dex was ready to explore *something* together. He trusted Luc enough to chase the good feelings, and there was so much he wanted to try that he had no desire to do it with anyone else.

But what was the point in dating if they weren't mates? What was the point if they were, and Dex would reject the fated bond? They were doomed either way.

Dex couldn't lose his chance to see his parents. He had to move on and live his life, deal with his grief, and not let it rule his whole world, but he wanted to share it all with them one day. He loved his mom and dad, and no matter how much he might love someone else, it would never cancel out his love for them.

Dex needed both.

But if he belonged to Luc, how could he have it all?

He made Nico's espresso, and thankfully, Nico seemed done reaching out, or whatever he'd been trying to do.

"Thanks, Dex." Nico sighed into his coffee as if the caffeine gave him strength.

"You better not complain that you're tired," Onyx said as he rejoined them, setting two mugs and a serving bowl on the counter. "I'll take these, but I was wondering what else you make. I assume there's more than what's on display?"

"Yeah. I've got a studio full of stuff. I'm starting an online shop."

Onyx's face lit up. "That's awesome. Ollie hasn't mentioned it."

"I haven't told Ollie." Dex quickly rang up the items. "I

wanted to get it going first. See how it went. I'm not the best with promoting my work."

He stopped short of voicing his worry that no one would buy his pottery, thank god. No need to look completely incompetent in front of Onyx.

"I can help you with promotion ideas," Onyx offered without hesitation. "An online store can help you get your stock into more brick-and-mortar shops, too. You could have wholesale information listed, or a note to contact you for large orders."

"That's a great idea."

Onyx paid for the items, and Dex wrapped them in paper. The demon checked his phone. "You better be free on Saturday night."

"I am." Dex had lied to Holt about dinner with friends, hoping something would materialize.

"Good. I'll text the group. We're starting the nightlife section of the tour. Harper is going to have a field day."

"I might even be allowed to tag along," Nico added.

Onyx stuck his nose in the air. "If you're lucky. Don't forget you can text the group, too, Dex. Anytime."

"I know." He playfully rolled his eyes. Why were they being like this? It wasn't as if he didn't know how to socialize. "I get it, I'm one of you now."

Onyx's haughty air evaporated. "You are. See you Saturday."

But was Dex truly one of them? Could he ever be if he didn't bond with Luc?

16

LUCIFER

Luc waited for Onyx in the main showroom of Gallery Four, feeling antsy.

He should have said something about seeing each other again before Dex left the loft, but Luc hadn't wanted to push. Now that it had been a few days, Luc worried he'd misread Dex's departing mood. He'd been quiet, and Luc had told himself to give him time to think.

What if he had been waiting for Luc to initiate more?

Luc was obsessing like only an unmated demon could.

Every one of his senses urged him to seek out Dex. When you'd lived countless lifetimes and disregarded one of the ultimate rules to fall to Earth and find your mate, it wasn't unbalanced to make your mate the center of your world. But Luc was committed to acting at least a little bit human.

He unlocked his phone, opened his message thread with Dex, and sent a text.

LUC:

Hi. How's work this week? I've been thinking about you.

Hopefully, that was close enough to a normal message a young man might receive.

Even though Luc had modernized Hell in an effort to reacclimate demons to human life before freeing them, a disconnect remained.

Should he ask Dex out on another date? Courtship seemed inadequate in a way it hadn't before. Dex was aware of mates and was probably already questioning Luc's interest. Dating didn't seem to fit. They had to broach the topic of what they were to each other. But when?

No immediate response from Dex popped up.

He better not be cooped up in his depressing condo, or out drinking himself under the table again. Maybe Luc would have to check in—in a more stalkery sense—if he didn't hear back, though, in all likelihood, Dex was probably working or busy with some other non-destructive activity.

At least he would know Luc was thinking about him.

He pocketed his phone and turned his attention to the painting in front of him. Onyx had excellent taste, and Luc enjoyed knowing he wouldn't be thrown out for visiting the gallery this time.

The front door opened, and Nico walked in, his steps faltering as he noticed Luc. "I see we're both early." His tone didn't waver. Impressive. Such a steadfast witch would be good for Onyx.

"Your mate is meeting with his employee." Luc waved a hand toward the stairs. "Once the human leaves, we can get started."

Nico nodded and crossed his arms, his expression hard.

Luc cast about for something to say to break the tension. What kind of small talk did you make with your brother's mate when he made no secret of distrusting you? Perhaps he should ask Nico's star sign or mention the weather.

Before the awkwardness became unbearable, the human who worked in the gallery breezed down the stairs. "You two can go on up. I'll lock the door on my way out."

Nico directed a friendly nod at the man. "Thanks, Scott. Have a good night."

"You too, Nico. And you, Onyx's mysterious brother. More and more of you keep popping up." Scott's eyes lingered on Luc. "Not that I'm complaining."

He turned to go, and Luc trudged up the stairs with Nico in tow. The sound of the front door closing and locking with a beep echoed off the cavernous space, and the gallery lights faded to a low glow.

Onyx waited for them in his office at the end of the hall, lounging back in his desk chair, a crystal glass of blood in his hand. "Can I get anyone a refreshment?"

Nico strode forward and planted a kiss on his mate's lips. "Not my cup of tea, little butterfly."

Onyx ran a hand down Nico's chest. "I have bourbon for you."

"In that case, I'd love a glass, but don't get up." With a parting kiss, Nico went to the shelving built into the side of the room and opened a cupboard, revealing a glass decanter full of amber liquid.

"Luc?" Onyx shook his glass, eyebrows raised.

"No, thank you. I don't need anything right now." He sat in one of the sleek chairs positioned in front of Onyx's desk.

"Really? Not even with your mate around? You don't want to get too hungry like Ash and demon-out on him."

A laugh bubbled out of Luc, seeming to surprise Onyx as much as himself. "Dare I ask?"

Onyx leaned forward. "Ash almost bit Harper while they were having sex, and had to run off before his wings popped out."

Poor Ash. "That won't be a problem. It's not like I have to pretend to be human around Dex."

Nico returned, a drink in his hand. "Knowing who you are isn't a guarantee that Dex won't freak out if you change forms unexpectedly."

Luc gritted his teeth. "It won't be a problem."

Onyx and Nico shared a look.

Luc wasn't telling them he'd fed on Dex. That Dex liked fear and forceful play, and 'demoning out' was so far from a problem that it was almost funny. It was none of their business.

Would Dex allow Luc to drink from him again? They might never share blood as mates, but they could have this small intimacy.

Blood exchange was once a sacred connection between bonded mates and no one else, until demons discovered that keeping their immortality on Earth came with a price.

Onyx sipped his drink. "Fine. If you say it's not an issue, then it's not. What did you want to talk about?"

"I have an idea." That was putting it strongly, but confidence was key in most endeavors. "I don't believe the council will ever allow us to return home, but witches don't have to share our fate."

"Witches?" Onyx and Nico exchanged confused looks.

"It's not right for witches to be damned for demons' transgressions. I want to argue for their entrance into the rightful afterlife."

Nico's eyes narrowed in Luc's direction, but he didn't speak.

Onyx said, "That's very noble of you, but how will that help you bond with Dex?"

Luc's grip tightened on the armrest. "It might not. This isn't about Dex. Not completely. Something has to be done about the souls in Hell. No one but those of us who chose to fall should be punished."

A knowing look crossed Onyx's face. "Only those of us who chose. Meaning mates should also be allowed into the Eternal Realm."

"Exactly. If the council listens to reason and lets witches in, they can't deny our mates unless they admit to punishing them for being associated with us, and for no crime of their own. There's no reason mates shouldn't be allowed to travel between realms."

Onyx's face fell. "Except that travel itself is forbidden, hence us being stuck here."

Luc couldn't deny it. This plan wasn't perfect. "We have to start somewhere. There's no refuting our claim when it comes to witches, and if it goes well, we can push for more. I'll bring my case to the gate, but I don't think anyone will listen."

Onyx caught Nico's eye. "Gee, I wonder why."

Luc ignored that. "I need help. I'm here to ask for your support. I can't bring the argument forward alone. There needs to be a united front."

Onyx finished his drink and set the glass aside. "What good will my support, or even Ash and Dante's, be? We're always on your side. The council doesn't know you fucked that up and had to earn our trust back."

Onyx spoke as if Luc had succeeded in earning his trust. Did he mean it, or was it nothing more than a slip of phrase?

Luc couldn't dwell on it. This wasn't about him. Centering things on himself was his fatal flaw.

"I was hoping for more than your support. I'd like help getting other demons on my side, and I don't mean Ash and Dante. I'll talk to them later."

Would they stand with him? Would anyone but his brother?

Onyx raised a brow. "You realize what scrounging up support will look like, right? No one is going to trust you, Luc. They'll assume you're after power."

"But no one believes witches deserve to be in the Realm of the Damned. Demons will support the cause. There's no way for me to gain power from this. Demons will see that."

"Perhaps."

Luc clenched his fist. "I have to try. Even if no one trusts me now, in time, they'll see that I'm not up to anything. Demons will come around."

"You might need serious time for that. I guess you have the length of a mortal life to figure this out, but will that be enough?"

Luc's chest seized. This couldn't take Dex's lifetime. That was cutting it too close. "What about support outside demonkind? Nico, would you, Ollie, and Harper agree? What about others? Even vampires want entrance to the Eternal Realm."

Their souls went to the Realm of the Damned if their immortal life on Earth ended, regardless of whether they'd been a witch or human before turning.

"No living witch or vampire would argue against you," Nico agreed. "But how does that help? Surely the Eternal Realm already knows that we want to be spared from the Realm of the Damned."

"They know theoretically. We have to make them see the reality. It'll be much harder to deny our claim, looking into the faces of the innocent beings they're damning."

Nico seemed even more wary than before. "Can anyone but demons get to the gateway?"

Onyx shot a worried look at Luc. "I don't know."

"I don't either. Anyone who goes would be risking themselves. If they can't get back to Earth, they'll probably have to enter the afterlife."

Onyx wrapped a possessive arm around Nico. "And if the

council doesn't allow any vampires or witches we bring into the Eternal Realm?"

"Then they'll be trapped in the gateway."

There was a heavy silence.

"It will show that we're serious," Nico said eventually, earning a sharp look from Onyx. "As long as anyone coming knows the risk, then it's their choice."

"Nico," Onyx hissed.

"We'll talk about it later. I'm not saying I'll go. But we have to be very clear before taking volunteers."

Onyx's arm seemed to tighten around his mate.

"I'll be explicitly clear," Luc promised. He wouldn't trick anyone into joining. That would be counterproductive as well as cruel. "I don't expect any mates to come to the gateway. We aren't sure the Eternal Realm will extend their acceptance that far. At least not yet."

"Good." Onyx's eyes burned, locked on Luc.

He silently vowed to force Nico to stay behind if he had to. By any means necessary. He wasn't risking Onyx losing his mate.

Luc cleared his throat. "So, do we know any witches or vampires willing to risk their eternal lives for all the damned?"

Nico grinned, shaking his head. "I might know someone. He's going to be even more shocked than the day he met you, Onyx."

They shared a smile, and some of Onyx's tension seemed to leak away. "*Ugh*, Rowan. He'll love how important this is, and how important he'll be if he helps."

"Only you could shed his willingness to risk himself in a bad light."

"It's a skill." Onyx lifted his chin. "Let's rally the troops. I hope you like strippers, Luc."

As the sun set, Luc and Onyx landed on the roof of a building in the Business District. Nico looked relieved to be back on a solid surface.

The phone in Luc's pocket vibrated, pulling a smile from him. No one had his number except Onyx and Dex. He extracted and unlocked it.

DEX:

Hey! Work's good. You trying to say you miss me or something?

LUC:

Missing you is only the beginning. Can I see you?

"What are you grinning at?" Onyx appeared at his elbow and peered at the phone screen.

Luc quickly pressed the device to his chest. "Dex messaged me."

"Since when is he talking to you again?" Onyx punched him in jest. "You could have mentioned that sooner."

Luc's face heated. Was he blushing? He never blushed. "I didn't come to talk about Dex."

"You should have. This is all for him. I know helping witches is the right thing to do, but you wouldn't have gotten it in your head to try if it weren't for finding your mate."

"No, I'm a terribly selfish person. Thank you for reminding me."

Pinching his arm playfully, Onyx took on a gentler tone. "That's not what I meant. Dex inspires you to do better. That's not a bad thing. So, what's he texting you about?"

Luc rubbed his arm, his phone buzzing with a new message.

"He's just replying to me. Ollie talked to him, and I saw him last weekend."

Onyx's eyes flashed. "Way to bury the lead."

"It's complicated. Letting him go might kill me." Luc's voice cracked, and he coughed to cover it.

Fuck. Why was saying it out loud far more painful?

Onyx grabbed him, fingers digging into his arm. "Then don't let him go. Don't stop with freeing witches. Create a world where you don't have to lose Dex."

Luc laughed bitterly. "Create a world?"

"Yes," Onyx growled. "You believed you could change the world once upon a time, when Dex was merely an idea. Now he's real. So, what are you going to do?"

The challenge hung in the air.

It was true, he had believed he could change the world back then. And he had, just not the way he'd hoped.

Luc's fire sparked. "I'll do whatever it takes."

"Then stop saying you'll lose Dex. Believe you can do this. You've believed stupider things with ten times the conviction. Get your shit together." Onyx glared with fire in his eyes, his cheeks red and feathers standing on end.

Fire roared to life in Luc's chest. Not in anger. Love flooded him, burning away his bitterness.

He had to stop acting like he was doomed.

Luc ruffled Onyx's hair, eliciting an indignant snarl.

"Thanks, brother. Good thing I've got you keeping me in line. Feel free to slap me next time I get like this."

"Gladly," Onyx muttered, frantically fixing his hair.

Luc turned to find Nico staring at them fondly.

With a smile, he led them toward a service door. "Rowan and his coven are meeting us on the top floor."

"I hate to ask, but they aren't the kind of coven that worship me, are they?" It was usually witches who worshiped Satan, not vampires, but it was better to be sure.

Nico snorted. "Fuck no."

"Thank goodness." Luc detested his followers.

He'd never asked for their devotion. Thinking they owed him for their magic was one thing, but there was no need to take that belief and use it as an excuse to harm others or commit vile acts in his name.

They went inside and headed along a hall to an open door. Nico entered first, Onyx at his heel. Luc followed, his wings and other features tucked out of sight, same as Onyx.

The room was bare and windowless. Luc couldn't imagine what it was used for. A tall, slim man in a suit with long black hair stood in the center, his hands resting casually in his pockets.

"Nico, you continue to astound me with the company you keep."

"I'm full of surprises. Let me introduce you to Lucifer."

Luc resisted rolling his eyes. "Please, call me Luc."

One of Rowan's dark brows rose. "Pleasure to meet you, Luc. The Valero Coven welcomes you."

He didn't introduce the dozen vampires surrounding him. Not even the three standing closest—two large men and one tiny woman with a formidable air—who were hovering behind him like shadows.

Luc got straight to it, explaining his plan to gain entrance to the Eternal Realm for witches and vampires.

"The council claims to be altruistic and will be loath to admit otherwise. They'll have to concede when faced with the fact they've punished innocents, or risk upsetting the balance of power in the Eternal Realm," he concluded.

Rowan took a moment to digest. His posture hadn't so much as shifted the entire time Luc spoke. "If all that's needed is a well-reasoned argument, why wasn't this done long before now?

Saving witches in the beginning might have stopped the creation of the vampire species."

"I don't disagree. At the time, I was focused on stopping any further spread of magic, and no one in the Eternal Realm would have listened to me."

"That's why we're here," Onyx added. "The Eternal Realm needs to face its mistakes. Demons can't change this alone."

Rowan's lips thinned. "I support your cause in principle, but how do you plan on making that happen?"

Luc stepped forward. "We can't, but you can. Come with us to the gateway and show them. You might not come back, but you could help change the fabric of your world and the ones beyond, ridding the universe of the Realm of the Damned."

Rowan smiled a cold, calculated smile. "And they say the Devil will tempt you. Let my coven discuss it, and I'll be in touch."

17

———

DEX

Dex lay in bed after a long day at work and a productive session at his pottery studio, staring at his phone like it might disappear if he blinked.

Come on. Why wasn't Luc replying? Dex's heart pounded with each passing second.

His message was on read. Luc had seen it. Shouldn't he be jumping at the chance to feed from him again?

At last, the typing dots appeared, and a message came through.

LUC:

> I might be hungry by then. But you will be too.
> Can I take you out for a meal?

It wasn't a no. It also betrayed no enthusiasm for what Dex offered. Did he have this all wrong?

A little voice reminded Dex that Luc wanted to give him *everything*, not just a good time.

Luc wanted to date, not be a booty call, which sounded good on the surface, but Dex didn't want to find out if he and Luc were fated. Couldn't he enjoy a few orgasms before they got into a relationship and acknowledged that they were doomed, mates or not?

Besides, he was already going out to dinner this weekend and couldn't invite Luc to join Onyx, Ollie, and Harper. Maybe Luc could meet him at the club afterward. It would be the perfect place to try out one of his fantasies.

DEX:

> I'm going out to dinner with friends on
> Saturday night. Sorry.

> Want to meet me after dinner and buy me
> breakfast?

LUC:

> I can do that. Where should we meet?

DEX:

> I'll be at a club. Why don't you see if you can
> hunt me down?

Even typing the words had Dex's senses on high alert. Goosebumps erupted over his skin, and his breathing shallowed. He almost couldn't believe he had the guts to ask. Would Luc know he meant it literally?

His phone rang and he jumped, scrambling to answer Luc's call. "Hello?"

"Dex, are you suggesting I stalk you through a nightclub, capture, and feed on you?"

He swallowed. "Yes. Feed on me...fuck me. Anything goes." He meant to sound confident, but his voice wavered, his core tightening and cock stirring.

Luc growled, sending a shiver through Dex. "I'd love to hunt you, but there are rules if we're playing like this."

"Okay." Dex would agree to just about anything if Luc would grant him this wish. *Anything.*

He'd only had a taste of his true desires and needed more. He was dying to give in to the urge to run from Luc. To do his best to get away and fail. To fully surrender himself to Luc at a time in his life when everything was so tumultuous. To feel the fear he hated and couldn't escape knowing it would be okay in the end because Luc held it all in his hands.

The idea had been stuck in Dex's head since Luc had mentioned ensnaring him.

What would that be like? A huge, winged man following him through the city, overpowering him, and forcing him to be his plaything. Taking any and all decisions away from him. He wouldn't have to worry about a damn thing except taking what Luc gave him.

Dex had jerked off imagining it more than once already.

Whatever the rules were, Dex would agree.

Luc's deep, commanding voice had him captivated. "Rule one: you can't get drunk. No alcohol or other substances, or we aren't playing."

"Yeah, no problem. I'll stay one hundred percent sober." Dex rolled his eyes. What an easy price to pay.

"Two: you need to use your safe word if you change your mind."

"I know. I will."

"And..." Luc said with the air of someone who'd been interrupted. "I need to know if you still want me to ignore you when you say no or stop, or if you'd like me to listen this time."

"Ignore it. I want to be overpowered." The last word came out soft and breathy, and Dex felt like he was hanging on by a thread, ready to tip over into something amazing.

Luc's tone matched Dex's, airy and almost tender. "We can do that, but I'll need another way of checking in as we play. Since you chose red for stop, you'll tell me yellow to slow down, and green if you're good to continue. How does that sound?"

Dex nodded eagerly to the empty room. "I can do that."

"Good. Now, can we discuss condoms?"

Dex swallowed. "Sure, but I'm not on PrEP." He didn't hook up often enough to bother. He'd had sex once all summer, and his dry spell before that had been, well, *extended* was a kind way to put it.

"If that weren't an issue, would you be interested in getting fucked raw?" Luc asked as calmly as if they were discussing the weather.

Dex couldn't find words, his mind suddenly overrun by image after image of Luc breeding him.

Thankfully, Luc didn't wait for a reply. "I'm immortal. I can't carry human infections—my magic destroys anything I come in contact with—so there's no safety reason for protection."

Dex sat up. "Really?"

Luc's tone turned unreadable. "You can check with your friends if you don't believe me."

"I'm not doubting you. I just didn't realize being immortal meant you're immune to everything, but it makes sense. I trust you, Luc. You wouldn't say it if it wasn't true. You don't lie to me, remember?"

"I remember. Thank you for trusting me," Luc said softly. "When I fuck you, there can be nothing between us. Unless you prefer otherwise."

Dex's core clenched involuntarily. "No condoms, okay? I want it." Fuck, he sounded desperate. Good thing he didn't have to pretend to be chill with Luc.

"Okay." Luc sounded satisfied, once again collected and commanding. "We should go over our limits."

Dex hesitated, lying back and getting comfortable. "Like what? I'll use my safe words if I need to."

"Yes, you will, but I don't want to put you in that position unnecessarily. Give me an idea of what you want from this hunt and how far you'd like things to go. You enjoy being fed on, but what else?"

Dex's throat ran dry. He could do this. He could tell Luc anything, no matter how it sounded.

"I...I want to be scared," he rasped. "I want to run and try to get away, but for you to catch me. I want you to take control and do...anything." His voice turned soft and far too breathy, eyes falling shut.

"Anything I want?"

Dex's "yes" sounded like a plea.

"What if I wanted to feed on you in public? What about public sex?"

Dex's face flamed. "Like with people watching?" Would he be into that? He didn't know. Maybe. Heat flared in his cheeks, and his gut twisted.

Luc chuckled, but not unkindly. "No. We can't have humans seeing what I'm going to do to you, and we'd need their consent before getting anyone involved like that. I meant having sex in a place where only my illusions keep prying eyes and ears away. Somewhere we'd be discovered if not for magic. You'll see them. They won't see you."

Dex imagined Luc biting him in a club as people danced beside him. Luc slipping his hand into his pants, and... "I'd be into that. Public is fine for biting and, um, sex."

Luc could have his way with him right under everyone's nose. Dex hadn't ever considered such a thing, but like imagining Luc stalking him, now that he had, he burned for it to happen for real. What said 'being at someone else's mercy' more than being taken whenever, wherever they wanted, regardless of anything else?

Luc hummed appreciatively. "Can I use an illusion to prevent people from hearing you scream? What about preventing them from seeing you flee before I catch you? It would make it impossible for anyone to intervene."

Dex bit back a moan. That shouldn't be hot, or maybe it should. It would let him feel completely out of control, while Luc had the power to shape everything around him. "Yes to all of it."

"Perfect. Are there any sex acts you don't enjoy? You said you want me to do *anything*, but I need a little more from you. I'll do anything I want, but only within our agreed bounds."

Dex couldn't believe they were having this conversation. He'd expected Luc to resist or insist that Dex didn't want to do this. But he'd accepted Dex and knew exactly how to make this happen.

"Dex..." Luc's gentle coaxing sent a fresh wave of heat sweeping through his body.

"Sorry. No watersports. Cum, spit, and...um, blood are fine. Blood from your bite, I mean. Not from getting hurt."

"Playing like this should never injure you, and I'm only interested in bleeding you on my fangs, my dear."

"Yeah," Dex breathed. "Me too. Just your fangs."

"So, biting is okay. No other blood play. Do you like pain?"

Dex shivered. "Yes."

"Tell me more."

"Your bite hurt at first, and that made it...better. You can choke me or tie me up. Or gag me." Now he was just listing things he wanted to try. He closed his eyes, and Luc's voice seemed to surround him.

"You liked the pain of my bite. What about other pain?"

Dex's stomach swooped. "I'm not sure."

"That's all right. We can leave it at biting. It's the perfect pain/pleasure touch, or so I've heard."

"Yeah." Dex stroked his neck involuntarily. It was too bad Luc wasn't with him now.

"When you say choke you, are you talking about having your breath restricted?"

Dex swallowed. "I want to struggle against you but not actually be restricted, no. So not actually choking. I want your hand on my throat. To feel owned."

Luc hummed, thoughtful now. "I can do that. You're so breathless, telling me what you want. Have you done any of this before?"

"No." Dex braced himself for Luc's reply, for him to backpedal and say Dex wasn't ready.

A growl sounded down the phone line. "Would you like me to show you what being hunted and owned is like?"

Dex moaned, palming his erection through his jeans. "Yes, Luc."

"Don't worry. I can give you what you need. I promise I'll scare you just right. Give you the kind of ownership you crave."

Dex panted into the phone, unbuttoning his pants, and slipped his hand inside.

"Are you hard right now?"

"*Mmhmm.*"

Luc's chuckle wound around him, the heat of embarrassment following. Luc probably wasn't hard from a conversation, but whatever. Dex didn't hate the squirming in his gut.

Luc's voice dropped lower. "How would you feel if I told you not to touch yourself?"

"What?" Dex's eyes popped open, and his hand stilled.

"You only come with my permission. No jerking off. Nothing unless I allow it. What do you say?"

"That's not fair," Dex whined, yet he automatically withdrew his hand from his aching cock.

"You don't have to obey. If you're not interested in orgasm control, then I don't want to push you. It was just an idea. We can take it or leave it."

Dex should say he wasn't interested. Giving Luc control over whether he jerked off in the privacy of his own home should be going too far. But the idea of letting Luc command him filled him to the brim.

"No, I'm interested. I want to try it. I won't touch myself."

"Do you promise? I won't let you come until I capture you on Saturday night, and maybe not even then."

Dex squirmed. "I promise. Please, Luc."

"Please, what? Take charge of you?"

"Yeah. I like it." This way, he could be at Luc's mercy even when they weren't together.

"I should have known you'd be into this, and I promise, if you're good, I'll reward you."

Should have known how? Saturday was suddenly too far away. "You could hunt me tonight."

Real amusement tinged Luc's laugh. "No, I don't think so. If you wanted me sooner, you shouldn't have told me to wait until the weekend."

"But that was before."

"Too bad. You'll have to wait." Dex could imagine Luc's red lips twisting into a smug smile.

He hated and loved that Luc wasn't giving him his way. Forcing him to wait was better than letting him call the shots.

How amped would he be by the weekend? Finding out would be torture.

DEX HELD the door as Harper, Ollie, and Onyx spilled out of the restaurant and into the night. Finally. This meal had been far more relaxing than their previous one, but Dex would be lying if he said he was sad it was over.

He itched to get to the club, his mind wandering to Luc cornering him and taking what he wanted every other minute.

He'd texted Luc the details of where he'd be that afternoon. Was he there waiting? Hopefully. Dex would detonate the second Luc touched him at this rate.

He hadn't so much as stroked his cock, and he'd been hard an excruciating amount over the last few days.

"Which way to dancing?" Harper asked, his cheeks flushed from the wine he'd had with dinner. Dex had dutifully declined a glass.

Onyx linked arms with Harper. "We're a few blocks away. Come on. Our mates will meet us there."

Ollie linked arms with Dex. "I'm so glad you're out with us."

"Me too." Dex's gut twisted, some of his excitement fading.

They might have mates waiting, but did he? Did he even want to be Luc's mate?

Dex couldn't think about it. Not now. Tonight was for fun and hopefully the best sex of his life. Nothing more.

"I can't believe I got Dante out to a club," Ollie said as they fell in step behind Onyx and Harper. "He's not much of a dancer."

"I'm sure he'd do anything for you," Harper shot over his shoulder.

Ollie laughed.

Dex forced a smile. He wasn't jealous. He wasn't thinking about mates. Not about how Luc claimed he'd give him everything, and he definitely wasn't thinking about what that might mean.

Dex couldn't have everything. Not like Ollie and Harper.

What he could have was a wild night. And an orgasm if Luc permitted it.

They turned a corner, continuing through the busy part of the Arts District. Bars and restaurants lined the street. Dex hadn't spent much time in this part of the neighborhood. It was farther from the university than he'd ventured when he'd briefly lived there at the start of college. There was a far more upscale vibe this close to the Business District, especially compared to the Docks, where Dex usually went clubbing.

A line had already formed outside the gay club Onyx was taking them to. Of course, he didn't have to wait. He led them inside and straight to a VIP area with its own bar.

The place was packed. Even the exclusive area seemed to be at capacity.

Dante, Ash, and Nico waited for them at the VIP bar. Nico and Ash both had their shirts off, and as soon as they all finished kissing their mates hello, Onyx whipped his off as well.

"Are we dancing?" Onyx shouted over the music.

"Drinks first," Harper shouted back, and Ollie nodded eagerly.

Nico already had one, so he moved out of the way, allowing Harper to lean against the bar and wait to be served.

Dex scanned the crowd, searching for any sign of Luc. He wasn't in the VIP area, and tucked in the corner as they were,

Dex couldn't see most of the club. Apparently, there was even an upstairs dance floor.

"Looking for someone?" Onyx asked.

"What? No. Taking it all in." Dex turned his back to the room.

"I haven't been here in years, but I figured it was a safer bet than dragging everyone to a leather night."

Dex laughed. If Onyx was talking about the same event Holt had mentioned, he was glad they hadn't gone.

"I'd be down for that," Harper said as he moved away from the bar, sipping a drink.

Onyx's eyes seemed to flash. "Well, okay then. I'll file that away for future reference."

Nico wrapped an arm around his mate. "What are you planning?"

Onyx pursed his lips. "Nothing."

Nico didn't look convinced, but let it go, pulling Onyx closer. Dex tried not to stare or have any jealous feelings about how sweet and possessive the gesture was.

Ollie hurried over, holding out a shot for Dex.

He shook his head. "No, thanks. I'm good tonight."

Ollie pulled his hand back, the clear liquid sloshing. "You want it, Harper?"

"Let's share." Harper took the shot and had a sip, his face scrunching at the taste. "Wow, maybe not." He handed it back for Ollie to finish off.

Dex had another look around, finding not so much as a hint of familiarity in the surrounding figures. Luc would make him wait, wouldn't he?

They didn't linger by the bar. It was too loud to have a conversation, so there wasn't any point once the drinks were done. Ollie dragged Dex to the dancefloor, pushing through the throng of people.

It was even harder to see who was around in the midst of it all. Lights flashed and the air seemed to vibrate with the beat. It would be difficult for Luc to find him. They could be five feet apart in this crowd and not know it.

Was this going to work?

Dex pushed the question aside. He had to forget about Luc and enjoy himself. He hadn't been clubbing much this summer, only a few nights here and there, and letting loose would do him good.

He pulled Ollie close, and they danced like they had hundreds of times before. Dex relaxed into the familiarity, vowing to stop pushing Ollie away. Knowing he could rely on his best friend, he had to do a better job of reaching out.

They moved as one, no space between them. It was the first time at least one of them wasn't single and open to hooking up. Admittedly, Ollie had no idea Dex wasn't looking for a one-night stand.

Over Ollie's shoulder, Dex caught a glimpse of Dante watching them closely.

Dex leaned to speak in Ollie's ear. "Dante doesn't mind that I'm dancing with you?"

Ollie shook his head. "He'd rather hang back, but I'm determined to dance with him at least a little."

Dante held himself stiffly, more like a statue than anything, but didn't appear uncomfortable. Not with that content, almost wondering expression on his face. Dex could believe he was satisfied watching his mate have fun.

He couldn't help taking stock of his surroundings one more time. There were so many people. Harper and Ash danced like there was no one else in the room, and Onyx was almost hypnotizing as he moved. Nico certainly looked under his spell.

Dex's heart clenched. Being around couples had never

affected him before, but these weren't couples. These were fated mates. They'd be together forever.

It doesn't matter. I don't want that. Dex had to convince himself.

He failed, imagining dancing with Luc along with the other demons and their mates. He imagined belonging to this group as much as everyone acted like he did.

Dex's chest tightened. Why did he have to want the impossible? Ollie wouldn't party with someone who'd attacked him, no matter what he said about forgiving Luc. The Devil wasn't part of this group, and neither was Dex, so he danced like the music pulsing in his ears was all that mattered.

Eventually, they had a break, and Ollie went to say something in Dante's ear.

Dex scanned the dance floor. "I'm getting water," he shouted to Harper before pushing into the throng of people.

He headed toward the main bar, gaze snagging on anyone tall. He caught sight of a man with wavy black hair and his heart skipped, his insides tightening in anticipation. Dex pushed closer, and the man turned, revealing an unfamiliar face.

A weight settled over Dex. He shouldn't have asked Luc to hunt him when he was out with Ollie and the other demons. It would have been better on his own. Then he wouldn't be thinking about mates and forever.

Dex reached the bar. No one around even reminded him of Luc.

He pushed forward, waiting for the nearest bartender to look his way. The man moved quickly back and forth, pouring drinks and grabbing bottles of beer with impressive efficiency.

As the bartender paused for a moment to take an order, a flash of the club's lights revealed a figure looming behind him, his face in shadow, horns curling along his head, and eyes glowing crimson. A split second later, the figure was gone.

Dex's pulse raced, and he looked frantically around. Luc was lurking behind the bar, hiding behind an invisibility illusion.

The bartender was back in motion, flitting back and forth, meaning Luc couldn't still be there. Magic didn't make it possible for people to walk through you. Right? But then, where had Luc gone?

Fingers trailed down the nape of Dex's neck. He yelped and spun around.

"You good?" the short, stocky man behind him asked.

Dex cupped the back of his neck with his hand. "Did you touch me?"

The man frowned. "No."

Behind the guy were more men waiting to be served, none of whom paid him any attention. Dex pushed past, away from the bar. Had Luc touched him? How? He couldn't have been behind Dex with so many people packed in on all sides.

Dex skirted the edge of the crowd, the hair on the back of his neck standing on end. He looked everywhere. No Luc.

"You lost, sweetie?" a man probably twice Dex's age asked.

"No. All good." He moved away, pretending not to notice the way the man leered.

Maybe he'd imagined the touch. It had been feather-light. More likely, someone had breathed down his neck a little too hard.

Dex caught a glimpse of Ash and Harper and pushed toward them. Even if the touch had been in his head, he hadn't imagined Luc behind the bartender.

His skin prickled. The hunt had officially started.

By the time he reached the group, Dex was breathless, and not because he had to fight through the crowd. Luc could appear at any moment.

Dex couldn't stop looking for him, even though he doubted

Luc would reveal himself before he wanted to. It was impossible for Dex to see Luc coming when he had magic on his side. There was nothing Dex could do but wait, and fuck, he twitched with anticipation, his neglected cock half hard.

He had to get off. God, he hoped Luc would let him.

Ollie seemed to have convinced Dante to dance, and they were sweetly wrapped around each other. No way Dex was butting in. He danced by himself, trying his best not to look over his shoulder every few seconds.

Harper broke away from Ash and grabbed his hand. "Dance with me."

Dex could barely hear his shout over the music. He moved in close, and they found a rhythm.

Harper had taken his shirt off while Dex was at the bar and sported a black lace bralette. He'd skipped the glasses for the night, his makeup sparkling. He looked so damn happy, it was impossible for Dex not to smile and lose himself in the music.

Dex's skin seemed to vibrate. His body pulsed to the beat, and sweat dripped down his back.

"*Dex...*" a low, seductive voice whispered, breath tickling Dex's ear.

He gasped, his body jolting out of rhythm as his pulse thundered in his ears. He whirled around. No one was there except Onyx, plastered to Nico's chest, writhing to the ever-pounding beat.

It should've been impossible to hear a whisper, but Luc's taunt had reached him all the same.

"You okay?" Harper shouted.

Dex faced him and laughed it off. "Fine."

As he got back into the groove of dancing, he swore he heard the ghost of a chuckle, and tingles skittered down his spine.

This wasn't what he imagined Luc hunting him in a club would be like, the unexpectedness adding a layer of foreboding that kicked Dex's heart into gear. Even when nothing else happened, and Luc's chuckle faded into memory, Dex's senses stayed on alert.

Ash crowded behind Harper, and the three of them danced. Onyx joined in, pulling Nico along, and soon, Dex and Onyx were pressed together. For once, Dex wasn't nervous. He could forget that Onyx was one of the most important people in the Shearwater Landing art scene and see him as a potential friend.

Their group moved with the music, breaking off and coming back together.

"Are Ash and Harper making out behind me?" Onyx shouted in Dex's ear.

"Yeah," Dex confirmed, glancing over Onyx's shoulder.

The lights flashed blue, illuminating Ash devouring Harper, his hand tangled in Harper's hair. The lights flashed red. A dark figure towered behind them, features obscured by shadow and eyes glowing. The lights flashed green, and the figure was gone.

"What's wrong?" Onyx shouted.

Dex had stopped moving. "Nothing." He began to dance again.

Onyx grabbed his arm. "No, really. Your eyes nearly popped out of your head." Onyx craned his neck to look behind him.

A chuckle tickled Dex's ear, and he shivered.

Onyx narrowed his gaze. "Something is up with you. You look freaked out."

"I'm not." Dex shook his head, smiling brightly. Too brightly.

"That's not helping." Onyx stopped dancing completely. "You've been looking over your shoulder since we walked in. What's up?"

Nico leaned in close. "You can talk to us."

Dex groaned in frustration. He shouldn't have done this

when he was with people. "I don't know what you're talking about. I'm fine."

"Is it Luc?" Onyx asked, and Nico's eyes widened.

Dex was momentarily stunned.

Onyx's mouth dropped open. "It *is* him. Is he stalking you? He said he wouldn't. I could kill him."

"No," Dex shouted, grabbing Onyx's arm. "It's not like that."

"Then why are you so jumpy?"

Dex clenched a fist. Fuck. He didn't want his night ruined. "Because I asked Luc to stalk me tonight. It's a game, okay?"

Onyx blinked. "You asked...*oh!*" A sly grin twisted his lips. And he seemed to get exactly what Dex was saying.

Dex's face flamed.

Onyx leaned closer. "No need to be embarrassed. I get it. Whatever floats your boat. As long as my brother isn't putting you up to something you aren't into."

"It was my idea. I have a safe word. It's fine."

Onyx beamed at Dex as if he was...proud? That couldn't be right. "Don't let me kill the mood."

"Too late," Dex grumbled, and Onyx laughed.

"I'm guessing you won't be riding home with us?" Nico asked.

"No." The lights flashed purple, and suddenly, Luc stood behind Onyx, his fangs descended, his lips drawn back in a snarl.

Dex swallowed. He wouldn't be going home with anyone but Luc.

18
———

DEX

Dex danced with Onyx and Nico until his feet hurt. Harper and Ash seemed to have disappeared, and Ollie had taken Dante home.

"Want to check out upstairs?" Onyx shouted.

Dex nodded and followed him and Nico through the writhing bodies. He should break away to give Luc a better opportunity to come for him.

People made out in the stairwell, and Dex's gaze lingered on the dark corners, searching for a looming figure with glowing eyes.

The dancefloor on the second level was sweltering and not as crowded as below. The air hung thick with the scent of musk and alcohol. Suddenly, the fresh scent of a campfire on a cold night filled Dex's nose. He breathed deep, and it intensified.

"I see you." Luc's voice rumbled in Dex's ear.

Even though no one would be there, he turned. The nearest people danced a few paces away. Dex swung his arm through the empty space and came across nothing.

It was time to get this hunt going for real.

"I'm going to the bathroom and then I'm heading out," Dex said to Onyx and Nico.

Onyx lit up like a Christmas tree. "Have fun, and call if you need us."

"Anytime," Nico added, like Dex was his kid and not some guy he hardly knew.

Dex was glad the dark lighting hid his blush. "I appreciate it."

"Okay, we'll leave you alone." Onyx grinned.

Dex hurried away before Onyx said anything else.

Why was the demon so happy that Luc was hunting him through a club? It was as if Onyx wanted Dex and Luc to get together.

Dex shoved the thought away as forcefully as he could and pushed through a door to the restrooms, finding the dimly lit hall deserted. The door clicked shut behind him, muffling the music, and Dex's ears rang.

Two steps down the hall, the single overhead light flickered. Dex paused, then kept going. There seemed to be a bunch of private restrooms all along the hall rather than one shared room. He tried the first toilet door, but it was locked.

The light flickered again.

At the second door, deep grunts and the slap of skin on skin met Dex's ears. He hurried to the next one. The light flickered and went out, leaving him in complete darkness.

He froze.

The sounds of sex intensified. Moans and whimpers filled the hall around him as if someone was getting fucked right beside him.

Something scraped along the floor, harsh and grating.

Dex sucked in a breath. No one was in here with him, and none of the doors had opened. What was that?

There was another scrape, then a thud, and heavy breathing.

"*Fuck me harder*," a deep voice moaned.

Dex reached out, completely blind in the dark. He patted a hand along the wall, searching for the next toilet door, found it, and pulled the handle.

It was locked.

Screw it. This had been an excuse to wander away. He didn't actually need the restroom. Dex turned back the way he'd come.

How had no one else entered the hallway? Surely not everyone behind a locked door was fucking. And no one else had come in from outside to wait.

The light flickered, and Dex stopped in his tracks. The bulb flared to life, revealing Luc standing beneath, his wings spread, filling the narrow space. His eyes glowed. The light went out, and his red irises disappeared along with everything else.

Dex's panting breaths were harsh to his own ears. What should he do?

The moans of the people having sex swelled louder than ever. Dex was caught. Would Luc press him against the wall and fuck him? Feed on him?

Dex stumbled back. Luc blocked the way out, but the urge to run was more insistent than his aching cock. He couldn't give in this easily. He took another step backward.

Dex's back collided with something firm. He yelped, spinning around, but he couldn't see. A hand wrapped around his throat, and Dex screamed.

A low laugh filled the pitch black room, the sounds of sex taking on a savage edge. Dex twisted his body, hitting the hard chest in front of him, spurred on by the firm grip on his neck. He struggled, his breaths ragged, and managed to pull free, taking a staggering step back.

Luc's growl scraped along Dex's clammy skin. "It's time to run."

Dex tore down the hallway, hoping like hell he was headed toward the exit. He slammed into a wall and stumbled back. Loud footsteps echoed. Dex couldn't hear the music from the club. Even the moans had stopped. For a second, he wasn't sure where he was.

What if magic had trapped him or transported him somewhere?

He lunged for the wall, feeling along until he came to a door. It didn't budge. Dex whimpered, and a chilling laugh washed over him. With all his strength, he pulled on the door. It burst open, and Dex fell forward, the flashing lights of the dancefloor blindingly bright as the music drowned out all other sound.

Recovering his footing, Dex ran. He shouldered someone out of the way, but the guy didn't seem to notice.

Dex tore down the stairs and skidded to a stop. Which way was out? Nothing but a wall of bodies stood before him. He glanced over his shoulder, and there was Luc, at the bottom of the stairs, and for the first time that night, not cast in shadow.

Luc's red wings filled the stairwell. His horns gleamed in the flashing lights, not a strand of hair out of place, his eyes completely red. A thick red tail wound over Luc's hip, his chest bare, dark hair standing out on his pale skin. He wore a pair of suit pants and nothing else. Baring his fangs, his growl drowned out the thundering club music.

"*Mine.* You can't escape me."

Dex's heart skipped. His chest constricted, and he was consumed by the needy desire to belong to Luc forever. To never escape, no matter how hard he tried.

Whirling around, Dex pushed into the dancing crowd. A frantic look over his shoulder revealed Luc had left the stairway.

He was coming for him.

Dex surged forward, trying to shove people out of his way. Normally, people moved when you jostled by, or at least pushed back, but no one reacted. It was as if they couldn't feel Dex touching them. He pulled a man's arm, and he didn't so much as flinch. The guy beside him looked straight through Dex.

This was more than invisibility.

Dex shoved harder and harder, his muscles tensing as everything from his back to his fingers seized.

It was like he wasn't really there. Like he didn't exist. A ghost.

"No," he muttered, primal panic taking over. Dex shoved a guy with all his strength, and he didn't budge. "No!"

Luc's laugh tickled his ears, and Dex let out a helpless sound. Luc had said no one would be able to intervene, but Dex hadn't known *this* was possible.

Luc's control was complete.

Dex scrambled between people, slipping through any gaps he could find, his chest and back sliding along sweaty bodies. Someone elbowed him in the ribs, and he grunted. Ignoring the pain, he forced his way through the next gap.

What if he couldn't get out?

No. He had to.

"Move!" he shouted in someone's face.

They didn't even flinch.

Dex squeezed around the guy and stumbled, falling into yet another oblivious person. This part of the dance floor was even more packed than where he'd come from. He had to get to the edge of the crowd. Go around the room, not through.

As he wedged himself through a gap, all the space between the men dancing around him seemed to close. They pressed tighter together, moving as one.

What?

A wall of bodies formed in front of Dex. There was no way out without ripping the men from each other's arms or climbing over their heads.

He turned the other way. There! A gap. Dex pushed forward, aiming for a space between two couples, but as he reached it, the gap closed. The four men pressed in, leaving him no way through.

All around, the bodies closed in. The immediate space around Dex opened as the men nearest melded into the perimeter, leaving Dex in an empty circle, people writhing all around him.

Luc was doing this. He was controlling the crowd. A chill trickled down Dex's spine as he spun in a circle.

There was no way out.

Over the heads of the crowd, Dex caught a glimpse of red wings. His throat ran dry, and his hands trembled.

The wings drew closer.

He backed away as far as he could, hitting the wall of dancing men and getting no reaction. Luc had so much power. He could do *anything* to Dex.

Dex was realizing how much he'd underestimated the depth of the Devil's powers. It was terrifying to be this helpless. A thrill like no other, even though, deep down, he was sure Luc wouldn't take more than what he offered.

It was perfect.

The crowd on the opposite side of the circle parted, and Lucifer stepped into the clearing, his glowing eyes fixed on Dex, his mouth open in a snarl.

Dex's neck throbbed, his pulse dizzyingly fast.

Luc lunged forward, and the crowd seemed to surge with him, closing in around Dex. Luc's tail wrapped around Dex's hips, his arms around Dex's body. He pushed against Luc's chest and his skin burned hot beneath his fingers.

"No," Dex whimpered.

"Yes, you're mine." Luc tangled a hand in Dex's hair and yanked his head back.

Color splashed across Luc's face as the lights strobed. The red glow of his eyes turned into flame, and he pulled Dex tight against him, his tail constricting. Dex squirmed, his hard cock rubbing tantalizingly against Luc's thigh.

A moan tore from his parched throat, and his whole body vibrated.

Luc bent to Dex's neck and ran his fangs along his skin.

"*Luc*," Dex whimpered, the sound lost to his own ears.

The Devil pressed his lips to Dex's cheek. "Remember, you can't come. Not until I say."

With lightning speed, Luc's fangs pierced Dex's throat.

Dex screamed as pain and pleasure exploded beneath his skin. He clawed at Luc's chest, pushing him away, bringing him closer, he didn't know.

His cock throbbed. Dex rubbed against Luc and almost exploded with the first roll of his hips. It was torture to stop, but he did. He wouldn't come. Not before Luc gave him permission. Luc owned him, and he would be good for the Devil.

Luc's fangs sent pleasure through his veins, and an agonized cry filled Dex's ears. He realized it had come from him. It was too much. Too good. He shook and whimpered, his heart thundering so fast he might faint.

"Please," Dex whispered.

Luc withdrew his fangs, licking his lips. He swiped a thumb over the wound on Dex's neck and brought it to his mouth, sucking the blood off. "Mm. Such a good boy holding back for me."

Dex bit his lip. If he moved, he'd come in his pants. *Fuck.* A strangled sound left his lips.

"So, so good for me." Luc stroked Dex's cheek.

Heat pooled inside Dex, growing hotter with Luc's words, and his fingers flexed on Luc's chest. "Please."

The fire danced in Luc's eyes. "Would you like another chance to escape?"

Words wouldn't form. *No.* Dex needed to *come.*

Luc gripped Dex's jaw, holding him in place. "Dex." The warning in his tone was unmistakable. "You know how to end this if you need to."

Stopping was the last thing on Dex's mind. He shook his head, hardly budging within Luc's grasp. "Don't stop. Green. I need to come. Luc, please."

"Not yet. I like you trembling with need. All *mine.*"

Dex stomped his foot like a child, lost to any other action, and Luc smiled. Fire burned Dex's insides, and he loved it as much as he hated it.

He took a breath, trying his best to steady himself. Agonizing moments passed, and at last, he wasn't about to blow his load.

Now that he was thinking more clearly, he wasn't ready for this to end.

"All right," Dex gasped. "Give me another chance."

Luc released him so fast, he would have fallen if not for the tail around his hips. "Don't let me catch you." The command was more growl than spoken word.

Dex's chest heaved. He was still hard, but his growing need to escape overshadowed everything else.

The wall of men encircling them remained. They'd drawn back without Dex realizing, giving him space, but no way out.

How was he supposed to get away?

The beat changed, and a gap in the crowd opened like a biblically parted sea, leaving a clear path to the exit. Dex took off at full speed, racing down the dance floor.

The club door banged open in front of Dex of its own

accord. Luc must be giving him a way out, but Dex didn't turn around to check how closely he followed.

He burst into the night, air cool on his sweat-slick skin. The bouncers didn't even flinch, and everyone in line ignored him. Dex's skin crawled. With an agonized roar, he took off down the sidewalk without a care for where he was going.

Feet pounding the pavement, Dex ran. His arms pumped, his breath tearing harshly from his lungs. Lights turned green as he came upon them, and he flew across intersections without looking.

Luc had control. Dex was safe to be terrified and flee through the night. He knew it in his bones. He couldn't hear Luc behind him, but he was there, manipulating the world around them. His attention burned into Dex's soul.

Dex turned a corner and ran harder. He didn't know where he was. He turned again, finding the next street almost completely deserted.

He chanced a look over his shoulder. Luc stood in the middle of the intersection, nothing but a silhouette with huge wings beneath the city lights.

Dex didn't stop, running farther from the populated area. His muscles burned. He wouldn't last much longer.

One more corner. He could make it that far, and then, he didn't know.

Dex skidded around the bend and crashed into Luc. Hands closed around Dex's biceps and squeezed, a snarl filling the night. The scream that came from Dex seemed to have a mind of its own, shredding his throat until he sputtered incoherently.

Somehow, he wrenched from Luc's grasp and twisted away. Run. He had to run. This was his last chance to escape.

Luc grabbed Dex and hauled him back. He couldn't get enough air to scream. Dex struggled, tripping and losing his balance.

He fell, his arms flying out to catch himself, but Luc's arms wrapped around his middle and hauled him upward, saving him from the impact and setting him gently on all fours.

Then, Luc was on him, his body bracketing Dex.

Luc's breath was harsh in his ear. "Mine."

Dex had no control over the sounds coming from him, more animal than human, and he'd never been harder, his clothes too much and not enough friction for his poor, denied cock. His palms stung as he scrambled for purchase on the sidewalk, resisting the urge to touch himself.

Luc tore Dex's shirt in two and pressed his hot chest against Dex's bare back. With another violent tug, Dex's pants ripped. Then his boxer briefs. Luc shredded the fabric until Dex was exposed to the knees.

"Please, please," Dex found himself chanting, his words slurred, the night air providing no relief to his exposed, straining erection.

Luc's fangs found his throat, and he bit down with an obscene moan. Dex whimpered with the pleasure, not even registering the pain.

He was naked in the street, Lucifer mounted on top of him, taking what he wanted. Dex thought he might pass out with the effort it took not to grab his cock. He might not even need to touch it at all. His body was on fire, so good he couldn't hold back.

"*Luc!*" he wailed, voice loud and high-pitched.

The Devil withdrew his fangs. "Tell me you're mine."

"I'm yours. Please. *Please.*" Dex's arms gave out, and he would have face-planted into the pavement if Luc hadn't caught him.

Luc's hand snaked along his chest and gripped his neck, his forearm secure against Dex's sternum. His lips returned to Dex's throat, brushing gently against his skin.

"Come for me," he growled, then fisted Dex's cock as his fangs sank back in.

Dex exploded. He couldn't even tell what part of his body the orgasm came from. It was as if his very blood—his whole being—was the source of his pleasure. Dex sobbed. He couldn't see. He could do nothing but feel.

Luc growled into his neck and worked his cock without mercy. Dex wasn't even capable of humping into it. He had no control. Everything was Luc. His very soul belonged to Luc.

It was bliss.

When the oversensitivity started to hurt, Luc released his spent cock, and Dex didn't know if he could be anything other than a whimpering mess ever again.

Luc pulled back, licking Dex's neck as a strange sound, nearly a purr, emanated from his throat, his erection hard against Dex's lower back.

Would Luc fuck him? Here in the street?

"I'm yours," was all Dex could mumble. "Yours."

19

LUCIFER

Luc scooped Dex into his arms. Dex's pulse thundered, his breaths coming in short, shallow pants, and Luc's body thrummed to the frantic beat.

Mine.

"Breathe with me, Dex." Luc laid a hand on Dex's chest. "Look at me. Deep breaths. That's it. In. Out."

Dex's eyes locked on his, and he dutifully copied Luc's breaths. At last, his heart rate began to settle. The steady beats grounded Luc—bringing them closer together—and took the edge off Luc's potent need to claim all of his mate's body.

Not in the street. Not yet, but soon.

Dex's eyes fluttered half closed. He wrapped a loose arm around Luc's neck, leaning his head against his chest.

So sweet, his little mate.

Luc's heart clenched. "Hold on," he whispered, the growl gone from his tone.

He launched into the air. Dex whimpered, clinging to Luc's neck, and Luc only clutched him tighter.

His. Dex was his, and Luc was far from done with him. "I've got you. You're mine, and you're staying with me."

Dex's fingers flexed against Luc's neck, and he pressed his face to Luc's chest. "Yes."

Luc's wings pumped at full speed. Fire flared within him. He doubted he could have retracted his demon features if he'd tried. The need to claim Dex coursed through him, throbbing along with his own pulse and nearly blinding him.

He'd found his mate, toyed with him, hunted him, given him pleasure, and his mate had said he belonged to him.

The mating spell echoed in Luc's mind as he landed in front of his loft and kicked the door open. Claiming Dex would be a perfect end to the night, but the bond had never been on the table, and instinct would never override reason.

Luc could want something and not take it.

But that didn't mean the night was over.

Dex lifted his head and glanced around as Luc carried him up the stairs to his bed. "You decorated." Dex's voice was soft, dazed, and maybe even amused.

"We need more than a bed, especially if you're going to be my prisoner."

Dex stiffened, his pupils blowing wide. "W-what do you mean?"

Luc carried Dex past the couch and table to the bed and tossed him onto the mattress. Dex's cock slapped his stomach, already hardening. Luc pulled off Dex's shoes, ripped the destroyed jeans from Dex's calves, and tossed them away.

He wrapped his hands around Dex's ankles. "You failed to escape, and I captured you. You aren't going anywhere, my dear."

Dex moaned, arching his back. His hand neared his cock, before quickly jerking back.

"Good boy. No touching yourself unless I say. Now, hands above your head."

Dex complied without hesitation, stretching his body and

bringing out the definition in his arms as he reached for the headboard.

Luc let fire dance in his eyes. With a flick of his fingers, leather straps wound around Dex's wrists, securing them together. Another flick, and a second strap melded to the cuffs, attaching itself to the headboard as if the leather had grown out of the wood.

Dex twisted to look over his shoulder, tugging on the restraints. "*Luc.*" He whipped back around, his eyes wide, and tugged to no avail. "You can't."

"Can't I?"

Was it too much?

Dex had said he'd never played like this before, and the fantasy of being restrained might not have prepared him for the reality. Same with the fantasy of saying no and not being listened to, even though they'd gone there before.

Dex shook his head, words seeming to fail him.

"I need you to give me a color," Luc said calmly, almost gently, with a hint of command, the fire in his eyes dying to a smolder.

Dex's chest heaved up and down. He closed his eyes and his body went lax. "Green."

"Good boy." Luc caressed Dex's ankle, trailing his fingers along Dex's calf and kissing his thigh. "And what would you say if you wanted me to stop?"

"Red."

"That's right." Luc kissed him again.

Dex's eyes opened, his relaxed manner seeming to loosen his tongue. "Nothing permanent, and we're green."

Luc froze. Nothing permanent? Of course not. "You're not my captive forever. Just for tonight."

Dex squirmed, eyes closing once more. "I know, but I want to be yours."

He sounded as agonized as Luc felt. Had he realized the truth? That they were fated to a nearly impossible situation.

Whether he'd landed on the truth or not, Dex needed him. It was clear in his body language, in his voice, and Luc could give him what he needed within the confines of this scene. He could fulfil Dex's fantasy of being his—of belonging and being owned—even if it wasn't enough.

Even if it wasn't everything they were destined for.

Fuck. Luc's grip tightened on Dex's ankle. He had to give Dex *more*. He had to free them from their doomed fate.

Fierce determination scorched Luc's soul like he hadn't experienced in two thousand years. He would find a way. He'd settle for nothing less than giving his bonded mate the universe on a silver platter.

Luc surged up his mate's body, cupping his throat. "You are mine, Dex. Look at me."

His lids fluttered open.

"*Mine.*" Luc infused the word with everything he had, leaving no room for question.

Dex nodded, his words breathless. "Yours. What are you going to do to me now that you've caught me?" His hint of melancholy had fled, a needy whine taking its place.

Luc straightened, looming over his captive mate. "Whatever I want. Whatever will please me most."

That had been part of Dex's fantasy—Luc doing 'anything' he wanted. Deciding for Dex what came next. Luc would grant his mate any wish, give him anything he wanted no matter how difficult, but this was easy. Fulfilling his mate's needs transformed every little action into something important, and Luc felt powerful in the best way.

This was the kind of control he craved. Taking over was as much his fantasy as Dex's.

Dex's breathing shallowed, and his heart rate picked up. He

squirmed in the sheets. "Please. Come on. What are you waiting for?"

"Are you being impatient?" Luc chided. Seemed he needed to remind Dex who was in charge.

"No." Dex shook his head like pleasing Luc was more important than his own needs. Or like pleasing Luc was as much of a need as his desire to be used.

Luc's fire smoldered. "I'd hope not. You can wait while I get ready. Can't you?"

Dex bit his lip. "Yes, I can. I'm waiting."

"Good." Luc soaked up the renewed flush to Dex's cheeks before sitting on the bed, facing away and undoing his shoes, taking his time with the laces.

After a long moment, Dex whined. "What are you doing?"

Aww, his mate sounded tortured, and after only the briefest diversion of Luc's attention. Luc smiled. "Taking off my shoes. I can't get this knot untied."

Dex made an indignant sound. Yeah, he didn't believe the lie, but he didn't protest, trying so hard to be good for Luc.

Luc put his shoes and socks away, and at last returned his attention to Dex. His soft brown cheeks were flushed even darker, sweat lining his brow. Dex's erection hadn't flagged in the slightest.

"So good for me. A patient little captive. Ready for anything." Luc licked his lips, and Dex sucked in a breath. "I can't resist you, so it's a good thing I don't have to."

"No, don't resist. Please."

Luc took off his pants.

Dex's gaze dragged over him, straining to see Luc's newly exposed skin, head tilted as much as possible. "I can't touch you," he whined, his arms flexing as he tugged on his bindings.

"No, tonight you're mine. If you're good, you can touch me next time."

Dex nodded, eager to please as ever.

Luc loved giving them something to look forward to. It was vital for Dex to know his desire extended past this moment. That way, he could enjoy without worry. Dex liked fear, but that didn't mean Luc should leave him wondering or afraid about what lay between them. Dex had to know he was secure. He was safe with Luc.

And Luc had to remind himself that this was their beginning. Having something to look forward to opened him up in a way he'd forgotten existed. It excited him like nothing else.

Luc lowered his underwear and fisted his cock, the physical pleasure almost an afterthought compared to the heat in his heart.

Dex's tongue poked out, and he licked his lips almost like he couldn't help it. Luc's fire flared.

Claim.

He spread his wings and beat them, working off the urge to let his primal side take over.

Dex gasped, his gaze drawn away from Luc's cock in wonder. Air swirled around them, Dex's scent everywhere.

A hint of smoke tinged the air.

Luc climbed onto the bed, his tail winding back and forth, and he grabbed Dex's ankles, spreading his legs.

Dex moaned, arching his back and tilting his hips. "What are you going to do to me?"

"Hmm, let's see..." Luc purred as he bent Dex's knees, planting his feet on the mattress. With his thumbs, he spread Dex's cheeks, exposing his hole, and Dex's muscles clenched beneath his touch.

"Yes, this will do." Luc ran a finger over Dex's pucker. "You're here for my pleasure. My captive, to whom I'll do whatever I desire. A hole for me to use."

Dex whimpered. "Please."

"You've been dying for me to fuck you, haven't you?" Luc scraped blunt red nails against Dex's hole, eliciting a moan.

"Yes, I wanted you the first day we met. It's your fault it took this long."

Luc chuckled, meeting his mate's defiant gaze. "And now look at you. Tied up and at the Devil's mercy. Isn't it better this way?"

"Y-yes." Dex's voice shook. He spread his legs wider, lifting his hips in clear invitation.

Luc growled, fire bursting in his chest. His eyes burned, and he snapped his wings again, powerless to resist his mate. "*Mine.*"

Magic slicked Luc's fingers, coating them generously in lubricant, and he thrust one inside Dex. He arched off the bed, crying out as Luc worked him.

"I'm going to fuck you hard. Like you belong to me. So hard, you'll feel me inside you for the rest of your life. So you know that I'll *never* let you go." Luc said it like a promise, like a threat, like the most sacred vow he'd ever made.

Dex clenched around him. "Yes." His eyes were wild, a deep flush darkening his face and neck. "Yes, Luc. Please."

With a growl, Luc added another finger. He thrust, and Dex moaned helplessly, bringing his hips to meet Luc's hand. His cock leaked onto his stomach, and he tipped his head back, baring his throat.

Need thrummed through Luc's veins as he opened his mate with brutal efficiency. "Does it hurt?"

"No, it's good. So good. More." Dex thrust onto Luc's fingers.

That was what he needed to hear. Another swell of magic slicked his cock, and he withdrew, lining himself up. He grabbed Dex under the knees, tilted his hips, and pushed in, forcing Dex to accommodate his girth.

Dex gasped. "*Argh*, Luc. Ooh."

Luc tasted smoke. Dex was tight around him. He pushed forward, savoring this first invasion, Dex's first acceptance.

"You're perfect, Dex. Come on my cock like a good captive. Lose yourself for me."

"*Luc*," Dex cried, a sob of relief sending a shudder through his body.

Luc was all the way in, their bodies pressed together. His chest tightened. He had his mate. This was the beginning of the rest of time. He wasn't letting Dex go. He'd do anything to belong here. To return to Dex over and over.

Luc pulled back and snapped his hips, eliciting a moan from Dex, whose eyes fluttered closed. He couldn't hold back any longer. He threw Dex's feet over his shoulders and fucked him hard, the base of his tail vibrating with every thrust.

Dex's high-pitched cries filled the cavernous loft and bounced off the ceiling. "Fuck me." He threw back his head and came, release flooding his stomach, his tight hole strangling Luc's cock.

Dex's earthy scent filled the air, and pleasure raced down Luc's spine. With a snarled, "*mine*," he filled his mate with his seed, claiming his body, if not his soul.

Dex was his. Luc would make it so if it was the last thing he accomplished in his life.

Luc lowered Dex's legs onto the mattress and pulled him close, keeping his cock buried deep. With a spell, Dex's restraints fell away, but he didn't immediately lower his arms.

"You can relax, my dear." Luc brushed light fingertips along Dex's cheek.

He whimpered.

Luc pressed a kiss to Dex's lips and brought his arms down one at a time, massaging his wrists and shoulders, stroking his skin as he relaxed.

Dex's palms were red from being on all fours in the street. Luc brushed a thumb over each in turn, healing the agitated skin with magic. Dex sighed, his body clenching around Luc's spent cock.

Luc groaned and kissed Dex's soft lips, his earthy scent taking on a floral quality. "You've been a good captive."

Dex's relaxed muscles tensed. "Don't let me go."

"I'm not. I'm keeping you close, telling you how much you pleased me. How good you were. I'm not saying you were a good captive because I'm letting you go."

Dex nodded, trembling slightly.

Luc rolled them onto their sides, his cock slipping from Dex's body. He stretched the wing nearest the mattress back and out of the way, the other folding over them like a cocoon.

"Don't go," Dex whispered again.

Luc tightened his arms around him. "I'm not going anywhere. I'm right here with you. I've got you." Dex's body gave another shudder. "You're safe, Dex. I'm here and you're safe."

He squirmed, pressing closer. Luc welcomed him, draping his tail over Dex's thigh and kissing his forehead.

"I don't want this to be over," Dex whispered, the hint of urgency in his tone setting Luc on alert.

Dex needed reassurance, but Luc had to find the right way to express it. Clearly, saying he wasn't leaving wasn't enough. "Why don't you want it to be over?"

"I—I don't know. It's overwhelming. I don't know what to do."

Luc rubbed Dex's back, his heart clenching. "You don't have to do anything, sweet boy. The scene is done, but I've still got you. You don't have to worry. I'm not going anywhere. You're good. So, so good. You gave me so much pleasure, everything I wanted."

Dex clung to him, nodding against his neck. Luc murmured more reassurance in Dex's ear, cuddling him like the precious soul he was, praising him and giving him love, even if Luc didn't use that particular word.

"Whatever you're feeling is normal, Dex. You can tell me. You can say or do anything without worrying about what will happen next. I promise."

Dex's grip on Luc loosened, and he shifted until their eyes met. "Anything?"

"Yes, anything. I want all of you, remember?"

"Yeah." Dex's lips twitched upward. "I feel better now. I don't know why I got so scared for a second."

Did he not know, or was it just hard to voice? "Would you like to talk about it?"

Dex hesitated. "Okay, but I don't know what to say."

"You feared me leaving. Was it rejection that scared you? Is that what the scene ending felt like?"

"No..." Dex took a moment to put his words together. "Having you in control was a relief. I didn't have any worries. That hasn't happened in a long time. I've been low-key afraid for years, holding back because I was scared of losing anyone, and I hate it. I've got so much happening in my head, and the idea of it all coming back hurt. I didn't want this to be over because then I'd have to face it all again."

Luc felt his mate's pain. They might not be bonded, but Dex's emotion was plain on his face, the set of his shoulders, the way his fingers flexed against Luc's chest. Luc welcomed it all.

"Even when you're not my captive and I'm not controlling you, you can count on me and share your worries."

Dex bit his lip. "I know. But being free from it all was so...

well, freeing." He huffed a laugh. "That was articulate." He swallowed and tried again. "Being scared like I wanted was even better than I imagined, but when the actual stuff I'm scared of was coming back, I didn't want to let go. It was too much all at once."

"I'm sure it was. Fear is a powerful emotion." Fear could do horrible things. It had led Luc to his darkest moments. "Wanting to avoid what frightens us is only natural."

"Yeah...but I also crave fear. Obviously. I asked you to scare me, and being hunted was the most thrilling thing that's ever happened to me. The adrenaline. The raw desire. It was so pure and hot. Is that weird?"

"Wanting to be scared and enjoying it? No. Your desires aren't weird. Recognizing that you can take something you struggle with and make it yours is a powerful thing."

Luc knew that from experience. His desire for control could take him to bad places, but he could mold that desire to reflect his morals and take charge for the good of his partner. That's what gave him pleasure and got him off, and it had nothing to do with what he'd done, trapping everyone in Hell.

His desire for control wasn't weird or wrong in and of itself, and Luc wasn't afraid he'd cross any lines with Dex. What Dex wanted was always at the front of his mind, even when they played with denial. Dex wanted to please Luc. He got pleasure out of being good and putting Luc first, and felt free when he wasn't in control.

If Dex didn't enjoy these things, Luc wouldn't ask them of him.

Dex seemed thoughtful. "Getting off on being scared does give me a deep kind of satisfaction, but you make it sound like I'm mastering my fear."

"Aren't you?"

Dex's cheeks flushed, and he tucked his face out of sight, but not before Luc caught his smile. "I don't know if I'm mastering it. It's more like I'm giving it to you," he whispered.

Luc's breath stuttered. "Then I'll guard it with everything I have."

"I like giving you things to look after. Um…" Dex's face froze like he'd surprised himself with that admission.

"Wonderful, because I like looking after you." Luc's fire smoldered at the way Dex's whole body softened, melding into him even more. "Tonight was hot. Exciting. I've never hunted someone like that, watching for hours, drinking you in. Biding my time. I loved every moment. What else did you like about tonight, other than giving me your fear?"

Dex relaxed and answered like the words were bursting from him. "Struggling and being naked in the street with you on top of me, and knowing you were watching when I couldn't see you. I liked being your captive. Your plaything," he added eagerly.

Luc nearly purred. Perhaps Dex considered it less vulnerable to admit he enjoyed being Luc's plaything than saying he liked being taken care of, but Luc wondered if the two weren't connected.

A plaything and a captive were both for Luc to look after—Luc's responsibility—and it was no mystery why Dex longed to be cared for. He might not be looking for a Daddy, but he seemed to crave the nurturing he'd lost from his life as much as Luc longed to nurture his mate and use his affinity for control for good.

"I liked all those things too," Luc said. "Especially you as my captive. Would you do any of it again?"

"Yeah." Dex laughed like the question hardly needed asking. "I'd do it all again."

Luc's chest warmed. "What about controlling your pleasure. How did that go?"

Dex lifted his chin. "I didn't touch myself, just like I promised."

"Such a good boy, but I meant, did you enjoy it? Would you like to do something like that again?"

"Oh." Dex pressed closer to Luc, averting his eyes. "I didn't realize we'd stopped. I want to keep going."

A low purr filled the air. "You do? Why? Tell me why you enjoyed it."

"I don't know. It was like we were connected all the time. Like I was doing something for you and earning something I wanted."

Always connected. Like they would be with their mating bond. "In that case, let's see if you can earn another orgasm."

Dex nodded eagerly, and Luc covered Dex's mouth with his. When the kiss ended and Luc drew back, Dex's eyes remained shut. He had to be exhausted.

"Don't fall asleep. We have to clean off and eat something."

Dex opened one eye. "I'm not hungry."

"Maybe not, but I drank substantially from you, so you need to eat before going to sleep."

"Fine." Dex closed his eyes again, a tiny smile on his face.

Luc cleaned them with magic and evaporated the mess from the sheets. He propped Dex on the pillows and fetched him water and a small box of cookies.

Back on the bed, Luc pulled Dex onto his lap. Dex squirmed, rubbing his ass against Luc until Luc's cock hardened.

He gripped Dex's hips. "Eat your cookies, little tease."

Dex held still and ate quietly for a few minutes. "Can I touch your wings?" he asked in a rush like he couldn't hold the words back a second longer.

Luc's wings rested against the headboard, wingtips draped

over the sides of the bed. He ruffled his feathers, bringing one wing around and lightly stroking down Dex's spine.

"Touch all you like."

Dex ran a hand along the ridge of Luc's other wing. "All of you is so warm. Your feathers are like silk." He shivered as Luc stroked the exposed skin of his back from neck to ass.

"Your skin feels divine beneath my feathers, too."

Another shiver wound through Dex's body. "Don't stop." He braced both hands against Luc's wings and rubbed their chests together.

"Careful," Luc warned as Dex's hard cock leaked against his stomach. "You aren't getting off again tonight."

Dex moaned, his motions slowing to a stop. "Okay. I'll be good."

"Yes, you will." Luc kissed his nose. "We should go to sleep if you're done eating."

Dex stroked Luc's wing. "But then the night will be over."

"Is that a bad thing? We can do it all again. I'm not abandoning you. You may not be my prisoner, but you're mine, and I'm yours."

Dex withdrew his hand, running it along the healed skin of his neck as if searching for Luc's bite. "You're right, none of that's bad." A yawn drowned out the last word.

Luc set the empty water glass and the single uneaten cookie on his new bedside table and pulled Dex beneath the blankets. "Sleep, and we'll go to breakfast in the morning. Nothing is over, my dear. That's a promise."

20

———

DEX

"Dex," a low voice hummed, sending shivers down his spine.

"*Mmm*," he groaned and pressed his face further into the pillow.

"Wake up," Luc taunted.

The covers disappeared from Dex's back, leaving him exposed to cool air.

"Hey." Dex reached blindly behind him, but couldn't find the covers. He turned his head and peered at Luc.

"Good morning." Luc's red-lipped smile was as bright as the sun streaming through the windows. His wings were gone, but his horns still framed his face. "It's time for breakfast."

He sounded so damn excited that Dex's heart clenched.

A buzzing sounded from the other side of the bed, and Luc turned away. "Someone sent you a text message."

"You have my phone?" Dex rolled onto his side, rubbing a hand over his face. He was lucky his phone hadn't been lost in the street, where Luc had shredded his clothes.

Heat flooded his body. God. He'd really done that. And he'd do it again. If Luc told him to run naked through the Sunday morning crowd, Dex would jump to it. No hesitation and no regrets.

"I grabbed it when I tackled you." Luc handed the phone over. "It should be charged."

"Thanks." Leave it to Luc to remember the little things when he was giving Dex the night of his life.

Dex unlocked the phone. Fuck. He'd forgotten brunch with Ollie.

OLLIE:

What time do you want to come over? I just woke up.

DEX:

Me too. Can I come by this afternoon instead? Lunch? Or we can do dinner?

OLLIE:

For sure. Come by later this afternoon. We can game and get pizza.

Dex liked the message. Would he tell Ollie he'd canceled because he was with Luc? Before he could worry about Ollie's reaction, a message from last night caught his eye.

ONYX:

Hope you had fun.

At least it was a private message and not in the group chat. Dex still frowned. Did Onyx mean at the club or with Luc?

He quickly replied, saying he had a great night, leaving things as vague as Onyx had.

"Is everything all right?" Luc asked.

"Yeah, I'm meeting Ollie later, and, um, your brother messaged me."

Luc's brows rose. "I heard you tell him what we were doing."

Dex's face heated. "He seemed happy about it."

"I'm not surprised."

Maybe Onyx had some idea of Luc's preferences, but knowing Luc was the kind of man to hunt a lover through a club didn't explain why Onyx had seemed happy to see him with Luc. Nothing but being Luc's mate explained it.

Did everyone think they were mates? Was that why Ollie had encouraged Dex to talk to Luc?

Dex *felt* like Luc's mate. How he knew what mates felt like, he couldn't say, other than his connection with Luc was tangible, almost physical, as it drew them together. Not a physical attraction to Luc's appearance, but something more solid.

"I've got clothes for you." Luc stood from the bed, naked, back fully covered with tattooed wings, and headed for the dresser. His red tail hung over his ass, the thick base resting along his crack. The tip flicked back and forth near his ankles.

Dex's insides tightened. Who'd have thought tails were hot? Damn.

Luc turned, holding a pair of shorts and a pair of jeans. "Which one?"

Dex pointed to the jeans. Luc put the shorts away and tossed the jeans on the bed, along with a pair of black boxer briefs.

Luc had gone out and bought Dex underwear. He'd done all this knowing he planned to rip Dex's clothes to shreds. It was sexy, but also made Dex's heart ache.

He climbed out of bed and pulled on the underwear and pants. Luc handed him a soft T-shirt, and he slipped into it. "Thanks for all this."

Luc cupped his cheek. "You're welcome."

Dex sat on the bed and watched Luc dress. His tail disappeared, becoming a tattoo wrapped around his hips, the tip trailing down his left ass cheek. Dex's fingers itched to trace the ink.

Luc pulled on underwear and a pair of dark gray slacks. He never seemed to wear anything casual. Another soft-looking sweater was unearthed from a drawer, and Luc pulled it over his head, catching it on a horn along the way.

As Luc emerged, Dex realized that his red lips probably weren't due to cosmetics—he hadn't put anything on and the color hadn't smudged or faded—it had to be natural.

Dex rubbed his chest as an empty feeling opened inside him. Waiting for someone to get dressed the morning after sex wasn't something he'd done since his early college days, before his parents' deaths. Before everything had changed.

Even as he was in the middle of it, Dex missed this kind of intimacy. He hadn't over the years, but now, looking back, he wished he hadn't gone without it. If only Luc had found him years ago.

Dex had told himself to focus solely on sex, but after exploring his true desires, he wanted more. Could he have Luc as a boyfriend? As a mate? He didn't want to lose this achy feeling or hide from connection, even if the two of them were doomed, and he couldn't have forever the way the other mates could.

Luc ran a hand through his hair, his smile faltering. "What is it?"

Dex gripped the edge of the mattress. "Am I your mate?"

Luc's eyes crinkled around the edges, and his smile returned in a brittle contrast to what it had been. He closed the distance between them and kneeled before Dex, pulling his hands from the mattress to cup them in his.

"Yes, Dex. You are my mate."

Dex sucked in a breath, butterflies exploding inside him. He was right. He was Luc's. His fingers dug into Luc's palms. "How do you know for sure?"

"I felt our connection the moment I saw you. Before, actually. I bought one of your mugs and couldn't figure out why I was so drawn to it until I followed you to Dorthy's."

"I felt it too. I couldn't stop thinking about you."

Luc squeezed Dex's hands. "I haven't stopped thinking about you since we met. I can't believe I found you. I was sure, down to my soul, that I never would. It didn't seem real at first."

Didn't seem real? "But you were so calm when we met."

Luc laughed. "Not on the inside. I hadn't been genuine with anyone or free of my past in centuries, and it rattled me. I was out of my depth." Luc's tone hardened, his eyes wide and pleading. "I'm sorry I gave up on finding you and did such horrible things, and I'm sorry I used losing you as an excuse for my actions."

"You didn't." Losing Dex before they'd even met couldn't have pushed him over the edge.

"I did." Agony tightened Luc's words, and his eyes glowed with the faintest hint of red as he gripped Dex tighter. "I stopped caring when my quest to find you failed. My world was misery, and instead of finding hope, I clung to self-pity and indulged every horrible thought I had. I wish I was the kind of man you didn't have to excuse. One you could love without hesitation. I wish I'd never lost hope."

Dex wanted to say he hadn't hesitated, but he couldn't, and that was okay. Caution was natural. Luc's past was a part of him and affected their relationship. But Dex's conflicted feelings over what Luc had done weren't nearly as strong as they'd been. He knew who Luc was.

Luc was plagued by the remorse he felt. He didn't want to be that person anymore. Ollie seemed determined to forgive Luc, and Dex wanted to give Luc the chance to be the best version of himself. He still had to talk to Ollie and be honest with him, but finding some level of harmony between the three of them seemed possible for the first time.

Ollie was right. They had fate on their side.

Dex pulled a hand free from Luc's grasp and traced one of his horns. "You can't undo the past, but you've changed. I believe who you are with me is the real you. And I want all of you. You don't have to be someone else."

The glow faded from Luc's eyes. "I'm glad. I like who I am with you."

"Good." Luc should like who he was, even if he didn't like who he'd been. "You can have love in your life. Things can get better again."

Life would get better for Dex, too. He wouldn't always be drowning in grief. Coming through the other side was within reach. If he could believe in a better future for someone as flawed as his mate, why not for himself?

Luc stood, running a hand through Dex's hair. "My life is already better."

But was it enough? Dex swallowed. "What about when I die? I can't... I'm not..."

"I know, my dear." Luc's fingers teased Dex's scalp. "Don't worry about me. I'd never ask you to give anything up, least of all the afterlife."

Dex choked down a sob before it escaped. "There's no other way?"

"I'll find one." Luc's eyes flared red, his hand tightening in Dex's hair. "I'll do everything in my power to create a world where we can bond and you can enter the Eternal Realm. I destroyed everything looking for you. I can put it back together, make it better than it was, so you don't have to lose anything. I'll try my best. I swear."

"Wait. It's possible?" Dex's voice shook. Nothing Luc had

said before suggested there were options, but Luc's grip was so secure that Dex's doubts scattered.

Luc's expression hardened. "I won't lie, the odds are against us, but there is a chance. We can have hope, and nothing can take that away. I'll do my best not to fail you again."

"Fail me? You couldn't. A minute ago, we were doomed, and now you're saying there's a chance. What else could I ask for?"

"You could ask for anything." Luc tugged Dex's head back and bent to kiss him, his tongue invading Dex's mouth. "Anything, my dear Dex."

He whimpered, mind straying to last night. "Make me yours."

The scent of smoke filled the air. "You're already mine. We'll figure out how to make it last."

DEX AND LUC sat at a café by the river on a patio overlooking the southern end of the riverwalk. They hadn't gone far from Luc's loft, and the all-day breakfast spread was exactly what Dex needed.

Being awake all night, getting tackled and claimed in the street before being made a prisoner gave him an appetite. Who knew?

Dex was on his second coffee and contemplating a third as he considered Luc's idea.

Luc hadn't wasted any time proving he was ready to make Dex his forever. He'd outlined his plan to approach the Eternal Realm and argue for the entrance of all who'd been damned unfairly, starting with witches and vampires. Dex had a momentary freak-out at vampires existing, but got over it quickly.

Luc's plan concluded with asking for entrance for bonded demons' mates, but would his logic be enough? There seemed to be no arguing with accepting witches or vampires into the rightful afterlife when they were as innocent as any human, and yet, they'd been denied all this time.

As Dex had said before, existing wasn't a crime, and anyone who claimed otherwise was the real villain, but villains didn't usually admit they were in the wrong and change because someone pointed it out.

"Why do mortality and magic have to be separate?" Dex couldn't figure out the big deal, no matter how hard he tried. "There's nothing wrong with having a less rigid, richer, more diverse universe, right?"

Luc cocked his head, his attention seeming to sharpen. "That's a very good point."

"So why is the separation so important? I get that humans were never *supposed* to have magic, but not reincarnating isn't inherently bad. Eternals have one life."

It was all so arbitrary. Rules for the sake of rules and nothing more. At least in Dex's eyes.

"Magic and mortality as opposing forces is a fact of the universe. A sacred balance that must be maintained."

"But is it?" Dex leaned forward, his coffee forgotten. "Nothing bad happened when the two forces combined. The world—the universe—didn't end."

"No." Luc stroked his chin. "There was no reaction at all, except for the council's anger."

"Maybe they aren't opposing forces at all. Who's to say magic and mortality were never supposed to combine? Who's to say *this* wasn't fate?"

"No one." Luc's eyes narrowed. He spoke slowly, as if thinking out loud. "Fate is an unknown. Perhaps the universe doesn't have to be defined by opposing forces. Maybe it never truly was."

"Exactly. Magic and mortality seemed to come together fine."

Luc stilled, coming to attention. "Which proves the two don't exist in a rigid binary. And if mortality and magic aren't inherent opposites, what is? Not even life and death sit in opposition with reincarnation and eternal life. What if it's not about balance at all? And if not, there's no reason that magic can't be in all realms, other than someone decided it was forbidden."

Dex's heart leapt as if he'd had that third coffee after all. "Agreed. And while we're asking questions, why can't Eternals be on Earth? Human souls exist in the Eternal Realm. It's not like the two realms balance each other either."

"True, though humans only exist in the realm of magic as souls. The mystical piece of humanity." Luc scowled, his brow creasing. "The council could claim that souls belong in the Eternal Realm while living humans—bound to demons as mates—don't."

Dex laughed. Never mind how arbitrary all these lines seemed; did Luc realize what he'd said? "So you're saying all humans—even me—have a mystical, *magical* piece inside us?"

"Yes." Luc's frown deepened. "Your soul is your essence. It transcends mortality."

"So magic was always a part of humanity. Always a part of this realm. Giving witches the power to cast spells didn't even bring magic to Earth. It was already here in a different form."

"Fuck." A laugh burst from Luc, and he covered his mouth. "You're right, Dex."

"I am?"

"Yes..." Understanding broke over Luc's face. "What you're saying is that everything I was taught about the sacred balance is a lie."

What a revelation, but Luc didn't seem upset. He seemed excited.

Did the Eternals in charge know the truth, or did they believe the lies they preached? Either way, Dex didn't see change coming easily. "Do you really think all you need to do is present an argument proving the council wrong? Surely they won't give in."

"Not without a fight. Not if it's this big. We need more. We need a show of force behind our argument. A consequence if they don't listen." Dark emotions twisted Luc's expression. "That's why I trapped everyone in Hell. To create a consequence. Maybe that isn't the way to go."

Dex grabbed Luc's hand. "It's not the same. Most demons did nothing wrong, and you still punished them. You regret it, and your hesitation proves you're different now. You're trying to stop unjust persecution. The council and the Eternals in charge aren't innocent. They're the ones punishing witches for existing. Any consequences will be more than deserved."

Luc's hard features softened, expression so tender that Dex's breath caught. "My fierce little mate. I can't argue with that. What would you suggest we do to them?"

A wave of energy filled Dex like he was ready to take the council on right this second. "What do they fear most?"

Luc's eyes flashed. "The same thing anyone in power fears."

21

———

LUCIFER

"I'm meeting another demon today to see if he'll support me," Luc said as Dex finished the last of his coffee. "Would you like to come with me?"

Dex set his cup aside. "Now?"

Luc pulled out his phone. "Yes. Onyx confirmed he's ready to see us."

Dex hesitated, readjusting the positioning of his cup. "You want me to come?"

"More than anything." Luc captured Dex's nervous hand. "Your support means the world, but if you don't want to meet more demons, especially ones who hate me, then I understand."

"You're going to ask someone who hates you to help?"

Luc shrugged. "If I didn't, I'd have no potential allies."

Dex's face fell. "Doesn't being hated bother you?"

Luc opened his mouth to deny it, but his mate deserved the more complicated truth. "Yes, it bothers me deeply, but I can't think about the love I lost or how I turned everyone against me without getting sucked into a very dark place. I can't dwell on it if I want to do anything about it, and if I don't do anything, it will always be this way."

Dex's hand tightened in his. "I'll come with you."

Luc raised Dex's hand and kissed his knuckles, taking great pleasure in the flush darkening Dex's cheeks.

He led Dex back to his loft, where they could take off from the roof.

Luc hadn't dared hope he'd have not one, but two people on his side, supporting him after everything. Onyx might grumble every step of the way, but Luc wasn't as afraid he would change his mind anymore. Onyx's fierce affection hadn't gone anywhere, even when Luc had trampled all over it.

And his mate. Dex's belief that he was redeemable pushed him to new heights. He wanted to be everything Dex saw in him. He could be good and loving, a positive force like he'd envisioned himself to be when he first had the idea to fall. An idea that hadn't been as horribly flawed as he'd believed for the past thousand years.

He hadn't been wrong to flee a controlling society.

Luc had questioned many things in his life. Challenging authority had always been a point of pride. But he'd never questioned the fundamental facts defining his world.

Dex's fresh eyes had opened Luc to new truths. Pulled back blinders that Luc's mind hadn't even conceived of. Luc would change the realms for Dex, but he couldn't have done it without him.

Magic had always existed on Earth. Mortality and mystical forces had always been combined. The fabric of the universe had never been binary. It wasn't some delicate balance that needed to be guarded. Something that Luc could ruin. Why couldn't beings exist in many forms on a spectrum of life?

"Thank you." Luc cupped Dex's cheeks. Wind swirled around them on the exposed rooftop, wrapping them in scents of earth and fire.

Dex's brow quirked. "For coming with you? No problem."

"Not only that." Luc's fingers tightened. His fire swelled, chest tightening and eyes burning, but not with flame. Luc blinked, and a tear fell hot down his cheek. "For showing me the truth."

Dex gripped Luc's sweater, tugging him closer. "What truth? That magic was always here?"

"Yes." The tension in Luc's chest released, and a lightness radiated outward, filling him with intense relief. "For millennia, I believed I'd led the way to destroying the sacred balance of the universe. It was one of my greatest mistakes. The one that triggered all my other deepest regrets. The one that proved I was wrong to fall. That I was wrong at my core. But it wasn't a mistake. I couldn't have destroyed a sacred balance that doesn't exist. Coming to Earth wasn't inherently wrong. The rise of witches wasn't a blight on humanity. You called this a richer, more diverse world."

"It is." Dex's determination could have taken Luc to his knees.

He stood strong for his mate. "That's the truth you showed me. The explanation of the realms I was raised with is just that, an explanation, not an inherent or irrefutable fact. I didn't ruin something that can never be fixed. I'm not worthless."

A heavy weight lifted from Luc and crumbled into dust. He wasn't suddenly perfect, all his actions excused, but the guilt that had poisoned so much was gone, and without it, Luc could see a path to redemption.

He could make up for all of his real mistakes. Atone and humble himself to the people he'd wronged. And one day, he might be free of it all. Nothing had been so deeply destroyed that he couldn't try to undo it.

Dex embraced him, and he buried his face in Dex's hair. "You're not worthless, Luc. You never should have believed that breaking the Eternal Realm's rules made you less than."

"No," he agreed. He shouldn't have.

Luc had still done bad things and gone against his own morals. But he would never act like that again. Nothing was ever so ruined that you should stop trying to be better. And it was never too late.

Luc landed on Onyx's roof, with Dex cradled in his arms.

Onyx tapped his foot, arms crossed, and scowling, but his pissy look cracked as Luc set Dex on his feet. "You didn't say you were bringing anyone."

"I'm not bringing *anyone*. I brought my mate."

Onyx's eyes widened. "You told him?"

"I'm right here." Dex gave a breathy little laugh. "I guess that answers my question of whether everyone knew."

Onyx turned to Nico, who waited patiently beside him, a smile breaking out on his face.

Luc's heart constricted. Onyx was happy for him, overjoyed even.

A silent conversation seemed to pass between Onyx and Nico, and when their attention landed back on Luc, they were both grinning.

"I can change the name of the group chat back." Onyx dug his phone out of his pocket.

Nico laughed. "*That's* your first priority?"

"Shut up," Onyx muttered without malice.

Luc didn't ask.

"How are you feeling?" Nico asked Dex.

"Good." Dex shifted closer to Luc, Nico's attention following the movement.

"You're bringing Dex to help?"

"Obviously." Luc wrapped his arm around his mate. "Dex's insight is key."

Nico gave a small nod as if he approved, and Luc found it encouraging rather than an irritating reminder of judgment, as he might have before.

"Done." Onyx pocketed his phone and flung himself on Dex, hugging him tight. "Welcome to the mate club."

A surprised laugh burst from Dex, and he hugged Onyx back.

Luc's cheeks ached from smiling so hard. Onyx may have never longed for his mate the way he had, but he clearly loved everyone's mates as much as he loved his brothers.

They parted, and Onyx narrowed his eyes at Luc, a petulant growl filling the air. Then, like something snapped, Onyx flung himself on Luc and wrapped him in a crushing hug. If he'd been human, Luc would have popped.

"Stupid, miserable brother," Onyx growled. "You better be happy."

Luc ruffled Onyx's hair, and his growl turned to a snarl. He lurched back, fixing his hair, his eyes burning.

Luc shook his head, warm fuzzy tendrils enveloping him. "Love you, brother."

Onyx's face softened, color creeping into his cheeks. He sniffed, his nose lifting. "You better. Let's get going. Nico..." He turned and grabbed his mate, pulling him close before scooping the bigger man into his arms.

The warm fuzzies continued to spread. Onyx's hug—his love—was a gift Luc hadn't believed he'd receive again.

He gathered Dex into his arms, and they flew across the city. Luc could face any task with these men at his side.

"Didn't think I'd ever be back here," Luc said as he landed beside Onyx in a familiar courtyard.

"Right?" Onyx set Nico on his feet. "Seems rude to ask us to meet at the place he held us captive."

"Captive?" Dex gripped Luc's arm.

"Don't worry. Valac agreed to a truce. We're safe." He wouldn't have brought Dex otherwise.

Not that Luc had spoken directly to the demon who'd planned to permanently kill him. Onyx had arranged this, but Luc trusted Onyx with his life. And his mate's. Onyx was good to his core and wanted this to work out as much as Luc did.

His love ran deep, and Luc wished he'd never taken it for granted or taken advantage of it.

Luc looked around. The courtyard was deserted, as bare as he remembered, nothing but dirt and drab buildings on all sides.

A door to the right opened, and Valac strolled out, his white wings folded at his back, and gray horns standing tall. The demon, Isaac, followed close behind. He'd helped Valac imprison Luc and Onyx. The others in their gang were absent, at least for now.

Dex pressed close to his side, and Luc settled his hand on his mate's lower back.

Valac stopped squarely in front of Luc, his arms crossed. "I hadn't planned to take this meeting."

Luc swallowed a cutting retort. "I appreciate you changing your mind."

Valac rolled his eyes. "That's got nothing to do with you."

Onyx sighed like he'd had enough a century ago. "Yes, yes. Animosity is running high. We're all well aware that none of us are friends. Can we move on?"

Valac grunted. "Fine. But only because doing the right thing is more important than anyone's personal feelings."

Luc cut a look at Onyx. He'd said he'd kept the details of their plan quiet when contacting Valac. How did Valac know how important their quest was?

"I was suspicious when I heard you wanted to meet," Valac went on. "Surely you weren't trying to rally supporters so soon after claiming you weren't after power. And you wouldn't come to me with any bullshit. This stunk of a trap."

Couldn't he see it wasn't a trap now that they were here? "This isn't a trick of any kind. I can explain."

"Yeah." Onyx rushed to Luc's defense. "I'd have given you more information if you'd asked."

"Would you?" Valac cocked his head. "It doesn't matter. I doubt you'd have brought your mate to anything that might go wrong." His gaze strayed to Nico, then to Dex. "Who's the human?"

Luc swallowed a growl, his hand flexing on Dex's back. It wouldn't do to snarl and egg Valac on. He said calmly, "Don't be rude. Humans aren't beneath us."

Valac's lips parted as if in shock. "My apologies." He tipped his head to Dex. "I didn't expect any humans to be in on this, that's all I meant."

"I'm surprised as well."

Luc had been so focused on the demon in front of him, he hadn't noticed anyone else enter the courtyard.

Rowan strode toward them, the same three companions he'd kept close in their previous meeting at his heel. The vampire went straight for Nico, and the two embraced.

"What are you doing here?" Nico asked.

"Valac called to warn me that Lucifer was up to something, and I said I had a good idea of what it was."

Luc hadn't heard anything from Rowan or his coven. If he'd decided against helping, convincing Valac would be more of a challenge.

"You could have told me," Nico chided.

Rowan huffed. "Where's the fun in that?" He turned his attention to Luc. "I'm in. The four of us"—he gestured to his companions—"will go with you to the gateway, but no one else from my coven is permitted. I won't risk them."

Luc bowed his head. "I understand. Your support is no small offer."

"No, it's not. But this is too big to ignore. I can't pass this by and claim I stand for what's right." The vampire's impeccable posture became even straighter, his hand smoothing the front of his pristine suit.

"So you already know what we're planning?" Onyx asked Valac and Isaac.

They nodded, though Valac added. "I'm not sure I believe it."

"Why?" Dex asked, and all eyes turned to him.

"Rotten people don't do good deeds."

"He's not rotten." Dex's voice didn't waver, and pride filled Luc to the brim.

Pity transformed Valac's stern face. "Do you even know who you're standing beside?"

Dex wrapped an arm around Luc. "My mate."

Valac's eyes narrowed. "Is that supposed to sway me?"

Luc tensed. He was so tired. He'd schemed for so damn long and would be happy never to do it again. "I'm not here to sway anyone, and neither is Dex. You don't have to help, Valac. I'd like to show that demons support everyone's right to enter the Eternal Realm, but it's more important to have vampires and witches make a stand. We're doing this for them and for our mates, and because we want to."

"I believe witches and vampires should enter the Eternal Realm," Valac said, like he was offended Luc might think otherwise.

"Gee, thanks," Nico said.

There was a tense moment of silence, where Valac looked distinctly guilty.

Rowan prowled forward, challenge hardening his features as he fixed a glowing stare on Valac. "Will you join us, or are old grudges too strong?"

Valac growled. "I told you, I stand for what's right. Same as you. But I don't believe the Devil does." He jabbed a finger at Luc.

"Then let him prove it," Dex said.

22

DEX

Dex arrived at Ollie's with a large pizza, nerves eating away at him.

"Yes, you have food. Thank god." Ollie pulled Dex inside like he couldn't be happier.

"Bad hangover?" Dex asked, trying to relax.

"No, I don't get them now that I'm bonded to Dante. But I've done nothing but game all day and seriously need to refuel."

Ollie flopped onto the couch, and Dex set the pizza on the coffee table. Ollie didn't hesitate to dig in.

"Dante's not here?" Dex had expected him and Harper, but no one was around.

"He went home half an hour ago. We wanted to give Harper and Ash the day in the big house, but Harper will be home soon."

"The big house?"

"Dante and Ash's place. It's this massive mansion in the nature reserve. Dante's gaming room his unreal. We'll have to show you."

A mansion in a nature reserve seemed contradictory, but

Dex didn't ask. Even if Luc didn't have an evil lair, it seemed strange, lair-like living situations might be a demon thing.

"I'd be down to check it out. I still haven't made it online with you and Dante. Text me next time and I'll hop on."

"Deal." Ollie grinned around a huge bite of pizza.

Dex's stomach was too twisted to eat. "I need to talk to you."

"Sure." Ollie wiped his mouth on one of the many napkins Dex had brought, and sat up straighter.

Fuck, he had to say it. No more fluffing around. "I've been seeing Luc."

There was a beat of silence, and Dex's chest tightened.

Ollie grabbed his hand. "That's okay, Dex. You don't have to say it like you're admitting something you shouldn't be doing."

"I know. And I'm not as conflicted as I was, but it's still weird to talk about with you. I know I'm Luc's mate. Is that why you're okay with it? Why you said to call him?" Dex didn't want Ollie feeling obligated to forgive Luc because of him.

Ollie didn't seem upset, but he hesitated, and Dex's doubts rose. "That's not why I said to call."

"Then why?" Dex was desperate to know.

Ollie turned serious. "Luc being your mate showed me a different side of *him*. Luc wouldn't be fated to you if he were all bad. Being your mate means there has to be something in him to forgive. It's fated. No one destined for you could be unforgivably evil. You proved that Luc is...or has the potential to be good. And he proved it by telling me he'd let you go to the afterlife. There's more to Luc than I know, even if what I know is terrible, and in the end, it's fated for the good to come out on top."

Dex's head spun with the force of Ollie's determination. "You're putting a ton of trust in fate."

Ollie shrugged, matter-of-fact rather than dismissive. "I'm all in. Fate gave me Dante. It showed me that I can face my own shit and have the life and relationship I always wanted. Besides, I want this for you. I want you forever, Dex. You're meant to be a part of our group."

"Ollie, it's not that simple." Dex hoped it would all work out, but there was no guarantee. Luc could do everything in his power, and the Eternal Realm could still decide that mates were banned and force Dex to choose.

Ollie scowled. "I know. But Luc promised me he'd try to fix it. I told him to, and he listened to me. That's why I'm going to forgive him. He's giving me you, and you're worth facing anything, no matter how hard."

Dex's chest tightened. "Fuck. I'd never ask you to forgive him."

"No, you wouldn't, but I can still do it for you if I want to." Ollie grabbed another piece of pizza like that was the end of it. "Why don't you tell me about Luc. Why do you like him? He must not be awful if he's got your attention."

Dex laughed. Not awful was practically a glowing endorsement under the circumstances.

He grabbed a slice of pizza, planning to tell Ollie how sweet Luc was. How he offered to help store his parents' belongings. But what came out was, "Has Dante ever bitten you?"

Ollie choked on his bite of pizza, and Dex thumped his back until he stopped coughing and cleared his throat.

"Fuck yeah, he's bitten me." Ollie's growing smile turned feral. "I'm guessing Luc showed you how good it feels?"

Dex nodded, trying to hide his own smile and failing.

Ollie leaned closer. "Have you ever bitten back?"

Dex's mind ground to a halt. It had never occurred to him. "Should I?"

"Definitely. It's incredible."

Dex's face flamed. Biting Luc was intriguing, but he preferred to be at Luc's mercy. Being bitten appealed because he had no control. It freed him, and that wouldn't be the case if he bit Luc. Dex didn't want to do something so domineering. Unless Luc ordered him to. If Luc made Dex bite him, if it was something he wanted and demanded, then Dex could see himself trying it.

He cleared his throat. "I'll keep it in mind. But it's more than sex between us."

Dex told Ollie all the important things, leaving nothing out, and every soft piece of Luc he shared seemed to bridge the gap that had been growing between him and Ollie. He found himself talking about his parents, Luc's support, and how bad the last year had been, and the headspace he'd gotten stuck in.

Ollie grabbed Dex's hand. "I didn't know things had been so hard for you."

Dex pulled away. "That's because I hid it."

"Why?"

Shit, Ollie sounded hurt, and Dex couldn't meet his eyes. "I didn't want to burden you."

Ollie made a small, sad sound. "It wouldn't have."

"I'm sorry. I don't mean that as a guilt trip. Holding back was a me problem. I didn't want to face how bad things were, and telling you meant I had to stop denying it to myself."

Ollie seemed to understand. "I'm glad you told someone. And that you're moving out soon. I want to help any way I can, Dex."

"I know." He pulled Ollie into a hug. "You've helped me so much. Asking for more was too hard."

"Then I'm especially glad you have a mate."

Dex hugged him tighter. "Even Lucifer?"

Ollie pulled back, biting his lip. "I can't believe I'm saying this, but yes. He'll help you and do anything for you the way Dante would for me. Now, let's game. I can't think anymore today. I may not be hung over but I didn't get a lot of sleep."

Dex laughed and grabbed a controller. Sounded good to him.

THAT NIGHT IN BED, Dex's phone vibrated as he settled in to sleep. He flicked the light on and checked the message.

LUC:

How was your evening?

DEX:

Exactly what I needed.

LUC:

Good. I wanted to check in after everything that happened today.

DEX:

With Valac?

LUC:

That, and us being mates.

Aww. Luc looked after him like no one else ever had. Dex smiled goofily to himself and called Luc.

He answered on the first ring.

"What is it?" Concern filled Luc's voice.

"Nothing bad. I couldn't be bothered typing."

Luc laughed. "I thought young people didn't like talking on the phone."

"Oh my god, could you sound any older?"

"Probably."

"True. And you're right. I'd never call Ollie, but this seemed like an important conversation. And I like your voice."

"You like my voice?" Luc sounded smug. "Good to know. So, how are you?"

"I feel better than before I asked if we were mates."

"So do I. It's a relief to have it all out in the open, but I wanted to see if anything had changed now that you've had more time to think."

Changed how? Dex felt more settled. Less doomed. Less overwhelmed. "Nothing's changed. I'm good. Better than good. Happy. I even talked to Ollie about it, which I'd been avoiding. He said you'll take care of me."

Luc sucked in a breath. "He did?"

"Yeah. Why? Is he wrong?" Dex teased.

"Of course not. Ollie is a very unique human being. I don't know if anyone else would see things the way he does."

"Right? He's the best."

Luc chuckled softly. "He is." There was a pause. "Since all is well, I have a few more things I'd like to check in on."

Dex snuggled further into his blankets. Being cared for soothed him down to his soul. "Like what?"

"How does our hunt seem now that it's been a little longer?"

Dex's body heated. "Like the best night of my life. I want to do it again."

Luc rumbled. "Me too. There are so many potential hunting grounds to play in."

Dex moaned softly.

"Patience, Dex. We'll get to it."

"Okay." He'd gladly wait, even if immediate gratification tempted him.

"That brings me to the other thing I'd like to check. Have you been good for me?" Luc's tone was heavy with meaning.

"Yes," Dex said urgently. "I haven't come or touched myself even though I thought about it in the shower."

"Good boy."

Dex shivered, his cock stirring. "What would happen if I wasn't good?"

Luc's voice dropped low, his words hard as steel. "I'd be very disappointed."

Dex's stomach lurched. "You wouldn't spank me?" His breath hitched as he imagined it, and the sinking sensation disappeared.

"Not when it sounds like you're eager for it. If you want to be spanked because you'll enjoy it, we can do that, but not as a punishment."

"Okay."

"I don't want to punish you for disobeying me, Dex." Luc's hard tone became tinged with something more urgent. "I won't spank you unless it's strictly for fun. Serious corporal punishment leaves a bad taste in my mouth."

Fuck, Dex hadn't even considered that, but it should have been obvious. Punishing Dex could trigger all the things in Luc's past he was trying to move away from, and might make him feel bad about himself and what they were doing.

Luc continued, "Don't mistake me, I'll be very disappointed if you don't obey. Controlling your orgasms pleases me deeply, and I expect you to please me."

"I will," Dex promised. "I want to please you."

All Dex needed was to be sure that Luc cared if he got off by himself or not. If the command was empty, what was the point? But showing he cared didn't have to be through punishment.

"I know you want to please me," Luc said, as tender as he had been stern. "You already have. But if you fail, I'll let you know that I expect better, and you'll have to try harder. If you do, I'd rather reward you for being good. Does that work for you?"

"That works. I wasn't planning on disappointing you, but I wondered what would happen." Dex hated the idea of disappointing Luc, enough to make him want to obey. More than avoiding punishment would have.

"Of course you wondered. If we're going to continue on like this, dealing with disobedience has to be addressed. I just thought we'd ease into it."

"I'm feeling very eased."

Luc laughed. "In that case, I'd like you to touch yourself until you're as close to coming as you can stand, then stop."

Dex sucked in a breath. "Right now?"

"Yes. Unless playing over the phone is unappealing."

Unappealing. Luc was funny sometimes. "It's not."

Luc purred down the line. "Get some lube and make it feel good. Don't try to be quiet."

Dex shoved off his boxer briefs and grabbed the bottle of lube from under his bed. "I'm hard and I haven't even touched myself yet."

"Mm. So desperate."

He really was. Dex dribbled lube on his cock and fisted it, sighing in relief. He had to be careful or he'd fuck this up. He stroked slowly, teasing his cockhead. When he was sure he wouldn't blow, he quickened his pace, his breathing growing heavy.

"I can hear each slick stroke," Luc purred in his ear.

It couldn't be that loud through the phone. "Is that demon hearing?"

"It is, dirty boy. If I were there, I'd smell your arousal building, hear your little heart fluttering. All for me."

Dex moaned and dropped his hand.

"So close already?" Luc teased.

"I told you I like your voice."

"You did indeed. Can you give me a little more? I was starting to enjoy myself."

Dex bit his lip and gripped his cock. The first stroke had his head falling back, and he moaned. "I'm too close."

"Then wipe yourself clean and put your underwear back on. The ones I bought for you."

"Okay."

Dex did as he was told, bringing the phone with him to the bathroom. The damp cloth was unpleasant against his cock, but not enough that his erection deflated. He washed his hands and hurried back across the hall.

"I'm all clean," he announced as he put the black boxer briefs on.

"Good boy. Are you still hard?"

"Yeah." Dex covered his hot face with his arm.

"Don't do anything naughty. I'm going to get myself off in the shower. You have a good night. Sleep well."

Dex whined. "I will. Thank you. Good night, Luc."

When the phone disconnected, Luc's presence stayed with him.

23

LUCIFER

Luc flew to the nature reserve on the cliffs overlooking Shearwater Landing. The web of illusion Dante, Ash, and Onyx had created around the sanctuary couldn't repel him any more than it had when he'd first come around. Not even after he'd given back their magic.

But that didn't mean Luc could get inside.

He hovered above the clifftop, invisible to mortal onlookers, but not to the shearwaters. He revealed himself to the birds on purpose, and a group quickly surrounded him, squawking at deafening levels.

"Dante, I'd like to talk to you and Ash," he said to a bird.

It screeched in his face and flew off.

A few minutes later, Dante and Ash emerged from the tree-tops, sunlight glittering off their wings.

"What do you want?" Dante growled, his curling lip giving Onyx a run for his money.

"To talk to you. I don't have your phone numbers."

Ash tutted. "That's not a mistake. Go away."

"No. I'll respect your boundaries, but first I need to tell you what I'm planning." Luc refused to do this through Onyx. It wasn't the same as getting support from the vampires or Valac.

"Planning?" Ash shot a look at Dante. "You can't be serious."

"If it was anything bad, I wouldn't tell you—"

Dante bowled over him. "We don't trust you, Luc. Finding your mate doesn't change that. Nothing comes at face value with you."

"For a long time, that was true. But you'll see that's not how I operate anymore."

"Or we won't see, and be much happier for it." Ash turned away and flew back the way he'd come.

"Everyone else knows." It was a desperate, manipulative move, but Luc wasn't giving up easily. He'd respect their wishes to stay away once he had this off his chest.

As expected, Ash swung around. "Everyone who?"

"Onyx, Dex, Valac, Rowan."

"Rowan?" Ash glared from Luc to Dante in confusion. "The vampire?"

"Yes, Nico's friend. It goes without saying, Nico knows as well. And Dex will probably tell Ollie, if he hasn't already."

Dante's nostrils flared. "Fine, talk."

It was too much to hope that Dante would lower his protections and let Luc land. He'd have to do this hovering there like an overgrown bird.

Luc let his bitterness go. "I'm sorry."

Dante made a rude sound. "That's what Dex is going to tell Ollie?"

"No. I'll get to that. But I can't until I come to you as the man who used to be your friend. I am so deeply sorry for what I did to both of you. For not talking to you. Or listening to you. For disrespecting you. For giving up and not caring about you because I'd stopped caring about myself. And for hurting you in every conceivable way. I was wrong to treat you the way I did. It was selfish and cruel. When you're ready—if you ever are—I'll make amends however you deem fit."

There was a long silence save for the squawking shearwaters.

Ash hovered as unmoving as possible while keeping himself in the air.

Dante sighed. "Ollie already said he'd forgive you if you gave him Dex."

"And I'm humbled by the chance he's given me, but this isn't about Ollie. This is about the three of us. I hurt you, too, and I'm sorry."

"I never dreamed you'd apologize." Ash's tone was flat and almost baffled. "If you did, I assumed it'd be fake. But this is real. I don't even doubt it anymore. You seem different than you were in the tower and when we rescued you from Valac."

Luc flew closer. "I am different. Dex believes I can be better. I believe I can be better. None of us are irredeemable. The Fallen didn't inexorably destroy anything. I wronged you all, but it's not unfixable."

Dante closed the remaining gap between them. "What do you mean?"

Luc explained everything he and Dex had discussed, emotion giving his voice a frantic edge, words tumbling from him like a cleansing rain.

Ash's eyes blazed. "Magic was here all along? It can't be that simple."

"Why not?"

He growled. "Because if it's all arbitrary, then we did nothing wrong."

Luc clasped Ash's shoulder, and Ash didn't pull away. "You did nothing wrong."

Ash let out a long breath. He'd held on to a great deal of

guilt even though he wasn't responsible for witches any more than Dante, Onyx, or countless others.

Luc's heart ached. "You saw something bad in yourself that didn't exist, Ash. Falling wasn't wrong, and that unworthiness was never deserved."

Ash's eyes widened. "How did you know I...? I never told you how I felt."

"I know you, brother. I heard it in your voice. Felt it in your presence. I had the same judgments lurking in my mind. We've always been similar in this way."

Ash grunted, the sound distinctly affectionate. "We have. We're two sides of the same self-critical coin. But we can't stand for this. They can't keep holding morality over our heads when there isn't any point."

"The point is power," Dante said heavily. "The universal balance is the justification for the council's existence. For the regulation of mates and Eternal children."

"Then it sounds like their time has run out." Ash clasped Luc's arm. "Tell us what you're planning."

Luc's PHONE vibrated as he flew back into the city.

DEX:

Can I see you today?

LUC:

That depends. Would you still want to see me if I told you that you're not coming no matter what?

Dex's reply came through immediately.

DEX:

Yes. Obviously. Come over to my place?

Luc's fire smoldered. His mate was inviting him into the dreaded condo. Allowing Luc to see what hurt him most. Trusting him. And he didn't even complain about his denial.

What a wonderful mate.

LUC:

I'll be there soon.

After detouring to his loft to grab a shirt, Luc stopped in the bakery on the ground floor of Dex's building and bought a selection of treats before they closed.

Dex greeted him at his front door, hands shoved in his pockets and shoulders hunched. "So this is it."

Luc entered, scanning the family pictures framed on the walls. "It smells like you."

Dex snorted. "As long as I don't stink, I'll take it."

"You smell better than any flower. Any perfume."

Dex's cheeks darkened. "At least I don't smell aroused."

"Not yet." Luc flashed his eyes, fire sparking.

"Before that happens, I'll give you the tour. That door there is my parents' room. This is the bathroom and my room. And through here"—Dex ushered Luc out of the hallway—"is the living-kitchen area."

The condo may have smelled of Dex, but it didn't feel like him. It looked like a family home, mature, and decorated by someone who liked cool colors and ornamental figurines. Everything was tidy and pleasant, but it wasn't Dex.

Luc set the box of treats on the counter separating the kitchen from the living area.

"What's that?"

"They're for later." Luc pulled Dex close. "Thank you for inviting me into your home."

Dex looked at the floor. "I figured I should show you before I move. I put an offer on a place, and they've accepted. All that's left is finishing the paperwork."

Luc squeezed Dex's shoulders. "Congratulations. Has your condo sold?"

"We're going to see if there are any more offers from the last open home, and then pick one. I've had a few already, and they all more than cover the cost of the new place."

"Wonderful. How do you feel?"

"Sad and excited. It's a weird combo."

"There's space for both emotions." Luc cupped the back of Dex's neck. "Tell me what you're most excited about."

Dex's expression brightened. "Decorating my new place. I need to start scoping out estate sales for furniture. I don't want too many mass-produced pieces."

"I'm sure Onyx can help you find what you're looking for. Have you seen his house? It's spectacular."

"No, I've never been to his place, but I'll ask him, as long as he sticks to my budget. Harper seems to have a knack for thrifting, too. Between the three of us, we'll figure it out." Dex hesitated. "Would you want to help?"

Luc's heart fluttered. "I'd love to, but check with Harper first. I haven't apologized to him, not directly at least."

Dex smiled encouragingly, like he believed Luc could gain Harper's forgiveness. "We've got time to work it out."

"We do." Luc covered Dex's lips with his.

He'd be eternally grateful for Dex and his open heart. Luc burned to create a life with him. Build a home together. Keep Dex close and watch their lives blossom.

Dex's thoughts seemed to be going in a different direction. His cock hardened against Luc.

"What's this?" Luc cupped Dex's bulge and squeezed.

Dex moaned, his earthy scent flooding the air. "Nothing. I'll be good. I promise."

"You won't beg to come?"

Dex shivered. "I'll try not to. No promises about begging. But I won't come. You told me I wasn't allowed. An orgasm isn't why I wanted to see you."

"I know. It isn't why I wanted to see you either, but now that I'm here, I want to play with you. See what I can give you other than an orgasm."

Dex gripped Luc's shoulders. "Can I be your plaything? Like before."

"Is that what you want, my dear?" Luc stroked Dex's cock until he was rolling his hips into the motion.

"Yes, Luc." His little mate was breathy and so eager. He positively melted under Luc's touch.

Luc pulled his hand away, eliciting a sweet whimper. "Kneel for me so I can use you."

Dex's face flushed, his eyes wide with excitement. He stepped back and got to his knees, clumsily finding his position. "Like this?"

Luc clasped Dex's shoulder and pulled him taller, so his ass didn't rest on his heels. "There we go. Look how pretty you are."

Dex ducked his head like he was trying to hide his smile. That wouldn't do.

Luc guided his face forward until their eyes met. There. Luc's fire ignited beneath his skin. "What did I promise last time we had sex?"

Dex's posture stiffened. "I...I'm not sure."

"That's okay. You weren't exactly in a state to be taking notes. I said you could touch me next time."

"Oh, right. Can I?" Dex's hands twitched where they rested on his thighs.

"You may. I'll always keep my promises. You can touch me as much as you want, but you can't touch yourself. Not even one stroke."

Dex nodded eagerly.

Luc pulled his sweater over his head and tossed it toward the couch. He released his horns and wings, keeping them tucked tightly in the small space.

Dex gasped, and Luc extended the tip of a wing toward him. He stroked Luc's feathers, his touch delicate. Reverent.

A low purr started in Luc's chest. He took the opportunity to undo his belt and lower his pants and underwear, and Dex's attention immediately found his cock.

His gaze lifted to Luc's face. "I can touch?"

Luc's pulse thrummed. "You may."

Dex clasped Luc's semi-hard length, stroking him as he fondled Luc's balls. Luc released his tail, the base tingling as Dex coaxed him to hardness.

Luc ran a hand through Dex's hair, stroking him softly before taking hold. He moaned as Luc's grip tightened. "Kiss my cock."

Dex leaned forward and kissed Luc's cockhead, licking the drop of precum beading at his slit, his eyes fluttering closed, and Luc's possessiveness flared. His mate already seemed to be falling into the pleasure of his command.

"Good boy," Luc murmured, pulling Dex's head back. "You can touch me however you like with your hands, but since you're my plaything, I'm going to use your mouth for my pleasure. Shall we see if you can take it?"

"Yes. Please." Dex opened his mouth and waited.

Luc brought his tail around and stroked Dex's cheek with the tip, then traced his plush lips. His tongue poked out and caressed Luc's tail.

He hummed and pressed his tail into his mate's mouth. "Suck."

Dex closed his lips around it and hollowed his cheeks, teasing the tip with his tongue. Luc groaned in appreciation. The tip wasn't as sensitive as the base, but the sensation was still divine.

He pushed farther into Dex's mouth, wiggling his tail against Dex's tongue. He squeaked and sucked hander, his hands traveling from Luc's thighs to trace his abs.

Luc pumped his tail in and out, going a little deeper each time, the tip slim and easy to take. Luc hit the back of Dex's throat, and he sputtered, but hardly faltered as he sucked.

"Good, Dex. So good. You'll do nicely for my cock."

A long, low sound of longing vibrated around Luc's tail.

Luc withdrew, snaking his tail down Dex's body, smearing spit along his face and neck. Luc teased each nipple through Dex's shirt, then traced the hard outline of his cock.

Dex's hands gripped Luc's hips. "Please."

"Please, what? Let you come?"

He shook his head. "Please fuck my mouth. Use me."

Luc smiled, his fangs lengthening. His tail abandoned Dex's straining cock and encircled his throat, not squeezing, but wrapping all the way around like a collar.

"*Luc*," Dex moaned, his pupils blowing wide. "Please."

"I've got you." Luc tightened the hand in Dex's hair. "I'm going to use you, don't worry. If you need me to stop, tap my leg twice."

Dex blinked.

"Did you hear me?"

"Yes." Dex nodded, but Luc held him so tight by the hair, he hardly budged.

"Tell me what you'll do if you need me to stop."

"I'll tap your leg twice."

"Show me."

Dex double-tapped Luc's thigh.

"Good boy. Now open up."

Dex opened his mouth and stuck out his tongue. Luc fisted his cock, brought it to Dex's lips, and pushed inside. Dex's eyelids fluttered, and he moaned around Luc, his hands running over Luc's abs and chest.

Luc let go of his cock, tangled both hands in Dex's hair, and thrust steadily as he'd done with his tail. He went deeper on each stroke, but took his time. He wanted to savor this.

Dex's wide-eyed gaze didn't leave his face.

Luc hit the back of Dex's throat, and he held his cock there. Dex's muscles spasmed around him deliciously. "That's it."

He pulled back and thrust forward, faster now, steadily increasing his pace.

"What a good mouth," Luc praised. "You know exactly how to take my cock."

Dex whined and choked as Luc filled him to the brink.

"Good little mate. What a perfect hole for me."

Dex's body shuddered, and his hands flexed on Luc's ass.

Luc thrust harder. "You like being my hole? My plaything?"

Dex gave a strangled sound of pleasure, and Luc fucked him faster, reveling at the sight of spit dripping from his mate's mouth, his eyes half closed. Dex tugged on Luc's ass like he couldn't get enough. He was a perfect picture with Luc's tail around his neck, skin slick with saliva, face flushed, and mouth hot and wet.

He was all Luc's. He owned Dex, even if they weren't bonded. Luc's to play with and take to new heights. Luc's to nurture and love.

Luc's moans filled the air. "Touch the base of my tail, and I'll give you my cum. Fill my eager little hole."

Dex scrambled for Luc's tail and wrapped both hands

around the base to stroke the smooth skin. Pleasure sparked, and Luc came in his mate's mouth, seed spilling over Dex's lips and down his chin. Dex sucked hard, doing his best to swallow what Luc gave him.

He growled. Nothing had ever brought him as much pleasure as marking Dex. Having his mate in the palm of his hand. Giving him what he wanted in a way that satisfied Luc down to his soul.

Luc didn't pull out. He left his softening cock in Dex's mouth, and Dex sucked the tip in rhythmic, almost meditative swallows. The scent of his arousal hung thick in the air.

"So good, Dex. You've pleased me so very much."

Dex whined and closed his eyes tight, sucking softly and seeming to bask in Luc's approval.

At last, Luc withdrew and inspected his mate from head to toe. "Did you come in your pants?"

"No." Dex's eyes flew open. "I was good."

Luc didn't doubt him, but gave a sly smile anyway. "Show me."

Dex's hands went for his pants without hesitation, and Luc soared as if he were high. Dex wanted so badly to be good.

He carefully loosened his joggers and pushed them down, his underwear too, and exposed his hard and leaking, yet unsatisfied cock.

"Yes, you were good. And so pretty for me." Luc licked his lips. "You can put yourself away now."

Dex bit his lip and fixed his clothes.

"I appreciate you not playing with that needy cock."

"Thank you," Dex said, breathless.

Luc unwound his tail from Dex's neck and scooped him into his arms, carefully moving to the couch, wary of the pants around his ankles. He settled into the cushions with Dex on his lap, and he lay his head on Luc's shoulder. Luc gently wiped the remaining spit and cum from Dex's face. He was still hard, but Luc didn't touch him. He'd been teased enough for now.

"I'm impressed."

Dex lifted his head. "You are?"

Luc hummed. "You were everything I needed, and you didn't give in to your own desire."

"I want to please you. I totally gave in to that desire, and got exactly what I needed out of it, so I'm not exactly being selfless," Dex whispered.

"You don't have to be selfless. I want you to indulge the desire to please me. How could I not? You have to like this, too." Otherwise, Luc would feel nothing but inconsiderate for using Dex like a toy.

"I do. It's so fucking hot." Dex lay his head back down. "I didn't know if I'd make it without coming."

"But you did, and I'm so proud."

Dex choked on a strangled little moan.

"You like making me proud?"

He nodded into Luc's neck. "Yeah, I do."

"You make me proud in so many ways. By being my perfect fucktoy, and by being a strong mate who believes in me. By facing your fears, and letting me see you. I'm proud of all of you, Dex."

"Not coming shouldn't make me feel capable. Especially when everything has been so overwhelming for so long, and I feel like I can't get anything right. But it does."

"Of course it does." Luc shook his head. "You're very capable. Whether it's accomplishing something big or small."

Dex laughed, the sounds soft like a tinkling bell. "I like the way you think. You get me."

Luc kissed the top of Dex's head. "We see each other's true selves, and it's fucking magical."

Dex laughed again. "So magical."

Luc kissed his lips. "Now, are you ready for your reward?"

24

———

DEX

"Reward for what?" Dex asked.

He was floating, the ache in his cock a distant feeling. Luc's hard body soothed him, and his praise gave Dex something deeper than an orgasm.

"For being good and not coming."

Tingles wound through Dex. "What kind of reward are you talking about?"

"A special one. You won't always get it, but when I deem it appropriate, you'll earn something extra."

Dex sat up, desire sharpening his senses. "What is it?"

Luc's red lips stretched around his fangs. "A special bite. Anywhere you like."

Excitement and dismay warred in Dex. "If you bite me, I'm gonna come. Then I'll fail."

Luc gripped Dex's chin between his thumb and forefinger. "No, you won't. You know how to be good for me. You've earned a reward. I won't push you. I'm done playing for now."

Luc's bite was akin to getting his prostate pegged. Dex couldn't take that in his current state, but he trusted Luc. If he said he was done playing, then he was.

"Okay. How is this going to work?"

That proud look from earlier filled Luc's face. "Holding back a little when I bite changes the sensation. All you have to do is tell me where you'd like my fangs."

That was easy enough. "Will you bite my ass?"

Luc chuckled. "Most definitely."

Dex's face flamed as Luc lecherously licked his lips.

He tipped Dex onto the couch, then stood and fixed his pants. "On your stomach," he ordered.

Dex lay on his belly, arms folded beneath his head. Luc pulled Dex's joggers and boxer briefs down to expose his ass, but didn't free his neglected erection.

"I don't want to come," Dex said desperately. Even the pressure of the couch cushion was nearly too much. Not humping it took serious effort.

"I know." Luc rubbed Dex's back gently. "I won't tempt you. Not when I told you it wasn't allowed. This isn't a trap. I wouldn't do that to you."

"Okay." Dex forced himself to relax, and his muscles slowly unbunched.

"Very good." Luc caressed Dex's ass, running his fingers along his crack, but didn't touch his hole. He grabbed the globe closest to him, pinching Dex's skin.

He bared his teeth. "A reward for my perfect boy."

Dex groaned as Luc lowered his head and bit, sinking his teeth into the swell of his ass with a sharp sting.

Luc took slow sips, and the pain faded into a steady pulse of pleasure. Softness radiated from Dex's ass, and instead of bringing his arousal to a peak, it smoothed out his pleasure. Sensation rolled through Dex's body, closer to a massage than the near orgasm Luc's bite usually triggered. He was in no danger of coming and breaking his promise.

Dex sighed and arched his back, pushing into Luc. He

rubbed Dex's spine, his head, his neck, and sent steady soothing pulses through his bloodstream. Dex closed his eyes and drifted, becoming more and more relaxed.

Eventually, Luc pulled off, licking the wound to heal it. "Sleep now, little mate. Then we'll have dinner."

Drifting off was the easiest thing Dex had ever done, knowing Luc was there to take care of him.

25

DEX

Dex gripped Luc's neck as he flew them toward the cliffs north of the city. "I know I can't come with you, but I hate this."

His stomach flipped, and he clutched Luc tighter.

It wasn't flying that had him in knots. Soaring through the air wasn't too bad as long as Dex didn't look down. He was safe in Luc's strong arms.

But Luc was making his move against the Eternal Realm, and Dex wanted to tell him to wait. It had come around so quickly, and felt like walking into a black pit, not knowing what lay within.

What if Luc's plan didn't work and Dex had to live the rest of his life knowing it was Luc or his parents?

"I hate it, too, Dex. But everything we need is in place."

"What if you don't come back?" Dex closed his eyes. He hated this fear more than Luc going without him. Fuck. Losing someone he loved—or was growing to love—was the same old worry that had plagued him for years.

"There's nothing to indicate that the council wants me trapped anywhere but on Earth. Remember, I'll do everything in my power to come back to you. And my power isn't small, even if it's not all-encompassing."

Why wasn't that as comforting as it should be?

"I know, but I don't want to lose you. Dammit. I thought I was getting better at dealing with this." Maybe playing with fear wasn't more than a trill. Luc had spoken of mastery, but Dex didn't feel a shred of confidence anywhere inside him.

Luc's hold tightened, his wings beating faster. "You are getting better at dealing with fear. You're facing it. Completely banishing a fear isn't the only way to conquer it. That's not always possible. But you're talking about it, asking me to help you through it, and not trying to hide. As tempting as it seems, we can't have complete control of life. Most of the time, there's no guarantee, even if we wish there was."

Dex swallowed, his throat dry. "You say that like I'm not the only one wishing."

"You're not. My desire for guarantees got me into a hell of a lot of trouble, and I'm slowly letting go of my urge to control outcomes. I'd rather channel that desire into positive outlets, like taking charge of you when you need it and want it." Luc took a deep, shuddering breath. "I can't control anyone who doesn't want me to, regardless of what magic allows. That's a dark path, doomed to fail. But I can try my best to make things happen. Not being in control doesn't mean I'll fail."

It didn't, though Dex supposed he'd been acting as if it did for years, and it sounded as if Luc had too.

Dex couldn't do anything about losing friends or loved ones, and on some level, he'd assumed that helplessness made him doomed. He couldn't stop death, couldn't control it, and he'd let fear of inevitable loss overwhelm him, living as if the loss was already happening.

Dex cleared his scratchy throat. "You're right. We have to try."

"We'll try our hardest and focus on hope. That's all we can do."

The words could have sounded defeatist, but Luc was determined. Confident. As strong as his arms were around Dex, a strength Dex took comfort in. Luc stood with him. He couldn't control everything like he did when they played, but this was enough.

Luc reached the cliffs and soared through the trees to land on a deck attached to a large home Dex swore hadn't been there a second ago.

Luc inspected the area as if he'd never seen it before either. "It's probably overkill leaving you here for protection, but none of us like having our mates out of reach."

Dex had the next few days off work after shifting his schedule around. Just in case. Though hopefully, he wouldn't be at Dante's house for more than a day.

"Overkill doesn't bother me. Besides, Harper made me promise to come over and keep him company."

Harper's plea had nearly been convincing, except for the fact that he was better friends with everyone—except Ollie—than Dex. He suspected Harper wanted him to feel welcome.

There'd been a ton of coordinating over the past few days. Ash was venturing to the Eternal Realm with Luc, Onyx, Valac, and the vampires, leaving Harper and Nico behind. Apparently, everyone had decided Dante's house was the safest place to wait.

Luc set Dex down, keeping an arm and a wing wrapped around him. A small flock of gray birds circled overhead, then suddenly swooped down to inspect them with sharp, beady eyes.

"I still can't believe he let me in." Luc laughed, low and bitter.

Dex frowned at the birds. Their behavior seemed unusual. "You mean Dante?"

Luc nodded, stroking his chin. "I spoke to Ash and Onyx, and they didn't give much away, but I assume Dante isn't coming with us. He supports the cause, of course, but doesn't share Ollie's optimistic view of me."

Dex felt the pain in Luc's words. "Inviting you here has to be a sign he's considering forgiving you."

"I hope you're right." Luc gave Dex a small smile. "Let's go in."

The glass doors leading inside were open, and the living room was full of people. Onyx and Nico lounged on a couch with two women. A man Dex didn't recognize sat opposite, and a demon was looking out the window, her light gray wings folded at her back.

Ash was in the kitchen, pointing at a bunch of containers while Harper listened, a patient expression on his face.

Ollie and Dante were nowhere to be seen.

Onyx jumped from the couch. "You're here at last." He threw an annoyed glare Luc's way, like he was late to the party, before hugging Dex. "Good to see *you*."

"You too." Dex fidgeted. You'd think he was a long-time member of Onyx's family or something. "Is Rowan coming over?"

"Here?" Onyx drew back as if shocked. "No, we're meeting him at the club."

Ash joined then and nodded at Luc. He smiled almost shyly in return, like he couldn't believe Ash wasn't taking back his acceptance.

Luc wanted the other demons' forgiveness so deeply. Dex couldn't imagine how agonizing it must be. Maybe the agony was deserved, but punishment didn't have to go on forever.

Ash cleared his throat. "The food is all organized."

"No one's starving, that's for sure," Harper added under his breath.

Ash pulled Harper against him. "What kind of mate would I be if I let you starve?"

"A terrible one." Harper caught Dex's eye, his lips twitching in amusement.

Ash laughed, and Onyx said, "Glad that's all worked out. Where the hell is Dante?"

Luc stiffened against Dex's side. "Isn't he staying behind?"

"I'm staying behind," one of the women on the couch said. She stood and maneuvered across the room to hold out a hand to Dex. "I'm Pamala."

He shook it. "I'm Dex, and this is Luc."

"Oh, I know who he is." Pamala seemed to stand taller, giving off a regal air.

Luc's stiff posture remained, and tension seemed to settle over everyone. Pamala must be a demon, though there was no way for Dex to tell from her appearance.

Luc placed a hand on Dex's shoulder, while his attention remained on Pamala. "You're here even after I imprisoned you?"

She waved an airy hand. "What can I say? I'm a sucker for a cause."

The corner of Luc's mouth twitched. "Aren't we all. I appreciate you staying behind. You'll have my unending thanks for looking after my mate."

"As long as you look after Lillian and Maxwell, there's no need for thanks. Besides"—Pamala turned her attention to Dex—"I hear you're a friend of Ollie's."

"Yeah, I am. Are you?" How many demons did Ollie know?

The demon by the window turned to face them, revealing a crisscrossed length of fabric binding her breasts without restricting her wings. She raised a brow. "Friend? Is that what you call someone who kidnaps you these days?"

"*Ren*," hissed the man whom Dex presumed was Maxwell.

"What?" Ren shrugged. "Did Pamala *not* kidnap Ollie?"

"Pamala only kidnapped me to try and save her friends. It was a misunderstanding," Ollie said as he came in from the hallway on the other end of the room. "She's Ellie's mate," he added to Dex.

"Ellie has a mate?" Dex didn't know Ollie's coworker well, but they'd hung out a bunch over the years.

Ollie nodded. "Awesome, right?"

"Yes," Pamala said primly. "And it's nice to socialize with you, Ollie. Now that Dante has calmed down."

"Who said I've calmed down?" Dante filled the doorway, his wings towering over his shoulders.

"You did." Pamala braced her hands on her hips. "You said we were good."

Dante stalked forward. "We are. Like Ollie said, it was a misunderstanding. I'd have acted similarly in your shoes." He turned to face Luc. "I'm coming with you."

Luc took a step back. "You are?"

"Of course. You're doing the right thing for the first time in a thousand years. I'm not missing it."

Luc's lips stretched in a wide, unrestrained smile, and Dex's heart leapt. Luc would earn back his brothers' trust. Dex was sure of it.

Nothing was so broken that you couldn't try to fix it.

Ollie wrapped an arm around Dante, lifting his chin as he met Luc's gaze. "You can do this. I know you can."

"Thank you, Ollie. Together, I believe we can."

The tension returned to the room, this time with a crackling undercurrent, like lightning about to strike.

Onyx stepped forward. "All right, no more declarations.

Let's get on with it, or we'll be here forever. We can all have a big moment when we get back."

Luc playfully shoved Onyx in the shoulder, and he shoved Luc back.

Nerves coursed through Dex. There was no way around this. All he could do was wait. That, and give his mate one more kiss.

26

LUCIFER

Five figures waited on the roof of Rowan's building rather than the four Luc had expected. He cut a sidelong glance at Onyx.

Onyx shrugged. "Nico didn't say anything had changed. Damn vampire."

Luc landed first, Onyx and the five other demons close behind him. It was good that Onyx, Ash, and Dante had brought their own allies, and that Valac's crew weren't the only fallen Eternals joining them, considering they'd been hunting Luc, Onyx, Ash, and Dante not long ago.

Luc hadn't had much to do with Lillian, Maxwell, Pamala, or Ren over the centuries. Ren, he hardly recognized, so she must have kept to herself. The other three had never liked him, but hadn't been as vocal about it in the Realm of the Damned as Valac.

He wouldn't hold it against them. How else had he expected demons to react? He'd never desired a court of pleasers or favor seekers, same as he'd never wanted to be worshiped by witches on Earth.

Not that Luc held it against anyone who'd tried to get close to him in Hell either. How much could he judge them for siding with evil when he was that evil? They'd all had to survive the best they could. At least now, they were all free.

It was time for everyone to start over. Even if the masses hated him, the team currently standing at his side believed he could change, and maybe that was all it took to turn the tide of hate.

Rowan approached, his stride unfaltering. "You're early. Good. Let me introduce an additional supporter, Catalina, a lone witch whom I've known for decades."

Luc held out his hand to the woman, and she shook it. "You've agreed to come with us knowing you might never return to Earth?"

Catalina looked about fifty, gray streaking her dark brown hair, and showed no sign of hesitation or unease. "It's important for a witch to join you, and I'm no more afraid of being stuck in a gateway for eternity than in the Realm of the Damned. Witches deserve to be free."

"You do," Luc agreed.

A flutter of wings announced Valac's arrival. He landed on the roof, followed by Isaac and his five companions. Everyone was here.

Luc nodded to Valac, who returned the gesture. "It's time."

He could have spent years gathering support, recruiting more demons, more witches, more vampires. He could have arrived at the gateway with an army. But a show of force risked sending the wrong message.

They weren't aiming to fight, only to demand what was right. There was no reason to delay, and they needed to act soon. Luc had freed the demons, and witch souls deserved the same. The longer Luc waited to make that belief known, the more he risked his demands being misconstrued as a scheme.

"Ready to go for a ride?" Valac asked Rowan, flapping his wings.

Rowan let his fangs drop. "More than ready."

Valac scooped the vampire into his arms, and his companions did the same for Rowan's coven members and Catalina.

Luc's heart skipped, and he caught Ash's eye. "Ready?"

"For this? Never. But let's go."

Onyx patted Ash's shoulder. "It's just the gateway, not home. You've got this."

Ash smiled tenderly at Onyx. "Thank you."

Dante gazed at the pair of them with naked affection. He'd always had the biggest heart, more capacity for love than anyone Luc knew. His dark gaze fell on Luc, shifting slightly but not going cold. "We're on your side, Luc."

Luc's fire sparked. "You really trust me with this?"

"I do. Now, lead the way."

THE OUTER GATEWAY was unnaturally silent. The stillness should have been unnerving, but it wasn't. It was calm brought to life, an emotion turned physical.

Luc had been in the gateway once before, but hadn't stopped to take it in. Screams of rage had followed him out of the Eternal Realm. He'd flown from the council's wrath as fast as he could, gladly leaving the half-realm behind without a backward glance.

Today, he led their group through the mist and over a rolling field, warily taking it in. All Luc could see was the grass below. It swayed without the help of any wind, creating a soothing shift of undulating greens while the distance remained shrouded in white fog.

As they moved, the mist parted, becoming thinner and revealing more of what lay ahead, but never clearing enough to give a wider sense of their surroundings. Magic fizzled in the air.

It guided Luc along with each wing stroke and prevented him from veering off in any other direction.

"We're so close to home," Ash murmured. "I can feel it."

"Me too," Onyx whispered back. "It's familiar even after all this time."

A strong pull tugged on Luc's chest. Unlike the mating connection, which was as much a part of him as his wings or eternal fire, this pull was external.

The magic of the gateway wasn't the only thing guiding him. The Eternal Realm was beckoning. Home called.

All the demons must have felt it, but what about Rowan and his followers?

Luc glanced over his shoulder at Valac and Rowan. It was impossible to tell what the vampire was thinking with his impassive face, but he didn't seem to be having any adverse reaction to leaving the Human Realm. Catalina also seemed fine.

Finding the half-realm might not be possible without eternal magic—or the magic of a human soul unbound from its body—but the gateway didn't seem to be harmful to living, non-Eternal beings. Rowan and Catalina seemed to belong here as much as they belonged on Earth.

A low, melodic hum caught Luc's ear, steadily growing louder until it became a pleasant background melody. The tugging on Luc's soul seemed to pulse in time with the sound, the two feeding off each other and amplifying his urge to move forward.

To get closer.

Beside him, Onyx rubbed his chest. "It sucks being this close. Fuck, I knew it would be hard, but somehow, not like this."

Luc had never truly missed home. He hadn't considered the Eternal Realm home in two thousand years. Being banned enraged him on principle, but returning had never been the plan. Even when he'd believed he'd failed and would never find his mate, Luc hadn't longed for 'home.' How could he long for such a controlling place?

Onyx wasn't the same. He'd never wanted to leave, and still, he'd chosen to stand at Luc's side.

Luc brushed Onyx's wing with an outstretched hand. "I'm here for you no matter how hard it is. You can do this."

Onyx's cheeks flushed—rosy rather than lavender since his horns were hidden—and a tiny smile pulled at his lips. They stared at each other for a long moment. Onyx cleared his throat. "I know."

"Good." Luc's heart clenched, and he flew on.

In the distance, an archway became visible, its gray stone glimmering in the sun. The mist cleared, and a winged figure appeared beneath.

"Stop!" the Eternal's voice rang out, echoing as if they stood in a vast cavern rather than an open field.

Luc flew forward until he was close enough to see who it was. "Hollis, we're here to speak to the council."

The Eternal, Hollis, growled. He was tall and slim, his green wings in perfect complement to the grass surrounding them. Gray-green horns stood tall in his black hair. "Lucifer. Here, after all this time. Leave now."

Luc landed, and everyone else followed suit. Onyx, Ash, and Dante stood closest, at his side as if they'd never left it. Ren, Lillian, and Maxwell crowded behind, obscuring Valac and their unexpected guests, who were hidden by illusions.

Hollis marched forward, leaving the gateway. Not that it was unguarded. Even if they overpowered Hollis, none of them would get through. Magic sealed the Eternal Realm from everything outside it.

Luc met Hollis halfway. "I can't leave until I speak to the

council. I'm not here to demand entrance. All I ask is that you call a representative to talk with us."

"What good will that do? You shouldn't be here at all." Hollis's stern features pulled tight, and he glanced around, warily taking in their group. Was he nervous? Afraid?

Hollis hadn't been a close companion of Luc's, but they'd known each other and been friendly. His presence at the gate was better luck than if any other guardian had greeted them.

"I have a message. If you'd like to hear it, I'll oblige, but I'm not leaving until I know it's been passed on and someone from the council comes to meet me."

Hollis's lips pressed together in a tight line. "I don't want to hear it. That's not my job. I can't let you in, and nothing you say will change that." He scrubbed a hand over his face like he was tired. "I have to report this regardless of your message. The council will know you're here. We have a special spell for you and everything."

"Oh?" Luc snorted. He wasn't surprised.

Hollis shrugged, seeming to relax a fraction. "Your arrival constitutes an emergency, but what the council does once I sound the alarm is out of my hands." He snapped his fingers. A red puff of smoke appeared and popped with an echoing boom.

Hollis glanced over his shoulder into the mist obscuring what lay beyond the archway. There seemed to be no immediate reaction.

Luc's pulse thrummed. This was it. His confidence threatened to waver. "You don't seem too upset to see me," he ventured, hoping to distract himself from his growing unease.

Hollis scowled. "What you did was wrong, but I can't pretend seeing you isn't a welcome break in the monotony. No one believed we'd see the Fallen again."

Onyx stepped forward. "So, in other words, you missed us. How sweet."

Hollis cocked his head, brow furrowing deeply as he inspected Onyx. "I'm sure there are more than a few Eternals who've missed you."

Onyx's tone turned unreadable. "My absence has been a great loss, I'm sure."

"I wasn't being sarcastic." Hollis stepped closer. "Are you all right? What happened to your horns?"

Onyx sniffed. "Nothing. You can retract them, you know."

Hollis's eyes widened. "Why?" He touched one of his horns protectively.

"Hollis!" a voice boomed, and he flinched, whipping around. "Get back from there!"

Hollis launched into the air and flew through the gateway, into the mist.

"Think he'll be on our side?" Onyx muttered under his breath, barely audible over the ambient melody filling the half-realm.

Luc stroked his chin. "He might be swayed. This was a warmer welcome than I anticipated."

"Isn't that because you've slept with him?" Ash asked. He'd moved closer on silent feet, Dante too.

Luc arched a brow. He had, but that was beside the point. "Haven't you?"

"Probably." Ash's brow furrowed. "I honestly can't remember."

"Who cares?" Dante hissed. "This isn't Earth."

That was a good point. Shame around sex wasn't normalized in the Eternal Realm. No one believed sex was immoral in any form, as long as consent was freely given. Who slept with whom wasn't of much concern. Each Eternal had at least one mate, and many mated pairs were monogamous, but many more weren't, and unmated Eternals didn't date like humans.

The mist around the gate hung thick, making it impossible

to see more than the vague impression of Hollis's green wings. Shadows loomed beyond, but who they belonged to, Luc couldn't say.

He turned his back on the gate. "Are we ready?"

"Yes, though I'd love to know more about who's slept with who." Rowan gave them an amused, fang-sharpened grin.

"You wish, vamp." Onyx huffed.

"What? I can't be amused while I risk my immortal life?" Rowan waved a hand. "I can't imagine orgies of winged beings to get me through?"

Ren snorted, trying and failing to contain her laugh. "Maybe we should tell the council that banning witches and vampires holds back their sex parties. They might roll over easier if they knew treasures like Rowan were being wasted on Earth and the Realm of the Damned."

"That"—Onyx pointed at her—"is our new plan B."

Rowan's face lit up. "So you think I'm a treasure, Onyx?"

"What? No!" Onyx sputtered.

Maxwell muttered, "Fuck, we're doomed."

"Be serious," Luc snapped, his heart thundering. "Don't let Hollis's attitude put you off your guard."

Tension rippled through the group, and Rowan slunk into the background, staying hidden with the other vampires and the witch as planned. Even with the illusion, it was better they remained in the background, keeping any evidence of the concealment out of the spotlight.

Hollis and the mysterious others remained shrouded in mist. Luc beckoned Valac and his supporters forward. As they settled around him, the tug on Luc's chest grew, pulling until he almost flung himself forward.

Magic sizzled against his skin. Luc wouldn't get through the gate if he tried. He had to stand firm.

At last, the mist parted and Hollis strode forward, his face drawn. "The council refuses to see you."

Luc laughed. "I'm sorry you have to play messenger. It's too bad they can't face me themselves like mature beings."

"It's not a failing or sign of immaturity to stick to one's convictions," Hollis said stiffly. "The council told you never to return. You must leave immediately."

Shadows still loomed in the mist. How ridiculous. How insulting that they stood out of reach, refusing to face him.

"No." Luc raised his voice as he directed his gaze beyond Hollis. "I won't stand for the council's injustices any longer. Witches deserve to enter their rightful afterlife. You've punished them for too long."

Hollis's eye widened, and he glanced over his shoulder into the mist.

"That's right, witches," Luc continued. "Banning their souls to punish the Fallen is immoral and goes against the balance of life you claim to protect."

A growl erupted from the mist and echoed through the archway. One of the shadows loomed larger, and black wings came into focus.

The Eternal, Malachi, strode forth, his massive horns like a stag's antlers and his body twice the size of the average Eternal. "Lucifer, wayward child of light. How dare you act as if you care for witches after being the one to damn them?"

Malachi's deep voice set the blood in Luc's veins vibrating, and he suppressed a shiver. "I didn't damn witches. No demon damned them. We may have birthed them, but you—the council —damned them. You created the cursed realm. Not us."

Malachi had to be at least twenty thousand years old and had been on the council for much of that time. There was no lead councilor, but he was revered by many.

"Semantics." Malachi waved a wing dismissively, sending mist waffling over Luc. "Leave."

"No." Onyx stepped forward, wing to wing with Luc. Ash pressed closer on Luc's other side, and Dante moved beside Ash.

The other demons advanced, their group spanning almost the entire expanse of the archway. Catalina stepped out from between Valac and Isaac, and they lifted the illusion from her.

"We will not leave. Witches won't be damned any longer. Why can't our souls enter the Eternal Realm?"

Malachi took a staggering step backward, his massive footstep sending vibrations through the soil. "What is this?"

"I'm a witch." Catalina stalked closer until she was beside Luc, in front of Malachi. "I'm not a *what*, I'm a person. A soul you have deemed unworthy. Less than."

Hollis flinched.

Malachi's eyes burned red. "Witches are not less than."

"Aren't we? That's how we're treated. Less than our human counterparts."

"No. The Eternal Realm assists mortal souls in reincarnation. Witches are not fully mortal. Magic should never have entered humanity, never touched Earth, and disrupted the natural order."

Luc clenched his fist, and everything seemed to heighten. The same old argument angered him like never before, but his time to speak would come.

"You don't reincarnate." Catalina pointed at Malachi.

"I am an Eternal being."

"So you're better than me?"

Malachi growled. "I do not answer to you. This is the way of the universe. If you are displeased, send your complaints to Lucifer. He created you."

Rowan stepped forward, his three coven members at his

side, all four unmasked from illusion. "The universe is only this way because you decreed it. The Realm of the Damned is your creation, and we're asking for change."

"More witches?" Malachi's lip curled. "No... Vampires. *Demon slayers.* Destroyers of eternal life. How dare you show your faces here after breaking the ultimate rule?"

"Are you kidding?" Onyx snarled. "Ultimate rule, my ass. You didn't care when Andras was killed. Those murderous witches escaped punishment and walked away with eternal life. Don't pretend you're outraged now."

"Exactly. Thank you, Onyx." Rowan clapped him on the shoulder. "I am not a demon slayer, and have broken no Eternal rules, ultimate or otherwise. Are you going to punish me for the sins of my father—not even that—my great-etcetera grandfather? I didn't create the vampire species any more than I created witches or the Realm of the Damned."

"No. I didn't say you'd be punished for another's crimes." Malachi glared, eyes burning with red fire.

"So, it's wrong to punish one person for someone else's crime?" Catalina cut in. "If you believe that, let witches enter the rightful afterlife or be a hypocrite."

"I am not a hypocrite. The council does not indulge baseless demands or bow to pressure. The state of the realms was broken when magic infected Earth. Nothing more can be done." Mist gathered around Malachi, obscuring him from view and swallowing Hollis along with him. "This conversation is over."

27

LUCIFER

"You can't walk away from this!" Luc shouted into the mist. "We aren't done!"

No response came.

"The Fallen didn't bring magic to Earth!" Luc screamed into the void. Malachi wouldn't have left. He'd hear. He had to. "Mortal souls are magic. Humans have magic at their core, the same as Eternals. The sacred balance is a lie!"

Heavy silence followed.

Luc heaved a breath, his fire raging. He surged forward, pounding on the magic barrier sealing the gate shut. Sparks flew as he pummeled the invisible force, sending red-hot pain up his arms.

"Face us!" Rowan yelled.

Ash snarled, and the demons around him joined in, their voices raising to a deafening level.

The magical barrier vibrated and pulsed. There was an ear-popping sonic boom, and a force hit Luc in the chest, throwing him backward.

Luc's ears rang as he soared through the air and crashed into the ground. His vision blurred, head heavy, as a high-pitched ringing drowned everything out.

He struggled to his feet. Onyx lay beside him, one wing crumpled at an odd angle. Luc lunged for him. He screamed, but couldn't hear his own voice. Nothing penetrated the ringing in his ears.

He rolled Onyx over. His lips moved, but Luc couldn't hear him. He pulled his brother to his feet and helped set his wing. It would heal, but he couldn't fly until then. Fuck.

Luc snarled. He gripped Onyx's hand tight, refusing to let go even when his brother tugged on him.

Beside him, Ash helped Dante to his feet, and Isaac was bent over Catalina, limp on the ground.

Shit.

A witch's body wasn't much stronger than a human's. They fought illness better, but didn't heal as rapidly as vampires and certainly not like demons.

Luc raced over, pulling Onyx with him.

"You heal her organs, and I'll get her spine!" Isaac shouted to Lillian as she kneeled on Catalina's other side, but his words sounded faint and far away.

Luc and Onyx stooped to help, Valac joining in. Soon, every demon was pouring magic into Catalina, healing each broken piece inside her.

Her heart fluttered, but didn't stop. At last, Catalina's eyes flew open and she drew a shuddering breath.

Onyx slumped against Luc, and the need to hold his brother was all that kept Luc from collapsing.

"Thank all that is damned," Dante said. "If she'd died..."

"They can't do this!" Ash's snarl popped Luc's ears, and suddenly, everything was loud again. "They can't attack us like this. Hurting innocent beings is vile."

Ash stomped toward the mist-shrouded archway, Valac at his heel.

Rowan stirred in the grass and sat up, looking dazed. Lillian murmured with Catalina, and the other vampires groaned as their immortal magic put their broken bodies back together.

"Shield's up," Luc ordered. "We can all lend power to protect our guests."

Fire flared on all sides. Red coated Luc's body, Onyx bathed in blue beside him, and a multitude of colors surrounded Catalina and each vampire.

"I'll stay back for now, until the vampires are healed," Lillian offered.

Luc nodded and marched toward the gate with Onyx.

"Come out and show yourselves, cowards!" Ash roared into the mist.

"We aren't leaving unless you kill us," Onyx yelled out. "Are you going to break the ultimate rule and admit it's all bullshit? Or own up and do what's right?"

Luc rested a hand on Onyx and Ash's shoulders.

Dante caught his eye, black flames raging in his irises. "Don't back down."

Luc let the strength of his raging fire fuel him. He wouldn't, especially not with his brothers at his side.

"We've seen the truth," Luc called into the mist. "The universe is not built on opposites. Straying from one box or another has no effect on anything. The realms don't balance each other. Life does not balance death. Magic is not in opposition to mortality. It never has been. All things exist in varied forms. Witches are not wrong for existing between what we thought were the only two ways of being. There is no reason some souls should be damned other than to satisfy *your* need for control."

But Luc might as well have been yelling at no one. Silence

filled the air. Even the ambient music of the half-realm had ceased.

The ground vibrated.

Dante growled. "Get ready."

Ash pulled Dante and Luc back from the invisible barrier. "We need space to move. Brace yourselves."

Valac and his supporters joined them. "No matter what's coming, we're not backing down."

"No." Luc reached into his well of power. "There's no coming back from this."

He was doing this for Dex—he longed for an unending life with his mate, there was no denying that—but it had become so much bigger. His heart's desire had brought him to a reality more important than any individual dream. Dex had shown Luc a better world. Everyone deserved that world, and no one had the right to stand in the way in the name of a sacred truth.

"Lies!" Malachi's voice boomed out of the mist.

"They are not!" Luc shouted back. "Discovering this new truth doesn't have to be bad. We can change our beliefs. Letting witches into the Eternal Realm threatens no one."

All it threatened was the council's power. Eternals would question them in ways they hadn't before, but that wasn't bad. If anything, it was good. Unless you were a councilor clinging to power and unwilling to change.

"Your attempt to bring chaos into this realm will fail." Malachi reemerged from the mist, flanked on each side by a dozen Eternal guards.

Hollis was conspicuously absent.

In a flash of eternal fire, the guards launched into the air, lightning crackling at their fingertips. Luc, Onyx, Ash, Dante, and their supporters rose to meet them.

28

———

DEX

"You weren't kidding about this game room," Dex said to Ollie.

Dante's game room was as big as Dex's new condo. There was a TV on each wall, an elaborate desktop set-up, and even a few arcade machines in one corner.

Ollie chuckled. "Told you Dante has everything."

"I guess it's easy to collect it all when you've been there for each new development."

Ollie flopped into a beanbag. "Let's play something. I know it feels weird to fuck around while everyone is in another realm, but sitting around is even worse."

"Good point." Dex lowered himself into the other beanbag.

"I can still feel Dante through our mate connection, so I'll know if anything big happens, even if I can't tell exactly what."

Dex looked at Ollie more closely. "You can *feel* Dante?"

"Yeah, when we want to share. Dante blocks out my emotions most of the time."

"Isn't reading each other like that weird?"

Ollie laughed. "It was at first. I might have panicked—a lot— but now, I like being connected. Especially at times like this. It means I can help Dante and support him even though I'm not with him."

Dex's heart sank. He couldn't help Luc from afar. Fuck. It felt wrong to sit around gaming while Luc faced the unknown.

What if he and Luc were supposed to face this together? What if Luc couldn't do it alone? He had support, his brothers back at his side, but what if it wasn't enough?

Sitting here safe and sound, Dex wasn't risking anything. How could he expect someone else to change the world for him?

If this fight had been about letting mates into the Eternal Realm and nothing else, that would have been one thing. But it was way bigger than that. Staying behind suddenly seemed like putting himself before everyone else.

Dex had been too focused on what *he* wanted. On his parents and Luc. His own loss and worries. He'd been thinking too small.

What if the only way to change the universe was to show the Eternal Realm that he—a human—was willing to risk it all to abolish the Realm of the Damned and shift the perspective on magic and mortality?

"What's up?" Ollie nudged him in the shoulder. "You look freaked out all of a sudden. I promise the mating connection isn't anything to worry about. Luc won't read your mind."

"No, it's not that. I—I should have gone with them."

"What! No." Ollie grabbed Dex's arm. "You could get stuck in the gateway. You could die and never come back to Earth. You'd lose your time with Luc. With me."

Dex's chest seized. "I know. But if we win, I'll get it all. You, Luc, my parents. If we lose, there's far more at stake than me and my life. I want an undivided world."

Ollie's understanding look was tinged with something more frantic. "I want that too. And we'll get it. The plan is sound.

The truth is getting out no matter what. Luc made sure of it. There's no reason for you to go."

"I don't know. I have a bad feeling." Dex closed his eyes as an increasingly sick sensation twisted his insides. What if he was making the biggest mistake of his life? "I don't think I'm supposed to be here waiting safely to see if someone else can fix everything for me. I have to try to fix it too."

"No," Ollie nearly growled.

Dex opened his eyes. "I'm sorry. I love you, Ollie. But I don't think they'll let mates enter the Eternal Realm without me. Even if Luc gets his way on everything else. Even if witches are freed. If the Eternal Realm has to face those they've damned, then a human mate needs to be there as much as a vampire or witch."

"No." Ollie shot out of the bean bag. "That's stupid. Pamala will never take you. She promised to keep us safe."

"But being safe isn't helping anyone but us. I'm not saying we all have to go, but I can't sit here."

Fuck, he'd screwed up. He never should have let Luc leave him behind.

Dex couldn't explain why this change had come over him so fiercely. It was almost like magic. Maybe fate was giving him a sign.

"Something is telling me I'm doing the wrong thing. I was distracted by my fear of losing Luc before, but if I hadn't been, I might have realized he needed me the way I need him."

Ollie let out a sound of frustration. "That doesn't make sense."

It did to Dex.

He climbed out of the bean bag. "Why not? If this is all fate, like you keep saying, how do you know I'm not meant to be there with him? I'm the one who realized the whole magic/mortality universal balance thing was nonsense."

Ollie shook his head. "Luc wouldn't want you to go. He'd never want you in danger. You're his mate. He'll protect you at all costs."

He would protect him, but Dex disagreed with the rest. "Luc would want me to go if it was what I truly needed to do. I don't know how to explain it, but something is telling me my presence there will change things."

Luc had faced his fears for Dex. He could do the same. And together, they could make the world better for everyone.

29

LUCIFER

Lightning flashed, reflecting off the mist, and filled the gateway with violent splashes of color.

Luc clashed with a guard and fought to strike past her shield. Ash caught hold of another guard and threw him into the mist.

"This is pointless," Luc bellowed as he dodged a blow. "Fighting serves no one."

"Then leave." Malachi's voice echoed.

Someone caught Luc from behind, and strong arms around his middle dragged him to the ground. A shadow loomed over him, and hands wrapped around his throat, crushing him.

Onyx appeared at his side and blasted the attacker off.

He held out a hand to Luc. "We have to stand firm. They can't kill us without breaking their own rules and bringing the chaos they accused us of sowing onto their own realm."

Luc clasped Onyx's hand and strengthened his shield. It was time to deliver the final truth.

"Falling was never wrong," he screamed at Malachi. "Magic and mortality have always been interwoven—"

Red lightning hit Luc's chest. Malachi's power obliterated

Luc's shield, stopping his heart. *No.* Luc had to lay out the consequences for ignoring them. They had a failsafe.

A second wave of power knocked Onyx back, leaving Luc alone on the ground.

Malachi stepped forward, shocking Luc before he could recover. "Stop this nonsense, Lucifer. No one wants to hear it."

Luc received another shock, and he couldn't speak. If his claims were nonsense, why bother silencing him?

Two figures appeared in the mist, one with white wings, the other black. The mist parted, and they stalked closer. Luc was trapped, unable to move as the two beings he'd hoped to never see again closed in.

His mother and father.

Isabella and Cenric had sat on the council for thousands of years before Luc had been born. They were less senior than Malachi, but their presence chilled Luc in a way Malachi never could.

"Lucifer." Cenric gazed down at him with glowing eyes. "How disappointed we are."

Malachi delivered another shock to Luc's system. For once, Luc wished a stopped heart prevented him from hearing those around him.

Cenric continued as if his son hadn't been harmed right in front of him. "Falling wasn't enough? Disgracing us and this realm wasn't enough? You had to ruin the magical order further, and now you have the audacity to return?"

Luc fumed. He'd be screaming if he had control of his body. How could they stand there after hearing the truth Dex had discovered? How could they condemn him? How could any of them hear this truth and not want to honor it?

Had they known all along, or were they that afraid of the unknown? So self-obsessed, they wouldn't risk losing power, no matter the cost.

Isabella bowed her head. "It would have been better if you had never returned."

A scream tore through the air, and a flash of blue streaked across the sky.

Malachi shocked Luc, turning toward the blur, but it was too late. Onyx landed on Malachi, plunged his hand into Malachi's chest, and ripped out his heart. Malachi's body went rigid and toppled, hitting the ground with a crack, dead until he regenerated the vital organ.

Onyx landed beside Luc and threw Malachi's bloody heart at their parents' feet. "You know, the only things I never missed about this realm were you, Father, and you, Mother. You think your disapproval means anything to us?"

"So you never longed for home?" Cenric cocked his head, hands raised as if to placate Onyx, but his gaze was knowing. "You never regretted your foolishness?"

Onyx winced, and Luc shot to his feet.

He growled, his voice bordering on the edge of incoherent. "Onyx is not a fool. You're the fools for never loving him like he deserved."

Cenric seemed not to have heard him. He was good at that. Acting like no one else existed. His raised hands glowed, and a satisfied smirk twisted his fine features.

The pull of the Eternal Realm tugging on Luc's chest lurched, the intensity skyrocketing.

Luc screamed. It was as if all his innards had been ripped out. He clutched his stomach and looked down, but everything was intact. The tug of the Eternal Realm cut through his soul.

Onyx collapsed, writhing on the ground, his mouth open in a silent scream. Luc's pain was physical and thus bearable, but Onyx had longed for home for two thousand years.

Luc dropped to his knees, reaching for his brother. "Stop it! You're monsters. He's your *son*. Stop!"

"Leave and we will stop," Isabella said with maddening calm.

Luc patted Onyx's chest uselessly, grabbing frantically as if he could save him. There was nothing he could do. He couldn't even sense the spell torturing him and was unable to counter it. Luc's breaths grew shallow, coming too fast. His head spun. No. They couldn't torture Onyx. He didn't deserve this.

Luc was sinking. He didn't know what to do. He was losing everything.

A squelching sound caught his frayed attention. Cenric screamed, and a blade erupted from his sternum. He collapsed, his heart destroyed just like Malachi's.

Isabella gasped, but Luc had eyes for no one but Onyx. He'd stopped moving.

"Onyx." Luc shook his brother, unable to stop himself.

The tug on Luc's chest faded to a dull ache. Thank all that was damned that it had stopped.

"Fuck," Onyx groaned, clutching Luc's hand, and Luc sagged in relief.

"Traitor!" Isabella's scream cut through the air.

Luc whipped around, not letting go of his brother.

Hollis stood over Cenric with a bloody sword, chest heaving. "It's true, isn't it? The sacred balance is a lie."

Isabella fumed, but Hollis didn't give her time to respond.

"When Eternals hear this, everything will change. They're already whispering that their mates could be trapped in Hell." He jabbed his bloody sword in Isabella's direction. "They could be trapped, and there's no point? Those souls could be here! With their Eternal mates!"

"Shut up, Hollis." Isabella was as cold as ice. "Those whispers are unfounded. None of this nonsense will ever get out. No one in the Eternal Realm will hear Lucifer's lies. Know your place."

All other fighting seemed to have ceased. Everyone watched, waiting for the next move.

Ash strode toward them, streaked with blood. "It's already out, Isabella. There is no unringing this bell."

Her nostrils flared.

Luc pulled Onyx to his feet, and Valac and Dante joined Ash, blood marring their skin as well. They all seemed unharmed, or at least healed.

Ash crossed his bulging arms. "Our message is coming to the Eternal Realm whether you like it or not—"

Isabella sneered. "Witches and vampires will never be allowed in. So, who's going to spread your lies, hmm?"

"They aren't lies." Dante snapped his wings. "Humans will bring the truth about the realms with them when they die. They've always held the truth. Their souls are proof. It's fitting that they'll be the ones to tell the Eternal Realm how things really are."

"Humans?" Isabella scoffed. Cenric stirred at her feet, body twitching, but she didn't spare him a glance.

"Yes, humans," Valac declared. "No matter what happens here, the truth of magic and mortality will spread through the Human Realm. We have humans, witches, and vampires ready to spread the message wide. Even humans who don't believe what they hear will carry the knowledge. When they die and enter the Eternal Realm, they'll see it's real and spread the word. You can't stop this. You will face the consequences of your lies no matter what. Your own people will bring them to your door when they hear."

Isabella's mouth fell open.

Satisfaction wound through Luc like a snake. "It doesn't have to be this way, Mother. You can welcome this change. Be the one to bring truth to the Eternal Realm. You can welcome witches, and then when humans come bearing news of the reality of mortality and magic, it won't be a problem. Their message will reinforce the change you facilitated rather than undermine your authority."

Malachi rose behind her, coated in blood. "No."

"So *you* choose chaos?" Luc stared the massive Eternal down. "*You* choose to fight against what is real to maintain your power? *You* chose upheaval in your realm when Eternals hear the truth?"

"Your plan won't work." Malachi pushed past Isabella, who stood as if stunned. "Eternals won't listen to humans. What do they know of the universe? Nothing will change."

"That's not true," Hollis shouted, his eyes wide and flaming. "Eternals are already questioning the Realm of the Damned."

"And you encouraged them?" Malachi strode to Hollis and gripped him by the throat. "Your duty is to protect the realms."

Luc's fangs pierced his smile. "Sounds like he has been."

Malachi's glare landed on Luc. "No. This ends now. Your message will not get through. All in the gateway will fall in line —swear unbreakable oaths of silence—or die."

Gasps echoed around them, fear in the faces of guards and Luc's supporters alike.

"Traitor," Hollis choked out, fire burning in his eyes.

Luc tasted smoke. His fire burst forth and crackled in the air around him. "Killing us changes nothing. Even if you slaughter us all, leave no witnesses, and hide your betrayal from the rest of the Eternal Realm by claiming any missing guards fell to Earth, the truth of magic and mortality is coming."

"We'll see about that." Malachi's burning eyes flared. "Well, you won't."

Permanent death. Luc had *never* believed the council would go that far. Maybe he was a fool after all. He'd had no idea what power he'd gone up against. He'd believed a sense of morality—

fucking decency—sat at the center of everything, even if the council had been corrupted by power.

He'd been wrong.

It seemed the ultimate rule only existed when it was convenient. How many others had died and been wiped from the universe to uphold lies?

Fuck. Luc had failed. He'd lose everything.

His mate.

His chance to fully reconnect with his brothers.

But it was worth it. If he had to go, this way was better than any other. Malachi was wrong about one thing. Change was coming. Human voices would be heard even if Luc wasn't around to see it. In the end, the truth would prevail.

Luc's heart bled at the loss of his mate, but Dex would see this fight through when he passed through the gateway, and Luc's damned soul warmed as he pictured it.

"*Luc!*" a faint voice screamed.

Luc's heart stopped, and ice slid down his spine, cold cutting through his raging fire. *No.* He turned, gripping Onyx for support.

In the distance, Dex ran through the swaying grass, his face flushed and eyes wide. "Luc! I'm here. I stand with you. We can do this together."

What?

Luc's eyes filled with tears, the drops turning to steam as they fell. His fire burned too hot to stand. His mate was here. His Dex. Love shone in Dex's wide eyes as he ran as fast as he could. He'd come for Luc.

But why?

Pamala ran beside him. Now they would die too. Luc's gentle mate had forfeited his life.

Dex would die here and see his beloved parents sooner than he ever should have.

Like a snapping bowstring, Luc launched into the air. He flew to Dex and scooped him up. "My dear. My love. What are you doing?"

Dex clung to him. "Helping you. I couldn't stay behind. It was like a nightmare. Not coming with you was wrong. I know it."

With a blinding jolt, everything clicked into place, hitting Luc like lightning to the heart. His sob turned into a laugh. "You're right. You've just saved us all."

30

———

LUCIFER

Luc carried Dex to the front line, where everyone stood frozen, watching them approach with everything from horrified expressions to indifference.

"What the fuck?" Onyx snarled, fear cutting his delicate face. "Dex, *no.*"

"How could you?" Dante yelled at Pamala.

"Who is this?" Malachi's voice boomed, drowning out everyone else. His cutting tone stung Luc's frayed nerves.

He set Dex on his feet and grabbed his hand. "Malachi, Mother, Father—I see you recovered—may I present to you my mate, Dex Colt. My unbonded, human mate. My living, mortal mate."

Luc smiled like the villain he'd been, fangs down, a hysterical triumph setting his fire roaring so fiercely he could almost hear it.

"What the fuck is wrong with you?" Onyx hissed, but Luc's attention was fixed on the three council members.

At last, the penny dropped.

Malachi hissed, lips curling back. He threw Hollis—who

he'd still had pinned by the throat—to the ground. Isabella gripped Cenric so hard his arm cracked, and he grunted.

Onyx sputtered incoherently. Luc might as well spell it out. His brother was clearly too stressed to think clearly, and he deserved to know they'd been saved.

Besides, Luc couldn't deny his smug, vindictive side.

He loved sticking it to authority. Dramatically.

"You can slaughter us to try and stop what we know from getting through, but a crime like that must be covered up. No witnesses. It could have been done. We demons and the Eternals you deemed traitors would have ceased to exist. No one in the Eternal Realm would have asked where I'd gone when they hadn't seen me in thousands of years. You could easily fabricate an explanation for the missing guards. The witch and vampires would have gone to Hell. There would have been no one to expose you for so grossly breaking the ultimate rule. It would have been a perfect crime. Except, along came Dex. The man who saw the truth of the universe and enlightened me. The source of truth, if you will. Kill him, and he'll go straight to the Eternal Realm to ruin you all."

There was a beat of silence.

Onyx cackled, worthy of a villain. "Checkmate, mother-fuckers."

"Wait!" Dex tugged on Luc's arm. "You were about to be killed?"

Luc smiled, no longer feral, but soft. "It's all right, Dex. The danger is gone. You saved us."

Dex trembled, and Luc pulled him close. Over Dex's shoulder, Luc's attention landed on his parents and Malachi, who all appeared shell-shocked.

"Shall we make a deal? It's the only way for you to save face. You didn't actually commit mass murder—merely considered it —so your eternal lives are safe, but you don't want to be shunned once everyone hears about this. Maybe you should let witches and vampires in. At least then you can say you did something right."

Cenric gave his head a tiny shake, like he was trying to dislodge something irritating. "You're asking us to restructure the universe. That isn't... We can't..."

"This battle is lost." Malachi drowned out Cenric's stammering, his eyes flaring bright before going out and revealing golden irises. He cleared his throat, his stance shifting from aggressive to authoritative. "We didn't know magic and mortality could coexist. It simply wasn't the way. The Realm of the Damned *had* to be created. But now that we know better, we are correcting our mistake. The Realm of the Damned will be abolished and all souls welcomed into the Eternal Realm."

His spin on the story curled Luc's lip, but he let it go. If the council wanted to pretend they hadn't known it was all a lie, fine. Some of them probably hadn't been aware. Luc wasn't even sure if Malachi had known, or if his violent reaction was as much shock as it was an instinct to cling to power. It didn't matter anymore. Not when things were being put right.

Cenric and Isabella shared an unreadable look.

"Looks like you got your way, Lucifer," Cenric said as if he were five years old. "This doesn't mean any of the Fallen are coming home. The rule that Eternals must not enter Earth exists regardless, and the council can enforce it if we wish."

Ash growled, his fist clenched at his side. "If you wish. *Hmph.* The reason behind the rule was to protect a balance that doesn't exist, but you're right, when we left, we accepted that we would never return. It was our choice, and we aren't asking to come home. The Fallen will remain on Earth as long as all other beings are welcomed."

"Yes, fine," Malachi boomed as if losing patience.

They had to wrap this up. Luc hurried to add, "All beings, including bonded demons' mates."

Malachi's face scrunched, confused. On anyone less terrifying, the expression would have been comical. "What do bonded mates need from the Eternal Realm?"

Dex cleared his throat. "Um... Hi. As a mate who wants to bond, I'd also like to complete my mortal life cycle. My loved ones are waiting in the afterlife, and I need to see them again."

Malachi growled, and Dex shrank into Luc's arms. "Lucifer will never be allowed into the Eternal Realm. This is not negotiable."

"Dex isn't asking you to allow me anywhere. Permit him to visit his family and stay in the Eternal Realm for a time before returning to me on Earth. Any other mate should be allowed the same."

Malachi rubbed a bloody hand over his face, making him even more terrifying. "Fine. We can't deny that now. Not if we admit—agree—that the sacred balance isn't as cut and dry as we believed. Humans should be allowed to complete their life cycle, even if it is their last. There will be two realms once more. But no other travel between realms is permitted, and falling to Earth is still forbidden. Humans deserve their mortal world. That, at least, we can protect."

Whether it was a genuine desire to protect Earth or a way to hold on to the last shred of control over Eternal beings, Luc couldn't say. Maybe one day, falling wouldn't be a crime. The Eternal Realm was on the brink of change, and Luc had no idea what Eternals would push for.

He'd be on Earth with his mate, and that was more than fine with him. "How do we know you won't change your mind? How will Dex get into the Eternal Realm?"

Malachi stepped to the side and waved his hand before him, clearing the mist from the archway to reveal a deep valley flanked by lush mountains and roaring waterfalls. "He's welcome to enter now."

Dex made a sound like a hurt animal, and his fingers dug into Luc's side.

Luc cupped his face. "It's all right. You can go. I'll be waiting right here when you come back."

"I don't want to go now." A tear slid down Dex's cheek as his gaze wandered to the eternal valley before them. "I want to live my life and come back when it would have ended if I weren't living forever. It's too soon."

Luc kissed his forehead, his fire dormant and heart bursting with love. "Then that's when you'll come. When it feels right."

Malachi called the mist back with another wave of his hand. "When he is ready, he will be admitted once, same as any other like him who bonds with a demon. Witch, human, or vampire."

Hollis marched toward Malachi, fierce for someone who was half of Malachi's massive size and had already had his throat crushed by the brute. "Make an unbreakable oath. They shouldn't have to risk you changing your mind."

"You dare give me orders?" Malachi ripped the necklace marking Hollis as a guard from around his neck. "You are dismissed from the gateway's service."

Hollis lifted his chin. "I was quitting anyway."

"Can you just make the oath, Malachi?" Onyx snapped as only he could at a time like this. "I want to get the fuck out of here. My longing for the Eternal Realm has been cured. I have a mate waiting, and all the family I need on Earth."

He glared at his and Luc's parents, who stood like the unfeeling statues Luc had always known them to be.

Luc would gladly never see their mother or father again.

Did they regret any of their actions? Luc hoped Onyx wasn't hurting. Cenric and Isabella weren't worth it.

Malachi stooped and selected a stray pebble to bind his

oath, and promised that all demons' mates would be allowed one entry into the Eternal Realm.

He handed the glowing pebble to Dex. "No need to bring this with you. The magic is binding either way, but take this as a token. As proof."

With that, Malachi disappeared into the mist, Isabella and Cenric following close behind.

When she was almost completely out of sight, Isabella paused. "I'm sorry this didn't work out better." She disappeared.

"What the fuck was that?" Onyx gestured into the mist. "That wasn't an apology for shit. Damnation, part of me forgot how awful they were. Sorry, Luc. You did a great job of showing your remorse. Especially given they're who raised us."

A laugh burst from Luc. "That's a low bar, Onyx. Doing better than our parents was the bare minimum I expected to accomplish in life."

"Right?" Onyx's lips quirked.

Luc scooped Dex into his arms. "Come on. It's time to go home."

31

———

DEX

Dex clung to Luc as he flew through the strange gateway realm. They sailed over the vast field until the mist swallowed them completely.

Dex's skin prickled. Air seemed to press in around him and a bright light stole his vision. When it cleared, they were flying over the ocean. On Earth.

Dex couldn't explain how he knew they were in the Human Realm, other than it felt fundamentally different than being in the gateway. Almost like someone had turned gravity back on, but not Earth's gravity, something deeper. A gravity within his soul?

Luc flew on, leading the group over the expanse of blue until Shearwater Landing came into view on the horizon.

A large containership sailed into the port, with other boats milling around the outer harbor. Dex had never seen his home from this angle, city sparkling under the setting sun. The sight soothed him as much as Luc's embrace.

"We're going to Rowan's," Valac announced, carrying the vampire in question.

"All right," Luc agreed. "We're headed to Dante's. Thank you for your help."

"There's no need to thank me, Lucifer. I'm grateful I could assist. It seems we're on the same side. Who'd have thought?"

"Not me," Luc said with a hint of surprise. "See you around."

Valac nodded and veered off, his demon friends following with the other vampires and a woman Dex hadn't seen before.

Ren picked up speed toward the city, calling, "I'm off," over her shoulder.

"We'll be going too," Pamala said, gesturing to Lillian and Maxwell. "I'm sure we'll see some of you at Ellie's birthday party if you accompany your mates."

"You will." Dante's expression turned sheepish. "I'm sorry, Pamala. I—"

"Don't worry about it. Thank the realms I listened to Dex." She flew away before Dante could say anything else, her companions following.

Onyx brushed the tip of his wing along Dex's arm. "We're all thankful she listened to you."

Luc gripped Dex tighter, gathering speed. "More than thankful. How did you know?"

Dex's chest erupted with latent butterflies. "I'm not entirely sure. The sense that I should have gone with you overwhelmed me until it started to physically hurt, and I couldn't think beyond getting to you. You shouldn't have had to go without me."

Luc growled low. "Yes, I should have. It's good you weren't there any sooner. Catalina almost died. It took all of us to save her."

Dex's stomach lurched. "It's almost as if it was meant to happen this way."

Luc hummed thoughtfully. "It seems so."

They'd reached the cliffs, and Luc swooped past the trees to land on Dante's deck. As if they'd been waiting on the threshold, Ollie, Harper, and Nico burst from inside.

"You're okay! Oh my god, Dex. Dante!" Ollie rushed forward, his eyes red and puffy.

"He saved us." Dante scooped Ollie into his arms and buried his face in Ollie's curls.

Ash and Harper were wrapped around each other, and Onyx seemed to have collapsed into Nico.

"What happened? Did they let witches in? Where's everyone else?" Ollie asked, wiggling in Dante's hold as he looked around.

Luc clung to Dex, showing no signs of wanting to put him down. "Everyone is safe, and yes, the Realm of the Damned is being abolished. Dex will see his parents when he's ready, and you can enter the Eternal Realm, too, Ollie. As can you, Harper."

Harper disengaged Ash's passionate kiss with a smack of lips. "Me?"

Dex laughed.

Luc snorted. "Yes. Ash can fill you in. I think we all need some time with our mates."

A purr emanated from Luc's chest, and Dex wanted to rub against him like a cat. He wasn't even drunk this time.

"Wait!" Onyx spun away from Nico, but couldn't seem to let him go. "Luc, wait."

"What is it?" Luc stepped closer to Onyx.

"I love you." Onyx's eyes shone. "You're forgiven for everything you ever did to me. Okay?"

"Okay, little brother. And don't worry, I'm not going anywhere. You couldn't get rid of me if you tried. You're my family. Not those Eternals who turned their backs on us. I promise I'll never hurt you again."

Onyx hiccupped, like he was choking back tears, and Nico kissed the top of his head.

"Come see us soon?" Dante spoke as if he wasn't sure he should, taking a half-step toward Luc and Dex.

Luc sounded just as hesitant. "I will. If you're inviting me."

"I am."

"Me too," Ash added.

"Thank you," Luc whispered, agonized yet hopeful.

"You're welcome. Now, go be with your mate." Ash grinned, his eyes flashing, and Harper giggled.

Luc launched into the air, and Dex swallowed a gasp of surprise.

"Have fun mating," Ollie yelled after them. "And you better text me, Dex."

"I will," he shouted back before burying his face in Luc's neck. "They all know we're about to have sex, don't they?"

Luc snorted. "As if they aren't about to do the same. Believe me, no one will be thinking about us in about five minutes."

"True." Dex's core tightened, and it all hit him. They could mate now. He could bond with Luc and be his forever.

Luc flew them over the city, seeming in less of a hurry than he'd been in getting to Dante's. "We can do more than have sex," he said softly. "But we don't have to mate until you're ready. We don't have to do it tonight."

Dex's chest tightened. "Do you want to?"

"More than anything in my life. But I can wait."

Why wait? This was the reason Luc had faced the Eternal Realm.

Okay, it had been bigger than that, but they'd accomplished everything they'd set out to do. The world would change for the better. Dex could have Luc and never lose him. He could spend eternity with Ollie. He could be a part of the demons' family. And he didn't have to sacrifice his parents for any of it.

"I don't want to wait."

A long, low whine filled the air. "Fuck, Dex. Are you sure?"

"Yes."

Luc's wingbeats quickened, and he tore across the city. "I'm going to devour you, little mate. I'm claiming your soul. Your very essence. You'll be mine, and there's no undoing it. Mine, Dex. Forever."

Dex moaned, his eyelids falling shut.

Luc landed at his loft and whisked Dex inside and up the stairs. "Do you have your pebble?"

"It's in my pocket."

Luc set Dex on his feet beside the bed. "Place it on the side table."

Dex fished the faintly glowing gray stone from his pocket and set it beside the lamp. When he turned around, Luc was naked, his eyes a brighter red than Dex had ever seen.

A shiver wound through Dex's body, and his cock stiffened.

"On the bed," Luc ordered.

Dex kicked off his shoes and scrambled up.

"Tell me your safe words," Luc demanded.

"Red for stop, green for all good, yellow for slow down."

"Good boy." Luc's wings pumped, sending smoke-scented air wafting around Dex. "After we're bonded, we'll be linked telepathically. We won't share thoughts, but we will sense each other's feelings. I hear it can be controlled to an extent, but there will be times when hiding from each other will be impossible. We can discuss this further and wait until you're comfortable."

"No. I want to mate now. Ollie already told me about the bond's emotional connection. I want to feel you and show you all of me. I need to be yours, Luc."

Luc tipped his head back and growled, the sound long and

low, almost agonized. Then he pounced on the bed, and Dex yelped in surprise.

In a flash, Luc was on him, his hands seemingly everywhere at once. It took Dex long seconds to process that Luc was ripping his clothes to shreds.

He was naked and panting less than a minute later. "Luc, please."

Luc hovered over Dex, who was splayed on his back like an offering. "*Mm*. Greedy little mate." He wrapped his hand around Dex's hard cock. There was a tingling sensation, and wetness bloomed between Luc's palm and Dex's sensitive skin.

"Yes." Dex arched into Luc's lube-slick touch, but Luc took his hand away.

"Touch yourself for me. I want to see what I missed on the phone the other night."

Dex hastily grabbed his slick cock and stroked. "Like this?"

Luc sat back, purring loudly as he watched. "Just like that. Jerk it until you're about to come, then stop."

Dex whimpered. Fuck. Luc hadn't given him permission to come. He hadn't come in so many days, it might as well have been forever. "I'm not gonna last long."

"Try for me. You can do it."

Dex fucked his fist, the slide of the magical lube combined with Luc's hungry gaze—like he was on the brink of devouring him—was too much to take. Dex's balls drew up, and he groaned.

He stopped, dropping his cock like it had burned him. He leaked precum, but he didn't tip over the edge.

Sweat gathered along his brow. He'd done it. But oh, god, if he moved, he might come and ruin everything.

"Good boy." Luc's red gaze burned as he took in Dex's naked body. "So good for me. I love seeing you squirm, trying so hard to please me."

"Did I please you?" Dex panted.

"Yes. I'm so proud of your restraint, especially after I haven't let you come all week. And after such a hard day." Luc wrapped his hand around Dex's cock, his grip too tight to handle.

"Luc, stop. Wait. I can't take any more."

Luc didn't stop. "I know, my dear. I want to see you come. You have my permission."

He squeezed Dex, jerking him slowly, and Dex came all over himself.

"Such a good, dirty little mate. My perfect fucktoy. I'm going to make you mine, and you can come as many times as you want while I do it."

"I can?" Dex nearly choked on the words, the sound strangled.

"As many times as you want. This is going to be like nothing you've ever done. Like nothing I've ever done." Luc flipped Dex over and lifted his hips into the air.

Dex spread his legs and pushed onto all fours. "Mate me."

Luc growled, fingers digging into Dex's hips. "First, I'm going to breed you."

Dex's vision blurred, and an aftershock of pleasure rocketed through him. "Yes. I need you."

Luc traced Dex's rim with a delicate touch, and a tingle of magic followed. Dex sucked in a sharp breath and lurched forward, but Luc held him in place as a soothing sensation spread within his channel. Luc pressed a finger into Dex's ass with a wet squelch, having slicked Dex on the inside with magic.

"Holy fuck." Dex buried his face in the bedding and thrust back onto Luc's finger.

Luc worked him with his hand, opening him with slick sounds that had never turned Dex on more. "Look how ready you are for me." Luc aligned his cock. "You're already mine. It's deep in your soul, isn't it?"

"Yes." Dex pressed back, and Luc pushed forward, breaching him and stuffing him to his limit.

Luc sank in until his body was flush with Dex's ass. He bent forward and bracketed Dex's body with his, surrounding Dex with his campfire scent. Luc's tail teased Dex's cock, then snaked along his body to wrap around his neck, applying no pressure, yet grounding him. Owning him.

Dex moaned. Luc's tail moved like a snake, soft against his neck as it coiled without tightening. The tip wound over Dex's face and teased his parted lips. He mouthed Luc's tail, trying to latch on.

With a pleased sound, Luc thrust into Dex's mouth.

His lips brushed Dex's ear. "Bite my tail if you need me to stop. Don't worry, you won't hurt me. Okay?"

Dex nodded and bit gently to show he understood. Luc rumbled in satisfaction and filled Dex's mouth, just shy of triggering his gag reflex. He pulled his hips back and thrust. Dex's resulting cry was wonderfully muffled.

"Good boy, stuffed full. I own you. See? Mine." Luc thrust again and again. "My mate. Mine to breed and use whenever I want."

Dex's moans left the realm of human sound, turning animalistic. He shoved his hips back as Luc drove into him. Luc's tail pushed farther down his throat, and he choked, eyes watering, his cock hard and swinging between his legs.

Luc tilted Dex's hips, changing the angle, and hit Dex's prostate on his next thrust. Dex screamed around Luc's tail, and Luc roared in response.

"Mine." Luc fucked Dex so hard, he'd feel it for days.

Yes. Dex never wanted Luc's tail to unwind from his neck. Never wanted his cock to leave his hole. He came, sobbing for more, tears streaming down his cheeks, and spit dribbling down his chin.

Luc growled and thrust harder until his body stiffened and he roared, "*Mine.*" He panted in Dex's ear. "Forever. I'll never let you go."

Dex whimpered and moaned. He was gagged, stuffed like a spit roast by one man. Fuck. An aftershock hit, and another spurt of cum spilled from his spent cock.

Luc nuzzled Dex's ear. "So good and we've hardly started."

Dex thought he might pass out. Hardly started? Holy fucking hell.

Luc slowly withdrew his tail, and Dex sucked on it, reveling in the silky slide over his tongue. It loosened around his neck and fell away, leaving his skin bare.

"Wait." Dex's plea came out strangled.

"*Shh.* It's all right. I'm not going anywhere. I'll put it back soon, but I need access to your neck. Your blood." Luc scraped his fangs along Dex's skin. "To mate you, I need your essence, and you'll need mine."

Dex shivered. "Then bite me. Please."

Luc thrust his hips. Fuck, he was still hard. "My pleasure, mate." He sank his fangs into Dex's neck, eliciting a sharp sting.

Dex pushed back onto Luc's cock, overstimulated but unable to stop himself. Pleasure bloomed in his neck and rolled through his body. He could have stayed like that forever, but Luc withdrew his fangs and began to chant in an unknown language, thrusting in time with his words.

The air crackled with energy. Magic. This was it.

Luc fucked Dex harder, his chant transforming to a melodic growl. Dex's arms gave out, and he buried his face in the sheets and took it, each jolt of his body reminding him he belonged to Luc.

When the magic and Luc's thrusts all seemed to come to a

head, Luc pulled him to his hands and knees and sank his fangs back into Dex's neck.

With each pleasurable pull—Luc growling, sending vibrations through Dex's blood—something opened within Dex. A presence loomed, and Dex longed to reach it. To join it.

Was this the bond? Was this Luc?

His body vibrated, an orgasm washing over him almost without him realizing.

The presence seemed to envelop Dex, a wild possessive urge taking over and leaving a deep well of love in its wake.

"Luc," Dex moaned, screamed, he wasn't sure.

Luc pulled his fangs from Dex's neck with a snarl. "I've got you. Take my blood and you'll be mine forever."

A bloody wrist appeared in Dex's vision. He reached for it and fell forward, his other hand too boneless to hold him up. He was a ragdoll, a fucktoy, and he was flying. Luc's overwhelming presence lit him up inside. His excitement and need filled Dex to bursting, as intense as the cock splitting him open.

Luc rocked back and hauled Dex onto his lap, his legs splaying to either side of Luc's knees as Luc's cock slid impossibly deeper.

"Here." Luc wrapped an arm and his tail around Dex's waist, holding him securely against his chest, and pressed his bloody wrist to Dex's lips.

Dex latched on and drank like a newborn pup having its first feed, a rich, smoky flavor coating his tongue. Hot yet refreshing, like the first breath of air after being underwater.

"I feel you, Dex." Luc gasped. "Come home. Let me hold your soul and keep it safe for eternity."

Dex's eyes rolled back, and the heat of the growing bond overwhelmed him, showing him Luc's burning desire and smoldering affection. His demon, who wanted to scare him, thrill him, hold him tight, and care for him.

"I'm home," Dex panted, Luc's blood dripping from his lips. "I'm yours forever, Luc." To prove it, he sealed his mouth around Luc's flowing essence once more.

Luc's grip tightened, and he stiffened beneath Dex, his orgasm shooting down their newly formed bond and hitting Dex like a freight train. Dex came harder than he had in his life, a feat that shouldn't have been possible after multiple orgasms, if not for magic.

"My mate." Luc kissed Dex's hair as he sucked on his wrist. "My Dex. I'm going to hold you close like you're the most precious thing in the universe."

Dex withdrew, a small, frazzled laugh bubbling out of him.

Luc's tail tightened around him. "You are the most precious thing in the universe, my dear. I love you."

Softness overwhelmed the bond, and Dex had never experienced such a tender emotion.

"Oh my gosh, Luc. I can feel your love." His head spun, his body so wrung out, he'd gone limp all over.

"Of course you feel it." Luc kissed his cheek and slowly separated their bodies so he could lay Dex down and wrap himself around him. "Take in my love. Feel it. Let it wrap you up." Luc kissed Dex's cheeks, his nose, his lips.

Magic tickled Dex's body, cleaning their mess, and his eyes fluttered shut. He wanted to say he loved Luc too, but words wouldn't come. Even his tongue was like jelly.

"I know," Luc whispered. "I can feel your love, too, and I've never been happier."

Dex smiled, and Luc pulled him tighter against his chest. He had the rest of time to find the exact right words. For now, he could fall into the experience and let the bond wind around his heart, bringing them together.

He was Luc's, and Luc was his.

32

———

DEX

One week later.

DEX SEALED tape along the top of the last box. "I think that's it. We're all packed."

Luc moved the box to the pile next to Dex's bedroom door. This was all that was coming with him to his new condo. Fuck, it didn't seem like much.

Other than the boxes, his parents' place was completely empty. Their belongings had been taken to Luc's that morning, and the furniture had been collected for donation earlier that week.

Luc rested his hand at the small of Dex's back. "How does it feel?"

Dex leaned into him, the tape dispenser held limply at his side. "You know how I feel."

The mate bond wrapped around Dex as securely as the hand at his back. If Dex concentrated on Luc rather than himself, he could feel Luc's calm, open presence. A contrast to his own feelings.

Experiencing more than your inner self was mind-boggling. Dex hadn't given it much consideration before bonding, and could admit he'd been unprepared, but nothing could have gotten him ready for the open line to Luc's affection.

It was the most beautiful thing Dex had ever experienced, and every time he reflected on their bond, he was grateful all over again that he hadn't had to choose between this and the afterlife.

"I may know how you feel, Dex, but I still want to talk about it." A flash of unease shot down the bond, and Dex's heart clenched.

He dropped the tape dispenser and gripped Luc's sweater. "I know you do. Sorry."

Luc pulled Dex against him. "There's no need to apologize. This is a hard moment. I imagine it's difficult to put into words."

Dex pressed his face into Luc's firm chest, his soft sweater tickling his cheek, and gathered his thoughts, trying his best to organize all the tangled sensations running through him.

"I feel the same as I have for weeks, but also...more. Raw. I didn't realize how exposing it'd be to share all this through the bond. You feel *everything* I do, and that's so intimate."

Luc ran a hand through Dex's hair. "I treasure the intimacy and promise to hold everything you share with me with the utmost care."

Dex had no doubt. The sensation of the bond—of Luc— wrapped around him was pure safety. "I treasure it too. I just didn't realize I could be any more seen than I already was. I thought I'd given you all of me, then I packed this last box and... It's not bad. I..." Dex's throat thickened.

Luc let the silence hang, giving Dex room if he wanted to say more without pressing him, but Dex had no words left.

After a long moment, Luc's deep voice surrounded Dex in a soothing resonance. "Sharing sadness is an incredibly intimate act, and I want to hold this piece of you as much as the rest. I don't only like you when you're expressing your sexual desires, or only when you're happy and having fun. When we met, I wanted to destroy the sadness you carried, but that was before I knew better. There's no need to destroy this. That would be a travesty. I want to share this with you. Your love for your family is precious, and I'm honored to be a part of it. I'm thankful that I'm here for this part of your life. You live with your whole heart."

Dex was speechless, his pulse pounding in his ears. He almost didn't want to pull his face from Luc's chest, but he did.

Dex smiled at his mate, cheeks hot. "So do you, you know. I didn't realize it was possible to be so determined, so focused and intense, and at the same time so sweet, but that's what's in your heart. It's *you*. I'm sad to leave this place behind, but excited for the rest of my life. I'll always wish my parents were here, but saying goodbye is okay. I'm glad you're here with me. I don't feel alone like I would have if I'd had to do this without you."

Luc stroked Dex's chin and placed a soft kiss on his lips. "Would you like to stay a while?"

Dex took in the empty room. "No. I'm ready to be done. Let's bring these boxes to my new place."

Luc pulled out his phone and called the moving company waiting on standby to say that everything was ready. "Why don't we get coffee and a pastry downstairs while we wait?" He held out his hand.

Dex took it. "That sounds perfect." He led Luc out of the empty condo, taking one last look. "On to something new," he muttered as he shut the door, the words bittersweet, but taking a weight with them as they faded from his lips.

"To something new," Luc echoed.

DEX AND LUC crossed the river, coffees in hand. They took their time, pausing to check out the shops on Dex's new block before entering his building. As Dex unlocked the condo door, a sense of pride flooded the bond, and Dex couldn't help smiling.

It was ridiculous that Luc was proud of him. He hadn't done anything noteworthy.

Dex glowed anyway. Pleasing Luc energized him. It made him whole like nothing else ever had, whether it was pleasing Luc sexually or otherwise.

The boxes arrived at the new condo shortly after Dex and Luc. They arranged them on the living room floor in a patch of sun cascading in from the glass door to the balcony.

Dex's mind strayed to the night before. Bonded sex was a whole new world, and fed all of his kinks. Luc's praise and approval went from verbal to physical. Their desires fed off each other, transforming into an ever-growing feedback loop like nothing Dex had ever dreamed of.

There was only one thing Dex didn't like about their newly enhanced sex life.

"What is it?" Luc asked, no doubt feeling the stab of disappointment that had hit Dex in the chest. Luc abandoned the box he'd been about to open, concern lining his face.

Why did he have to think about this now? Dex had been avoiding this for a reason. "It's stupid," he muttered, his face flaming.

Luc's expression hardened. "What did I tell you about calling yourself stupid?"

Dex looked at his feet, then up again. "That I shouldn't because I'm not."

"No, you're not. So...care to share?" Luc raised a brow. He

sounded stern, but affection and concern flooded their connection.

Dex couldn't help opening up, words coming out in a rush. "I can't be good for you anymore."

Luc's eyes widened. "What do you mean? Of course you can."

Fuck that hadn't come out right. "Not like before. You can't tell me not to come and use me now that we're bonded. I can't hold back when you finish."

Dex came every time Luc did. Every sensation Luc experienced during sex, Dex experienced too. Feeling Luc's orgasms through the bond always triggered his own orgasm, no matter how recently he'd come or how much he tried to hold it off.

Dex twisted his hands together. "I love being used and denied. Doing something solely for you. I didn't realize it would go away when we bonded."

What a trivial worry. Even if he'd known, Dex wouldn't have chosen not to bond. He was being greedy, but still, the disappointment lingered.

"Oh, Dex." Luc cupped his cheeks, a smile tugging on his red lips. "That particular pleasure hadn't gone anywhere. You need training, that's all."

Dex's core tightened, and heat flooded him. "Training?"

"You like that," Luc teased, wicked amusement tickling the bond. "Yes, training. Blocking strong emotions and sensations is difficult, especially during something as unrestrained as sex, but it's not impossible. We can practice. And even if we can't block each other's pleasure entirely, I can train you to handle my orgasm. With practice, you'll build a tolerance. I bet you'll hold out longer and even be able to bear it one day."

Dex groaned softly. "Training like that's going to take forever." Fuck, he was breathless.

Luc's fangs lengthened. "Not forever, but a while, I'm sure.

And I can't wait to get started. Think how much I'll enjoy bringing you close and stopping. Holding you on the edge. We'll learn what works for us. And even if my orgasm triggers yours, I'll still be in control of you. You can't come without me or touch yourself without my permission. You can still be good for me."

Dex went from disappointed to hard in his pants. "You're right." He'd been too focused on one thing to see all the new possibilities.

Luc's eyes flashed. "And no, we aren't starting now, you desperate little thing. You can stay hard and wanting while we unpack your boxes."

Dex made a childish, overdramatic sound, but he was grinning ear to ear. "Okay, fine, but can we start soon?"

"We'll see." Luc's excitement sparked, fading to a smoldering sense of love that flooded their bond and brought them even closer together.

33

LUCIFER

Three months later.

Luc paced the mezzanine floor of his loft, rounding the bed and dresser, and stalking past the sitting area. His heart fluttered, and his stomach was worryingly unsettled.

His phone buzzed in his pocket, and he stopped.

DEX:

Are you okay?

He'd sensed Luc's nerves through the bond. Luc smiled, his jitters calming as Dex sent warm, soft affection his way.

LUC:

I'm fine. I'll pick you up in ten minutes.

DEX:

Can't wait. You've got this!

Luc's feathers ruffled, and he stood taller. There was

nothing wrong with a little self-doubt in the face of what tonight represented.

Teetering on the brink of everything he'd ever wanted was surreal. His mate was happy, flourishing as if a weight had been lifted from his shoulders. Dex's new condo had injected joy into his heart, and he seemed focused on the future rather than stuck in the past.

Luc also had his eyes on what lay ahead for the first time in centuries. Some days, he awoke hardly believing it was real. *He had his mate.* That was more than enough, but Luc had been given far more.

The guilt he'd carried around since the first witch had been born cracked and fell away, the last remnants of dust disappearing in the wind.

Even that amount of healing would have been enough, but Luc had been blessed with more. Dante had invited him over for a family dinner. They'd all be there. His brothers and their mates.

Luc grabbed a sweater from his wardrobe and tied it to his belt. His loft was still mostly empty, other than Dex's parents' belongings which were stored carefully and tucked out of sight.

There was no need for most of the loft. Luc liked the mezzanine floor and kept his occupancy centered there. It was like living on a balcony, giving him plenty of room for his wings. But he wasn't planning to stay in the loft long term. He had dreams of creating a home with Dex.

This would do until then.

Luc left the loft and flew up the river. Dex waited for him on his apartment's small balcony. Luc cast an illusion to match the one covering him, so no one would notice Dex disappear, and landed on the railing, perching like a gargoyle, his tail flicking back and forth.

"Careful." Dex grabbed Luc's hand and kissed him.

"I won't fall."

Dex laughed. "I never imagined *this* when I bought a place with a balcony, but seeing you fly in and land at my door is my favorite thing about living here."

Luc purred, tangling a hand in Dex's hair. He tilted Dex's head back and kissed him deeply.

Their forever home would have an enormous balcony. Perhaps every room would have one. That way, Dex could always look out and see Luc coming home.

Dex pulled back from the kiss, cheeks flushed, and cleared his throat. "We should go. You don't want to get distracted."

"Don't I?" Luc chased Dex's lips, pulling the bottom one gently between his teeth. "Last time I checked, it was me who told you what to do. Not the other way around."

Dex groaned. "I'm not trying to deny you. I'm reminding you that you want tonight more than whatever your libido is telling you."

Luc laughed. "I can't want anything more than you."

"Then it's a good thing you don't have to choose. Come on, you know what I mean."

"You're right. I'm nervous about tonight and trying to distract myself. I don't actually want to be late." Luc wouldn't be inconsiderate like that, especially not to Dante.

He scooped Dex into his arms and launched into the air, swooping low over the river before pumping his wings and soaring over the city. Cool air whipped by, and the city lights glittered below. Soon, the city would be decorated for the winter holidays, Dex had said. He was adorably excited to see the Christmas lights from the air.

Eventually, Dante's nature reserve came into view.

The eight of them hadn't been together since the day Luc led his team to the gateway. Luc had seen Onyx and Nico the most out of everyone since then and had met with Ash a couple of times. He hadn't seen Dante, Ollie, or Harper at all. Dante had said to visit, but Luc had hesitated, unsure if all could be forgiven. He didn't want to push Dante, Ollie, or Harper into accepting him.

He landed and set Dex down beside him so he could retract his wings and pull on his sweater.

"I like this one." Dex ran his hands over the red fabric.

"You like all my sweaters."

Dex shrugged. "They make you soft and cuddly."

"Cuddly?" Onyx's sharp tone cut through the night air.

Dex wrapped his arms around Luc. "Very cuddly."

Luc flashed his fiery eyes at Onyx, who curled his lip.

"I'll take your word for it. Now, hurry and get in here." Onyx jerked his head toward the house. "It's too cold for the non-demons to leave the door open."

Luc ushered Dex inside, and Onyx shut the door behind them. The mates were huddled on the couch, looking at something on Harper's phone, while Ash and Dante were occupied in the kitchen, pouring drinks.

"We're all here," Onyx announced, stealing everyone's attention.

Luc's face heated, and he gripped Dex's hand. "Thank you for having me."

"Eww, don't be so stiff." Onyx swatted his shoulder.

Luc cleared his throat. "My apologies, dear brother. Please forgive me for forgetting how to socialize."

"*Ugh*. That was the stiffest shit I've ever heard." Onyx shook his head, apparently giving up, and went to perch on Nico's lap.

"You apologized like that just to bug him, didn't you?" Dex whispered.

Luc flashed his mate a conspiratorial grin, his initial unease softening to something manageable. "What good is family if we can't rile each other up?"

Dex laughed.

"Let's grab a drink." Ollie appeared at their sides and pulled Dex away. "Ash is practicing his mixology skills. You want one?" he shot over his shoulder to Luc.

"Why not?" He followed them into the kitchen.

The fact that Ollie could look at him at all was a miracle Luc might never get over. From what Dex had told him, Ollie was more interested in bringing the group together and spending time with Dex than focusing on how much Luc had hurt him. His determination to share everything with his best friend was admirable, but Luc's guilt for hurting Ollie hadn't been banished as completely as his guilt for falling to Earth.

Ash handed a drink to Ollie and Dex before catching Luc's eye. "I made negronis. Want to try one?"

"Go on." He accepted a glass and had a sip, rolling the liquid around on his tongue. "I don't know what it's supposed to taste like, but it's not bad."

Ash barked a laugh. "That's better than Dante's reaction, so I'll take it."

Dante flicked his tail. "How did you expect me to react? I don't like alcohol, and that was the most bitter thing I've ever tasted."

Ollie chuckled and had a sip. "Oh. That's strong."

"Yeah, I'm not having more than one of these." Dex caught Luc's eye, his cheeks flushing as a hopeful tendril of lust wound down the bond.

"Probably a good idea," Luc agreed, sending his burning desire back. "Always smart to keep your wits about you."

"I got a little too drunk *one* time." Dex huffed, his amusement taking the edge off his whining.

"At least Luc was there to take care of you." Ollie's gaze darted to Luc, then away.

Dex had told Ollie about the night Luc had found him

drowning his sorrows at Dorthy's. As far as Luc could tell, there wasn't much the two didn't share. They'd become even closer over the past few months. Dex had confessed to Luc that he'd been holding back from Ollie and was glad to put that behind him, along with the heavy emotions that had caused him to withdraw in the first place.

"I'll take drinks to Harper and Nico." Ollie set his glass down and grabbed the tray that Ash had arranged with two more drinks.

"No, I've got it." Dex took the tray from him and hurried off, giving Luc the moment he needed, but hadn't asked for. Had Dex sensed it through the bond, or did he know him that well?

Likely both, and that gave Luc the courage he needed.

"Ollie, can I talk to you?" Luc asked before Ollie could follow Dex into the living room.

He paused. "Yeah?"

"I wanted to say thank you. Again. I know Onyx thinks I'm being stiff, but I mean it. Before this can be a comfortable family dinner like I'm sure you're all used to, I have to let you know how much I appreciate what you've given me."

Ollie's cheeks flushed, and Dante wrapped an arm around him. "I didn't give you anything. You gave me Dex. I wanted to thank *you*."

"Me?" Luc looked at Ash for clarity, and he grinned unhelpfully.

"Thank you for giving Dex the life he deserves. He's so into you. I've never seen him like this with anyone. Not even close. I want us to be friends, so stop apologizing to me. Okay?" Ollie glared like he'd been practicing. His level of menace wasn't bad.

"Okay," Luc said on a shaky laugh. "But you don't have to be comfortable with me any time soon. We have years ahead of us. There's no rush to get over what happened."

"We know." Dante nudged Luc with his wing. "We're

focusing on the future, not the past. On who you are now. You should do the same."

"Focusing on the future sounds like a good motto to me," Harper said as he sidled up to Ash, drink in hand.

"Thank you. All of you." Luc was breathless, and everyone stared at him with varying levels of exasperation. "Last time, I promise."

"I still can't believe the Realm of the Damned is gone," Harper said, mercifully changing the subject before Luc broke his promise and spewed more gratitude. "The Eternal Realm better be ready for witches like my father."

"They will be," Luc assumed him. "Bad people die all the time. A soul's lifecycle is about healing. Even though witches won't reincarnate, they'll enter the same reflective stage as humans upon arriving. By the time someone like your father is walking around the Eternal Realm, I'd say he'll be different than you remember."

Harper's nose wrinkled. "I don't know what I think about that. I guess it's good, but it almost sounds like a second chance."

Ash frowned in response to his mate's distaste, as if anything that displeased Harper offended him. "Second chance or not, it's a positive thing. Witch souls in Hell didn't enter any part of the reincarnation cycle. It's better that your father changes than being left to fester."

Harper huffed. "True."

"Some souls are stuck in the healing stage for years, even centuries," Ash went on. "I'd say your father will be occupied for quite some time, given how far he has to go."

Ash and Dante had supervised the destruction of the Realm of the Damned, along with Valac. The three had stood at the gateway as the damned souls traveled through.

Hell was gone. Luc could no longer disappear to that cursed place when he needed to escape, and he'd never been more grateful. Hopefully, he'd never need to run like that, and if he ever had the urge, he liked to think he'd stand and face whatever scared him.

According to Valac, word of the Realm of the Damned's destruction had spread like wildfire through the demon population. Luc's participation had changed some demons' minds about him, but he wasn't as weighed down by their opinions as he had been.

He had his brothers, and that was what mattered most. There was no need to reconnect with anyone else, at least not right away. Maybe one day. It was something to look forward to.

The news that witches and vampires were no longer damned hadn't spread as quickly, but it was out there. Rowan, Catalina, and Nico had gotten the story circulating, but had been met with varying degrees of disbelief. Skepticism was fair. The magic world as a whole would likely take a long time to accept the truth.

Luc had told Rowan that he'd help deal with any Satan-worshiping covens who resisted the new reality. All Rowan had to do was ask, and with any luck, worshiping him would die out eventually.

"Hollis said he might join us one day," Dante said, shaking Luc from his thoughts.

"Really?" Luc couldn't picture it. "He'd fall? Why now?"

"The same reason you did. He'd rather not live under the council and hopes to find his mate here one day, but he wants to see how the transition in the Eternal Realm goes before he leaves. To make sure the council doesn't twist things around." Dante's eyes flared. "I told him we appreciate him keeping an eye on things."

"That's very good of him." Luc couldn't get his head around more demons falling after all this time. But why wouldn't they, now that they knew coming to Earth wasn't an assault on the sacred balance of the universe?

Strict duality didn't dictate the realms, and falling wasn't inherently wrong. The Eternal Realm could still ban travel between the two, but there was no moral reason not to come to Earth. The ability for Eternals to leave without guilt might actually help the Eternal Realm change for the better. If the council didn't want people looking for a better life elsewhere, they'd have to make living in the Eternal Realm seem like the best option.

"Hey, Luc, I was wondering..." Harper waited for Luc's attention before continuing. "Didn't you see Dex the day you followed me into Seaside Coffee?"

Luc's muscles tensed. "What? No. Dex wasn't there."

"Huh. I mean, he was there. I talked to him. Maybe he went out back after making my coffee, and you missed him."

"I didn't order coffee that day. I went into the restroom and disappeared back to Hell after you saw me. I didn't want Ash catching on. He was nearby." Luc threw an apologetic glance Ash's way.

Ash laughed. "Fuck, imagine if you'd met Dex then. You might have believed me from the start."

Luc's heart skipped. Would he have? That could have changed everything. He might never have hurt Harper or Ollie.

"It doesn't matter," Dante said, and Ollie nodded his agreement. "This is how things went, and in the end, we're all here in my house as I'd dreamed. That's what's important."

"You dreamed I'd be here with you?" Luc teased. No way that could be true.

Dante's eyes crinkled and he smiled like Luc hadn't seen in a thousand years. "In my wildest dreams, yes, Luc, you were here too."

EPILOGUE
DEX

Ten years later.

"We have to get going," Luc called from the front showroom.

"Give me a minute," Dex shouted back. He threw a plastic tarp loosely over the day's creations and went to wash his hands at the sink.

He'd been throwing mugs on the pottery wheel earlier that afternoon and had gotten distracted making teaspoon rests to match, with the extra clay. Now they were risking running late.

"The front's all closed up." Luc appeared in the doorway to Dex's pottery studio. "You're lucky I can fly."

"You're lucky I've cleaned already, or I'd throw clay at you."

Luc's eyes flashed. "The last time you did that, you begged me to spank you for being so naughty. We definitely don't have time for *that*."

Lust zipped down the bond. "There's always later."

"*Mm.*" Luc wrapped his arms around Dex and untied his

apron, slipping it over his head. "What a lucky boy you are, mate."

He was. Working with Luc had gone even better than Dex had imagined. They'd opened the Colt Ceramics brick-and-mortar store three years ago. How had time gone so fast?

Dex had never planned to run his own shop. His online business had taken off, and he'd had to resign from Seaside Coffee to keep up. That had been the dream, and it was six years ago now.

The in-person shop had been Luc's idea. He'd wanted to build Dex's brand and give him the opportunity to create and sell one-of-a-kind pieces.

Selling his pottery online and in other people's shops had been the height of Dex's ambition, but with his own shop, he could do sculpture alongside his homewares and sell both.

When he'd moved in with Luc, he'd sold his little condo by the river and bought this shop in the Arts District. There was a showroom out front and a studio in the back. He even had his own kiln. Which was awesome, but not as amazing as Luc firing pieces for him with his demon flames.

All of the sculptures were created by him and Luc as a team. Dex did the pottery, and Luc transformed the pieces with fire. No one outside the magic world was aware that they were created that way, but most of the people who ended up buying them were witches or vampires.

Onyx had hosted a magic-inclusive opening for Dex and Luc at Gallery Four. It was one of the highlights of Dex's life, and he didn't see that changing, no matter how long he lived.

Other than creating art together, Luc ran the shop while Dex made mugs, bowls, and all his usual fare out back. They didn't actually see each other often during a typical work day, keeping them from getting on each other's nerves or falling into each other's arms too often.

Luc kept busy when he wasn't working by volunteering at Harper and Ash's center for witches in need. He seemed determined to spend his life giving back, and Dex loved that about him.

Dex wrapped his arms around Luc's neck. "Fly me home so I can change, please?"

"Since you asked so nicely..." Luc scooped Dex into his arms and carried him out the back door, pausing to lock it magically.

The flight home was short. There'd been a time when Dex couldn't have imagined permanently moving out of the Banks, but he loved living in the Arts District.

Ollie and Harper lived with Dante and Ash at the big house in the nature reserve, which had become somewhat of a home base for all eight of them. They had regular family dinners, and Dex had gotten to know Dante's gaming room well. So had Luc. Of all things, he and Dante had re-bonded over video games.

Luc soared toward the tallest building in this section of the city. It was much smaller than the high rises downtown, but it had a perfect view of the Arts District and the northern expanse of the river with the main city skyline off to the west.

Home.

Luc had designed it especially for them—commissioned an architect and everything—and renovated the old building he'd bought. Dex and Luc lived on the top floor, with offices rented out below, meaning they had the building to themselves on evenings and weekends. Though Luc had magically sound-proofed the penthouse for guaranteed privacy.

They landed on the main balcony, a huge expanse of concrete with glass barriers along the edge and seating and potted plants distributed throughout. The whole penthouse was like living on a sheltered balcony. Every room had a view, with smaller outdoor spaces on the other three sides of the building.

Dex could look out at Shearwater Landing no matter what room he was in.

He'd called it their nest when Luc had first flown him here, and the nickname had stuck.

"I'll be quick," Dex promised as he hurried into their bedroom, leaving the glass door ajar behind him.

They were meeting everyone at a wine bar Onyx liked—even though he didn't drink wine—as a surprise for Ollie. He was meeting Dante soon to tell him if he'd gotten the teaching job he'd applied for, and Dante wanted the family ready for the news.

Of course, they'd all wanted to be there. They'd come running to each other's sides no matter the occasion, big or small.

Luc leaned against the doorframe. "I'll hold you to that. You've got five minutes."

Dex kicked off his shoes, pulled his shirt over his head, and dropped his clay-stained jeans. "If I'm quick and good for you, do you think I can come tonight?" He let his hand trail down his stomach, Luc's eyes tracking the motion.

"Put your clothes on, little tease, and I might let you."

Dex grabbed the first pair of pants he found and shoved them on.

His training to hold back from coming while Luc orgasmed had gone really fucking well. The process had been hot itself, but Dex had loved the resulting success even more. Luc could use him as many times as he wanted without Dex coming, and it had been a while since Luc had given him the privilege of an orgasm of his own. Not his longest period of denial, but getting close.

"Maybe I'll make you run home, and if I don't catch you, you can come," Luc mused.

Dex whirled around to find Luc looking at his fingernails,

casual as can be. He'd even managed to keep the bond closed off so Dex couldn't feel him.

He could imagine Luc as this distant, unimpressed man he hadn't yet earned the right to please.

Dex's heart pounded. "Do I get a head start?"

Luc met his gaze, fire in his eyes. "You know what? Today I'm feeling fair. I'll give you a real chance. Whatever the distance is from the wine bar to here in miles, times your average running speed, minus a minute. But no more than that."

Dex swallowed, his pulse thumping. "Deal." He slipped on his running shoes, rather than ones that matched his outfit.

Luc grinned slyly, taunting Dex with a jolt of pleasure down the bond. "Grab a shirt and we'll go."

Dex pulled on a clean shirt and followed Luc onto the balcony. Whether he made it home or Luc caught him and fucked him in the street, he would have a fantastic end to the day.

Who knew life could be this fun? Not the Dex of ten years ago, that was for sure.

His grief never disappeared completely, but it had become something he could live with. A part of his story, not the whole thing.

Dex was in no hurry to enter the Eternal Realm. He had Malachi's pebble next to a photo of him and his parents as a reminder of what awaited him. In a few decades, he'd take the journey the pebble represented, but he needed to live his life first. It was what they would have wanted for him.

Maybe in the centuries to come, Dex would meet his reincarnated parents. Perhaps they'd be friends. It was a wild notion, and reminded Dex how much possibility was truly out there. How much love there could be in the world, in every form.

He'd had his parents' love, and that would never cease to

exist. They would never cease to exist. He had Luc's love, which would grow and change with him like its own living thing. He had his demon family's love, and he'd have love and friendships he hadn't yet imagined.

And that was only his perspective. When Dex considered the love of others, the world was so damn full.

There was Luc, who'd believed no one would ever love him again, and yet Dex loved him every day. Luc's brothers loved him. Their mates, too. Dex could feel the eight of them becoming closer, drawing together like a solar system forming around a new star.

Luc gathered Dex into his arms and kissed his forehead. "Whatever you're thinking, it's giving me full-body shivers, my dear."

Dex tilted his face and captured Luc's lips with his. "I'm thinking about you. Us. Our life and family. How much I love you."

Luc purred. "I love you, too, Dex. More than words could ever say."

The bond opened up. Luc's feelings reflected Dex's, surrounding them both in a fire that would burn for eternity.

Their eternity.

The End.

Looking for more Luc and Dex? Don't miss *Training*, a steamy bonus epilogue available for free to my newsletter subscribers. Join now and see newly-mated Luc and Dex begin their exploration of the mating bond in the bedroom.

WHAT's next for Shearwater Landing? Rowan finds his mate in *His Eternal Temptation: Bound in Blood Book One,* a chosen mates MM romance kicking off an all-new series about the Valero Vampire Coven.

WHAT ABOUT THE greater Shearwater Landing magic world? Discover the Lockwood Coven in *Her Ghostly Embrace.* If you ever wondered what happened to the woman who was meant to marry Harper back in *Lovers of the Damned* book one, this is her story.

I hoped you enjoyed Luc and Dex's story.

Reviews are invaluable to authors. Please consider leaving a review for *Devil's Mate* on your favorite review site or the site where you purchased this book to help others find magical books they'll love.

HIS ETERNAL TEMPTATION

Bound to the enemy.

Rowan Valero rules Shearwater Landing. Some see him as a ruthless vampire, others as a protector of the disadvantaged. In order to be both, Rowan must know his enemies from his friends. Who to trust and who to keep outside his walls.

And no one may have his heart.

Lane Blackburn is desperate. Nothing short of a deadly curse could have brought him to Rowan's door, but here he is, hoping the vampire he had a misguided crush on will save an old enemy's life.

The last time Rowan saw Lane, the witch was a spy sent to seduce him. So why does seeing him on the brink of death tug on Rowan's heartstrings? Is it Lane's choice to waste his would-be last breath on a warning, or is it more?

Rowan saves Lane, but it comes at an unforeseen price. The curse binds him and Lane together. They can't be more than a few feet apart without Lane returning to the brink of death.

It's the kind of mistake that could bring Rowan's empire crumbling to the ground, or worse: expose what lies hidden in his heart.

Pre Order

HER GHOSTLY EMBRACE

Kiss girls and scorch the earth.

Gia Balzano's life is ruled by two inescapable facts: she's the daughter of Ashton Lakes' ruling crime boss and their family ties are forever. But Gia is a prisoner in her own home, and when she finds out everything was built on a lie, she has to break free.

Aurora Thornfield is bound to an evil coven. Her magic is useless against her captors—her family—and there's only one way to escape their control: sever all earthly ties and free her soul. There's just one problem. Once Aurora's spirit leaves her body, she can't find her way back to her mortal vessel.

Aurora is a ghost trapped in between life and death. All is lost until the day a beautiful woman walks into her, and screams.

Gia didn't know magic was real, and if every day since fleeing her family wasn't stranger than the last, she might not accept the truth. But Aurora draws her in like no one in this world ever has, and Gia has a feeling that together they'll have the power to conquer anything.

Pre Order

ACKNOWLEDGMENTS

First of all, I'd like to thank every single person who has come on this *Lovers of the Damned* journey with me. Thank you to every reader. Without you I wouldn't be writing these books. I get very mushy every time I hear from someone who enjoyed one of my stories, but even if I haven't heard from you, know that am so grateful for you.

I'd also like to give a huge thanks to Laura from Hummingbird Editing. All the chats we had while I was writing this series and needing to figure things out—like how I'd get Luc past what he did to Ollie—were so helpful and honestly fun. Working with you on edits has been amazing, and I appreciate all your feedback and suggestions more than I can say.

Thank you Rachel O'Rourke for taking a look an an early draft of Luc and Dex's story, and sharing your feedback. I don't often share my writing at that early stage and you were a great person to put my trust in. Your comments were so greatly appreciated.

Thank you Callie from CJ Editing for your keen-eyed proofreading and for your kind words and excitement for the series. It's been so lovely getting to work with you.

Thank you Molly from We Got You Covered Book Design. The covers for this series are fabulous and it was such a pleasure to work with you.

Thank you Angelika for your illustrations, bringing the Lovers of the Damned couples to life. Working with you was such a pleasure.

And most of all, thank you to TK for supporting my demon-dreams—all my writing dreams really—and for reading all these books about tails.

ABOUT THE AUTHOR

Colette (she/they) is an author of queer paranormal romance novels living in New Zealand. Colette loves to write couples who take care of each other and show their soft sides in love, even when they're prickly in other facets of their lives. Sugar, spice, and magic are key ingredients in all of Colette's books.

Colette can be found on Instagram @colette_rivera and on Facebook under Colette Rivera Author. Colette can also be found on their website coletterivera.com where you can sign up to their newsletter for bonus epilogues and updates.

Lovers of The Damned

Demon's Mate

Demon's Heart

Demon's Desire

Devil's Mate

Shearwater Landing Shorts

I Think I Found a Vampire

Moonlight Falls

The Fall of Elijah Gray

The Seduction of James Gray

The Cursed Sebastian Storm

The Heart of Moonlight Falls

Love & Magic

Give a Witch a Chance

Keep Your Witches Close

One Wicked Night

Witch Boyfriend Wanted